Nina Jones was born and educated in England but home for the first twenty-one years of her life was various locations in the bushlands of Northern Nigeria.

She now lives with her second husband in a village near Saffron Walden, Essex.

BUSH TOWN BLUES
A '70s African Tale

BOOK TWO

NINA JONES

BUSH TOWN BLUES
A '70s African Tale

BOOK TWO

Vanguard Press

VANGUARD PAPERBACK

© Copyright 2007
Nina Jones

A CIP catalogue record for this title is
available from the British Library.

ISBN 978 184386 327 4

*Vanguard Press is an imprint of
Pegasus Elliot MacKenzie Publishers Ltd.*

www.pegasuspublishers.com

First Published in 2007

**Vanguard Press
Sheraton House Castle Park
Cambridge England**

Printed & Bound in Great Britain

D e d i c a t i o n

You all know who you are!

But this book is especially dedicated to Barry, Magda,
Karl, Charly and Tom, not forgetting Ben and the boys.

With you all, there will always be a story to tell.

CHAPTER 1

November/December 1973

...You can hear the boats go by
You can spend the night beside her.....
Because she's touched your perfect body with her mind...

Early December.

It's night-time. A dozen white candles planted in a dozen little sand-filled pots, and the sand-filled pots in a dozen little places round the room. Tiny flickers of light, they dance with the shadows, dipping and dimming as the faint breeze from the open window wafts gently in. Leonard Cohen moans softly from across the room, and the air is pungent with the aromas of incense and marijuana.

On the floor we sit, cross-legged. I'm wrapped up in only an oyster-coloured shawl and Andy, a plain piece of cotton fabric is tied round his waist. He's reading to me.

'...history became legend, legend became myth, and for two and half thousand years the Ring passed out of all knowledge. Until when chance came and ensnared a new bearer. The ring came to the creature *Gollum, who took it deep into the tunnels of the Misty Mountains...'*

Andy pauses. Looks up from the book, and smiles. Holds out his hands, and draws me closer. 'Come away with me, Janni, come away. Let's find those Misty Mountains together.'

In the half-light, amongst shadows and flickers, I lean over and kiss him. Filled to the brim with happiness and joy. There's nothing in the world I want more than this, to go with Andy and search for those magic, elusive mountains.

'I've got some leave owing me. We could go to the Cameroon,' continues Andy. 'Hit Mambilla, and journey on to the Mountains of the Mists. It'll be a real trip, cosmic. What do you say? Are you up for it?'

'Of course.' I kiss him again, move over and snuggle my head deep into his lap.

Playing with my hair, he carries on making plans.

'We'll go by mammy-wagon. I don't think my bike's up to

11

making such a long trip. But that's half the beauty of travel, going native. Man, it'll be brilliant. We can sail down the Benue, camp on our very own islands, just me and my wee lassie.' His mouth touches my cheek; I feel his breath warm on my face. 'And we'll explore the bush and find our dreams.' He kisses the top of my head, twines my hair through his fingers. 'They're out there, you know, those dreams of ours. Man, they're fucking out there, and we'll find them, I promise.'

I don't doubt it. This is true free-spirited stuff, not pretend. I'm going on a journey with my lover, my soul mate, to a magic place far, far away; a boy and his wee girl, both of us searching for a new kind of freedom and a new kind of love. We'll be leaving behind an artificial society that mocks the true meaning of life, and together find the answers that are somewhere out there in the wilderness. These are his words not mine. I don't really understand, but it all sounds pretty profound.

'When are we going?' I murmur. Snuggled up, all warm and cosy here in my ivory tower.

'Christmas. Let's be true to ourselves, Janns, and not be part of the lie.' His voice is low, serious. 'For everybody else it's just the fucking silly season, another excuse to party, get pissed and tell dirty jokes. Man, that's not what Christmas is about. It's about birth and new beginnings. Our birth. Our beginnings. Our renaissance. I want to celebrate our rebirth up in the mountains. Get as far away as possible from Maiduguri as we can. It'll be out of this world. The two of us together. Just you and me.'

Leonard Cohen sings on.

....And you want to travel with him
And you want to travel blind
And you know you can trust him
Because he's touched your perfect body with his mind...

Andy rolls another joint. My head is still in his lap. Candles flicker, dipping and dimming as the breeze through the open window wafts gently in.

And I'm thinking. Christmas? Going away at Christmas.

And what will my parents have to say about that?

Two months together now, and the time had passed by like a dream. Every experience savoured, every moment with Andy more uplifting than the last. I pretty much floated in a state of constant euphoria, pinching myself sometimes to make sure I was awake.

12

There was only one big blot on my glorious and wonderful horizon. The parents. If they hadn't been dogging my every move, life, as I now knew, it would be total and perfect.

When I'd gone up to Maiduguri that first weekend with Lizzie I'd duly done the dutiful daughter bit and returned home to Gombe on the Sunday, as planned. That's not to say I hadn't toyed with the idea of sending a message to them via Lizzie saying I'd be staying in Maiduguri just a little while longer. I mean, I was having such a good time here, why would I want to go back to a shit-hole like Gombe? So I could play bridge with the lot down the road? Have a game of table tennis with Geoff? Hang about round at Barb's? Listen to Pru whittling on about her pending marriage to Ian? Worse still, play Scrabble with the parents? Worse, worse still, a game of hide-and-seek with Dick?

I mean, pur-lease! Who in their right mind would swap all this, a gorgeous bloke, a vibrant social life, and total freedom, for all that?

However, after much personal deliberation on the subject, I reluctantly bowed to the inevitable. That being, Mum and Dad would be truly pissed off if I didn't return home on the Sunday, as promised. You see, despite the newly acquired devil may care attitude (actually, it had always been there but there'd been no use for it up until now) there was still a semblance of the good girl within.

So with no minutes to spare, and the bus about to pull away, Andy and I roared into the lorry park with my bags all packed up and me ready to go.

Screaming, 'Stop! Stop!' I scrambled off the bike, hurled myself in front of the coach, and flagged down the driver. It was a miracle I didn't get squashed. The brakes were slammed on, the vehicle did a retching impersonation, black petrol fumes hissed from out of the front grill panel and the back exhaust, and everyone and everything inside the coach went hurtling forward. Including Lizzie. I saw her fly several feet down the gangway with my very own eyes.

Whoops! She was just a little bit livid.

Once balance was restored, she legged it to the front of the coach, threw open the door and stood at the top of the steps and glared. Hands on hips, foam on mouth.

'What the hell do you think you're playing at, Janni?' came the bellow, reminding me of a recent experience with a very angry, rampaging elephant.

My instant reaction was to tell her to go fuck herself but common sense prevailed. I needed an ally in Lizzie, not an enemy. 'Oh, Lizzie, I am so, so, so sorry. We had a puncture, didn't we, Andy?' I looked at my man, and my man nodded, quite willing to go along with the lie. It was partly his fault we were so late, anyway. He'd had a real problem letting me out of his bed; every time I made a move he'd grab me and pull me back, sending my blood pressure soaring to new heights previously unknown.

'Aye, that's right. Just as were about to leave. Sorry, and all that. We got here as fast as we could.'

Lizzie shook her head, unconvinced. But she helped me with my bags, and apologised to the driver, and told him we'd both be ready in just a second.

'Come on, say your goodbyes. Quickly,' she commanded, turning back to us. 'And I mean quickly, you're holding everyone up.' She remained rooted to the spot at the top of the steps, unprepared to go back to her seat until she had me firmly in her grasp. Sensibly, I followed orders and gave Andy a quick kiss and a hug.

'I love you,' he whispered softly, pushing my hair back of my face.

'I love you, too,' I breathed, my arms round his neck.

'Come on! Come on!' Lizzie's impatient voice jarred in our ears.

'See you next weekend.'

I leapt onto the coach. Lizzie banged the door shut, nodded to the driver, grabbed my arm and my bags and frogmarched me down to the rear of the bus. The dozen or so other passengers, all Nigerians, appeared quite unperturbed by the wait; hold-ups and unpunctuality were, after all, a national trend.

From the back seat, kneeling with nose pressed up against the side window, I blew Andy a kiss. Down on the ground, amongst the array of peddlers and waiting to be picked up or recently dropped off passengers, he caught it, put the kiss to his lips, and blew one to me. And I caught it, put the kiss to my lips, and blew one to him. And so it went on, until the bus turned the corner and Andy disappeared from my sight.

I went from kneeling position to sitting position, and sighed.

'What a weekend I've had, Lizzie.'

'I've no doubt, and you can keep it yourself, thank you very much.' And my travelling companion turned her back on me, and began studying the neem tree scene out of the window with great interest.

Wisely I changed tact. I mean, there were two hundred and forty nine miles still to go. Meaning hours and hours of silent treatment, if Lizzie stayed stuck in this mood.

'So, what did you get up to then? Buy anything nice at the market?'

Neem trees still took up a great deal of interest but there was a bit of a glance my way. And her uptight body wasn't quite so rigid.

'A couple of things.'

'Well, come on then! Show me!' Said a tad over enthusiastically but what the hell!

Lizzie rolled up her eyes. And gave a 'I'm really fed up with you, Janni' kind of sigh, but she unfolded her arms and began rummaging about in her big leather holdall.

'That's really nice, Lizzie,' I exclaimed, inspecting the papyrus painting of a mud hut and palm tree on black background. With African woman in typical African pose pulping the maize.

'No, it's not. It's horrible,' said Lizzie. And chuckled.

'Yeah, I suppose it is really.' I laughed. 'But I expect someone back at home would like it. A present, perhaps for your mum?'

'My gran actually.'

'Well, there you go. She'll love it.'

'And I also got this,' said Lizzie, warming up to the theme. Another dive in the bag and she pulled out a ten inch statue of a naked African man, carved from ebony. His prick was nine inches long.

'Bloody hell! Who's that for?' I exclaimed, inspecting the object d'art very closely. 'Not your gran, surely?'

'My Aunty Doris. She's got a thing about black blokes. I thought I'd send it to her for Christmas.'

'Well, you've certainly picked a winner, here. Aunty Doris will be over the moon!'

Lizzie chuckled again, now fully defrosted. The icy spell had thankfully passed. 'So, how was the picnic?'

'Fantastic.' And I told her all about it, well not everything, she wouldn't have approved of us overdoing the drugs bit, or the sex with Andy on the rock bit, but I gave her an overall picture. The ride to Bama, the trees in Bama, the humpback hill, the panoramic scene from humpback hill, the glorious sunset from top of humpback hill, our drive back down humpback hill, our encounter with the wandering minstrel, the bewitching music, the haunting voice, and the weird and wonderful star and crescent marks that were etched on his weird and wonderful face. 'Meeting him was magical! Totally cosmic, Lizzie. I'm telling you, it was almost as if he'd been sent to us. A mystical sign. Like he was casting an enchanted spell on me and Andy, a good luck token so our love would go on for ever and ever.'

Lizzie chortled. 'Don't be so daft, Janni. You really do come out with some rubbish at times. It's probably all that wacky-baccy you keep smoking. I'd ease up a little if I were you.'

I looked at her. Aghast. What a horrible thing to say.

'Well, you can think what you like. I know what I know, Lizzie,' I responded a tad humpy.

And left it at that. There was no point explaining the mysteries of romance to someone as inert and earthbound as Lizzie. I mean, she hadn't even turned up for last night's showing of 'Love Story' at the club. I'd kept an eye out for her as I sat cuddled up in my seat with Andy, watching this most romantic of cinematic performances (after 'Romeo and Juliet', it was definitely the best) unfold on a big, white sheet, but she didn't show. During the interval (when the projector had broken down – a total of four times in all) I spotted her mate Claire on my way to the loo. She was with a crowd of friends in the second to last row of seats.

'Hi, there,' I said. 'Where's Lizzie?'

'Overseeing a netball match.'

'What! You're joking?'

'I'm not,' laughed Claire, 'she said she'd prefer to have a game with the students rather than watch something as sloppy and as daft as a film with a name like 'Love Story'.'

See what I mean? Lizzie was a total non-romantic.

Back in Gombe, Monday to Friday went slowly. So slowly, sometimes I thought I was stuck in a time warp, destined to live the same second, over and over, and over again.

To help pass the time and speed things up just a little, I graciously agreed to accompany Lizzie, Kevin and Henry up to Bauchi on the Wednesday evening. A party was being given by some VSOs there, teacher friends of Lizzie's. I guessed the shindig would be boring, and I was right. It was boring. There were only ten people altogether, and that ten included the four of us. There was no dope, no nothing in fact, just a few nibbles, groundnuts and teeth-breaking, leaden cheese straws, and a bowl of fruit punch and a crate of Star beers. And the best the party-givers, a bunch so earnest they made me look positively wicked, could do on the music scene was play rubbish like The Jackson Five and Donny and Marie Osmond songs on a scratchy, old record player that was even more ancient than my parents' own turntable.

The only interesting aspect of the entire evening was Henry and Lizzie.

This was the first occasion both of them had really been in each other's company since 'the episode'. Following this most disastrous of unrequited situations, they'd spent their recreational hours, much like me and Dick, avoiding one another as best they could. Which in a bush town, as you know, is no easy thing. Tonight's get togetherness suggested that somewhere along the way an uneasy truce had been agreed (quite when this pact was made remains a mystery) and here they were in Bauchi doing their damndest to make good out of a not so good situation. It wasn't so hard for Lizzie. She treated Henry in much the same way as she had always treated him, think big sister act peppered with wry amusement and gentle ribbing. Henry tried to take it like a man but failed miserably. Red ears, red face, red neck, plus the stutter had returned, as had the shaking hands. He was a poor fucker, no doubt about it.

Anyway, after three long hours of enduring mind-numbing conversations with the likes of Shirley, originally from Bootle, now teacher of Sciences in Bauchi's Training College of Education, and Brian, Watford man, teacher of Mathematics in same Bauchi establishment (both were as boring as their dreadful subjects), we three in the Gombe gang decided, for a variety of personal reasons, to call it a day. Or rather a night, as it was now approaching 10pm.

So as quickly as was politely possible, we all piled into Kevin's dodgy old Land Rover and hurtled off into the bush and back home to Gombe.

'Thanks,' I said, meaning thanks for a really horrendously boring evening, as I jumped from vehicle onto gravelled path.

'You're welcome,' stated Kevin as if he'd just done me the biggest of favours.

'See you, Janni,' waved Lizzie from her seat in the front.

'See you, Lizzie. Bye, Henry.'

'Yah, see you soon,' from Quiff Man the Forlorn as he sat hunched up in the back of the Land Rover, all on his own.

Mum and Dad, as always, were both up. We went through the usual discourse. Good time? It was ok. Who was there? A few teacher friends of Lizzie's. What did you have to eat? Nibbles.

'Oh, by the way,' said Dad, barely looking up from his Polish newspaper that had arrived by post yesterday (sent courtesy of Aunty Helena from Krakow three months earlier), 'you had a visitor tonight while you were out.'

'Who?'

I'd just walked through from the kitchen and had a dirty great sandwich full of processed cheese and pickled onions (guaranteed to give you weird and wonderful dreams) halfway to my mouth.

'That young man of yours. Andy.'

I very nearly bit my hand off!

'Andy!!!!????? Do you mean my Andy??????!!!!!!!!'

'I presume so, unless you know another Andy,' responded Dad, now putting down the paper and raising an eyebrow.

'Was it him, Mum?' I almost, but almost, hoped she'd say that it wasn't. I couldn't bear to think I'd missed him.

'Yes, it was, darling. He said he was passing by.'

Passing by? When you live in Mauduguri you don't just happen to pass by a town that is two hundred and fifty miles away.

'What do you mean? Where's Andy now?'

I frantically looked around. Was ready for the off. Off in search of my Andy. Glanced at the French doors, almost expected him to be somewhere out on the veranda.

'Well,' said Dad, removing his glasses, 'he should be in Yankari by now.'

'Yankari?!!'

I wanted to run out of the house, jump on my bike and roar off there and then. Bugger the time and the distance.

'It was only a very fleeting visit, darling,' soothed Mum. 'Andy just came to the door, asked where you were, we told him, he didn't even come inside. He did say that they, I think there were another two boys with him, had to push on, something about a job that needed to be done very quickly in Yankari. Andy said to tell you he'd be back here on Friday night, and would see you then.'

I couldn't believe it. While I'd been spending an evening in Bauchi with a bunch of mind-numbing tossers, Andy, my Andy had been here in Gombe, had stopped here at my house, would possibly have invited me to spend another couple of magical days with him in Yankari. No doubt about it, I'd well and truly missed the boat. If

Mum and Dad hadn't been in the room I'd have screamed.

'So,' Dad was twiddling his spectacles round in his fingers, 'what are your plans for the coming weekend? Am I to presume we are finally going to have an opportunity to properly meet this young man that has stolen your heart?'

I looked at Dad. He had that expression that only fathers have. An expression that when deciphered means:

I will check to see if he's the right man for my daughter. I will spend time with him. I will ask him questions, many questions. I will delve into his background. I will ask him about his education. I will ask him about his long term plans.

That kind of expression.

Plus:

He will stay the weekend here in Gombe but there will be no hanky-panky under my roof. He will sleep elsewhere and my daughter will come home at an acceptable time.

Kind of expression.

I sighed, not sure about anything any more. The original weekend plan had been that I head up to Kwyaterra on my bike and meet Andy late Friday evening at the lorry park. We were going to spend another couple of nights at the Falls; just the two of us again. I hadn't quite worked out how I'd pass this by Mum and Dad and had been mulling it over in my head these last couple of days. Now plans might have to change. Dad, it seems, had taken charge.

'I think you'll like Andy, Dad,' I said with what I hoped was a more than convincing smile.

God help us both if he didn't.

'Without doubt,' replied Dad, putting his glasses back on. 'Without doubt.'

And he returned to his paper.

Andy arrived at ours at around six, Friday evening. Jim and Bruce were both in the Land Rover but declined an invite into the hornet's nest; they wanted to get back to Maiduguri as quickly as possible. And who could blame them?

As for Andy, well, as soon as his one foot stepped over the threshold, the Gombe Inquisition began. Polish style. This meant Dad welcoming Andy with open arms. Being over generous with the drinks. Feeding him as if he were one of the five thousand. Talking to him man to man (for hours on end), covering subjects such as religion, politics, and social and ethical issues. And finally, as a mine host gesture, Dad's *pièce de résistance*, personally taking

Andy to the Catering Rest House. Yes! Dad had very kindly booked him in for the whole weekend. And paid the bill out of his very own pocket.

How generous was that?

'I didn't get a look in,' came my moan to Mum as we waved the two of them off at midnight. (Yes, Dad had even provided a chauffeur service – his benevolence certainly had no limits.)

'Now, don't be silly,' retorted Mum, a tad impatiently. She was, after all, an extremely loyal wife. 'Dad just wants to get to know Andy. You know both of us have your best interests at heart, darling.'

'Hmm,' I muttered, totally pissed off.

Incredibly pissed off, in fact.

Andy was here for such a short while and I wanted to spend that time with him, alone. Not share him with the parents. And what with the Catering Rest House ploy, well that was Dad's way of keeping us conveniently apart. Any ideas we might have on the sexual side of things, I reckoned, were scuppered. Dad would be watching us like a hawk. Another weekend like this and I'd turn into a nun.

'I'm going to bed,' I said grumpily.

I turned on my heels and didn't even bother to wish my mother goodnight.

The next morning I was up very early. About quarter to six. The sun not quite wide awake and the moon still there in the sky. Quietly, ever so quietly, I swung my feet out of the bed and tiptoed over to my bundle of clothes on the floor. Dressed. And about to sneak over to the Rest House and share some intimate moments with Andy. But before I had time to put my plan into action, Dad was already fine tuning his.

Apparently he'd been up since the crack of dawn.

'Right, Peg,' he was saying to Mum out on the veranda, 'I'm off to pick up Andy. Tell Janni we'll be back about twelve.'

What?!

I'd have demanded an explanation but was in the middle of a piddle when I heard this conversation, and by the time I'd raced to the veranda the silver Ford Cortina was already halfway up the drive.

'What's Dad doing?' I raged, as the car veered left at the fork, and disappeared.

I'll give my Mum her due; she did look a mite embarrassed.

She gave me a sweet, sickly smile. 'He's taking Andy on a tour of some of his farms, darling.'

'Some of his farms?' I echoed hollowly. 'What do you mean?'

Mum smoothed her skirt and jangled the keys in her pocket. 'Well, darling, Andy expressed a wish to see some of Dad's work. The farming side of things. I suppose Andy's interested because their jobs are quite similar,' suggested Mum, trying to keep the tone light. 'So Dad thought he'd take him to see a few of his farms in action. And thought it best to leave early as some of the places he wants to take him are pretty remote and – er (she coughed) – far away.'

I shook my head in pure, utter disbelief. My eyes narrowed. 'When was this arranged, Mum?'

Mum shrugged. She frowned slightly, and sighed. 'I suppose last night, darling, when Dad dropped Andy off.'

I looked mournfully at the space Dad's car had left behind. Then I gave Mum one of my darkest looks, as if this was somehow all her fault. 'Why,' I muttered through teeth that were clenched, 'didn't Dad tell me? I might have wanted to go, too. Why, Mum? Why?'

'I don't think Dad really thought you'd want to, darling,' came Mum's simple explanation. 'And I suppose,' she added gently, 'he just didn't want to disturb you. He knows how much you like sleeping in.'

I shook my head. 'I don't believe this, Mum. I really don't.'

I could have sat down on the veranda and cried.

All week I'd waited for these two days. We should have been at the Falls now, sharing a sleeping bag, an early morning brew, and a smoke in our beautiful wilderness setting. Listening to the tinkle of the water as it splashed, watching the silver droplets twist up and twirl, admiring the red morning glory from under a wide, open sky.

I shouldn't be here, standing on the veranda with Mum, amidst flowerpots and deckchairs, perusing the same old scene, listening to the same old sounds.

'Why's Dad doing this, Mum?' Miserably, I plonked myself down in the dog basket, it was the nearest, comfy spot.

'Because he loves you, darling. Very much.' Mum sat down, on her three-legged, wooden de-ticking stool that was near to the basket, and stroked the top of my head. She'd be getting the bloody tweezers out next and searching for blood-sucking insects, the morning was getting that daft. 'You see,' Mum continued, 'after what happened with Johnny (I automatically flinched at the name) Dad and I were really concerned about you for a while. It broke our hearts to see the way you'd been treated by him and...'

I interrupted. 'Hang on a minute, Mum, what are you going on about? Andy's nothing like Johnny. And, anyway,' I snarled, 'what has Johnny got to do with Dad taking Andy to see a couple of his poxy farms?'

Softly, Mum smiled. 'Janni, Dad just wants to get to know Andy, that's all. It's an opportunity for them to have some time together. Believe me, darling, if we didn't care we would just let you get on with it, but we do care. Very much.'

Oh, for fuck sake, Mum.

And I offered a little prayer up to God.

Please, please, God, stop my parents caring about me. Please, please let them let me get on with my life. Oh, and please don't let Dad put Andy off me. Don't let Dad say anything that might embarrass me. Please, God. I beg of you (and never one to forget my manners) thank you, God. I would really appreciate it. Amen.

Dad and Andy came back at four.

Dad. Problem. Timekeeping. Remember?

I'd spent the whole of the morning, and half of the afternoon, like a cat on hot bricks. Or was it a tin roof? Anyway, hearing the car crunch on the gravel I was out there, all ready to drag Andy off for a drink up at the club. Well, actually not a drink up at the club, that was the official version for Mum and Dad's ears, I wanted to get him on his own, and have my wicked way with him at the Catering Rest House.

'Woowee!!!' whistled Andy, as we finally, oh bliss, made our getaway. 'What a day I've had!'

'I'm so sorry,' I said with feeling.

'Naw, that's alright. He's an interesting bloke, your Dad, if a little intense.'

We parked my bike up at the back of the reception area. Behind a massive great baobab tree. And several Land Rovers. Hiding the evidence. Didn't want Dad to spot the bike, if he so happened to wend his way over to the Rest House.

Dad. Elephant gun. Remember?

Hand in hand, ambling to chalet, oh my God, chalet number five! Numero cinque. Giorgio, whales on a beach, sticky sand, and all that that diabolical debacle entailed.

Still, within seconds, everyone, even my Dad, finally and truly forgotten.

Something good about the weekend, at long bloody last.

I took Andy to the lorry park Sunday morning. There were no buses going to Maiduguri but I don't think Andy would have got on one if there were. He preferred mammy-wagon travelling to luxury coach travelling because he was that sort of guy. Unfortunately, there weren't even any of these native contraptions leaving for Maiduguri, but there was one going as far as Kwyaterra. And according to Mr Official, who was hanging round with his badge and his sheaf of papers, Andy could catch another lorry at Kwyaterra, and go on to Bui. At Bui, he might be lucky and find one that was going to Potiskum. Mr Official wasn't too sure if there were that many lorries from Potiskum to Damaturu, or from Damaturu to Maiduguri, because it was a Sunday.

So you see, even in a predominantly Muslim country the Christian Sabbath was reverently observed. By most Muslims but particularly by those who were beggars. And particularly those beggars who happened to be lepers. And particularly those lepers who happened to ride donkeys. Donkeys with bells on them.

Ring! Ring! Ding! Ding! Unclean! Unclean!

Jingling away as they trotted down the driveway towards the house of the white man. It being Sunday, every white man (and their wives and their children) would definitely be at home. Yes, it was a good day for panhandlers, especially panhandlers without hands. Just stumps. Stumps of rotting, pink flesh. And holes where there should have been noses. And ears without ears. Oh, God how I dreaded the ring-a-ding sound.

Anyway, I digress. Back to Andy and his grand travel plans.

'What do you reckon?' I asked.

'Fancy taking me to Kwyaterra? Miss the middleman out.'

'Sure,' I said, grateful to have some quality time with Andy, even if it was on the back of a bike. I mean, apart from our quick one at the Rest House, the remainder of the weekend had been much like the start.

Saturday evening at six, Andy and I were invited to go off for a trot with my Dad. Which was fine, I wanted to show off my horse-womanship to Andy, let him see what an absolute natural I was. Except the both of them went galloping away and left me standing in the bowels of the riverbed on my own. We all met up half an hour later on the crest of the sandy ridge, where there were beautiful views of the plains down below and the majestic peak of Tangali Waja rising above. Andy was exhilarated and over the moon about the ride, and spent the rest of the jaunt home talking to my Dad about horses, and other boring equine subjects that I knew absolutely nothing about.

Then after a family supper together, Andy and I were about to pay another quick visit to the Rest House but Kevin zoomed up and scuppered those plans. We ended up having an evening at the club with everybody. And everybody included my parents. And everybody, including my parents, spent the evening playing tombola. And everybody playing tombola included us, me and Andy. I ask you, talk about a totally unromantic weekend.

The only highlight of the night came with the arrival of Dick the Prick. I heard the beast roar and instead of red flags flying in the wind, it was more celebratory balloons. I couldn't wait for Dick to meet with my man.

'Hello,' I said, expressing warmth and pleasure as Dick made his entrance. To say Dick was taken aback at my greeting is to underestimate. He was completely bowled over.

'Well, hi there! Good to see you, Janni!' For one blessed second methinks, he thought he was onto a winner; I'd changed my mind and was finally coming round to his way of thinking. That being, he was the man of my dreams and I was about to drag him off to a place in the hills where we could play sex games with each other. But then he saw Andy. Was introduced to Andy.

'This is my boyfriend, Andy from Maiduguri. I've told him all about you, Dick. Well, I've told him about everybody here, so he knows what kind of things we bush people get up to. Andy, this is Dick.'

They shook hands. Andy didn't actually know about Dick. Well, he knew about what happened, he just didn't know that Dick was the Prick in the brothel. So the greeting, on Andy's part was very amicable. But Dick appeared a bit like he had things on his mind. Pressing things on his mind. He mentioned a prior engagement, 'Hell! That I'd forgotten all about.' He gave us a wave, gave everyone a wave. And buggered off.

Anyway, here we were Sunday lunchtime hurtling our way to Kwyaterra.

We got to the lorry park in just under an hour. And sat on a convenient rock, having a few smokes while we waited, and planned our next encounter. I'd visit Maiduguri next weekend, and all the weekends thereafter.

No more rendezvous in Gombe. Well and truly, scrubbed off our list.

There was good news and there was bad news.

The good news was Dad quite liked Andy. *Quite, mind.* He thought him an intelligent, sensitive man. But thought his hair was too long, and some of his ideas a bit strange, and did query whether he smoked, 'This drug that is called pot?'

'Good God, no!' my shocked response. And hastened to add that I didn't either.

The bad news was Dad was still not giving me the green light; having said that, it wasn't on red either; just permanently stuck on orange.

'So you plan to go this weekend, but without Lizzie? Correct.'

'Correct.'

See what I mean? Dad and I were back at it again. Same bloody words, same bloody play, same bloody everything.

'And you plan to stay with Andy? At his house?'

'No. At Rosie's,' I lied.

Remember? Catholic parents. Sex before marriage. Abominable sin.

'Ah, Rosie. She is this young man Sam's sister, if I remember correctly?'

'Yes, that's right. She said I could stay at hers.'

'But, Janni, if I remember correctly, please tell me if I am wrong, Rosie is little more than a child. I believe you told me she is only twelve years old.'

'Thirteen, actually, Dad. It was her birthday last week.'

Dad shrugged. 'Thirteen. Twelve. It makes little difference. She is still very young.'

'For what, Dad? Me staying at her house? Oh, come on, Dad, what difference does it make. Rosie is very mature for her age, and very nice. You've met her, she was at the hotel swimming pool. And Sam. Wasn't he nice?'

'Indeed. But it concerns me that his parents allow him to go off like they do. I don't want people to think the same way about you. Or us. Don't you understand?'

Oh, for Pete's sake! Give me a break!

'I do understand,' I lied again. 'And I appreciate your concern very much. But, Dad, I'm nineteen, or almost nineteen, and if I was back in England I'd be doing what I want anyway. You'd be here, I'd be there, and you'd be none the wiser. I could be up to anything but,' I quickly added, 'I'm not. All I want to do is spend the weekend in Maiduguri, stay at Rosie's, and see Andy, as well. What's the problem?'

Dad gave out a very long, very exasperated sigh. 'If you don't see the problem now, you never will.' And up came the finger, wagging as always. 'But mark my words, one day you'll thank me for the time and effort I and Mum have put into your upbringing. I can't not let you go, as you said, you are an adult, and you must make your own choices. But, as a loving father I want to be sure those choices are the correct choices. Do you understand?'

No, of course I fucking don't understand.

But what the hell, I was going anyway, whether they liked it or not. Might as well try and leave on a right note rather than a wrong foot.

I tried to keep my voice, my objectionable self, out of my voice. My expression, I hoped, was sincere. 'I do understand, Dad. And I love you very much. And I'll be back on Sunday. And I'll be staying at Rosie's. And you know Andy, and you know he's a decent bloke…'

Dad interrupted. 'Yes, he appears decent. And very intelligent. But that doesn't mean he is the right person for you. Remember Johnny?' Inwardly, as always, I flinched at the name. 'Of course you do. We liked him, too. But look what happened there.'

See what I mean? Every which way I turned, and none of it right.

Finally, however, Dad gave me the green/orange light. I went up to Maiduguri by bus on the Friday with my parents' semi-blessings, and pretended I'd stayed at Rosie's, and spent a glorious weekend with Andy, and like the dutiful daughter came back on the Sunday, as planned.

This set the way for the next weekend.

Friday, by bus, to Maiduguri, lie about staying at Rosie's, fantastic time with Andy, back on the bus on Sunday. I've got to say the route to Maiduguri was as familiar to me now as the back of my hand.

The following weekend, Andy and I plotted and planned; more devious ideas so I could stay just that little bit longer. All this travel malarkey was actually getting on my tits. But of course it wasn't just the travelling part that was beginning to pall, it was the leaving

Andy bit that I hated. And Andy said it was the me leaving him bit that he hated. In short, we wanted to be together. All the time.

In the end we decided that I'd simply tell my parents that there were a few events going on mid-week, someone's birthday party, a good film on at the club, and I'd be back the following Monday or Tuesday.

Naturally, my proposal went down like a lead balloon. Initially. But after a long and lengthy discussion, with me doing a bit of hollering and shouting, and Dad doing a bit more hollering and shouting back, the parents finally bowed down to the inevitable and gave me permission to go to Maiduguri for a whole week.

I was over the moon.

Friday morning, I was up at the crack of dawn. Mum dropped me off at the lorry park. As was always her routine, she told me to enquire if the bus was running late, or, as in the case today, where the bus was. Our initial eye search of all the vehicles in this dusty, noisy, fume-ridden place, failed to locate number 10 Bus bound for Maiduguri. To appease my dearest mother, I sighed inwardly but went off in search of Mr Official. I found him having a drink in one of the shacks.

'Ah, good morning,' he said, greeting me with some familiarity. My frequent visits to the lorry park meant that he and I were getting to know each other quite well.

'Good morning.' I smiled. 'Could you tell me where the Maiduguri bus is? I can't seem to be able to find it.'

'Aha, Madame. I am very sorry but that is because it is not here.'

'Not here? When is it coming?'

'Not today, Madame. There is some engine failure. It is in the workshop in Jos.'

'So,' I asked, 'when is the replacement coming?'

Mr. Official took a swig of his drink, and shook his head sadly. 'There is no replacement, Madame.'

'What!' I exclaimed, going all panicky. 'No replacement! How am I going to get to Maiduguri?'

'That, Madame, I am not sure of.'

My heart sank. Now what the fuck was I going to do? Mr Official saw my forlorn face and took pity on me. He gave me an encouraging smile. Had obviously come up with a plan. He looked at his watch.

'There is a lorry, Madame, about to leave in the next half an

27

hour to Bui. And from there you can take another to Damaturu, maybe even straight to Maiduguri.' He smiled. Problem sorted.

I looked at him. I looked at the lorries, those awful, dirty, lethal and dangerous contraptions packed with chickens, goats, native paraphernalia, and native humans. And I looked at my Mum, parked up at the entrance of the lorry park in our silver Ford Cortina, with her head out of the window, awaiting the news of the whereabouts of number 10 Bus bound for Maiduguri.

'Ok,' I said. 'Give me one minute. I'll be back.'

I legged it over to Mum. Opened the passenger door and retrieved my luggage.

'Well?' asked Mum.

'It'll be here in a sec. Some delay back in Jos. So I'll just hang about until it comes. You can go, Mum. I'll be alright.'

'Are you sure? I don't mind waiting.'

'I'm sure.' Certain, in fact.

'Well, alright, darling.' Mum started the engine up. I leant over and kissed her. 'Take care. Won't you?' A little, mumsy kind of desperation had now taken hold. 'You will take care, won't you?' she said again.

'Of course.'

'Bye, darling.'

'Bye.'

We blew kisses and off she drove.

Hurling my bags over both shoulders, I legged it back to Mr Official. 'Which one is mine?'

He pointed to a mammy-wagon just like the rest. I paid for my ticket to ride and was given an official escort to the pile of shit that was my mode of transport for the day. There was a babble of Hausa as Mr Official explained my presence to the driver, and more babbles of Hausa as the driver got one of his lackeys to throw my bags on, and more babbles from everyone in the vicinity, as I was given a leg up. Crowds came to observe the unusual sighting of a young baturi woman master the art of climbing onto a mammy-wagon. Gripping the wood slats, I scrambled and pushed myself over the top (thank God I was wearing trousers) and several pairs of hands helped pull me into the caged-wagon.

'Na gode, na gode,' I kept saying. 'Thank you, thank you.' As various travelers, unsmilingly, shifted themselves and gave me space. Not that there was much space in the first place. But I managed to crawl over the piles of sacks, and the bundles of cloth-wrapped belongings, and the human and animal cargo, to a tiny pocket where sat my bags. I squeezed myself between several wooden crates that were jam-packed with chickens, all clucking away in a mad kind of frenzy, pecking at each other, flapping their wings, with no room to move. Like us humans, really. Feathers and shit dropped out of the sides, much of it over me. Their squawks, their smells, and other smells, unwashed body smells, stale wood smoke smells, yesterday spicy dinner smells, peanut smells, sack smells, and the dust, and the heat, and the discomfort, all made for a pretty hellish environment. But what choice did I have? None.

And that was how it was for the next four, long hours as we slowly, so slowly, chugged our way up to Bui. It wasn't that the driver was driving at some stupid ten mile an hour pace, indeed there were times when I had to hold onto my hair he was going that fast, what was slowing the whole journey down was all the stops. At every fucking village, every fucking mile, we stopped. Loads were dropped off, people climbed down, loads were thrown up, people climbed on. And we shifted, and we made new spaces, and every one looked grim, and nobody smiled, and the smells got worse, and the heat got hotter. And I thought, if only my Mum and Dad could see me now.

At long last Bui came into our sights. Desperate for a pee, I scrambled down the sides of the wagon, and surrounded by an entourage of inquisitive bystanders we all headed off to my little shack, where I was observed going to the loo. And then my ragged fans followed me round the lorry park as I made my enquiries and ascertained which lorry was next on my travelling list. I was in luck. One was going all the way to Maiduguri in the next hour. So, while I waited, I bought myself a bottle of Coke, plopped myself down on an empty wooden crate, and got one of my ready to smoke little joints from out of my bag. And there I sat, getting quietly stoned, smiling and sharing a joke or two with my groupies who refused to leave my side for the whole of my stay.

Some had their begging bowls out but I didn't part with a kobo, if I had the whole of the lorry park crowd, about five hundred or so souls would have been alerted to this generous fact, and I'd have been mobbed. And probably stripped of all my assets. So I stayed mean.

And some tried to flog me 'abinche', food. Meaty morsels on sticks, plus a few other odd-looking victuals but I declined. I think, more than anything, it was the flies, buzzing and writhing over these gastronomic delights that put me off. Anyway, I wasn't going to starve. Mum had packed me a little bag of goodies, an orange, a mound of sandwiches, a packet of biscuits, and a flask of squash. However, I was loathed to even eat my hygienically packed victuals, my hands were that dirty I could have planted seeds and watched flowers grow out of my palms. And there was nowhere to wash them. So I made do with a couple of boiled sweets purchased from a small boy who was also selling cigarettes and koala nuts from his little tin tray. Somehow, maybe because he looked so cute and doe-eyed, he managed to flog me the lot even though I hated koala nuts and had enough cigarettes on me to set up my own cigarette stall, if I so wished. Still, it made his day (it was probably the best day in the whole of his life), so that was okay. Except that once the news had spread, every bloody seller in the lorry park were now hot on my heels, trying to get rid of their rubbish on silly old me.

Dare I say it, but it was a joy to finally clamber on my Maiduguri bound lorry, and escape the scrum of sweetie, cigarette, and koala nut pushers that had now gathered from all the far corners of Bui. Once on the lorry, I did my Mother Christmas act, and began handing out to my somewhat startled travelling companions, a koala nut here, a cigarette there, that made them a little friendlier and give me a little more legroom. A little more, mind. Nothing to write home about, really

After ten long hours, it might even have been twelve because I'd lost all sense of time, we finally chugged our way into Maiduguri's lorry park. Never has a lorry park appeared so welcoming, despite the fact that there was no one there to welcome me. Andy obviously had checked out the buses, been told the bad news, assumed I wasn't coming, and gone home. Of course I expected this and so had to work out a plan. How to get from here, the lorry park, to there, Andy's house?

I walked.

By this time it was eleven at night, and there was really no other option. Jesus, it was a struggle. Tramping through the native part of town, with all the crowds and the mayhem, my legs and my body aching from a day cramped up in a lorry. My bags so heavy, I thought my arms would drop off. I was like a vagrant, a vagabond of no fixed abode. Dirty, dishevelled, smelly and tired. All I really wanted to do was curl up in a corner, any corner, and sleep. But I plodded on. And dreamed of Andy and his little house.

Finally, I left the clamour and chaos and found myself strolling down a still and silent road, beneath a dense canopy of neem trees. The air was warm, and the peppery and fiery smells of the African quarters were now replaced by fresh, leafy aromas. And the only sounds came from the hot buzz of the singing cicadas. Occasionally a dog barked, a motorbike droned by, as did a couple of cars. Other than them it was just me, all on my little lonesome. If I hadn't been so tired I think I'd of enjoyed the peace and the quiet, and the moonlight and the breeze in the trees. After a day in a hot, dirty, noisy, cramped-up, smelly mammy-wagon, believe me, an open road, devoid of sunlight, with peace and quiet all around is a longed for moment.

I put down my bags, with some relief, my arms and shoulders were killing me, and by the light of the moon peered at my watch. It was half past twelve. Bloody hell! I'd been on the road for more than sixteen hours and hadn't talked to or seen a single white person since saying goodbye to Mum at eight, yesterday morning. If only those intrepid explorers could see me now, I thought. I'd show them what being intrepid is really all about.

An hour later I was on an earthen path, the soft pad of my desert boots the only sound, apart from the chorus of crickets and the flitting of bats. And ahead of me, Andy's house, cocooned in darkness, as was every other bungalow on the Forestry campus. A few outside lamps were flickering but inside, the world and its mother, including Andy, were all fast asleep.

Quietly I crept up the veranda steps, and gently opened the unlocked door. Entered a room still pungent with the aromas of incense and marijuana. And Andy asleep on his bed. I put down my bags, and took off my dirty, smelly clothes. Tiptoed to the bathroom and had a shower. The cool water dripped over me, the dirt washed out, I could see the brown, liquid muck spiral down the plughole. And I inspected my poor, blistered feet. And I lathered my hair with soap because there wasn't any shampoo. And dried myself with a tea towel. And then slipped quietly back into the room. And still Andy hadn't stirred. I lifted up the net and slid in beside him. He opened his eyes. Moonlight flooded in through the window. He smiled, enveloped me in his arms.

I'd made it! I was finally home.

The next morning I slept in, until well after lunch. So did Andy. It was Saturday, after all.

At two-ish we pootled into town, and ambled hand-in-hand round the busy, bustling, and as always, very smelly market. Andy said he wanted to buy me something very special. It turned out to be a ring, a lovely one made of Bida brass. He said it was a symbol of our love, and placed it on my wedding finger. I felt I was floating on cloud number nine.

Then Andy spotted the Jolly Photo Studios.

'Fancy having a photo done together?' he asked, grabbing my hand and zipping me in and out of traffic and humans, to the other side of the road.

Of course I did. So we flip-flopped our way up the steps, into the little shop where a dazzling array of smiling and not-so smiling Africans greeted us from a variety of framed photographs displayed on the walls. There were happy couples in wedding gear, chuckling babies lying on mats, toddlers with frilly outfits giving the pose bit their very best shot, university graduates grinning from ear-to-ear as they clutched their scrolls and looked silly. And there were families, whole groups of them, all piled up together, dressed in their Sunday best, dead rigid, formal, and oh, so fucking serious.

'Ahhem,' coughed Andy, because no one was in the shop. On the second 'ahhem', Mr Jolly materialised from behind a curtain. He smiled. Rubbed his hands. Took off his glasses and gave them a wipe on the sleeve of his shirt.

'Madame? Master? Can I help you?'

We told him he could. Explained what we wanted. Thus so, and were invited to step behind the curtain. And pose.

'It is a question of capturing your love,' explained Mr Jolly. And he fiddled and faddled, and moved us about. 'Now, Madam, if you will be so kind as to put your arm a little this way, good, good. And, Master, your hand, if you please, right here.' And then he'd dart back to his camera, have a quick shifty through the lens, shake his head, sprint back, move my chin ever so slightly, Andy's shoulder a third of an inch until… 'Perfect!' Back to camera, and click.

We sat on the steps of the Jolly Photo Studios and waited. And smoked a couple of fags, and drank a couple of Cokes.

'It is done!'

It certainly was. Andy's looking down at me, I'm looking up; we're smiling into each other's eyes. A moment of love. A photo to treasure and keep.

'Look,' I gushed, and showed Hamish the black and white image. He took the pipe out of his mouth and gave it his full attention.

'Aye, that's not bad. You'll have to find a wee frame for it and hang it on the wall.' He smiled and handed it me back.

'And look,' I gushed again. And held out my left hand and wiggled my fourth finger.

'He must be serious,' chuckled Hamish. 'I dinna think he'd be handing out these kind of things just to any wee lass. I'm happy for you, Janni, no doubt about it.'

We sat back, me in the rocking chair and Hamish on his little stool, and enjoyed a moment of companionable silence. It was early evening, a good time to just sit with a tranquil companion, sip tea, roll a spliff, and rock yourself slowly, to and fro.

'Fancy a puff?' I asked. I leaned across, ready to hand Hamish over the smouldering joint.

'Och, no. There are times, like now, when I don't really think I need to alter the way I'm feeling. I'm feeling that good, why change it?'

I nodded but didn't really understand the drift. He was a weird one, was Hamish.

A motorbike purred along the sandy thoroughfare and stopped outside Andy's house. Our house. The rider was a Nigerian bloke, a big, black man with a big, black beard and he wore mirrored shades, even though the sun had sunk over the horizon long ago.

Black Beard dismounted his chopper, unhooked a bag from the rack at the back, slung it over him like a satchel, and mounted Andy's veranda steps. He tapped on the door, and waited. Tapped again, looked up and around, checked out Andy's bike that was parked up by the side, and knocked on the door once again.

'Can I help?' I shouted from across the way.

Black Beard turned. He smiled and took off his shades.

'Mr Andy, he is expecting me. Is he not here?'

'Hang on a minute.' I flounced out of my rocker and took Hamish's veranda steps two at a time.

'He is,' I replied, up near now to Black Beard. 'Wait, I'll go and get him.'

I entered the room that was pungent with the aromas of incense and marijuana. It was empty. The bed still unmade, the little anthology still on the floor, and Bob Dylan, still a-blowing in the wind from a tape in the cassette player.

'Andy! Andy!' I called. Then heard the rush and tumble of gushing water.

'I'm in here. In the shower.'

I half-opened the bathroom door. And stuck my head round. My man, all naked and brown was also all wet and soapy. He smiled. Gave a grin. 'Are you about to come in and join me?' said he, with a glint in his eye.

I laughed. That's what I loved about Andy. He always liked sharing things with me that were a little bit naughty. 'There's a bloke to see you.'

'Who?' asked Andy, as he flannelled his feet.

'I dunno. A Nigerian with a big, black beard.'

'Och, it's Bello. Where is he?'

'Out on the veranda.'

'Tell him I'll be just a minute.'

I shut the door and legged it back out to the veranda.

'He'll be just a sec.'

Bello smiled, took out a packet of fags and offered me one.

'Thanks.'

We lit up and waited.

Andy padded out in bare feet, two minutes later. All wet and warm, with a tea towel wrapped round his waist.

'Hi, there, man.' He gave the Nigerian a hearty embrace.

'Hey,' chuckled Black Beard, when their bodies were parted, 'let me look at you.' With hands on Andy's shoulders, he laughed. The laugh sounded not unlike a rumble of thunder. 'You're looking good, man.' Another embrace quickly followed.

'This is Janni,' said Andy, when hail-fellow-well-met greetings were finally over.

A hand as big as one of my Granny's cured hams clasped my little paw, while the other ham grasped my shoulder.

'Hey, my man, this woman is looking good.' And he laughed, showing off his brilliant-white teeth. 'Is she your woman?'

Andy nodded. Smiled. A light lit up in my tummy. His woman/Andy's woman. God, it made me feel so bloody horny and special.

'Hey, hey, hey, my man. You have done well for yourself. This woman is good. Good, good, good.' More laughter, more brilliant-white teeth. 'I am Bello,' he declared. 'And this man,' a glance Andy's way, 'is my friend. Yah. Dat is right.'

And, still with his ham in my paw, and the other still on my shoulder, the big, black bloke, with the big, black beard, fell about shrieking with mirth. Followed by a slapping of his thighs, a slap on Andy's back, and then he grabbed me and gave me a heartfelt embrace. I could barely breathe. And was lost in the bearded forest.

'Come on in, man,' invited Andy. This, I think, was a polite way of telling Black Beard that enough was enough. His hands were now squeezing my bum.

Still chuckling away, Bello released me but hung on to my hand, and we all moved off the veranda and into the house. Somehow I managed to retrieve my five incredibly squashed to the bone digits, and sat on the bed. Bello and Andy took a chair each and plopped themselves down, round a small, wooden table.

'Smoke?'

'Yah, man.'

Andy did the business and began rolling the joint. 'So, what have you got for me today, Bello?' he asked, as his tongue slid across the Rizla.

'Good stuff. Believe me, the best.' And he pulled his bag over his head and placed it on the table. Next, he took from it a very large packet that was wrapped in several layers of newspaper. He removed the outer page and revealed an inner page. He removed the inner page and revealed a plastic bag. He removed the plastic bag, opened it up and revealed a mountain of dried marijuana.

'This grass is the best. Grown in the mountains of Mambilla where the air is fresh and clean. Taste, go taste it, man, smell it.'

Andy, with his joint already lit, tendrils of smoke rising from between his fingers, used his free hand to pick up a small pinch of grass. He put the dried cuttings to his nose, sniffed, and then placed the stuff on his tongue, rolled it around, and swallowed.

'This is good, Bello.' And he passed him over the smoking, rolled-up version. Bello took a long, deep drag and then looked over my way.

'Come, come,' he said.

I got up from the bed and dragged a chair over.

'Taste. Taste.'

I followed Andy's example, picked up a pinch, sniffed, dropped the grass on my tongue, it tasted weird, and then swallowed. Half of the stuff still stuck to my tongue, the rest in bits down my throat. Not pleasant but not unpleasant. A bit like chewing on a dollop of mixed garden herbs.

'It is good. Yes?' Bello's quite bulbous eyes were on me. I thought they might just pop out of his head and land on the zanna mat carpet.

'Yes. It is good.' And I smiled, and tried to ignore the prickly sensation that was somewhere stuck round my windpipe.

'Yah, man! It is good!' And Bello fell about his chair, laughing, slapping his thighs, and then one hand on me, the still lit joint singeing my hair.

Finally, after much merriment, he looked seriously at Andy and said, 'Have we a deal?'

'Deal,' nodded Andy.

More guffawing to follow, more slapping of thighs, more singeing of hair, more brilliant-white teeth, more bulbous eye-popping.

Andy got up, went to a drawer and pulled out a bundle of money.

'As agreed, hey Bello?'

'As agreed.'

I moved away, went to change the tape, couldn't cope with more of the side slapping, eye-popping routine.

But Bello was for the off anyway. Business was over, time to shake hands and make leave.

'You are a good woman, yah man,' he said to me by the door.

I was still sorting through tapes. It was a good ploy, saved me from having to endure a bone crunching, hand-slapping embrace from the bloke with the beard.

I smiled, and said goodbye with a wave.

My days in Maiduguri settled into a nice, easy, gentle pattern.

During the week I'd get up with Andy around about seven. Yes, even I was surprised at my early morning efforts, but then if you've got something worth getting up for, it isn't that hard. We'd wake, with streams of golden sunlight pouring in through the half opened, un-curtained window by our bed, and hear the songs and whistles of a hundred different types of birds having a chinwag in the trees.

Andy was always the first one to stir. He'd nibble my ears and tickle my feet. And cover my face with kisses. I'd open my eyes, stretch out my arms, and together we'd move into a passionate embrace and the old bed would creak.

It was a glorious start to the day.

Afterwards, when the room was silent and we were still, we'd lie for a while, my head on Andy's chest, and bask like a couple of purring cats in a bed made up of dappled squares of brilliant sunlight. And in this dream-like state listen out for the clatter of breakfast pans from the little, outside kitchen, and the voices of Buggy and Hamish. This was our early morning alarm call.

'Time to get up,' Andy would whisper in my ear.

I'd smile, close my eyes, feeling my hair warm on my cheek, not wanting to move, and I'd say, 'Just another five minutes.'

Andy never argued the toss. He'd swing his bare feet out from under the net and onto the cool, cool concrete floor, have an almighty stretch, and then put on his wraparound towel. After a quick visit to the loo he'd pad quietly out of the bed-sitting room, through to the veranda and on to the kitchen.

'Morning, guys,' I'd hear him say from somewhere outside.

'Morning, Andy,' from Hamish and Buggy.

Five minutes later he was back with two steaming mugs of tea. Time for me to give a yawn, do a full stretch in the bed, and lazily fight my way out from under the net. Thus so, on with the blue silk kimono, a pad across to the bathroom, and then go put a tape on, usually something gentle like James Taylor or Carly Simon to herald the first blush of the day.

Supping our early morning beverage, and we'd also have a smoke. It gave a kind of warm kick-start to the rest of the day, made one feel benevolent to one's fellow human beings. Certainly it always brought a smile to my lips and made life seem nice and easy.

Twenty minutes later we'd be sitting on Hamish's little porch, drinking more tea, and spreading margarine and homemade marmalade on homemade rolls or charcoal, crunchy toast. And while the song-thrush sang from a nearby bush, and the robin-chat whistled a very beautiful range of liquid notes from its nest in a mango tree, the four of us would discuss what plans we each had for the day.

'Fuck, man, I've got a hangover. I'm taking it easy, I can tell you,' Buggy would say most mornings. And he'd be holding his head in his hands and downing more tea than was found in China, and popping the aspirins.

We'd laugh, shake our heads, and offer little sympathy.

Next was Andy.

'I'm off with Bruce to check over the plantation out at Baga. I might not be back until late afternoon.' And looking at me, he'd touch me lightly, push the hair back off my face, and ask, 'And what, my wee one, are your plans for the day?'

'Oh,' I'd reply, 'a bit of this and a bit of that.'

As a rule, I usually took myself back off to bed for a couple more hours, and got up again just in time to share Hamish's elevenses with him on his veranda. He was almost always around during the day as his office and studio was his front room and porch. After coffee, biscuits and a smoke on a fag, I'd let Hamish get on with his artwork, amble back to Andy's small bungalow and have a potter around for a while.

Funny how doing very little in one place is not at all the same as doing very little in another place. Here in Maiduguri, I enjoyed a couple of hours of time on my own and had little need for outside stimulation. I'd listen to some music, read a bit, smoke a couple more joints (that always helped), pen a few poems, have a dance round the room, or just sit in a deckchair on the empty, peaceful veranda, and listen to the tweets of the birds while I pondered on my many incredible things.

Like how much I loved Andy, and how much he loved me.

I'd sit with my knees up under my chin, and bask in the glow. And I'd smile at the memory of something he'd said earlier, and anticipate the pleasures that would come later that night. And thinking these thoughts, like the twirling, whirling velvety insects that danced round the red and yellow flowered bushes, those permanently inside me would flutter and spin and tickle around in my tummy.

Some mornings, I might have a visitor or two.

Someone, perhaps, just popping by on the off chance to purchase a small bag of grass. Andy had given me my instructions, where, what and how much. And I was happy to do business. It certainly was an opportunity to meet up with new '*my kind of people*' and others who I considered now as old friends.

'Hiya,' Richard would call out. 'Are you home, Janni?'

Well, of course I was at home. Music blaring, joss sticks burning, dope smoking, me singing, why would anyone think I'd be elsewhere when all this was going on?

'Come on in, Richard,' I'd say like the lady laird of the house. I'd jump out of my chair where I'd been reading my book, nothing fancy, Agatha Christie's 'The Murder of Roger Ackroyd' as it so happens. But as it wasn't a cool kind of book I'd tuck it under the pillow, or put it in a drawer, and pull it out only when my visitor or visitors had gone.

And Richard and I would share a fag, and a joint, and I'd ask the cook to make us both a cup of tea or open up a couple of bottles of Coke, and we'd sit out on the veranda and talk about this, and talk about that. Then after a while he'd look at his watch, and say, 'Fuck! Better get going.'

So quickly I'd potter off to the drawer and pull out the bag, dollop a load of grass in Richard's tin, he'd hand over some nairas, the money would be put in the drawer with the bag of grass, and that was it. Deal, well and truly done. And he'd get on his bike, and with a cheery wave, trundle off back to wherever he was working.

I'd just settle down to some more skulduggery with the famous Mr Ackroyd and another bike would pull up outside.

'Hi, I'm Mike,' the blonde man on the veranda would say.

'Hi, I'm Janni,' replies the girl, with the bare feet and the long flowing curls.

'I guessed. I've heard all about you.'

'All good, I hope?'

'Yep, all good. More than good.'

And Mike would smile, and my heart would miss a beat, and I'd think, God there's some handsome blokes here in Maiduguri. And I'd toss my hair back, just a little, and say, 'What can I do for you, Mike?'

He'd raise an eyebrow, or two. A tad suggestively? And flash me over yet another lovely beam.

'Andy told me to pop round. He said he'd just got a delivery of some more grass, good stuff. Said you'd sort me some out.'

And I'd smile, and toss my hair back, just a little again, and think, if only the girls back at school were here now to see my cool, cat performance.

'Yeah, sure, come on in.'

And handsome, blonde Mike follows me into the house, and I go through the motions, how much does he want, and would he pass me his tin. And afterwards, we'd sit out on the veranda, share a joint, and listen to The Byrds on the tape, and to the birds in the trees, whilst drinking ice-lemon tea.

It was all so very nice, and so very easy.

Sometimes it was the girls who'd be knocking on my door. Some came to buy dope, some just popped round for a chat. Sally, if she had a free hour, and Anne, Amy, and, of course, my little friend Rosie.

During that first week in Maiduguri, she bunked off school several times and spent her mornings with me. We'd pull up a couple of deckchairs and plant ourselves in a hot spot in the sun, and share our experiences, our strengths and our profundity of thoughts.

Bearing in mind our ages, one would think that there wouldn't be much of any of those three but we reckoned there was. Certainly we always had plenty to talk about; I felt totally and utterly relaxed in her company. I suppose, here in Maiduguri, she was my bestest of best friends. And Hamish, well, he came a close second. There wasn't much, I reckoned, that I couldn't tell him.

When Rosie was with me (or even when she wasn't), we'd join Hamish on his veranda for lunch, cheese and tomato sandwiches usually, or a bowl of the cook's homemade groundnut soup, and afterwards jump on her little bike and head off to one of the pools. There, we'd spend the afternoon lazing about and splashing around in the cool, blue chlorinated water under a hot, unbroken sky, with other members of the gang who'd managed to get off work or school just that little bit earlier.

If, after lunch, there were no one around to give me a lift, I'd take a stroll down the sandy path, through the dappled sunlight and emerald green woods, with the air full of the sounds of birds, to the club. And maybe encounter someone I knew on the way.

A purr of a motorbike, it pulls up beside me.

'Hiya, Janni.'

'Hiya, Phil.'

'Need a ride?'

'If you're going to the club?'

'Sure. Why not? Hop on.'

Again, all nice and easy. A chilled out kind of life.

On some occasions, my very own man took a break mid-morning and paid me a visit. He'd hurtle down the powdery track on his bike, and my heart would miss a beat.

'Hi,' I'd say from my spot on the veranda, while the butterflies inside went dancing mad.

'Hi,' he'd say.

And strolling over, he'd grab my hand and lead me to bed without saying another word. And afterwards, when he'd gone back to his plantation in Bama or Baga, I'd lie all warm and sticky on the cool, crispy sheets, and close my eyes. Drifting. Off for an extra half an hour of deep, contented, sweet-dreamy sleep.

Or he might leave work early afternoon, and take me somewhere far away in the bush. On the Wednesday we went right up to the Chad border and watched a camel race, just Andy and I, the only white skins amongst swarthy, turbaned gents with long, swirling robes, in a true desert setting. Red/brown mud-walled and flat mud-roofed buildings, and not a tin roof or a block of cement, or a brick or a pane of glass in sight. Just sand, more sand, and more sand. And dust. And a few prickly thorn trees and bushes. And of course, hundreds and hundreds of tawny-coloured humpbacked ships of the desert, thundering across the sun-baked track; a scene of billowing robes and tumulus dust clouds, yellow powder being tossed in the dry air by hundreds of hoofs. And a screaming frenzy from the excited spectators, a cacophony of sounds, trumpets blowing, drums beating, goats bleating, donkeys braying, the whole effect like one's taken an acid trip too many.

And not a female in sight, except me.

Afterwards, we drove across stony ground to Lake Chad, not the hotel but the expanse of water, the part that washes up against the shores of Nigeria.

Sunlight poured like honey on blue, silent ripples. The banks full of bulrushes, and turquoise, shimmering dragonflies flying and fluttering in and out of the tall reeds. Giant toads, and watery lizards, hunched and still, green, with bright yellow eyes and enormous black pupils, watched us while vivid blue and red-bellied kingfishers, enjoying a bath, were diving and breaking the liquid surface, again, and again, and again.

I can tell you, after a day spent in the company of camels, turbaned chaos, dry heat, and dust, with not a drop of water in sight, the lake was an oasis of calm, a welcoming sight.

We hired a boat, a dugout, from a fisherman who was pottering along the bank with a large, round, hollow calabash that had one hole as an opening, and a dangling piece of string. This was the fisherman's 'net'. Put a bit of bait in the inner sanctums; throw the calabash out into the water, hold on to the string, and wait for the catch. Quite simple really.

Anyway, in our floating log, we drifted off to a quiet place amongst the reeds and the bulrushes. And while the sun spread its red, orange tendrils in a sky now the colour of gold, we smoked and got a little stoned, read poems and dreamed. And made love, as egrets and herons and finches watched on.

It was pure, utter magic.

Other evenings, we'd amble over to Hamish's at around about six. Sitting out on his veranda, and watch the dissolving shimmer of heat as the solar planet slipped lower, and the first pale streaks of silvery-grey appeared in the sky. And when silver turned to blue velvet, cue for the cook to light the hurricane lamps, before the moon had taken its place in the sky. And together we'd enjoy the ambience, share a joint, a glass of beer, and take it nice and easy.

And I'd think to myself, like in the song, what a wonderful, wonderful world.

After supper, when we'd eaten our fill of garri, or it might be maize cakes, or a bowl of yam stew, all of us, or maybe just Andy and I would head for the club and join up with other like-minded folk. We'd spend the evening chinwagging under the fairy lights out on the patio. And there was always someone new to meet, always something of interest going on. And I loved it. Being part of the gang. And being with my man.

On the Thursday we went to a party. It was nothing like the damp squid do I'd been to in Bauchi, a few weeks previously. This event took place in Baga, and was hosted by Dutch volunteers, who knew how to have a good time. Quite a crew of us went. We managed to get hold of a Land Rover that was big enough to hold ten people comfortably, and about fifteen of us squashed ourselves in. A tad uncomfortable but who cared?

There's nothing like the feel of adventure as you zoom down a wilderness road with nothing but bush and darkness either side. The headlights pick up all sorts of things in a world that appears empty. A pair of bright, darting eyes. Two pairs of bright, darting eyes. A four-legged creature, a moment stuck on full beam, paralysed with fear, and then off, gone forever.

Halfway, I needed a pee. Asked Mark, who was driving, to stop; everyone fell out, the boys did the business right up against the vehicle, us girls headed off into the dark, scrambling over rocks, and tufts of grass until we found a safe spot because the blokes were now trying to spy on us with their torches.

'Behind here!' I hissed.

Meaning, behind this large solid mass, a three foot high, weirdly shaped anthill. And we scurried, and hid from the search beams and all pulled down our knickers.

Then screamed.

The anthill had moved.

'Oh, my God! Oh, my God! Oh, my God!'

'What?!!' shouted the boys. And with torches, they searched frantically for us, Andy and Buggy, and Mark, rushing madly around in the bush. And us screaming and hollering as the anthill now rose up and stood, and spread out things that appeared to be arms, and made a sound that appeared to be words. 'Yawwa, sannu',

42

I think it said.

Finally a light lit up our spot. Shined in on our six foot, mobile anthill dressed in a billowing, brown robe.

It's a fucking bloke!' yelled Buggy, to the others by the Land Rover and those still frantically searching. 'A fucking bloke in the bush.'

And everyone, including the fucking bloke in the bush, laughed. Even though, by the look on his face, he was really pissed off. Well, anyone would be. You think you're going off for a few minutes peace in a wilderness setting, away from the kids and the wife, and a bunch of white idiots stop their vehicle just at the spot where you are, and pile out and do a wee on your riga. It'd make anyone a little pissed.

Anyway, after apologies, and greetings, we all piled back in the Land Rover and set off once again. Left the bloke in the bush to his night-time mediation.

And we all sang as we puffed on our fags and our joints, and if someone was up in the sky looking down, they'd see two single head beams going along in an otherwise totally dark world, and think the vehicle was on fire, there was that much smoke billowing out.

Somewhere along the way we turned off, and bumped up some stony track to a bungalow shining bright in the inky night. A bonfire crackled and spat, and lit up the compound. The aromas of wood smoke and marijuana wafted and mingled with food cooking smells, alcohol smells, and the joss sticks and patchouli perfumed oils; a heady mix that blew your nasal senses for six.

Later, as I sat on a step on the veranda, with my joint and my drink, talking to Phil and someone called Bill, and Rosie and Jan, I looked across at my man talking to Mike and Amy, and someone called Mischa. I stopped listening to Phil and Bill, couldn't concentrate on what Rosie or Jan were saying. I was watching the glint of fire sparkle on the silvery snake, the strands of golden hair shine from the glow, the long fingers move in the air, the handsome face with its beautiful smile. And my heart soared. He's mine, all mine, I said to myself. And the butterflies whirled in my tummy.

Especially when Andy turned, looked my way. From across a bonfire, in a crowded, outdoor space, there was now no one else. Just the two of us, in our star-studded dream.

That week in Maiduguri went very quickly, very quickly indeed. Before I knew it, Monday was here.

Monday came, and Monday went.
Followed by Tuesday.
And I decided I wasn't going home.

25th Nov.
Darling Mum and Dad (I wrote).

*I'm sending you this note just to let you know I'm very well,
and having a great time. I'm still at Rosie's and her parents have
kindly said I can stay another week. There's quite a few things going
on, you see, at the moment. Sam's having a big eighteenth birthday
party on Thursday* (totally untrue but how would they ever know?),
*and midweek there's a dance on at the Lake Chad Hotel. With some
band playing. Apparently they're really good this band, so I'd love
to stay and hear them.*

(Now this bit was true. Well, the first bit, the dance and the
band playing bit at the hotel. Except, it was last Saturday. And there
was no way I'd ever go to a poxy dance where everyone there were
friends of my parents, either that, or their age, all dressed up in
glittery dresses and shiny, dark suits. Also, apparently the band was
hideous. A group of earnest Nigerians playing jazz and ballroom
dancing, fox-trotty tunes! Yuck).

*Please don't worry about me. I'm really fine, and am
remembering, Mum, to take my paludrine* (the last time I'd taken a
tablet was the day before I'd clambered on the mammy-wagon).

I'll see you next week.

Lots and lots of love and kisses. Janni xxxxxxxxxxxxx

I raced to the lorry park at eight, Tuesday morning, on the back
of Andy's bike, and gave the coach driver the letter. And a couple of
naira as payment for his services, hopefully he'd render.

'Can you please give this to my mother?' I asked the somewhat
bemused, but chuffed with the money, man as he sat behind his
large steering wheel. I explained she'd be the only white woman at
the lorry park in Gombe, and she'd be driving a silver Ford Cortina.
He shouldn't have too much trouble trying to locate her. 'Tell her not
to worry. Tell her you've seen me and I'm looking fine. Oh, and just
would you mind very, very much if (at this point I dug deep into my
bag and pulled out another note) if you'd tell my Mum I was with a
girl called Rosie. That this man here (pointing to Andy) wasn't here.
Do you understand?' And I handed over the note as a bribe.

'Yes, yes Madam,' and Mr Go Along With Anything driver, pocketed the extra naira and grinned.

'Good!' And turning to Andy. 'That's it, then. Shall we go?'

More take it nice and easy days lay ahead.

CHAPTER 2

December 1973

A week later and I was back at the lorry park. With letter number two.

1ˢᵗ December

Darling Mum and Dad,

I expect you're really worried but don't be. Everything is fine and I'm having a wonderful time. There's so much going on here in Maiduguri. Rosie's parents are really kind and say I can stay for as long as I want. Isn't that good of them? Obviously, you'll want to see me soon, and I promise I'll be on the bus next week. I really, really mean it. All I can say is please don't worry.

Give my love to Lizzie and Henry, and everybody else. And a hug to Woggles,

Lots and lots of love, Jannixxxxxxxxxxx

Ps Andy sends his love, too!!!!

PPs Don't worry about money because I'm not spending much!!!

Thankfully Mr Go Along With Anything driver was again behind the wheel of the bus. I gave him an extra naira for his services (on top of his usual regular payment), and instructed him to give this letter to the same lady as before. He assured me 'As Allah is Good' that he would.

'How was my Mother, by the way?' I asked, feeling a tad guilty. Very guilty, actually. But not enough to have me change my mind and jump on the bus.

'She be looking very very well, Madam,' nodded the driver, smiling. 'And she done tank me very very much for dat letter.'

'Oh, good. And she didn't look upset, or anything?'

'Upset, Madam?'

'Yes. Maybe a little angry?'

'No, she no look angry but I tink she have big surprise when I give dis letter to Madam and you no on the bus. I tink she be sad, if she done see you she be happy, that to be sure.'

More guilt to add to the pile. I hadn't planned to make Mum unhappy.

'Can you give my Mother my love, please. And tell her I'm well.'

'No problem, Madam.'

'Thanks,' I said.

And that was it.

And off I went.

Until next week. Same time. Same place. Same letter, just a different date.

A few days on, and I was painting a picture. Sat out on the little veranda, with a couple of green lizards and a regular army of black ants. I'd borrowed a box of watercolours from Hamish, and an easel, and paintbrush and was trying to capture the natural beauty of the flame tree opposite on a very large piece of white paper.

'Gee, but it's great to be back home/Home is where I want to be-ee', trilled Simon & Garfunkel somewhat inaptly from the cassette player by my feet. I lit up a fag and daubed a smudge of red paint on what was supposed to be a flame flower. Whoops! Too much water on the brush, and the red trickled and ran down the paper, converging in a blobby mass at the bottom of what was supposed to be the tree trunk.

'Shit!'

I stood back and perused. The painting looked a mess. What the hell? I was never any good at this kind of thing, anyway. I dabbed off the offending dribble using the hem of my skirt, and voila! Now I'd made a hole through the paper because I'd rubbed it too hard.

Meanwhile, a vehicle was pulling up alongside the bungalow. I heard a door open and then go 'clunk' as it shut, followed by the pad of footsteps coming this way. More visitors? I'd already entertained two lots this morning. A bloke called Kurt and his mate Meikle who were after some dope, and Sam who'd popped over for coffee and a bit of a chat.

'Hello, Janni. Glad to find you're in.'

'Mr Woodruff?'

Up the veranda steps Mr Woodruff came, mounted them two at a time. *What the fuck did Mr Woodruff, friend of my parents, want? Not some grass, surely?*

I put the brush in a tumbler full of pinkish, brown water, stubbed out the fag, turned off the music and smiled a welcoming smile.

'How are you, Mr Woodruff?'

'Very well, thank you, Janni. And yourself?'

'I'm fine, thanks.'

'I'm pleased to hear it.'

He scratched his head. Looked a tad embarrassed. *My God, maybe he is after some dope.*

'And Andy. How's he? I've not had a chance to catch up with him lately, with him over at Baga most days.'

'He's fine, Mr Woodruff, thanks.'

I smiled again. Obviously he wanted Andy, was Andy's boss after all. Then I had a horrible thought. Maybe Mr Woodruff had come to tick my man off, about his absenteeism from work yesterday, and twice last week. I madly tried to think up excuses if this was the case, I'd been ill, some awful accident, perhaps? Andy had raced to my side to deal with the emergency.

Awkward silence for a second or two.

Mr Woodruff scratched the side of his nose. I tossed my hair back, just a little. And waited. Hoped that what he wanted to say would be short and he'd soon go away.

'May I sit?' He pointed to the other deckchair on the veranda. A full to over flowing ashtray, fags, matches, and my bag were on the seat.

Fuck! This meant he was planning on hanging around for a while.

'Of course,' I said, clearing the space and dumping the lot on the floor. And remembering my manners. 'Can I get you a drink? A beer? A cup of tea, Mr Woodruff?'

'No. No thanks.'

He took a glance at my painting efforts, and hovered over the easel before plopping himself down. 'Enjoy painting, do you?'

I laughed. Nervously.

It didn't feel right. Him, Mr Woodruff, friend of my parents, making small talk with me here on Andy's veranda. There was something fishy going on, no doubt about it. This was definitely no casual 'oh, I'll just pop round and see Janni and look at her painting' type of call.

'I do. But I'm not very good. Not like Hamish,' I replied in a carefree and nonchalant manner, to hide my growing discomfort.

48

'Well, Hamish is quite exceptional. But,' peering at my watery watercolour that looked more psychedelic stick-insect than flaming flame tree, he said, 'this is a very pretty picture. Very nice indeed.'

And that said, he sat down. I flopped in my chair, too, and waited for Mr Woodruff to make his move. Like it was a game of chess.

Pawn takes Pawn? Or was it Bishop takes Queen?

Mr Woodruff coughed, cleared his throat several times. And flicked away a fly that was buzzing in and out of his ear.

'I've received a letter from your Dad today, Janni.'

There! I knew it! Bishop takes Queen. Shit! Shit! Shit!

'Have you, Mr Woodruff?' All innocent like. Plotting and planning my follow-up move. Like, let's take his king.

'Yes. Not for me to interfere.' He scratched his head again. Did another throaty kind of sound. 'But he's a little worried about you and asked if I'd come and have a word.'

'What about?' As if I didn't know.

'Well.' Mr Woodruff moved about in his seat. 'Really about where you're staying, and what you're doing mostly.'

I pulled myself up in my chair, stared Mr Woodruff straight in the eye.

'What do you mean? Where I'm staying? Dad knows where I'm staying.'

Mr Woodruff appeared to have some real problem with his throat. He was going for total clear out, swallowing lumps, and his Adam's apple bobbing up and down like it was going for gold. 'Now, that's not entirely true, is it, Janni?'

I was now on the edge of my seat.

'What do you mean, Mr Woodruff?'

'Well, according to your father's note, he says you've been telling him that you're staying at Rosie's, is that right?'

'Well, I am. Sort of.'

'Now, Janni. Come on.' Mr Woodruff gave me the briefest of smiles. One blink, and I'd have missed it. 'Everyone here in Maiduguri knows that you're staying here with Andy. And your Dad's pretty certain you are, too. He's no fool, Janni.'

I sighed. A very big sigh. A sigh that expressed total pissed-offness. 'I don't believe this,' I said. 'Why's Dad sent you here, Mr Woodruff? To try and persuade me to go home? Is that it?'

'No. Not entirely. That's up to you. Both your Dad and Mum acknowledge, as I do too, that you're eighteen, an adult but...'

'Almost nineteen, Mr Woodruff. More than just an adult.'

'I accept that, Janni. But that doesn't mean parents don't worry, whatever the age. And your parents are worried, Janni. Very worried. You've been gone for almost three weeks. They don't know how to get hold of you, or where you are? As a good friend of your Dad's, he contacted me, and my job is to assure them you're alright.'

'And I am.'

'Yes, you are. But I think they'd like to see it for themselves.'

I looked down at the veranda floor, and studied the march of the ants. A group had gone AWOL, sidestepped left and were scurrying madly round a crack. God knows why? There seemed nothing in it for them.

Mr Woodruff cleared his throat again. He really should visit the doctor and have his windpipe problem checked out. 'Shall I write your Dad a note? Saying you'll be back in the next couple of days? I've got a Land Rover passing through Gombe tomorrow. Better still, you can have a ride in it yourself. What do you say?'

Ah! The ants! One of them had found a crumb in the crack. All of them were going mad for the crumb. All of them were barking mad. Mad. Mad. Mad.

'Janni?'

Mr Woodruff leant forward in his chair, and with hands folded on hairy knees, waited my answer.

I smiled. It was a grim kind of smile. A smile that covered up a multitude of angry, pissed-off thoughts.

'No thanks, Mr Woodruff, about arranging transport, although that's very kind of you. Tell Dad I'll definitely be back, as planned, after the weekend. On the bus. And you will tell him I'm ok, won't you? Stop him worrying.'

Mr Woodruff got out of his chair. Relieved. His mission was done. Over and out. He put a hand on my shoulder and gave it a pat.

'I will. But, only if you promise you'll go back to Gombe and see them.'

'I promise.'

'Good. Well done.'

And he bounded down the steps, two at a time. With a spring in his tail. Or was it a coil up his bum?

I stood on the veranda. Watched Mr Woodruff climb into his Land Rover. Smiled, as Mr Woodruff looked back and gave him a wave. Continued to smile as Mr Woodruff put his terrain-busting vehicle into reverse. Shouted, 'cheerio,' as the vehicle pulled away.

And as Mr Woodruff roared down the sandy road and disappeared out of sight, I put two fingers up.

Step back in time. To the night before.

Remember?

'Come away with me, Janni, come away. Let's find those Misty Mountains together.'

Me all snuggled up, warm and cosy in my ivory tower.

'When are we going?'

'Christmas.'

And I'm thinking. Christmas? Going away at Christmas. And what will my parents have to say about that?

Rather a lot, it would seem. If Mr Woodruff's visit was anything to go by. Certainly, I was in a dilemma. I knew *what* I wanted to do. Stay put, take it nice and easy, and live the dream. But the parents were on the warpath. They wanted me home, wanted me back in Gombe. Mr Woodruff had delivered the summons. It was imperative I report back to base.

So, the following week, and I'm at the lorry park once again. But there's no letter to give to the driver this time, instead I hand him a ticket.

'So, you are for Gombe?' he said, a tad disappointed.

No letter meant no extra services required, meaning I wouldn't be handing him over any money. I empathised with him. We'd both be travelling back to Gombe disappointed.

'Now, don't forget your passport,' Andy advised me, as I hugged him goodbye.

'I won't.' And hoped that my parents wouldn't be that callous and hide it from me, somewhere deep in a drawer.

'And I'll see you next week. I'll be waiting. I promise.'

Andy pushed back the hair off my face, and kissed me. He kissed me in a way that sent my tummy rolling, and off into a double, triple somersault. And he held me. He held me in a way that sent the butterflies fluttering off into a swirling, twirling pirouette.

'Bye, Andy. I love you.' I almost choked on the frog.

'Love you, too. See you when I see you.'

And that was it. Mr Driver, who had been waiting quite patiently for his last passenger to find her seat, started up the engine. The bus hissed and spat out deadly black fumes. I took one step up and stood by the still open door. The bus juddered and quivered, I had to hang on to the handle to steady myself.

'Madam?'

My gaze still on Andy, as I shook like a piece of fruit in a jelly.

'Madam!'

Not a question this time. More a demand. Like, get out the fucking way because I'm about to close the goddamn door. So I moved up another step. Was at the top. Mr Driver got from his seat and slam, like bars in a jail. Back in his seat, and Mr Driver requested, 'Please, Madam, to sit before you fall down.'

'Bye,' I silently mouthed to my man on the other side of the metal and glass divide. A bucketful of tears gushed down my face.

'Madam. Please.'

Picking up my bags, I blindly made my way down the aisle. Sat in the nearest empty seat, pressed my face up to the window; couldn't take my eyes off Andy. The glass dripped with tears, small rivers meandered and converged in a big blob at the bottom of the pane. Windscreen wipers wouldn't have gone amiss; I was creating enough wet to surpass any tropical rainstorm.

With a judder, a lurch, and a sound like a bull elephant's belch, we moved off. Through the crowded throng, the sellers, and the beggars, and the drop offs and the pick ups, and everything else that is lorry park mayhem, slowly making our way to the busy main street.

And I'm up from my seat, and onto the other side of the bus.

'Excuse me, excuse me,' as I scrambled over passengers and luggage, and stood on somebody's foot. 'Sorry, sorry,' as that somebody, a big, fat Hausa lady with more tribal markings on her face than our tabby cat, Tabby, screamed from the pain. Followed by some word, I think the equivalent of 'fuck you' in Hausa.

But do I care?

I'm waving goodbye to my man. My lover. My soul mate. I blow him a kiss. He catches it, and blows one to me. I catch it. Hold it. About to chuck him another. But we're out of the lorry park, and he's gone. Gone. Gone. Gone. It's just neem trees and total desolation.

'You are what!!!????'

'Going away, Dad. Up to Mambilla, and on to the Cameroon.'

'With this Andy?'

'Yes.'

'For Christmas?'

'Yes.'

Dad threw down his napkin and banged his hands hard on the table. And when I mean hard, I mean hard. The table almost collapsed. Certainly everything on top, the salt and pepper pots, the plates, the knives, forks, the spoons, the mustard jar, vinegar bottle, the water tumblers, and Mum and I, shook.

Dad looked me squarely in the eye. 'I can't allow it.'

I held Dad's gaze. 'What do you mean?' Gripped the sides of my chair. Felt the blood rush to my head. 'You can't stop me.'

Dad's face, from blue to red, and back to blue. Then black. Black as thunder. Thunderous. I swear a bolt of lightning streaked from his mouth. Flashed. The air was electric.

'Are you defying me?'

Dad was up, out of his chair, stood over me, his face in my face; I could count the hairs in his nostrils.

I moved myself and my chair back, ever so slightly.

'I repeat. Are you defying me?'

My heart beat like a tom-tom. Boom! Boom! Boom! All round the room.

'Look, Dad... all I'm asking... is... (*fuck, I just couldn't find the words, the right words*)...if I can... I want to go... I am going...'

BANG!

Down came the hand again. Mum and I almost fell off our seats from the aftershock. And Woggles fled, flew across the room, out onto the veranda, and into his dog basket. I could hear him frantically pulling at his blanket, so he could hide under the cover. As for Jonathon, well he'd legged it ages ago. Was probably off to the market, even though the market was closed. Probably hang around there all night. I might have to go and join him.

'AND I AM SAYING NO! YOU CANNOT! WILL NOT! GO!'

Spittle flew out from Dad's mouth and landed on my hand. I ignored it.

'WHY?' I shouted back. 'WHY.'

'Because,' came the hideous growl, 'I am not having a daughter of mine travelling round the bush like some...what is it called? – hippy – with a man we hardly know.'

That was it!

I was up. Out of my chair. Kicked it. Kicked the leg of the table. Screamed.

53

'I'M GOING! WHETHER YOU LIKE IT OR NOT. I'M GOING.'

Now Mum was up.

'Stop it! Stop it!' She glared at Dad, glowered at me.

We ignored her.

'YOU WILL NOT GO!'

'I AM GOING!'

'Stop it! Stop it! The both of you! I will not have this in my house! UNDERSTAND?'

Me half in a scream. Dad about to whip up to a full force-ten frenzy.

Silence.

Total, utter silence. Could have heard the proverbial pin drop on the floor.

We both looked at Mum. Quite taken aback. Mum raising her voice was a rare thing indeed.

'Good,' said Mum, quietly. *Ever so quietly.* 'Now, Janni, Tony, the both of you, sit down. And let's, all of us, talk. This shouting and arguing is getting us nowhere.'

I hovered over my chair. Scowled at Dad. Dad, flushed with rage, shot me a 'if looks could kill' glare and remained standing.

'You're not going to change my mind, Mum,' I said, shifting my eyes on to her. Dad also looked to Mum. And said in a low voice. So low, so hushed, so ominous, it sent shivers through my body.

'She's not going. And that's final.'

Fuck the fear!

'I am! And you can't stop me.'

Think gladiators, think coliseum. Think fight to the death.

Dad's eyes were back on me. With lips the colour of bleach, blue orbs glinting like steel, he stuck his head out like a cobra ready to strike.

'WHAT DID YOU SAY?'

'I SAID YOU CAN'T STOP ME!'

The end was nigh. With a roar, Dad lunged. Thankfully, Mum stepped into the arena and saved me.

She came between us, spread out her arms and pushed us apart. I think Dad would have made light work of her too but he didn't. Instead, he lifted up his arms and looked to the ceiling and heaven. If he was after divine intervention, it never came.

'That's it! That's it! I throw in the towel.'

54

He picked up the nearest napkin at hand, and symbolically chucked it down, straight into a bowl full of tomato soup. The red tepid liquid splashed in a million directions, some on me, some on Dad. Blood had been spilled. Now we really looked like we'd been in a punch up.

'You speak to our daughter, Peg. I wash my hands of it. I cannot deal with her, or her behaviour anymore. She can do what she likes.'

And he stormed from the room. Went out the French doors. We heard the car door open, and the car door slam shut. The ignition switched on, a screech of tyres.

And lift off.

The rocket on power drive, destination orbit. Another galaxy. Another universe. Another world. Where eighteen, soon to be nineteen-year-old daughters do their father's bidding. Do not, do not argue the toss. Do not, do not, do anything. Just behave. Be good. Be obedient. Attend Mass on Sundays. Play Scrabble on Mondays. Ride horses Tuesdays and Wednesdays. Go out with blokes like Henry the Wonder Boy on Thursdays. Stay in on Fridays. Read knowledgeable books on Saturdays. And back to Mass, Sundays.

Well, fuck that for a game of soldiers. I'm out of here.

'What is it with you and Dad?' I screamed at my Mother. 'You're always spoiling it for me. Always. I've had enough.'

Turning on my heels, I made to leave the room, grabbed my bag and fumbled in it for keys.

'SIT.'

'What?'

'I said SIT.'

So I sat. Grudgingly. Threw my bag onto an empty chair.

Mum sat down too. He hands were a little bit shaky.

'Right,' she said. 'Now, in as calm a manner as we can, you and I are going to talk. And try and sort this dreadful, dreadful situation out. Get to the bottom of it. Understand?'

'No, I don't understand. Get to the bottom of what? You just don't see it, do you? Neither does Dad. I'm in love. Really in love, Mum. Over the moon in love. Can't you see?'

Mum nodded. It was a gentle kind of nod. She was the calm after the storm.

'Yes, I can see. And it's wonderful to be in love, isn't it, darling?'

'Yes! Yes, Mum, it is.'

'And you want to be with him, don't you?'

'Yes. Yes. More than anything else in the world.'

'And does he love you? Does Andy love you as much as you love him?'

'Oh, yes, Mum. We love each other to bits.'

Mum put her hand over mine.

'You're sure of his love?'

'Absolutely. One hundred percent sure.'

'Then,' said Mum, her face lighting up, there was a solution to this totally, horrific situation, 'why don't you ask Andy to spend Christmas with us? As a family. Give Dad and I a real chance to get to know him properly. Hmm? What do you think?'

What did I think? No, fucking way!!!!!!!

Like a lead singer in a rock band, I shook my head this way and that, banged my hand on the table, not quite as hard a thump as Dad's but enough to cause a couple of wobbles. 'You just don't understand, do you?'

I didn't wait to hear Mum's response. Got up, got a fag, searched the room for a box of matches, couldn't find any, went into the kitchen, opened drawers, banged them shut. Found some by the cooker, lit up, headed back to the table, slumped myself down in the chair, and puffed. Puffed like a chimney, anger rising, utterly and truly pissed off.

Mum was still bleating on. Couldn't understand my reaction. 'Why,' she asked, 'are you so anti him coming here? Why?'

'Because, oh, for God's sake, Mum, because… Because…'

Because I want to be with him, somewhere far, far, away, up in the Misty Mountains. Where the sun rises and the sky turns into a hundred different colours of gold. Where the solar planet meets the earth and the heavens explode into red balls of fire. I want to be with him on a dark night and make love under the twinkling stars. Be with him and imagine together we can fly to the moon. Travel with him, travel blind. As in the song. That's why. That's because…

'Because what?' said Mum, still awaiting an answer. She couldn't understand. Hadn't the problem been solved, hadn't she found the key to the oracle? Spend Christmas with the family. Me, her, Andy, and Dad. Oh, God what a nightmarish thought!

Enough was enough.

'I'm going out. Round to Lizzie's.'

'Stay, Janni. We need to talk, we need to sort this out.'

'Sorry, Mum, there's nothing to sort out. What's there to sort out? I'm going away for Christmas, end of story. I don't want to stay here in Gombe, end of story. I want to be with Andy in Maiduguri, end of story.'

That said, I got up, bundled my fags into my bag, picked up my keys.

'I take it then that you're not going to do as we ask. Is that right? You're going to go against our wishes?'

I hovered by the door.

Mum still in her chair, looked across at me. Her hands were all knotted up, her face all forlorn, her demeanour crumpled and sad. Was she about to cry?

The guilt hit me hard.

I wanted to run to her. Put my arms around her hunched-up little body and hold her tight. Tell her I was sorry. Assure her that everything was really all alright. There was nothing to fear. If she and Dad could only understand, I wasn't out to hurt them. I just wanted them to set me free.

This wasn't too much to ask for. Surely?

From the age of six, I'd been locked up in a boarding school. Subjected to hard labour for thirteen long years; no parole, no reprieve. Murderers, gold bullion robbers, knife-wielding maniacs did less time than me. After seven years or so they were out on good behaviour. At liberty to do as they pleased, kill someone else, rob another bank, go on the rampage, but oh no, not me, even though I'd behaved and done well in my exams.

Okay, so some of my school reports claimed I 'could do better', and suggested that at times I was 'inattentive in class'. But so bloody what?

And there was the occasion when Sister Joseph felt 'compelled' to write to my parents regarding a matter that gave her 'grave concern', it was an 'inappropriate remark' I'd made in a letter to a boy, a pen pal who I'd been writing to for over a year. I was fourteen years old, for God's sake, and the inappropriate remark was 'I'd like you to turn me on'.

I'd no idea what this phrase actually meant but one of my friends, Sarah, told me she'd overheard her older brother saying it to his girlfriend and she, the girlfriend, seemed to appreciate it. Apparently she went all giggly and gooey-eyed, grabbed Sarah's brother by the hand, led him away upstairs, and all sorts of fun noises could be heard from his bedroom.

So, trying to be all grown-up and impress a French boy I'd

never met (I got his name from the pen pal list dished out by our enlightened, lay language teacher who thought corresponding with a foreign friend was an excellent way to practise French in the written form, and who knows, oral form if an invite to France so happened to come along) and see what kind of reaction I would get from Gerard who, by the way, was the same age as me. I wasn't, of course, expecting him to drag me upstairs 'hands across the sea' and all that malarkey, that would have been impossible. All I was trying to do was get our relationship on a more deeper level. But I never got to find out what Gerard thought about the 'turn on' factor because, as I said, Sister Joseph, in her role as Headmistress or Prison Warden (both titles are apt) intercepted the letter.

She was doing her rounds and spotted me and Anne Watson giggling over it in prep. She marched up to my desk, black, billowing skirt like devil's wings (the cross dangling at her side was just a front) and grabbed the bloody piece of blue airmail paper out of my warm, little hands. And that was it. Next thing Satan's advocate is writing her own letter and over the sea and many miles it goes, not to Gerard but to my parents in their African home. What a nightmare. I'm tarnished even before I've begun.

'Your daughter has displayed sexual inappropriateness. This is a matter of grave concern.'

I mean, bloody hell, after all that, the tellings-off, the tickings-off, I still didn't know what the flipping phrase meant. We could have been discussing turning on a tap, for all I knew. Suffice to say that was the end of my pen pal phase forever after, Sister Joseph made sure of that.

But apart from that little debacle, there was nothing else really. My copy book was pretty un-blotted. Of course I admit I was one of the loudest pupils in my year, to be heard is a most dreadful sin, especially in the hallowed corridors of a convent school where the silence rule is most definitely golden. And I admit I was a fully paid-up member of the 'naughty girls' gang. But our misdemeanours were so infantile. We did things like drop our boaters out of the music room windows to see whose hit the ground first, and wore 15 denier stockings instead of 40 denier ribbed-tights, and gave each other love bites so we didn't feel too left out on Monday mornings when the day girls came in to school and showed off their real ones.

And I admit that by the time me and my mates were about fourteen, we were indulging and smoking the odd fag or two. But smoking is a rite of passage for every teenager on this planet. My

God, you weren't normal unless you'd bought your first packet of ten Number 6.

Thus I rest my case. Apart from stuff like this, we who were locked up were angels.

But angels have wings and this particular angel now wanted to fly.

Live the dream that I'd been fantasising for nigh on thirteen years. Well, perhaps not thirteen, up until eleven, I was quite happy with my lot, but when puberty struck and Jackie comics became the vogue, everything changed. The world suddenly appeared different. I looked out from my convent school bars and wanted, yearned for a slice of the action.

And here I was six or so years on, finally making a bid for freedom but Mum and Dad were still blocking my path. So despite the guilt, and anguish, and the pain that it was causing, I didn't run over, put my arms around my Mother and tell her I was sorry. I didn't do any of that.

I just said, 'See you later,' instead.

I jumped on my bike and roared out the driveway, turned right and made my way in to town. At the roundabout I went straight over (not the roundabout, that would have caused untold damage to me and my bike) and followed the road to Lizzie's. Blindly, I skirted in and out of those who happened to stroll into my path, dogs, goats, chickens, women with pots on their heads, men with billowing robes picking their noses, the usual suspects, until I arrived at the last bungalow on the college campus. I propped my bike up by the mango tree and leapt up Lizzie's steps, three at a time.

Ian was twanging away on his guitar and glorifying Jesus, Gordon was smoking a fag and reading a book, and Lizzie was doing her usual thing, marking some papers.

'Can I have a word? In private,' I said to my friend, ignoring the other two. And my friend did my bidding and we went to her room. And I threw myself on her bed and out came the moans. About half an hour's worth. Lizzie sat quietly, nodding from time to time, shaking her head every so often as she took it, all my woes, all my troubles, in. When finally I'd ceased up and had begun bawling my eyes out, only then did she speak.

'Why don't you go along with your Mum's idea? Invite Andy for Christmas?'

I sat bolt upright, used the hem of my pretty gypsy skirt to wipe the snot from my nose, and hollered and screamed.

'You're all the fucking same. I hate every one of you here in Gombe.'

Grabbed my bag, and without another word, fled. Out of Lizzie's bedroom, down the corridor, through to the sitting room.

'And you lot can fuck off, too,' I said in passing. To Gordon who was quietly reading his book, and Ian who was still creating songs of praise to his Jesus. And down the steps I went, marched to my bike, lifted my skirts and mounted. Over to the next house, the one behind the banana trees. Dismounted, chucked my bike to the ground, thought better of it, picked it up and propped it against a palm trunk, and headed into the house of my new best friend, Barb.

It was a nice family evening, the kids were playing tiddlywinks on the floor with their Dad, and Barb was making a new velvet cushion. She had a big mound of fluffy kapok and was stuffing it into a large, square of purple material.

'Hi,' I said from the door, smiling at each and everyone.

'Hi,' they all cried, including Dick with the Prick (he had no option). Followed by a twangy Canadian chorus of, 'Come on in.'

So I did.

'Can I have a word,' I asked my newest best friend. 'In private.'

'Well, of course, honey,' responded Barb, and she abandoned her chore. Dick looked a little worried, probably thought I was about to finally spill the beans. Well, he could think what he liked, I couldn't have given a fuck. In fact, at this moment in time, our misdemeanours in a brothel appeared like chicken feed compared to my current God-awful situation.

So, I followed Barb down the corridor into her amazing techno-coloured bedroom, and threw myself down on the marital bed. And for the next half an hour bewailed the knotty complexes of my life. How I was at my wits' end, hard pressed, hampered and walking amongst eggs. And like Lizzie before her, she listened, and unlike Lizzie, she commiserated and poured balm on troubled waters.

'Poor, darling. Poor you. What a beast of a problem.'

And I nodded, and said, 'Yes it was. And what am I going to do?'

'Well, honey, it's hard to figure out. I kinda wish I knew the answers.' Barb put her beautiful head in her hands and thought for a moment. Her long, black hair cascading over her honeydew shoulders as her brain went tick-tick-tick.

'I reckon,' she finally said, lifting her face up so the yellow fairy lights above her bed made her look almost golden, 'that you do as your Mom suggests.'

'What!' I half-bounced off the bouncy divan.

'Honey, don't look so pained. Andy loves you, he won't mind coming to Gombe and spending Christmas here. And your parents will learn to love him too. Give them time. Then, later, you can go wherever you want with him. With your Mom and Dad's blessings. And everything will be fine.'

That was it. I jumped off the bed with a bit of a spring, and said, 'Thanks but no thanks, Barb.' And under my breath I murmured, 'Fuck you.'

Down the corridor I went, bypassing the kids and the Prick, to the French doors with no more than a, 'See you.' I stumbled out, down the steps, mounted my bike, and headed off to nowhere. Just revved the engine and sped through the town not caring who I knocked over or down, past my house and up the hill, and out of Gombe.

About ten miles on, somewhere in the bush, I came to a halt. Got off my bike, and plonked myself down on the root of a baobab tree. Using the beam from the headlamp, I rolled myself up a joint. And when finished, switched off the lamp and sat in the darkness.

'Hello darkness my old friend
I've come to talk to you again'

Listened to the whirr and the buzz from the shadowy grasses, studied the craters and mountains on the moon, and blew smoke rings, and watched the gossamer mist waft and disappear into the air.

And I pondered my situation. And finally hit on a plan. I was going to leave home. Not forever but for now. Go to Maiduguri tomorrow. On my bike, it was my only trusted companion and had never failed me yet. Well, apart from the dog fiasco but that wasn't the bike's fault. And bugger Mum and Dad, and everybody else. I had Andy. And as long as I had Andy, I had all that I wanted.

Decision made, and finally and totally felt the bars of my life rise up and disappear. Uplifted, I clambered onto my bike, cut through the dark and headed back down the hill into Gombe.

Back at my parents' house (it was no longer mine) I ignored my Mum in her chair, and my Dad who was back and in his chair, and went to my room. And began packing. Not too much, I had to carry all my worldly possessions on the back of my bike. It wasn't easy making choices, which skirt to leave, which pair of shoes should I take? But finally it was done. And as I zipped up my worn out old bag, I remembered my passport. Crept in to Mum and Dad's room and quietly opened up one or two of their drawers. And found it, Allah be praised, sitting on top with Mum and Dad's, and some other important looking papers in my father's bedroom bureau. Tiptoed back to my room, and unzipped the bag and pushed it down, right to the bottom between the knickers and the T-shirts. And finally, seeing the book lying on my bedside cabinet, the one I'd not yet read, I picked up 'The Snows of Kilimanjaro' and popped it in the bag.

Thus so, and I was ready for my nightly ablutions, and thus done, I was ready for bed.

I waited until Dad had screeched off to work. And then made my entrance. Mum wasn't in the sitting room, she wasn't in the kitchen; neither was she counting bags of sugar in the larder.

'Where's Mum?' I asked Jonathon, who was busy giving the kitchen mat a hammering out the back. Dust blew everywhere.

'She be over there,' said Jonathon from somewhere in the cloud, and pointed to the vegetable garden. Mum was kneeling down, bent over the tomato plants, pulling out weeds. I strolled over and hearing my soft pads, she looked up.

'Hello, darling,' she smiled, flicking back a curl that had fallen into her eye with her garden-gloved hand. 'How are you?'

As if it was an ordinary day.

'I'm alright thanks, Mum.'

She carried on smiling, but behind the mask there was sadness. I must admit I felt a bit throaty myself, that old frog was beginning to croak. I squatted down, picked off a tomato plant leaf and began pulling it apart. For a while we were silent, both of us bogged down with our own personal thoughts.

Finally, I said, 'I'm off to Maiduguri today, Mum.'

Mum responded to this news with a watery smile. Not like Sonia's watery smiles, this one came with tears. Mum wiped them away with the back of her hand, just like she had done with the curl.

'I half expected you to say that, darling. I guessed after last night you'd be going.'

'I'm so, so sorry, Mum, all this arguing and everything. I didn't mean it to happen this way.' And I got hold of her hand and squeezed it tight.

'I'm sure you didn't. Growing-up is very hard, it makes us do and say things we don't really mean.'

'But I do mean them, Mum. I want so much to go away with Andy because I love him. And I'm angry because you and Dad, especially Dad, are always putting obstacles in my way. I'm an adult now. You've got to let me go.'

'We're not doing it for any other purpose than because we love you, darling. We just want everything to be right.'

I picked up another leaf and began the shredding process again.

'But it is right, Mum, yet you don't see it.'

Mum shook her head. 'It doesn't really matter who's right, or who's wrong at this moment, darling. All I care about is you. I'm not sure how I'm going to cope with the idea of you wandering around in the bush. When, one day, you have a daughter, then I think you'll understand.'

Another tear spilled down her face. This time, I brushed it away.

'Look, Mum, I'm only going to be gone for about a month or so. I'll be back in January. And I'll be fine. Please, please don't worry.'

'I'll try not to. If you promise you'll take the greatest of care. Promise.'

'I promise, Mum.' And I threw my arms round her, nestled my face in her sweet smelling hair.

'Dad and I love you, darling,' she whispered.

'And I love you both, you know that,' I murmured.

It was all getting far too sentimental.

'I'd better get going, Mum,' I said, pulling myself away from her comforting bosom. 'Many miles and all that.'

I got up from my crouching position. Mum, still kneeling amongst cucumbers, cabbages, beetroots and tomatoes, pealed off her gardening gloves and got to her feet as well.

'I'll give you a lift to the lorry park. I take it there's a bus going, today?'

I shook my head, took a deep breath, and came out with it. 'I'm going by bike.'

'Bike?! Whose bike?'

'My bike.'

Mum put her hand to her mouth. 'Oh, my God, no! Your little bike?'

'Yes, my little bike. It'll be fine. It's had a complete overhaul, as you know. And I've done a third of the journey, or almost, loads of times. It'll just be like going to Bui, coming back to Gombe, going again to Bui, and stopping off at Kwayaterra on the way back. I've worked it out. It's about the same distance.'

'But, darling,' said my Mother with dread in her voice, 'after Bui, you're in bush, until you get to Maiduguri. There's nothing there. What if you have an accident? Breakdown?'

'I won't have an accident. The road's straight, tarmac all the way. And if something does go wrong, then I'll hitch a lift on a mammy-wagon.'

'A mammy-wagon?!!!!'

'Yes.' And I told her all about my little adventure on one of those lethal contraptions just a few weeks before.

'My God! We never knew.'

'Well, now you do. And it's alright, I promise. Quite good fun, really. So please don't worry.'

I might as well have asked my Mother not to breath, both were quite impossible to do. But bless her, she put a brave face on things and tried hard go with the flow. We walked back into the house and she made me breakfast, the full Monty, watching me as I ate it all up. And then came outside as I made ready for my journey.

'What about Dad?'

I was tying my rather large bag on to the back of the bike.

'What about Dad?'

'Aren't you going to say goodbye?'

With the rope in one hand, and flicking a fly away with the other, I pondered on this, and how all this would be with my Dad.

'No, Mum. It might all end up in another row. And I don't think I can handle another row, what with the journey and everything. I want to travel with a clear head.'

'But, darling, he's your father. He loves you. It'll break his heart if you go away without saying goodbye.'

'Oh, Mum, stop it!' This was stuff I didn't want to hear. 'Look,' I said, a little more gently, seeing the pain etched on my Mother's face, 'I'll write Dad a note, explaining things. And I promise I'll keep in touch, you know that, Mum. I promise. And please believe me, I'll really, really be back soon. I'm not going away forever.'

Which was true. The half-truth was, I just didn't know exactly when I'd be back.

So, Mum let me get on with my packing, and went off and came back with a hamper full of sandwiches, cold drinks, flask of tea, like I was going on a picnic.

'I can't take all that, Mum,' I said, 'I'm overloaded as it is.'

'But you need food, darling. Drinks. You're travelling through desert regions.'

I made light of it and laughed. 'No, I'm not. There are villages dotted along all the way. I can always stop off and have a drink from a well, and grab something to eat from some village somewhere.'

Mum shivered. Not from the cold, it was very, very hot even in the shade of the flame tree where we were standing. No, her shivers were shivers of fear. She just couldn't cope with the idea that her beloved daughter might be drinking untreated, unboiled, unfiltered water and eating meaty morsels of diced-up bush dog. Neither could I, for that matter, but I'd face the horror if I had to, I was becoming that intrepid.

'Don't forget your paludrine,' she said, sounding mildly desperate, wanting me to hang on to something that was part of our expatriate way of life.

'I haven't.'

And plunged my hand in my bag and produced the little aluminium container, shook it, to prove that the small white tablets were definitely inside.

Appeased that all was perhaps not lost, Mum slipped her hand in her pocket, the pocket where the keys always jangled, and pulled out an envelope.

'Some money. To keep you going.'

'Thanks, Mum.' I put the envelope in my bag, and gave her a hug.

'Done!' I finally said, and patted my well strapped-on bulging bag. For Mum's sake, I'd also added the food hamper but would chuck it somewhere in the bush, near a village where someone would find it and go have a feast.

'What about Dad's note?'

I sighed – inwardly, so Mum couldn't hear – and headed back into the house, found pen and paper and sat at the table and wrote:

Darling Dad,

I'm really sorry to be a disappointment and am really sorry about hurting you. I love you very, very much and wish all this hadn't happened in quite this way.

I do promise, Dad, that I'll keep in touch, and will behave like a lady, and I'll take care on the journey.

I'll be home sometime in January but will keep you informed at all times.

I hope you and Mum have a very happy Christmas.

Your very loving daughter, Jannixxxxxxxxxxx

That done, I popped the paper in the envelope and left it propped up against Dad's pen and pencil jar on the desk. Then I had a final piddle, and pulled on one of Dad's old khaki bush hats, popped on my sunglasses and headed back outside. Mum, Woggles, and Jonathon were all waiting for me under the shade of the old, old tree. 'Green Green Grass of Home' sang in my head, and it was all rather sad.

Very sad, in fact.

All of a sudden I wanted to cry. Throw myself in my Mother's arms and sob like a baby.

What the hell am I doing?

You're going to meet with your lover, your soul mate, and go on a magical, mystery journey, the rational voice said in my head. So stop feeling blue and leave with joy in your heart.

So I smiled, kept a stiff upper lip. Let's face it, I'd had years of practice pretending I was brave.

'Bye, Jonathon.' I shook his hand, and gave him a kiss on the cheek.

'God be with you,' he said as we parted.

'Bye, you old hound.' I bent down and drowned my face in his straggly, matted fur.

And Mum. 'Bye. I love you.'

She held me close. 'I love you, too. Get a message to me as soon as you get to Maiduguri,' she just about managed to say.

Time to go.

I clambered on my little Honda 50cc, ready for a two hundred and fifty mile journey through the bush. Just me and my trusty old steed. Bloody hell! What an adventure.

'Bye,' I shouted.

Mum, Jonathon, Woggles, even Musa the horseboy came out from his stable and watched as I wended my way up the driveway. They looked a strange, little bunch.

'Bye,' I shouted again, as I reached the top and made ready to turn right onto the road. A cow, and a couple of donkeys meandered by. A vulture swooped, and perched itself on the branch of a tree. A lizard scuttled across a stone, and zipped back into the grass. A vibrant, blue woodpecker hammered away on the baobab bark, three butterflies fluttered and hovered over a pink bougainvillea.

And with a final wave, I left them all.

Turned the corner.

There was no going back.

The journey to Bui was a doddle. Apart from having to stop every ten miles or so to readjust my bag that kept slipping to the side, however hard I pulled and tied knots in the string, the road was straight, clear, and I managed to go at a steady fifty miles an hour. Not bad for an overloaded 50cc little motorbike. I reached Bui just after eleven, and stopped at the lorry park for petrol. I'd worked it out that I'd just about manage to get to Potiskum before needing another tank full, and that would be enough to get me to Damaturu. Fill up there, I'm on the road again, and Maiduguri here I come.

After Bui, I purred on down the tarmac that cut a black, shiny line through the bush. Ahead of me, around me, miles and miles of emptiness, the hills now gone, and everywhere flat. And it was hot, very hot. Even the wind created by the bike barely cooled me down, and I was glad of Dad's hat. Above me, the bleached, unbroken sky poured heat down on the baked earth, and the road ahead shimmered in a silvery haze, the horizon indistinct.

Thirty miles on, and I smelt charred wood and came upon burnt out land, a place where the sun's rays had been so strong they'd managed to set this particular bit of the world on fire. It must have raged. The few trees that had managed to grow in this arid, god-forsaken place were now blackened trunks, standing bare and skeletal above others which had fallen. And the ground itself was black, everywhere grey ash that stretched silently for several miles, bleak and devastated, in an already bleak, barren landscape.

Further on, and back amongst living grasses again and sun-warmed earth, I stopped and had lunch under the shade of a baobab tree. It wasn't as big as Martyn's tree, but it was wide enough to give me a little respite from the shining blob in the sky.

I ate a few of Mum's sandwiches whilst sat on the bark, and was glad that I'd not abandoned the hamper somewhere in the bush, after all. In fact, the thought of her dear, sweet hands preparing and packing the food, brought a bit of a lump to my throat. Reminded me of when I was a little girl, when my Mum used to get me dressed, ready for the plane trip back to England. Ten hours and four thousand miles later, I'd stand in my little bedroom at Granny's, looking out on a world of drizzle and fog, and think about my sunshine home in Africa and my now far away Mummy and Daddy.

'Let's get those clothes off you, poppet', my dear old Granny would say, very gently because she knew I was hurting. 'Get you all warmed and snuggled up in your pyjamas'.

And I'd answer with a, 'No, don't want to'. Didn't want to take off my dress, my knickers and socks, my shoes, or my cardie. Mummy's hands had tied the laces, her fingers had buttoned me up, she was the one that had pulled on the socks and the knickers, and if I took them off, well then I was severing all contact with Mummy. And that would break my heart. So, as a rule I stayed in my clothes until the following morning. And even then Granny had a devil of a job getting me to undress.

A mammy-wagon trundled by, from one of the branches above, a bird gave out a loud 'creeee-creeee-creeee'. An enormous grasshopper leapt, suddenly, over my foot. A beetle, a troupe of red ants, crawled over stones and through the sand. I heard the distant bray of a donkey, saw a single vapour of smoke twist and curl itself into the heat-thickened air. Far away down the road, a couple of women were walking, they had calabash pots on their heads, and if I listened very carefully, there it was, the thump-thump-thump pulp of the maize.

You think you're all alone in the wilderness but you're not. At first glance there's nothing to see, you hear the silence, feel the silence, but if you really look, really listen, life is everywhere, even in the loneliest most barren of places.

My spirits perked up. I saw what was around me, and it was good. More than good. It was great. Almost nineteen years in Africa and I'd never been this close, as close as I was now to the real Africa. All my previous encounters were through expatriate's eyes, it was a kind of touch but don't touch philosophy we white folks had. Look but don't look, see but don't see. Keep your distance, keep away, don't be part of, be apart.

But here amongst the baobabs and the grasses, in the deep and enveloping warmth of the late African afternoon, it was just me on my own in the middle of nowhere. I felt suspended, secluded; unreachable. Nobody's child, and answerable to no one. A free spirit in every sense of the word.

'Sannu,' said one of the ladies, as they passed me by.

'Sannu,' I replied, and gave them each a sandwich, ham and pickle, I think, slightly gooey but tasty all the same. The ladies were a bit taken aback, in fact their eyes nearly popped out of their sockets, but they clung on to the soggy morsels, giggled and curtseyed while still balancing perfectly, without even a wobble, their calabash pots on their heads, and walked on, munching their sarnies. And the flies buzzed around, but they didn't care.

It was time for me to move on. So with a final piddle behind the tree while a lizard looked on, I gathered up my scanty possessions and set sail once again.

I reached Potiskum when the heat of the day was fading, though it was still warm. Very warm. Unbearably warm. Sweat bucketed down my back, my neck, down the inside of my legs, in my shoes, even my bottom was all wet and sticky. And sore. Very sore. And my back felt like it was breaking. I had to keep readjusting myself, straighten up for a minute, then that position hurt, so I'd go for the hunchback position, no that wasn't any good, so I'd shift myself in the seat and try something else, but there was little else I could do. There aren't too many choices when riding a bike, especially when riding a bike for as many hours as I had.

It was a relief, an utter relief, to dismount at the petrol pump in Potiskum. Except when I dismounted I found walking a struggle. My legs were all bowed up and I did a rather grand impersonation of John Wayne, or was it more like someone who'd shat their pants? And my arms felt as stiff as boards, as did my hands; actually they were more arthritic, like old ladies, bent up and clawed. Still, I managed to wend my way over to a shack, with the usual crew of hangers-on, and buy myself a warm, fizzy drink. And I strolled round, and limbered up, and moved my shoulders and head around and about, and after half an hour I was ready to move on again.

To the west, the sun was already sinking below a flat, undulating horizon. And still about a hundred miles to go. And I was beginning to think maybe this wasn't such a good idea after all. I was that tired I had to stop. I sat myself down on the edge of the road, undid the tea flask and enjoyed that most English of beverages whilst in the heart of the savannah. And rolled myself a joint, and whilst getting a little stoned, pondered on the possibilities of finding somewhere half decent to have a kip in Damaturu, the dust bowl. But, based on my previous experiences of the place, the possibilities appeared to be pretty slim. So I sat on my rocky seat and felt somewhat low and despondent. Maybe I'd have to curl up right here, and go sleep with the snakes and the scorpions.

Then a miracle happened. In my life, miracles do have a habit of popping up when least expected. From over the horizon, coming my way was a Land Rover. And as it neared me, it slowed down, and when it was right by me, it stopped. Bloody hell! Middlesbrough Bruce!

'What the hell are you doing out here?' he asked, with his head out of the window.

I responded by jumping up and giving him a big kiss on the lips. 'My God! Am I pleased to see you.'

Bruce disentangled himself from out of his seat, opened the door and jumped down.

'Please don't tell me you've driven all the way from Gombe to here on *that*,' pointing to my little 50 cc.

'I have!'

'You're mad!'

Then, with much laughter and much hilarity, we picked up the bike and my loads, and shoved it all in the back of the Land Rover, with me in the front.

'Ready?'

'Ready,' I said.

And off we went. Maiduguri bound

CHAPTER 3

Maiduguri; late December 1973

Bruce dropped me off at the house in the woods at around eight in the evening. Everywhere was quiet, all three little bungalows shrouded in darkness, no motorbikes, and the rocking chair on Hamish's porch vacant and still.

'Seems like everyone's out,' Bruce commented, stating the bloody obvious. 'Sure you don't want me to take you round to the club, see if Andy's there?'

'No thanks,' I said. A definite no thanks. Grand entrances equals looking your best, and after a day sweating it out on a bike through hundreds of miles of sun-baked bush, I now probably looked like one of the witches left over from last year's Halloween party, hardly the way I wanted the world and its Mother, and Andy, to see me. Anyway, it didn't matter that they were all tripping the light fantastic elsewhere (as long as Andy was behaving himself, of course), because none of them ever bothered to lock their doors, even Hamish who had a wealth of precious art stuff tucked away in that little house of his. So I gave Bruce a hug and waved him goodbye, then let myself into the abode that I now (how exciting!) called home.

Half an hour later, fresh from a shower, I was basking in lamplight, reclining in my deckchair out on the veranda, feet up on a pouffe, joint in hand, Neil Young crooning in the background, cup of coffee by my side, and The Hobbit opened up at page forty-three. But I wasn't really concentrating on Bilbo Baggins's travels around Middle Earth; my own forthcoming adventures were far, far more exciting.

I imagined scenes of great beauty, rainbow-coloured skies, mountains swirling in mist, meandering rivers, and Andy and I in amongst it all, walking hand-in-hand, Romeo and Juliet style, so deeply in love. When thoughts about my parents filtered in, as they did from time to time, guilty, uncomfortable ruminations, I managed to dismiss them quickly, a quick puff on a joint seemed to do the trick, and return to my romantic daydreams.

Maybe he'll ask me to marry him?

71

I shivered deliciously as the concept of nuptial bliss floated around in my head. I could picture the setting. Andy proposing in the light of the moon, the gentle breeze flapping the hem of my beautiful gypsy skirt, the wafts ruffling our hair, his eyes looking deep into the windows of my soul, the soft Scottish voice. 'Marry me, Janni.'

Our two hearts beat as one. I feel we are going to float away in the moment. I am truly in Heaven. 'Oh, Andy, yes. Oh, yes, yes, yes.'

Three motorbikes purred up and gatecrashed my wedding. I was on a mountaintop dressed in a long white, silken dress, barefoot, a crown of red roses adorning my wild, tumbling hair. Andy's wearing white silk too, a robe pretty similar to mine actually, and he's slipping a ring on my finger. The same ring he's already given me, the one made of Bida brass, the wandering minstrel with the crescent moon and the star on his face has blessed the circular, metal band, and it is he who is now uniting us in marriage.

'Do you take this woman forever? To be your wife? To love and behold? Until death do you part?'

Andy smiles at me. A smile so sensuous, I feel I'm going to melt on the spot.

'I do.'

The crescent moon and star face now turns to me. 'Do you take this man, love, honour, and obey him? Until death do you part?'

I'm like a butterfly dancing in the breeze, a spring flower opening up and basking in the glow of the sun. I'm as happy, as happy can be. 'I do. I do. I do.'

'It is done. I pronounce you man and wife. You may kiss the bride.'

Andy enfolds me in his arms as a hundred doves are let loose, they flutter high in the crimson sky and form a heart shape, grey silk against golden light. And the minstrel sings. And the moment is pure magic.

The boys were home.

I couldn't wait to tell Andy about my trials and tribulations with the parents, my decision to defect to Maiduguri, and my intrepid journey by bike. Quickly I said hello and goodbye to our two neighbours, then dragged my man into the house – our house – and sat him down.

'Listen to this,' I said, all excited.

Andy listened.

My story unfolded.

When I got to the bit about me leaving home (don't know when I'll be back again, like in the song) I expected Andy to jump up, punch the air and shout 'Whoopee.' But he didn't. In fact he seemed a little taken aback. And his voice sounded strange. Like something was wrong. 'Och, man, this situation is getting too intense. Really heavy,' he said with a frown.

My stomach lurched. 'What do you mean?'

'This thing with your parents, for one.' Andy ran his fingers through his hair. 'I dinna want there to be any more trouble.'

'There won't be, I promise.' Jumping up off the bed, I went over to the little table where he was sitting. Put my arms around him, and sat on his lap. 'Anyway,' I said, pressing my cheek up against his, 'we're together now, and that's all that matters.'

'Aye,' he nodded. But, like a cool flame, he burnt indifferently.

'What's up?' I asked, totally mystified by the lukewarm response. Even his arms weren't around me, they flopped down by the side of his chair, and his face was turned the other way, the eyes looking at some invisible spot on the bare, whitewashed wall.

'Och, nothing.' He shrugged.

'Are you sure?'

'Aye.'

And that's all he said.

A long silence. A knot tied itself up in my tummy. I tried to hard to think of something to say, something that would lighten the mood. Couldn't, so said the first thing that came into my head.

'Did you miss me?'

Andy shot me a look. It was difficult to judge what was behind the deadpan expression. The knot in my stomach tightened. I swallowed. It hurt.

'Andy, tell me what's wrong?' Again he shrugged and again he turned away, back to the mysterious, invisible, fascinating spot on the bare, whitewashed wall. 'Talk to me, Andy. Please.' He didn't. Instead he picked up a pencil, and began to tap a beat on the table. In the silence, the sound boomed loud like a drum in my head.

Tap, tap, tappety, tap. Tap, tap, tappety, tap. Tap. Tap, Tap. Tappety, tappety, tap. 'Andy, talk to me. What's wrong?' I was beginning to sound like an old record, well and truly stuck in a groove.

Tap, tap, tappety, tap. Tap, tap, tappety, tap.

Alarm bells clanged. Invisible fingers pressed my panic button.

73

What was going on? The cold fish on whose knee I was sitting wasn't my Andy. My Andy was warm. This man was freezing. My Andy was passionate. This man was a block of solid stone. My Andy held me close. This man was for pushing me away. Remember the film, 'The Body Snatchers'? Aliens overrun a small town in America, take over the bodies of the local population so everyone still looks the same as before, dresses the same as before, has the same voices, but are actually cruel monsters from outer space. Well, when I was back in Gombe, these body snatchers must have come in the dark of night, stolen the real Andy, and left behind this identikit stranger. Just like in the horror movie.

And the nightmare continued.

In the black dream, I got up from Andy's lap. He didn't hold me back or try to stop me. I moved to the centre of the room.

Tap. Tap. Tap. Tappety, tappety, tap tap, tappety, tappety. Tap. Tap. Tappety tappety tap.

I perused the iceberg. Felt the cold blast, and shivered.

Tap. Tap. Tap.

Wanted to grab the fucking pencil and ram it right down his throat. That, or collapse in a heap on the floor and howl.

Tap.

'Oh, for fuck's sake, Andy, talk to me!'

Silence. Silence. Silence.

The pencil held aloft in the air. I saw the snake around his arm glint. Then the pencil was chucked. It bounced across the table and landed with a plop on the floor. Andy turned. Poker face, he looked me up and down. Perused me, as if I were a rather strange exhibit in a rather strange show. I waited for whatever was to come. If anything. The cold, stony silence was killing me. My heart was bleeding. The world as I knew it had stopped. But in that darkest hour there suddenly came the dawn. Just like that, he went from poker face to loving smile.

'Here,' he said, 'come here.'

I came. Collapsed with relief into open arms. Felt his breath warm on my face. Could hear his heart beating. 'What's up, Andy?' I asked, nuzzling up against him. 'Aren't you glad I'm here? Have I done something wrong?'

'Och, no, there's nothing wrong.' There was a pause. 'Just this thing with your parents, and you leaving them the way you have. It's all a bit sudden. Makes me feel a wee bit nervous. But I'm sure we'll work things out.'

'I'm sure too,' I said, not sure at all what he meant by this. Work things out? A bit sudden? What's sudden? What's there to work out? All along he'd wanted me to come to Maiduguri. All along he'd wanted me with him. All along he knew my parents were a total pain in the arse. But now everything was sorted. Done and dusted. The truth was out. They knew where I was, and even if they didn't like it, well so bloody what?

'What's going on in that wee mind of yours?' Andy tweaked my nose, ever so gently, gave me a really, really nice smile.

'I'm just thinking about how much I love you,' I replied with a heartfelt sigh.

'And I love you too.'

'Well, that's alright then.'

And it was. We were two blissfully happy lovers once again.

Until a couple of days later.

I was getting dolled up for a night out at the club. On went the eyeshadow, the mascara, the lipstick; it was no more than usual.

'You wear too much of that stuff,' he said, as I came out of the bathroom.

'What stuff?' I asked, looking at my bangles, and checking out my beads. I thought he liked me kitted out in this Romany jewellery.

'Your make-up. You look like Dusty Springfield.'

'Dusty Springfield?' I laughed.

'Och, a girl should look natural, you dinna need that crap.'

Crap! How dare he!

'You've never been bothered by my make-up before,' I retorted, a tad tetchily.

'It has bothered me,' he said sneeringly. 'Often. I've just put up with it, that's all. But I dinna like it, and you'd look a lot better without it.'

No I wouldn't.

'Are you saying I look like a tart?'

'I'm saying you wear too much.'

'And I'm saying I don't.'

And I didn't. Just a smidgen of eyeshadow, a brush of mascara and a hint of pink-tinted lipstick. Bloody hell, my Mum wore more make up than me, and Dad always said how lovely she looked. And Andy had always said how lovely I looked. So why, all of a sudden had it become a big, big problem?

'Suit yourself.' Andy shrugged, turned away. Sat down, put his feet up on a chair, and began reading his book, 'The Catcher in The

Rye', not out loud but quietly to himself.

Standing by the bathroom door, I perused him. Golden hair and silver snake, shining and glinting. Long brown legs stretched out, eyes down, every part of him still, like a figure in a painting.

What a bastard! I'd a good mind to grab the bloody book out of his hand, throw it to the floor, and jump on it. Then kick it round the room. And afterwards, tear out all the pages. Build a bonfire. Burn it. But I didn't. Instead I enquired, in as nice a voice as I could possibly muster, if it was still the plan that we go to the club.

No response, eyes remained locked on the book, the proverbial cat had bitten his tongue. Through gritted teeth, I repeated my question. 'Are we still going to the club, Andy?'

Now he looked up. 'I'm not. You can do what you like.' And returned to his page.

Well, fuck you!

I picked up my bag, and took out my keys.

'I'm off, then. See you later.'

He continued to read. Didn't raise an eye. Didn't say, 'hang on a mo, I'm only joking.' Didn't do anything. I marched to the door, stopped and wavered there for a couple of seconds, praying it was just a horrible game he was playing. But he didn't flinch, except to turn a page in his book. A great wall of rising silence hung between us, so heavy it would need a sledgehammer to knock it down.

Turning abruptly, I headed out into the warm blanket of night. Stood in the darkness. Afraid. Shivered. The knot in my stomach tightened. Tighter and tighter, and it hurt. I wanted to scream. Howl to the sweet, shining, luminous moon. Rid myself of the anger that bubbled and clogged up my insides.

Getting on my little bike, I sat astride it, and waited. Waited for over ten minutes. Expecting, hoping, praying, he would rush out, he would throw himself in my arms and beg forgiveness. But I waited in vain. For those ten minutes it was just me, alone in the quiet of night with a sky full of stars, and a veranda that stayed empty.

I turned on the engine, broke the silence. Brumm-brumm. Brumm-brumm. Slowly I steered the bike round the bungalow. Glanced through the window and saw Andy still sitting in his chair, smoking and reading. A nice, chilled out scene, like he hadn't a care in the world.

Pain replaced anger, or maybe pain is anger, whatever, my pain hurt, it hurt so much it felt physical, like I'd been kicked in the stomach, like I needed to retch. But I kept moving on, slowly cut through the trees, until I reached the dried-up riverbed, close to the cave of the bats. Dismounted, and sat down on a stump (I was doing a lot of stump sitting lately) and went over the last half an hour in my head.

What on earth was happening? Honest to God, I couldn't work it out. But I knew something was wrong and fear gripped my heart. Fear replaced pain, or maybe fear is pain, and pain is anger, because I felt all three, and all three took hold of my body and were as one.

'This is a fucking nightmare,' I said, out loud to myself. 'A fucking nightmare.'

I picked up a twig and drew strange shapes in the sand. And as I prodded and poked the sun-baked earth with the stick, and began stabbing the hard soil beneath, the anger emotion began to steam. It bubbled. It boiled. It came out fighting and saw off the fear and the pain. Fear makes one a coward. Hold your head down and don't say boo to a goose. Pain is agonizing, so excruciating. Stops you in your tracks, instant paralysis, can't do a thing. But anger's different. It gets you going. It moves you along. Anger creates a thirst for revenge, an eye for an eye, a tooth for a tooth.

Fuck you, Andy. Fuck you! Fuck you! Fuck you!

I jumped on my bike, and headed for the club. Everyone was there, well not everyone because Andy wasn't but he didn't count.

'Hi,' I said to everyone, as I made my entrance out on to the patio. And I tossed my hair back, quite a bit.

'Hi,' everyone chorused, as they made room for me around the table. I found myself sitting next to Mike. Deliberately sat next to Mike, he of the blonde hair and lovely smile.

'No Andy tonight?' he asked, raising that handsome eyebrow again.

'No Andy tonight,' I replied, tossing my hair back again, and giving him the glad eye. 'He's got a headache.'

'Oh, dear. Well, I hope he feels okay soon.'

'So do I.'

The quicker the better all round.

I stayed at the club until gone eleven. And for the most of that evening I chatted, nay flirted, with Mike. No doubt about it, he was dishy. But Mike wasn't Andy, and it was Andy I wanted. It was Andy I loved. I loved him so much it hurt. But anger spurred me on. And my anger bubbled all night. How dare he say I wear too much make-up, how dare he imply I look like a tart.

'Do you think I wear too much make-up,' I asked Amy, when

she and I had taken ourselves off to the loo for a piddle and a pout.

Amy, who was not averse to a bit of mascara and eyeshadow her self stood back, perused me, and shook her head. 'No. Why do you ask?'

'Oh, it was just a remark Andy made earlier.'

'About your make-up?'

'Yes.'

'What about it?'

I shrugged. Made light of the situation. Actually chuckled. 'Well, he said he thought I would look better without make-up, that's all. Said he preferred the natural look. I said everyone would run a mile.'

'I've never seen you without any make-up on, so I wouldn't know. But I imagine you'd look okay without it. Anyway, I shouldn't worry about what Andy says,' said Amy, touching up her lips with some Vaseline, 'most blokes say they'd prefer their woman without make-up. But if that was the case, why do the girls with the make-up get more blokes than the girls who go without. Do you see what I mean?'

Yes, I did see what she meant. Would Andy have fancied the scrubbed-up version before we'd got it together? Somehow I think not. Eyeshadow and lipstick gave out signals, it implied, here I am and aren't I attractive? It grabbed the bloke's attention. The natural look was the opposite, was insipid, colourless, drab and dull. It detracted rather than attracted. Maybe that was why a man, once he'd caught his woman, wanted the washed-out look to deter competition.

Well, fuck you, Andy. And the anger bubbled. And as the bubbles boiled, I flirted madly, and as the bubbles simmered, I still flirted madly. With every bloke, but especially Mike.

'You're having fun with old Mikey,' Anne chuckled, when once again I was back in the loo for another pout and a piddle.

'Not really,' I said, thinking, oh bloody hell, perhaps I have gone a bit over the top.

'He seems a bit smitten with you.'

'Well, he can be as smitten all he likes. I've got Andy, and no one comes close to him. He's the best.'

I said this with a flippant smile, but my heart suddenly felt heavy. And my stomach disappeared into a big, gaping hole. I needed Andy, and needed him now.

Ten minutes later, and it was goodbye to everyone, and it was goodbye to Mike.

Twenty minutes later, I was quietly opening and quietly closing the door. Stepped into a room pungent with the aromas of incense and marijuana. And Andy asleep on the bed. Well, he looked as if he was asleep, he didn't stir as I silently undressed and went about my nightly ablutions. And he didn't stir as I lifted up the net and slipped in beside him. And he didn't stir when I put my arms around him. Well, he did but only to turn the other way.

All night, and I lay in the dark with his back to my face. All night spent with the hideous four horsemen, Terror, Bewilderment, Loneliness and Despair. All night, and not one wink of sleep. Morning broke but I was blind to the glorious sunrise, didn't notice the dappled, golden lights on the bed. As far as I was concerned, in my world it was still dark. Very dark. Black. Black as the darkest corner of Hell.

Andy moved. Opened his eyes, watched me, unblinking, like a lizard. I didn't dare open my mouth. I lay lifeless, watching him watching me.

Finally he spoke.

'I'm sorry.'

Those two little words. That's all it took for the sunshine to come back into my life. The room lit up, it was golden.

'I'm sorry, too.'

Another nice and easy day lay ahead.

Only two days to go. We're leaving early morning Christmas Eve, the day after tomorrow. I'm thinking about what to pack in my bag. Shall I take three pairs of trousers, or shall I take four? Do I need these shoes? And what about that skirt? Will it be cold in the mountains? Should I take my cardigan *and* the shawl? And what about knickers? A pair for every day? Save me washing. How many have I got? One, two three, four, five...

I heard the motorbike purr up and the engine go silent. Seconds later Andy appeared at the door, he'd just finished work. He had on his old weather-beaten hat with the tartan patches, his ancient desert boots all scruffy and scuffed, a pair of cut-off denims with holes in the pockets, and a baggy white T-shirt. He looked delicious.

'Hi,' I said, and gave him a kiss. He almost moved away, as if he was expecting a bite.

'What's all this?' Andy picked up the pile of knickers, and gestured to the garments and shoes that were half-in, half-out of my worn out old bag.

'Stuff I'm taking with me. Why?'

'Why? Because we're going on a journey, man, not attending a fucking fashion show.'

Inwardly I sighed. Here we go again. Mr Moody was back.

Over the last couple of weeks, since the night of the tapping pencil, since my defection to Maiduguri, I'd seen a side of Andy that I'd not glimpsed before. And I couldn't work him, the problem, or it, the problem, out. He swung like a pendulum, one minute Mr Loving, the guy with the tender promises, romantic notions, and utopian dreams. Wonderful. He had the knack, as you well know, just one glance from him and I was floating, just one touch, one tiny, little touch and emotionally whisked off to a place of unimaginable beauty. And then just as I thought it couldn't get any better, it got worse.

Enter Mr Moody.

Mr Moody was a different guy, the opposite of Mr Loving. He knocked the promises, kicked the romance, said fuck to the utopian dreams. Horrible. He had the knack, as you now know, just one glance from him and I was crashing, just one word, one tiny, little word and scrambling about in the bowels of Hell. And just when I thought it couldn't get any worse, it got better.

This yo-yoing was doing my head in, and like the sweet chariot, at times I swung low. But I endured his moods because I loved him, adored him, had given up everything for him. Put all my pretty, shiny eggs in one beautiful basket. And with only one beautiful basket to my name, what else was a young girl to do?

And here we were again. Or rather here was Mr Moody again. Arguing the toss about my grand packing plans.

'Look,' I said, trying to get him to see the light, and keep it light, 'we're going away for about a month, and I need clothes to sustain me.'

Andy didn't see the joke.

'You've got no idea, have you? You think it's just a walk in the park. Look at this lot.' He gestured to my pile of tops. 'Fuck me, man, you're doing my head in.'

And that said, he walked out of the door. Just like that. Without another word. Got on his bike and roared off into the silver dusk of the evening.

I flopped on the bed, and sighed. Bent down and picked up the tin of grass off the floor, and with trembling hands rolled myself one hell of a massive, great joint. Puffed away, and thought about going over to see Hamish. Not that I'd talk to him about what was going on with Andy, I wouldn't talk to anyone about what was going on with Andy, unless it was good stuff. Oh, yes, I'd be more than happy to share the upside of things, of which, of course, there were plenty, but when Andy got moody with me then I went quiet. Very quiet. It was like if I dared admit there was trouble in Heaven then everyone would laugh in my face. *Ha. Ha. Told you so.* So I said nothing to nobody because it made sense. I knew Andy would come flying in sometime later tonight, would pick me up, and take me soaring back to paradise. It was just a matter of me biding my time.

So, even though I was emotionally in pieces, I strolled over to Hamish's and pretended everything was fine. We shared the pipe of peace on his veranda. And we talked about normal things like Christmas and who'd be doing what, when and how.

'There's going to be quite an exodus from Maiduguri in the next couple of days,' commented Hamish, leaning back in his chair. 'There won't be many of us left at all I reckon by Saturday.'

Which was true, most of the in-crowd was planning to head out, to Jos, to Yankari, to Mambilla. Hamish was staying put. Group travelling wasn't his thing.

'Where are you spending Christmas Day?'

'Och, I'll take it nice and easy and amble over to the club. They put on a good do. And I'll drag Buggy along for a laugh.'

'I bet he gets really pissed up at Christmas.' I said this with a smile. See what I mean, I really was good at this 'everything is ok' malarkey. Could grin, joke, do a dance. Anything.

'Aye,' chuckled Hamish, nodding his head, 'and he's already started. He was in a right mess last night, tried to get into my bed because he thought it was his. And we'll have more of that sort of thing right through to the New Year, and beyond. He kinna likes his tipple.'

'That's why he doesn't want to go away with the rest of the crew,' I laughed, 'because all the travelling will take up valuable drinking time.'

'Aye. He's a one.' Hamish got up as he spoke, went inside his little house, and came back with a small package. 'A wee Christmas gift for you and Andy.'

'Oh, Hamish, you shouldn't have,' I said, feeling terrible. I hadn't got him anything. Hadn't got anybody anything. Away from everybody at Christmas, so didn't think about presents although I had sent my Mum and Dad a hastily written card. *'Love you lots, see you soon, have a happy Christmas, from your loving daughter, Jannixxxx.'* But then nearly forgot to post it, they probably wouldn't get it now until the New Year. Still, better late than never.

'Och, it's nothing. Just a wee gesture.'

'Can I open it?'

'Aye, I canna see why not. You don't want to be carrying it about with you when you're travelling.'

So I undid the wrapping. And nestled amongst the cheap Christmas paper, the kind that tears easily, there was a beautifully framed photograph. Our photograph. Andy's and my photograph. The one taken by Mr Jolly.

'I sneaked in your house, I'm afraid, and pinched it, when you were both out last night. I hope you like the frame.'

Like it? I loved it.

The frame was made of wood, and ten little butterflies were intricately carved round the edge of it, and each had a different coloured pair of wings. All hand painted. All delicate and wispy, as if they really could flap in the air and fly away with the breeze.

'Oh, Hamish, it's lovely.'

'Aye, I remembered about you and your butterflies. The ones that go flutter when the feeling is good.'

I smiled. And wished the feeling was good this minute. That it was dancing butterflies, not twisted knots in my stomach.

'Are you all packed up and ready to go?' asked Hamish, tapping the charred contents of his pipe into the earthenware ashtray.

'Sort of,' I said, and the knots tightened as I cast my mind back to the bundle of clothes, the shoes and the knickers that still lay on the bed. And Andy's biting remarks. And the look he had on his face when he left.

'What time are you planning on leaving Saturday?' Hamish was now filling up his pipe with Grandpa's tobacco.

'Early. Andy says it's best we have a really early start. Around about six, I reckon.'

'That's early.' He struck a match, puff puff, and the inside of the pipe began to glow. 'Are you planning on spending Christmas Eve in Mubi?'

The sweet, aromatic smoke wafted up my nose, I was reminded of carefree childhood days spent sitting with Grandpa under the apple tree in his garden, amongst the roses and daffodils.

We were on the look out for naughty bunnies in the cabbage patch. Sipping homemade lemonade brought out by Granny, and munching buttered scones spread thickly with jam. Happy times! Oh, to be carefree like that once again.

'I think so. And then we're going to wend our way across to Yola, spend a few days sailing down the Benue. Camp on the islands, that sort of thing, before we head off to Mambilla and the Cameroon.'

'Och, it sounds like a romantic journey.'

'It does, doesn't it?'

And my heart missed a beat. The both of us far, far away. On our very own desert island. Him reading me poems, me wrapped up in a shawl, sitting around a crackling fire. And thinking about this made the butterflies flutter. And their wings loosened the knots. And the knots disappeared, the heaviness lifted and I began to feel good. Really good. Yep! I was going on a journey, a romantic journey with my man. And everything was going to be fine.

But the feel good factor didn't last long.

I spent the rest of the evening waiting for Andy to come home. Midnight, and he still wasn't back. He'd been gone six hours. Visions of him lying dead on the side of the road, vultures pecking out his eyes, flies buzzing round the broken, bloody body, a pack of dogs fighting over his dismembered limbs, had me going frantic with worry. I paced up and down, chain-smoked, alternating between cigarette and joint, and raced out to the veranda every time I thought I heard an engine purr. Nothing. But even worse, much worse than motorbike accidents and scavenging creatures out for a nightly bite, were the pictures in my head of Andy lying curled up in bed with another woman. Quite who this 'other woman' was I'd no idea, she didn't exist, but the thought filled me with dread all the same.

At one in the morning he came home. Hearing the familiar drone of the bike I was out, and down the steps of the veranda.

'Where've you been, Andy? I've been going out of my mind with worry.'

The headlamp switched from bright beam to dark, the engine went from purr to quiet, and both of us looked at each other through the shadows. It reminded me of another encounter, long, long ago.

Andy pushed the hair back off his face. I wanted him to push the hair back off my face. Instead he kept his distance, didn't even give me a smile. He just looked at me strangely. The knots in my stomach tied themselves up, double quick. Tightened. And a lump of concrete, a fucking great lump of concrete weighing a ton, embedded itself in my chest. 'I've just been round Sall and Richard's,' he said coolly, and gave a nonchalant, couldn't care less kind of shrug.

'Sally and Richard? Why didn't you take me?' I asked stupidly.

'Because,' he said with an exaggerated sigh, plopping himself down on the little veranda wall, 'I needed some space.'

'Some space?' I plopped myself next to him. 'Space from what?'

He thought about his answer. With head down, he studied the ground. The seconds ticked by. Finally, he came out with it.

'From you.'

'What?' I whispered, not sure I'd heard right.

He looked up, turned and faced me. 'I needed to get away from you.'

A cold hand, with talons as sharp as nails, got hold of my heart and squeezed. And squeezed, digging the nails deeper and deeper. My stomach heaved. I thought I might puke up on the spot. I looked to the heavens above, hoping for divine intervention. But God was nowhere. There was just the moon shaped like a lopsided smile, and a star twinkling merrily nearby. Like they were both taking the piss.

When I opened my mouth, when finally I managed to speak, when I was sure I wasn't actually going to be sick, I came out with just one little word.

'Why?'

Andy shrugged. 'Och, the fuck knows why. I'm not quite sure myself.' And he stared again at his feet, dug a little hole in the sand with the toe of his boot.

But I was desperate. I needed answers. Now.

'Come inside, Andy. Let's talk. Let's sort whatever it is that's wrong, out. Please.' I was begging, pleading. I had a hold of his arm, was hanging on to it for dear life.

Andy shook his head. And retrieved his arm. And moved away. 'I'm in no mood to talk. It's late. I just want my bed.'

He picked himself up, crossed the veranda and disappeared through the door. Dumbstruck, I remained rooted to the spot, but my legs felt like jelly. I half wobbled and had to hold on to the edge of the wall, and stayed like that for ages, not knowing what to do. In the dark. Alone. With warm, silent tears cascading down my face while a moon with a lopsided smile mocked me from high up above.

Finally I moved, but not far. Just sat on the wall and tried to take stock. Tried to untangle my tangled-up thoughts. What on earth was happening to us? To me? How had we got to this point? Were we ever going to get past it?

Keep quiet, keep quiet, said a rational voice from somewhere in my head. Maybe it was my Guardian Angel? *Keep quiet, and it'll be all right. Don't push. Don't do anything. Be silent. Be mute. Go inside. Roll yourself up a joint. Smoke it. Inhale deeply. Let the drug still the mind.*

I heeded my own sound advice. As Andy went about his night-time business, locking himself in the bathroom for a good twenty minutes, I sneaked indoors, retrieved my baccy tin, and headed back out to the veranda. And there I sat, with smoke billowing out of my mouth and tears tumbling down my cheeks. I couldn't even be bothered to wipe them away.

How long I stayed out there on my little wall is anyone's guess. Even when I heard Andy come out of the bathroom and switch off the lights, one by one, I still didn't dare go inside. I waited, rolled up another joint, and waited. Smoked some more, and bided my time, until I could bide no more. Crept quietly into the house like a burglar with a head full of dope, undressed, dropping my clothes in a muddled pile on the floor. Couldn't be bothered to wash, couldn't even be bothered to go to the loo.

Crawled under the net and slipped in beside him. Back to back. My face to the window. For the whole of the night, staring at the moon with its lopsided smile, and the twinkling star, who were both still taking the piss.

At his usual hour, Andy stirred. No kisses, no tickles, he just climbed over me like I was an abandoned, not much loved, fluffy toy, and slipped out of bed. I lay as still as could be, had lain still all night, as still as could be. Even when wanting the loo I'd not moved. It was almost like the pain in my head went when the pain in my bladder began. Kevin had once mentioned something about how you could transfer pain from one part of the body to another, but I hadn't really been listening. I reckon though, this must have been what he meant.

But now wasn't the time to carry on with the experiment. If I didn't make a move I'd be pissing in the bed, and the consequences would be horrendous. I was having enough problems with Andy without having to explain why I had a sudden, overwhelming desire to wash the sheets and buy a new mattress. So as soon as Andy left the room, and I could hear him talking with Buggy and Hamish from somewhere outside, I was out of the bed, and into the loo. God, what a relief! At least that was one part of my life sorted. Quickly I got dressed, pulled on jeans and a T-shirt. Decided to put on a brave face, like I always did, and have breakfast with the boys. It was a new day, after all. A new kind of dawn. Wondrous things might happen over a pot of coffee and a plate of buttered rolls.

But Andy was already walking back from Hamish's, had a half-eaten piece of toast in his hand. Obviously, he wasn't planning on hanging around. He gave me a look when he saw me. It was the kind of look that made me feel I didn't matter to him any more. He walked on, passed me by. Indifferent. No kiss or hug. Strangers we were on our way to our own different lives.

But I stopped. I turned. And called him by name. 'Andy?'

He was halfway up the veranda steps. Turned, he glared at me in the same way I've glared at lepers. 'What?' he barked.

'Nothing,' I mumbled, 'I'll see you later,' and walked on. I knew that if I broke down now I'd never get myself back together again, just like Humpty Dumpty, but even that cracked egg had the kings horses and kings men on his side. I had no one, just little, old me. So I tried to listen to the inner voice, tried to remind myself that even though things appeared bad at the moment, it would surely pass like all the other, not quite as bad, times before.

Give him space. Let him cool off. Everything will be all right, said she, the optimist with the now cracked, shiny eggs in the one beautiful, torn apart basket.

So I sat on the sunny veranda, sipped tea and spread marmalade on toast, and whiled away an hour or so with Hamish and Buggy. And gave out the message to them that life was so very good (I'm a brilliant actress). And when it was time for them to get on with their work, I trotted back to the bungalow, already planning that I would ride over to Rosie's and spend the day with her round the pool. Try to get through the day as best I could, by tonight I was certain we'd be back to normal.

Opened the door, the empty room still pungent with the smell of incense and marijuana, the bed still unmade, the little anthology still lying shut on the table, the photo of two happy, smiling lovers surrounded by a troupe of dancing butterflies still on top of the chest of drawers. And next to the photo, a letter.

A letter?

Propped up against an unlit candle that stood in a sand-filled, small, earthenware pot. Blue airmail paper, folded in half, and then half again. And one word scrawled across it in Andy's long, spidery handwriting. *Janni.*

A letter to me. A letter for me from Andy.

What was so hard to say to my face that he had to put it in writing? I picked up the flimsy paper, unfolded it, and read:

Forget Me Not – Janns, Forgive me if I'm not in love anymore, something has kinda died. But it was the most beautiful love I ever had in my life. I'll be leaving tomorrow on my own to go to the mountains and find some kind of living. I don't know why I feel this way, Janni, but I think you know and understand the way I am.

Take care of your wee self. You'll have a beautiful life because you are a beautiful person.

I'll see you when I see you
Andy.

Think Hiroshima. The bomb. The devastation. Think Armageddon. The end of the world. Think trillions of splinters, shards, and a million shattered dreams. Think dark abyss. Think hurtling down into a bottomless pit. Think monsters and nightmares. Think torture and pain.

I flopped like a rag doll, and sank. Drowning, and fighting for breath, with the letter still in my hand. Crouched in a huddle on the cold, cold, cold as ice, concrete floor, numbed with absolute, pure, unadulterated grief, I couldn't even cry.

I stayed in this position, on the floor, all day. A couple of times motorbikes purred up, they were from somewhere far, far away. And from another world there came knocks on the door. Someone out there was calling my name. But I'd roll myself up into a tight, tight ball and hide under the bed. And wait. Wait for the silence that follows the sound of footsteps as they walk away. Wait for the quiet, the stillness after the motorbike drones have finally disappeared. Then I'd crawl out on hands and knees, back to the cold concrete spot, with the letter still in my hand. *Forget me not – Janns.* And I'd read it again. *Forgive me if I'm not in love any more.* And read it again. *Something has kinda died.* Until the paper was all tattered and torn and my hands were covered in blue, inky smudges.

And as I read, I smoked. One joint after the other. Didn't bother with an ashtray, used the floor to flick the ash and stub out the smokes. Ground the little bastards so hard that by the end there was nothing left but black ashen marks on the concrete.

87

And that's how it was all day, on the floor, huddled and alone, in so much pain, and with so much fear, but, still unable to cry.

And that's how Andy found me.

It was a weird moment, him walking through the door. He stopped, looked down at me, and I, like a trapped animal trembling with fear, looked up. There was this stranger who I knew really well. Had shared my most intimate moments with, but now I was nothing to him. *Something had kinda died.*

Andy didn't say a word. Just sat down on the unmade bed and cupped his chin in his hands. And while he stared at the opposite wall, I stared at him.

Oh God, how I stared at him. All I did was stare. And all he did was stare and stare at the wall.

The silence ticked on.

Finally he said. 'What are you going to do?' His voice was quiet, soft. And he looked at me now as he spoke.

What am I going to do?

A little spark of anger flickered. It was just that, a flicker, but for the first time in this dreadful, dreadful day I felt something. And feeling something was enough.

'What do you think I should do?'

My voice sounded strange. These were the first words I'd spoken since this morning. I'd forgotten I could talk.

Andy put his head in his hands. Was like that for a while. I patiently waited. Let's face it, I'd been patiently waiting all day, another few minutes wouldn't matter. Finally he lifted his head up, and sighed. 'Honest to God, Janni, I don't know.'

And the flicker flared and began to heat up the anger. 'Well,' I said quietly, 'you should know. You're the one making all the decisions.'

Andy coughed. He twiddled his thumbs. 'This isn't easy, you know, Janni.'

And the anger slowly bubbled, not quite boiled, but steam was rising. 'Isn't easy for you, or isn't easy for me?'

Andy shrugged. 'For the both of us.'

And I said, ever so, ever so softly. 'I hate you. For what you've done to me. I hate you for being a liar.' And the anger bubbled, and the anger boiled. 'I hate you. I hate you. I hate you.' And I picked up the nearest thing to me, his book 'The Catcher in The Rye', and lobbed it straight at his head. Unfortunately it missed but it still gave him a shock.

'For fuck's sake,' he shouted.

I was up.

'You're a bastard, a shit, pissing son of a whore. A low, mean, lying fucker. And I hate you, I hate you.' I ran to him and tried to bang my fists against his chest, and slap his face. But he grabbed hold of my wrists, and held on to them. So I used my legs and kneed him in the groin instead. 'You bastard, you bastard, you bastard.' I was shouting, and hollering, and screaming. And Andy was screaming, and hollering, and shouting. 'For fuck's sake, Janni, calm down. For fuck's sake.'

But I wouldn't calm down, couldn't calm down, and with super human strength (amazing what you can do when you're totally barking mad) I pushed him back on the bed and fell on top of him. And still we were fighting, and I'm kicking and screaming, and he's got me in a hold, and my face is up against his, his lips are touching mine, and we're locked together. Still fighting, but now kissing. Eating each other, devouring each other like a pair of hungry wolves. And he's kicking off his boots, and I'm pulling off my jeans, and he's tearing my top, and I'm ripping his shorts, and, well, need I go on? I think you get the gist.

Sometime later, and we're lying in a heap on the bed. The evening light shines through the window, the blob in the sky has moved on to another part of the world and all that is left of it is the afterglow. For ages we don't speak, but we touch, and we stare into each other's eyes. Unblinking. And I wish we could stay like this forever. He pushes the hair back off my face, and tenderly kisses me. It's a beautiful kiss. I'm freefalling in space, dancing amongst stars.

'We're going to be all right, aren't we?' I say, breaking the silence.

'I don't know,' he answers. 'But we'll always have a special place for one another, whatever.'

I touch his cheek. Draw an abstract picture with my finger, strange circles on his face. And I'm thinking, I don't want a special place. I want him. For years, well ever since I realised boys and girls paired up, became an item, I've wanted a boyfriend, and now that I've found Andy, I want him forever. 'I love you, Andy.'

'I know.' And that's all he says.

So I ask him. 'Do you still love me?'

'Janni,' he replies, and I can taste his breath in my mouth, we're that close, 'don't ask me things that I can't answer. It's not fair on you or me.'

What does he mean by that?

'But you said you'd love me for always.' *And he did. He really did.* …And I will love thee always/until all the seas gang dry…

'Things change.'

'What's changed?' My voice wobbles, there's a lump stuck in my throat, and tears are gathering like storm clouds behind my hazel/brown eyes.

'I dunno. Everything.'

'Everything?' I raise my head, use my hand as a prop, and look down into his beautiful face. Blue, blue eyes stare back at me, and I want to kiss them and I want to touch the halo of hair that lie like golden threads on the pillow. 'What do you mean everything?' My wobbly voice comes out like a squeak, and the tears start cascading down like the Falls at Kwyaterra.

Andy moves, turns on his back, focuses his attention on the ceiling. 'You and me. It's just not working,' he says quietly.

'What's not working?' I cry.

'You. Me.' He looks at me with his whole face. 'For fuck's sake, can't you understand?' I'm dumbstruck, so he carries on. 'You keep pretending everything is ok but it isn't. Ever since you moved in, it's all got too much and I want – ', the last word shoots, like a bullet from his mouth, – 'out.'

No, I scream. 'You can't mean it, Andy. You can't. I love you and you love me. This is crazy.' And I beat my fists on the pillow, and bury my head on his chest. And hold him. Like I've never held him before, squeezing him, hanging onto him, for if I let go I'll fall and fall and fall. But he pushes me away. Sits bolt right up in bed, and throws off the sheet. 'This is no good,' he says matter-of-factly, like he's found a rotten tomato in his cheese/salad sandwich. 'How can we talk when you don't listen to anything I say to you?' He makes to get out of the bed.

'No, no,' I plead, 'don't go. I'll listen. I promise.' I sit up, and wipe my tears with the back of my hand. 'Please.' He looks at me, his legs are already over the side, his feet an inch from the floor. God, I want to hug him so much, nestle my face into him like he were a soft, velvet cushion. Tell him I love him more than anything else in the world. But I don't. I say, 'Please, Andy, talk to me. Please.' And he sighs. And I'm thinking, he's not going to stay, he's going to leave me like this, and what am I going to do? And he sighs again, but there's one leg up and back on the bed, and then the other.

And he shifts himself, as I do, and the both of us sit back against the pillows, side by side, and start again.

'Andy,' I ask, and this time I choose my words carefully, 'tell me what it is that's made you change your mind about me? Why it's all got too much?' And I try very hard to ignore the pain in my throat, and the imaginary axe in my heart, and my voice is quite steady, quite calm.

Andy doesn't answer straight away. We sit like solemn bookends. A watch ticks. A motorbike in the distance purrs down the road. Above us, a couple of mosquitoes buzz round our heads.

'I just don't love you anymore, I guess,' he says finally.

I'm trying very hard to be brave, as you know, I really am. But when someone you love tells you they don't love you anymore, being brave isn't easy. But I stay calm because I figure if I lose it now, I'll have lost him completely. Forever. And though I don't understand, at all, how we got to this point, and feel so pushed away, so inadequate, so not what he obviously wants, there's still a part of me, the spirit within, that reckons everything will be all right. Maybe? He loved me once. Then he can love me again.

'So, do you want me to go back to Gombe?' I'm struggling. For three reasons. The thought of leaving everybody here fills me with sadness, and going back to my life in Gombe fills me with dread. But severing my ties with Andy, well that's worse than the other two put together. Anywhere in the world without him, Maiduguri, Paris, London, and my life will always be empty as empty can be.

'It's up to you,' he says simply.

Meaning?

He does want me to go back to Gombe.

Oh, God help me.

Like The Scream, I'm on the bridge, I've got my hands to my wide, open mouth, and I'm giving it my all. But my despair is for my eyes and ears only. It's all within. Outwardly, I'm relatively composed.

It's part of the plan, you see. It's a clutching at straws plan, but it's a plan, nonetheless.

To Andy I say, very calmly. 'What about tomorrow? Going away?'

'What about it?' He's sitting up, and is putting a lit match to a fag. I get myself one from the packet and he strikes another match, it flares as I puff. I take a couple of drags.

'It was you that asked me to come with you, remember?'

'Aye, of course I remember.' Andy is watching the smoke as it curls from his mouth.

I am watching him. 'Well, I've really been looking forward to it.' A heart beat. I take a deep breath, and say, ever so smoothly, like a Cadbury crème egg, 'Can't I still come?'

'Oh, Jesus!' Andy's shrill cry makes me jump. He throws himself back on the bed, his eyes now on the ceiling. I lie down and join the ceiling watch. Well actually, it's the net watch but you can just about see the cracks and the cobwebs through the mesh. 'I can't believe I'm hearing this,' Andy mutters, as though from far away. 'I've just explained things to you, and yet you're still pretending everything's ok.'

'No, Andy, I'm not.' My voice is still calm; I'm doing a good job. I'm holding down the riot within. 'You've told me you don't love me anymore, and I understand.' Believe me, it isn't easy saying these words out loud but this is a part, a very important part, of my plan. 'And I do hear what you're saying, things haven't been good recently but –well – like you said, we'll always have a special place for each other and I reckon – well – we could still be friends?' He turns, I turn. We're nose to nose. I swallow. The frog doesn't go down but my voice isn't too wobbly. 'Couldn't I…' here comes the plan '…just come as a friend? A travelling companion?'

Andy takes a deep breath, and a long, hard drag on his fag.
'Please.'

The watch ticks. A waft of air shimmies through the open window. An animal cries in the distance. A lonely cry. But not as lonely a cry as mine.

He sits up, stubs out his fag in the ashtray that's on the bedside table, and rubs the back of his neck. Considering.

'Och, Janni, I dunno?' he finally says. 'It's not going to be easy, being with each other, with all this going on."

A flicker faintly flares. A light finally at the end of the tunnel.

'Let's at least give it a try, Andy. Please.'

Please, please, please. I'm begging you. Pleading with you. I'll stand in the corner with a bucket of shit on my head, if it'll make you say yes. I'll walk on hot coals, eat bush dog, climb Everest, kiss a leper. I'll do anything. Anything. But please just say yes.

He sighs. 'You don't give up easily, do you?' He's looking at me full on. I shrug. Try to give out that it's not really that big a deal. Even though my life depends on it, and his decision means everything to me.

Silence.

I can hear the ticking, tick tick tick of the watch. And I'm studying the cobweb in the corner of the room, there's a spider. I think it's eating a fly.

'Are you packed?'

'Sort of.'

'Whatever you take, *you* carry.'

'Fine by me.'

'That's it, then. We leave at six, tomorrow morning. And no fucking about.'

I smile. 'No fucking about, I promise.'

Maybe there are more nice and easy days to look forward to, after all.

We were up at five, and tramping across sand by six. Taking the back route to the Bama road. Andy walked in front, he was moody, but what the hell, I was with him and being with him was all that mattered.

Lagging behind, and I wished after just ten minutes of heavy slog through the sandy scrub that I'd not packed as much stuff as I had. My bag was heavy, very heavy, but I didn't dare moan. I just kept shifting it from one shoulder to the other, pissed off that mine wasn't a rucksack like Andy's, wished I could carry the fucking thing on my back in the nice and easy way he was carrying his.

And so we plodded on.

Even at this early hour the African world was wide awake. Out of the thorn bush popped a man carrying a large, brightly painted enamel tin full of bananas, on his head, on his way to the market. And from another direction two young women sashayed through the waste, swinging their arms in unison, one with a large bundle of wood, and the other a bucket of water. Both had tiny, little babies, maybe just a few weeks old, strapped to their backs, and their exposed tits, full with milk, hung low, and swung like their arms.

A bit further on we passed a waterhole. A group of women were washing clothes (rags really), some slapping frayed pieces of cloth hard on the smooth rocks, some knee-deep in the brown, murky water scrubbing away with large lumps of homemade soap made out of animal fat mixed with lye. And around them, the bushes emblazoned with tatty pieces of material hanging out to dry. Children ran in and out of the water, their small, dark bodies, with the sun already warm on their naked backs, glistening with drops as they splashed about, giggling and laughing. It made for a very happy spectacle, the kind of picture snapped by my Mum on her old Kodak Brownie, tales of African life, to be shown later to the aged grandparents back in England.

And of course, no bush scene is complete without the obligatory cow or two meandering their way through the scrub chewing on paper-dry cud. And there's always a man on an overloaded donkey trotting briskly, up down, up down, across stony earth, and a small barefoot boy chasing his herd of bleating goats, and a lone Fulani man with his crook having a piss in the sands.

And so we plodded on.

It took us a good hour to get across the sandy ridge and by the time we reached the road, we were frazzled. Well, I was. Andy was still looking pretty cool. We dumped our bags by the side of the already, despite the early hour, melting-with-heat tarmac, sat on them, and waited. And thankfully we didn't have to wait long, five minutes later a lorry came trundling down the road, filled with sacks, and when the driver saw us he stopped.

'Where you go?' asked the pock-marked man, with a fag in his mouth.

'Bama,' replied Andy.

'I go to Duiki.'

'Duiki is good.'

So we threw our bags up to the three blokes who were sitting on the sacks in the back, and then scrambled up the sides, and joined them. I must say I was glad that I'd put some practice in earlier, what with my previous mammy-wagon exploits, and was pretty nimble to say the least. I was sitting on top of a sack and ready to go within seconds.

'Are you okay,' Andy asked, as the lorry moved off. It was the first words he'd said to me since we first began our trek across the sands an hour ago.

If he was meaning am I okay about sitting on a sack, in the back of a lorry, then yes I was fine. There was quite a nice breeze blowing through my hair, and it was cooling me down. And the bush looked pretty spectacular. At this time of the morning the whole world was golden. The earth was yellow-gold, the trees and bushes were tawny-gold, and the sky was honey-gold. And very pretty it all was too.

But if he was meaning are you okay, meaning are you okay in yourself. Well, the answer was no. I felt very, very sad. Here I was doing what I'd always wanted to do, go travelling with the man I loved. Only problem was the man I loved wasn't too sure he loved me. And sitting on my sack, thinking about that, and a huge wave swelled up inside me. I could feel it sweeping me away under, into cold, dark empty waters, which was a bit strange because I was as far away from cold, dark empty waters as I could possibly be. But that's what a broken heart does to you, I suppose. Makes you dwell on the dark side of life even when the warm sun is shining.

'I'm fine, thanks.'

And that was all that was said for the whole of the forty mile journey.

At Duiki, a hamlet of less than a dozen mud huts, we were dropped off. As the man said, he was going no further. So we did our rock climbing simulation, a foothold here, a hand on there, and scrambled off the lorry. Then down came the bags, Andy slung his over his back, I hitched my burdensome weight up over my shoulder, and we went across the road and sat under a withered old tree with a group of aged pensioners. You know the type, ragged old men, in ragged old clothes, who have nothing better to do other than sit under a withered old tree, flicking away at the flies and picking their noses, as the world passes them by. Andy immediately struck up a conversation with them, speaking fluent Hausa, of course. He'd been in the country only two and a bit years and I'd been in Nigeria for most of my life, yet I couldn't speak the lingo anywhere near as well. And he was obviously enjoying the chat, as were the old boys, (I suppose it was a bit of a deviation from their usual fly flicking and nose picking routine) all of them laughing. Oh, they were all having such fun in the shade!

I sat on my bag and felt glum. Stared down at the dusty, red earth and watched a black ant with a large, fat body, waddle its way towards a small, rounded stone. Reaching it, the ant began to go a bit mad; it sort of jumped up like it was having a tantrum. Little legs were going all over the place, and I swear I heard a scream come from its funny little mouth. Anyway, I came up with a plan and moved the stone a couple of inches away. Immediately, the ant stopped flapping, had a quick look round (just to see if any fellow insects had observed the madness of King George the ant – that would have been most embarrassing, one does have to keep up appearances, you know) and with the coast clear, commenced again with the waddle.

Fumbling in my bag, I retrieved my fags.

Another burst of laughter from the gang of wizened

pensioners. Another chuckle from Andy. *Ha, ha, ha. It was all so very funny.*

I lit up, and tried to knock the tears in my eyes on the head.

'They're all nuts.' Andy had finally had enough of the wise cracks and banter. He came over and squatted beside me in the sand. 'Senile dementia, I reckon.'

I half-smiled. 'At least they seem happy.' *Lucky fuckers.*

'Aye,' nodded Andy, glancing back at the ancients. 'They don't have a bad life.' *Lucky, lucky fuckers. Wished I was an old man and could have a good life under a tree.*

'Where are we?' I asked to roll the conversation on.

'Duiki.'

'Yeah, I know. But how far are we from Bama?'

Andy looked up and down the silent, empty road. 'Dunno. About four miles, maybe five.'

'Not far then.'

'No.'

End of conversation. The minutes ticked by. The flies buzzed around. The road became hazy, shimmered as the sun moved higher into the sky.

A little boy, with snot running down his cute, little face, ran up to us, shouting and pointing. A car was coming, absolutely jam-packed; every tiny bit of space had a person stuffed in it. It slowed down. Stopped. The driver was so squashed up in his seat his head was already halfway out of the window.

'Where you go?'

'Bama.' Andy had already risen, and was hitching his rucksack over his shoulder.

'Two naira.' A hand was thrust out, ready for the cash.

'What! You must be crazy, man. It's only five miles down the road.' Andy pointed to the car, 'There's no room for us, anyway. Where are we going to sit? I give you fifty kobo. My final offer.'

'Two naira,' repeated Mr Obstinate, his empty hand still at arms length out the window.

Andy turned to me, and almost spat. 'Why is it? Why do they think that just because we've got white skins, we've got money?' And back to the driver. 'No way, Jimmy, we'll get another car. Go and steal from someone else.'

That said, he dropped his rucksack on the sandy ground, and perched his bum down.

'OK. OK. Fifty kobo.'

'Done. Come on,' he said, shooting a glance in my direction, 'get your bag.'

The driver jumped out, well, fell out more like once the door was opened, and shooed us round to the back. More doors were opened, more people fell out and had to be squashed back into place, and then it was Andy's and my turn. Andy had to sit on the luggage, and I had to sit on him. Then the doors wouldn't shut properly but that was probably a good thing, the smell of bodies was so terrible a bit of fresh air was a blessed relief. All I can say is, thank God it was only for five miles. Fifty miles would have been a nightmare in this motorised can.

And so we chugged on.

At the Bama lorry park, we gratefully squeezed and pushed ourselves out. There were plenty of mammy-wagons hissing and spewing, and being loaded and unloaded, but none of them were going to Mubi, our destination. So we wandered off and sat on some stone steps and drank Fanta. Both of us quiet, both of us lost in our own personal thoughts.

My mind wandered off. To the last time I was here, the only time I was here, the day of the picnic. I looked down the wide, dusty street, at the mud-bricked houses, at the avenue of trees, at the people in their ragtag assortment of traditional and second-hand Western clothes, and imagined me on the back of my lover's bike hurtling down this way with not a care in the world. Me and my golden boy.

What a difference a couple of months make.

'Shall we take a walk up the road?' Andy had put down his bottle and stubbed out his fag. 'See if we can thumb a lift. We may have to wait ages for a lorry. What do you reckon?'

'Yeah. Ok,' I said, pleased with the idea. It's not that I liked walking, especially with a large, cumbersome bag, but it was better than sitting doing nothing, and thinking about things to make you sadder than you already were.

So Andy slung his rucksack on his back, and I did the business with the bag, and we walked. And for a while it was fine in the shade, under the neem trees in dappled sunlight, but the further on we went, the sparser the trees, the hotter it got. Half a mile on, and it was open bush, and boiling. Another mile, and the sweat's pouring off us. And my bags getting heavier and heavier. And not one lorry or car passed us by, only donkeys. And I didn't fancy a two hundred mile journey on one of them.

Wearily we plodded on.

A hundred yards further up the road from us we spotted a stationary Land Rover. Getting nearer to it, and we saw the distinctive MNR (Ministry of Natural Resources) initials on the side of the doors. Right beside it, and Andy recognised the driver who was lying stretched out, across both front seats, having a bit of a kip.

Andy shook his legs. 'Hey, Hassan. How you doing, man?'

Eyes shot open. And up so quickly, Hassan banged his head on the steering wheel.

'Hey, Master Andy. I be good, man,' he answered, rubbing his sore bit.

'Are you driving this thing?'

'I be driving to Iska.'

'Can we have a lift?'

'Sure, man.'

'Where's Iska?' I asked, as I put my bag, oh bliss, in the back. My shoulders and arms hurt like anything.

'Only about twenty, thirty miles down the road but it's better than nothing, I suppose.' Andy gave me a half-smile. Like the man said, it was better than nothing.

I got in the front of the Land Rover with Hassan; Andy sat in the back. That hurt. In the old days we'd be joined at the hip.

We did nought to sixty in five seconds. It was just like being in the car with my Dad.

'You be Master Andy wife?' asked Hassan the Speed as he ploughed into a massive, great pothole. I flew off the seat and bumped my head on the roof.

'Sort of,' I replied. If only, I thought.

'He be a good man, Master Andy. He be my good friend. Yes, I like him too much,' as we swerved to avoid a wandering goat. Quickly I grabbed the dashboard as the Land Rover bounced in, and bounced out of another moon-sized crater. My whole being was bouncing too. It was like taking a ride on a speeding trampoline.

A couple of miles further on, in front of us, on an otherwise deserted road, was another fast moving vehicle. Hassan put his foot down. 'This man in dis car,' pointing, 'he be a friend of mine. Maybe he go to Mubi, maybe he be give you a ride?'

And so the chase began. It was Nigeria's equivalent to the Paris to Dakar rally. It was definitely like being in the car with my Dad.

It took ten miles of bumps, rocket launches, and stomach churning swerves, to catch up with Hassan's friend in the white

Peugeot. Initially, I think, Mr Peugeot driver thought he was being pursued by the enemy. The speeds both vehicles got up to was unbelievable, well unbelievable for anybody that hadn't ever had the experience of being in a car with my Dad. I was used to this type of manic driving. But even veteran speedos like me look forward to the moment when the vehicle finally lands, and we can put our feet back on terra firma.

Neck and neck, hailing each other through open windows, and both vehicles simultaneously did an emergency stop. It's a miracle that none of us in the front went through the windscreens, and Andy didn't go flying into space out the back.

Doors were flung open, customary greeting were made.

'Sannu.'

'Sannu da aiki.'

'Yawwa sannu.'

'Blahdey blahdey blah.'

Andy jumped out, joined them, and so it all began again. More Hausa greetings. More Hausa chat. I perused the scene from my seat in the Land Rover whilst smoking a fag.

An agreement was made.

'The guy's giving us a lift,' said Andy. 'Come on.'

And so it was out of the Land Rover, unload the bags, put them in the Peugeot, put ourselves in the Peugeot, and we're off again. Certainly we were having a high time trying out the different modes of transport. It was a bit like being a contestant in some weird marathon race where you had to change vehicles every ten miles, unload, load, and jump in the seat as fast as you could.

And they're off!!!! Up to the next hurdle!!!! And over the jump!!!! Into the next pothole!!!! And they've managed to hold on to their seats!!!!! And here comes a cow!!!!! And they're over it!!!!!! And look how they took that donkey!!!!!!

On a more tranquil note, the landscape around us was changing. Ahead of us, in the distance, we could see the purple hills of Gwoza. And beyond them, the Mandara Mountain range that stretches from Mubi in the north down to Mambilla in the south, and is the natural border between Nigeria and the Cameroon.

'It looks beautiful over there,' I remarked to Andy. This time the both of us were sitting squashed up in the front with the driver. Not Andy's choice. The back of the Peugeot was full of bits of machinery. We were still not really talking, but we were not not talking either, we were just sort of half-way between.

'Aye, it is,' nodded Andy.

'They look a bit Misty Mountainish, don't they?'

'Aye,' nodded Andy, 'they do.'

See what I mean. Talking but not talking.

My heart was actually breaking. So many times I yearned to put my head on his shoulder, touch his hand, kiss his cheek, as I had done, naturally, comfortably, without inhibition, so many times before. But now circumstances dictated I couldn't, and it was dreadful. But, in the true spirit of an adventurer, I put a brave face on things.

It was cooler in the hills of Gwoza and I was glad that I'd brought my shawl. Not that I needed it at this very moment, it was late afternoon, and still very hot. But I reckoned it would come in useful later, especially at night-time in the Manadara Mountains.

We got dropped off at the lorry park and found a mammy-wagon that was bound for Mubi. But, as was always the case, it wasn't going for a while. So with the usual bunch of hangers-on we ambled across the lorry park, and had a drink in a little bar. The thick, mud walls kept the drinking hole nicely cool, and the place was nicely dark. Believe me, cool and dark is just what you want when you've been travelling in the harsh sunlight for several hours. We plonked ourselves, and our bags, on a low wooden bench that straddled one side of the bare, inner mud wall, while our followers poked their noses, and giggled and gawped at us through the entrance that had no door.

We drank our drinks, warm Fanta and Coke, and said nothing. Smoked our fags, and said nothing. And when his fag was stubbed out, and his bottle was empty, Andy leant back against the cool, solid mud, pulled his khaki hat over his eyes, and feigned sleep. So I got up and walked back into the sunshine. A little boy, dressed in a pair of shorts that had so many holes in them you could actually see one cheek of his bare bum sticking out, came up to me with a tray on his head.

'Abinche, baturi?'

I'd actually forgotten about food. I mean, I'd actually forgotten it existed. I hadn't eaten since yesterday morning when I nibbled some toast for breakfast, sitting on Hamish's veranda. Straight after that repast came the letter, and the rest you know.

God, I was hungry.

'Let me have a look,' I said. In English, of course, using sign language. I couldn't remember the word for 'let me have a look' in Hausa (it had been a long day, and an even longer day, the day before). So, the little boy with the exposed little bum, took the tin tray off his head, and removed the dirty old sheet of newspaper that was supposed to act as some sort of hygienic cover. A fly flew out as the newspaper wrapping came off. About a dozen sticks of smoked meat lay in a neat line, and another fly that had been buzzing around the third stick from the left, flapped its wings and flew off to join its mate. Believe me, I must have been hungry.

'Nowa, nowa?'

Something kobo, he said.

'How much?' I asked again.

His five fingers flashed five once, five twice, five a third time.

'Fifteen kobo!' That was daylight robbery. I shook my head. 'I give you ten for two.'

He shook his head. 'Two for fifteen.' (This transaction was done in Hausa, I can count up to twenty, no problem.)

'OK, deal.' And I jangled my coins in my pocket, and counted out fifteen kobo, and in return I got two pieces of (dog?) meat on sticks. And a big cheesey grin from Naked Bum. I'd made his bloody day.

And so I munched on my stick, and tried not to think of the flies, and where the newspaper had been before it ended up as a cover on a tray, and if the meat I was eating was dog. And I ambled back into the cool, dark bar where Andy, now awake (he'd never been asleep), was smoking another fag and drinking another warm bottle of Coke.

'Want some meat?' I offered.

Andy chucked his cigarette on the earthen floor, and took the stick. 'How much did you pay?'

'Eight kobo,' I lied. The way things were, I'd be getting a lecture on our money situation if I'd told him the truth.

Four in the afternoon, and we were on our way once again, cramped up with thirty or so other passengers in a mammy-wagon, destination Mubi, two hundred and fifty miles to the south-east. My immediate travelling companion wasn't Andy, he was perched somewhere up the front, no my chum for the next quarter of a thousand miles was a revolting bloke who picked his nose constantly, whose breath smelt of dog turds, and who had black and yellow fangs that were chipped. And I saw a louse crawl out of his filthy, stinking robe. Instantly I was scratching my head.

And feeling very, very depressed.

I'd wanted to be near Andy but there was so little room on the wagon, what with the pots and the pans and us humans, so Andy decided to stand and hang on to the roof of the cab, which wasn't the most comfortable, or safest way, of travelling down the potted ruts that were laughingly called roads.

'Can't I come with you, Andy?' I asked, as he inched himself over people and loads, to the front, and I stood forlornly in my allotted space, enough room just for my bag and my bum.

'No,' he growled. 'Just sit the fuck down and stop being a pain in the arse.'

See what I mean? Not much loved lost, was there?

So miserably I sat down next to Mr Dog Breath and tried to ignore the nasal treasures he unearthed, as we rumbled up and over the hills. Shifting about, I eventually managed to twist my body ninety degrees in the opposite direction, and found the comfiest position was if I lay my head against my full to stuffed up bag, and used it as a pillow. And the bounces and the jolts became rather soothing after a while; it was a bit like being rocked in a cradle by a granny on speed. Somewhere along the way my eyes shut, my ears closed up, my head went into melt down. And I fell fast asleep.

When I awoke, it was dark. And cold. Very cold. So cold, I had to rummage about in my bag and get out Old Ma Coltsworth's shawl. Even then, with it wrapped tight around me, the wind still raced through my body and chilled my bones, and my teeth rattled, and my hair blew in a million directions. Oh, for a warm comforting bed. Oh, for my little bed back at home. Oh, to be back in Gombe! Yes, I really felt really that bad!

Thinking about Gombe, and I thought about my parents. And thinking about my parents, a new lump materialised and joined the permanent lump that was stuck in my throat. And the more I thought about my parents, the more I wished I was with them. And the more I wished I was with them, the more my eyes filled up with tears. And the more tears, the faster they trickled and splashed down my face.

I felt so bloody lonely on that mammy-wagon.

I don't think I ever knew what lonely really meant until now. All my life there'd always been somebody there. I know I go on about how awful school was, and it was, but I had friends, I had telephones, I could write and receive letters. And I knew my Mum and Dad, or my Granny and Grandpa were around if I needed them;

102

and if I was really in trouble, they'd be there, and to hell with the distance.

But now I was in the middle of nowhere with a bloke who didn't love me, and Mum and Dad, who really, really loved me, unconditionally, didn't even know where I was.

I'd abandoned them.

And all my friends. My real friends. No-nonsense Lizzie. Dear, sweet odd-looking Henry, and pompous know-it-all Kevin. The beautiful Barb, and bouncing Pru and her lolloping Ian. I even think, at this moment, I'd have been quite pleased to see Dick the Prick, I know he was a bastard but he was a familiar bastard all the same. And I could bank on the fact that he wouldn't be perched on the other side of the lorry, aloof and blowing cold, he'd be here with his arms around me making sure I was warm. Too warm, maybe, but warm nonetheless.

And so the tears fell. I tried to wipe them away with my shawl but as fast as one lot got sorted, the next lot were spiralling down. I don't know why I looked up. But I did, and through water-filled eyes, I saw something twinkle. One solitary star shone bright in the dark of the sky.

'God, it's the Christmas Star!' I murmured out loud. Nobody heard. The clanks, and the banging, and the shudders, and the howls of the wind made sure of that.

I'd completely forgotten it was Christmas Eve. But remembering it now, made me think of Dad. Dear, darling Dad. Christmas Eve was really special for him. Being Polish, it was a much more important date than Christmas Day. We'd all, the whole family, sit round the table for Christmas Eve supper. Beetroot soup for starters, delicious, and the next dish was traditionally carp, although we generally ended up with mudfish. And after pudding, came the breaking of bread. No ordinary bread, mind, this stuff was wafer-thin like the communion host, and was sent special delivery from relatives in Poland. I always found the bread ritual embarrassing; we were expected to go round the table wishing each other things like 'a wonderful future' and 'blessings from God'. Mum and Dad went really over the top. 'I love you darling, and every, every happiness, and God Bless, and...' oh, dear it was all so bloody, excruciatingly sentimental.

But tonight, this night, this Christmas Eve, would be my very first Christmas away from my parents. What were they doing now, this minute? Visions of my empty chair and a half empty table, and

Mum and Dad sitting sadly around it. On their own. Slurping their borsch. Wondering where I was. Worried sick.

I gazed up at the star. Dad said the Christmas Star, the first star in the sky, was very special. Every Christmas Eve we all trouped out, searched for it, and when spotted, we all made a wish.

'I'm here, Mum and Dad,' I whispered to the Star from my perch in the wagon. More tears fell, and got caught up in the wind. Like raindrops, they pitter-pattered and sploshed on my hand. 'Please, little Star, let them know I'm okay. And please, little Star, will you grant me this wish? Give me back my Andy. I love him so much. Give me back my dreams, little Star.'

The tears trickled, and the tears ran. And even though the wind was whistling, and the wind was howling, and the lorry grumbled, and the lorry growled, I had to put my face deep into my bag in the end, to muffle the thundering sound of the sobs.

The lorry screeched to a halt. My Dog Breath fell right on top of me, his face up to mine; his calloused claw on my bosom. He grinned. I got a face full of dog turds and black-yellow fangs. I pushed him off, and tried to shift myself a few inches further from him. Not an easy thing to do when you're jam-packed tight and no inch to spare. Dog Breath let out a high pitched cackle, and began babbling away, to me, to everyone. He was mad. Loony mad. But no one took a blind bit of notice.

We were in a lorry park in some place and most of the other passengers were all too busy collecting their possessions, gathering their stuff, and making a move. After a few more cackles, and a few more rambles, Mr D B got to his feet too, picked up his smelly old Hessian sack (that was probably full of dismembered limbs, I swear those dark marks on it were dried up blood stains). About to go, thank God, and Mr D B the murdering-bosom-leg-grabber, leaned over, again stuck his ugly face right up to mine so I got another full blast of canine shit breath, and gave another fiendish grin.

'Fuck off,' I hissed.

His revolting claw clamped my thigh.

'Hey! You! Bugger off, or I'll knock your rotting teeth in backwards, you'll fucking swallow them.'

Andy had come up from behind and was gripping the man by his shoulders. The insane-murdering-bosom-leg-grabber gave a final cackle, shrugged Andy off him, and without another word clambered (I'd like to have pushed him) out of the lorry.

'Thanks,' I said, straightening myself up, and resisting the urge to ask Andy to bend down and give me a much longed for and needed cuddle. 'I think he was just a bit mad.'

'Aye,' nodded Andy. 'But he's gone, and looks like nearly everyone else has, too.' People were still throwing loads down, and climbing off the mammy-wagon, but not that many new passengers were getting on. Ten down, two up. Twelve down, one up. Nine down, none up. 'It won't be so cramped for the rest of the journey.' Andy gave me a half-smile.

I gave him a half-smile back.

'Want something to eat?' he asked.

'Yeah. I'm starving.'

'Wait here, I'll see what there is.'

Andy was over the side of the mammy-wagon and off. I stood up, gave myself a full body stretch, and then worked my way through the heaps of sacks and paraphernalia so I could have a deckers at what was going on in the world down below.

Leaning over, and instantly, despite the late hour, a group of ragged urchins raced to and gathered round the lorry, crying with glee and holding up battered, old, tin bowls in the hopes that I would send a rainfall of kobos down.

I held up my hands, my empty hands. 'Ba changi, no money.'

It didn't make a blind bit of difference. The begging bowls stayed up, and more came by the second. I could hardly see faces there were that many tin receptacles being thrust in the air. I glanced over the ocean of waving arms and looked to see if I could spot Andy amongst the crowds, but there were far too many people, and it was dark, so I gave up the ghost, and made my tentative way back over the piles of obstacles to my bag. Sat down and waited, and lit up a fag.

Twenty minutes, and three cigarettes later, Andy's blonde head bobbed up.

'Here take this.' He passed me a warm package wrapped up in dirty old newspaper, then scrambled over the side and into the wagon. I'd already started to open up the food parcel. Inside were more smoked meat things on sticks, and some bread rolls fried in batter. Andy plonked down beside me. 'Sorry. It's all I could get.'

'It's fine. Thanks.'

And so we commenced with the feasting.

While we ate, a few more passengers had clambered on but still nowhere near as many as had got off in this unknown but highly popular village, and there was definitely more space to move around in. Andy, I'm pleased to say, retrieved his rucksack from where he'd been standing and put it down next to mine. It was a start. But communication was still minimal. He sat in silence for a long time, resting his back against his bag, looking up at the night sky.

I lit a fag, and perused my fellow passengers. One bloke reminded me of Giorgio. Well, his clothes reminded me of Giorgio. He had on a bright pink pair of trousers, an orange floral shirt, and a red and blue scarf tied round his neck. A cap, with the BP insignia, and a pair of mirrored sunglasses completed this rather startling ensemble. Certainly it made him stand out in the dark. He also had a transistor radio with him, all part of the 'look', and was fumbling around with the dial. Crackly sounds first, but he twisted on until at last, a radio station. The sweetest voices, a children's choir rang out in the cool African air, and the words of 'Silent Night' could be heard clearly, as if we were sitting in a church with the choir in front of us.

'You know,' murmured Andy, with his eyes still on the celestial heavens, 'I'd forgotten it was Christmas Eve. Today has seemed just like any other day.'

Hardly. But I wasn't going to argue the toss.

'Did you remember?' he asked, turning finally away from the dark dome above.

Our eyes held, for a moment. I tried to feel into him. Stir some soft into his eyes; remind him of what we had been. It was pointless. He drew on his fag and returned instantly back to the sky.

'Not until the first star came out. Then I did,' I mumbled.

'What's with the first star?' Andy was still looking up.

'It's the Christmas Star. When you see it you make a wish,' I said, watching him as though from far away.

'And I suppose you made a wish.' His eyes were back on me. His face a blank expression.

'Yeah, I did.'

Apparently disinterested in a girl and her wishes, Andy returned to his celestial thoughts, gazing back up at the velvet blue of the night. I felt hollow inside. But what could I do? Nothing. So I lit another fag and like him, studied the stars. Millions of them, the first one well and truly lost in the twinkling constellation.

Meanwhile, the lorry's engine spluttered and came to life, the lorry juddered and moved. We were ready to rock and roll once again.

Jesus, it was cold.

As the lorry picked up speed, the wind rushed through like an Arctic gale. All the Africans were out with their blankets, thick, warm blankets. All I had was a fucking crocheted, oyster-coloured shawl that was as much use as if I'd wrapped myself in soft tissue toilet paper.

'Are you okay?' From Mr Star Gazer himself.

'I'm freezing.' I'd had enough of putting a brave face on things.

'Hang on.' Andy delved into his rucksack and pulled out the sleeping bag. Tenderly wrapped it round me, and as I snuggled into the warm, he asked, quite gently, 'Okay, now?'

'Lovely.' And then I asked him, 'What about you?' He was that blue with cold it looked as if he might turn into a snowflake. Not that we have such a thing in Nigeria but there's always a first time, and this could be the night.

'Mind if I join you?' This was said with a smile that was almost as warm as the rest of him was freezing.

Would I mind?

I opened my arms, drew him in, and, like two little birds in a nest, we cuddled up together.

And the rest of the journey went like a dream.

CHAPTER 4

Mubi and the Benue River; Christmas 1973

It was Christmas morning and Father Christmas was at the foot of my bed.

'Ho, ho,' he bellowed, 'have I got some Christmas presents for you.'

And out of his sack came a quilt, a warm quilt filled with feather down. Next, a blanket made of the purest, softest wool. Father Christmas (I think it was my Dad behind the long, flowing beard) wrapped me up like a parcel. Oh, so warm. Oh, so cosy. Drifting. Drifting.

And now the reindeers were trying to wake me up. Rudolph was shaking me.

'Come on, Janni. Come on.'

Do I have to?

I half-opened my eyes. Opened my eyes and saw a galaxy of stars in a black-velvet sky. And Andy standing over me, saying, 'Janni, wake up. We're here.'

'Where?'

'Mubi.'

Eyes wide open now, I shifted myself into an upright position, and God did my body ache and feel bruised. But now was not the time to moan, Andy was already slinging his rucksack on his back. 'Come on,' he ordered, 'get your stuff.' Just like that, without a smile or a 'how are you doing?' We were back to square one.

Struggling to my feet and still in a daze, I tripped over something, my bag I think, and went flying. Next thing I'm crashing down on a woman who's carrying, or had been trying to carry, her entire kitchen collection, pots, pans, enamel buckets, bowls, you name it, it was probably there. 'Ayee,' she cried. There was a loud clatter-bang as the whole lot including the both of us went down and hit the floor of the lorry. Andy saw it all happen but did nothing to help us two damsels in distress, he just rolled his eyes up to heaven and said, 'Typical.'

'Sorry,' I muttered, as I disentangled myself from the woman and attempted to get upright again. 'Sorry,' as I tried to help my unintended victim at the same time and wasn't doing a very good job of it. We both wobbled like we were skating on ice and would have probably gone down for a second time if two good Samaritans, the cool dude with the tranny and an elderly Hausa man, hadn't rushed to our aid. Vertical at last, and the buckets and the pans, and Uncle Tom Cobley et all collected and returned to their rightful owner, a Kanuri woman with bog standard tribal markings and spider-leg hair braids. She gave me a look that implied 'fuck you' and clambered off the lorry. Bang! Crash! Oh, dear, there they go again. Fuck you, too, Miss Kanuri.

Meanwhile Andy, he of the 'I can't be arsed to help you' attitude was about to jump ship himself. 'Ready?' he enquired, as his leg and the rest of him went over the side.

'Ready,' I replied, even though I wasn't. Quickly I grabbed my cumbersome bag and heaved it up and passed it down. And after the bag, I was next in line. A foot here, a foot there, and jump, finally back on terra firma.

We'd been on the road since six this morning. It was now 11.30 at night. And very quiet here in the town of Mubi. As we trudged our way out of the lorry park, empty except for us few passengers who'd just disembarked, and headed down the main thoroughfare, the little stores – mud bricked edifices caked with a peeling white plaster slumped against one another – were all shut up and the streets pretty much deserted, which was very strange as most Nigerian towns, even shit-holes like Gombe, were usually heaving with chaos and noise at this time of night.

It's a bit Mary and Joseph, I thought.

We walked a long time up a vague road. A dazzling moon rose in the east. We passed dark buildings, their outlines sometimes illuminated by low fires. Voices murmured and drifted in the night.

Wearily, our feet dragged (even Andy didn't appear the cool cucumber he was this morning, more a drooping radish), our bags, well my bag getting heavier and heavier by each passing second, and our stomachs feeling as empty as the town itself. We walked past several native hotels, all closed up. *Christmas Eve? No room at the inn?* It was definitely all rather strange. I took a peep at my tummy, half expecting (half hoping even) there'd be a large bump. Jesus, I thought somewhat aptly, that would be a tale to tell to the world. *And would Andy be pleased?* I glanced at the grim-faced bloke beside me who'd not said a word since leaving the lorry park and thought sadly, probably not.

And so we plodded on.

For a while the silence hung heavy. Only our huffing and puffing, and the odd shuffle and scurry here and there, from a wandering dog or a rat in the rubbish, to fill the night air. But a little further on, and we heard the sounds of tinny, radio music. Nearer, and the music got louder, and nearer to the music we saw lights in the dark. They came from a small hotel bar.

'Worth a try?'

I nodded.

Inside, we were standing in a shabby, little room with three or four dilapidated tin tables and some very decrepit tin chairs and nothing else apart from the bar where sat the transistor radio playing African beat music. A few shifty looking blokes were lounging about drinking beers, and there were a couple of mournful looking women propped up against one of the grubby walls smoking cigarettes. Prostitutes? A brothel? More than likely, my experiences with Dick had taught me this much. But I didn't care, was too tired and too hungry to care. Brothel or no brothel. Stains or no stains. If there's a bed, I'll sleep in it. If there's food, I'll eat it. See what I mean? I was well and truly fucked.

A quick word with one of the 'ladies', and Andy turned to me. 'There's no room and they've run out of food. The only thing they've got is beer. What do you reckon?'

I sighed. Shrugged my shoulders. Allowed Andy to make all the decisions. Couldn't be arsed to come up with any ideas of my own. 'Come on,' he said, 'we need food and a bed, not beer.'

And so wearily we plodded on.

It was definitely a bit Mary and Joseph.

Down the dark, empty streets. We asked the few Nigerians who were roaming about if they knew of any hotels open this night but all we got was a shake of the head and the Nigerian version of a 'dunno'.

After we'd asked our sixth person and got the same negative response, and were trudging the road to God knows where, Andy, who was several yards ahead of me, turned. 'Fancy a rest?' he asked.

Did I?

Conveniently, there just so happened to be a large rock nearby, big enough for the two of us to sit on. Gratefully, we unloaded ourselves of our bags, plonked ourselves down, and got out the fags.

Andy gave me a light.

'Thanks,' I said, puffing.

110

'You're welcome,' he replied.

We both blew smoke rings in the air.

'It's a bit weird,' mused Andy, after a while, 'you and me here on Christmas Eve.'

'What do you mean?' I asked, as the wispy stuff rolled out of my mouth and floated away.

'No room in the inn, and all that. Like something really cosmic is happening.'

'Yeah,' I smiled, suddenly quite wide awake. I was thrilled to hear him say what I'd been thinking all along. It *was* cosmic. It *was* meant to be. We *were* destined to be together. Forever. 'Are you glad I came with you?' I hadn't planned on asking him this but in view of the fact that he'd quite obviously now seen the light, it sort of just popped out of my mouth.

He gave a noncommittal shrug. 'It makes no difference to me either way.' And that said; he went back to his puffing.

My heart went into freefall.

I took a long, hard drag. And had to pretend that it was the smoke that was making my eyes water. Not that he'd have cared. Whatever state I was in, he wouldn't have cared.

'I'm starving,' muttered Andy, breaking the unbearable silence that followed. 'My stomach feels like an empty pit.'

Food was the last thing on my mind now. The sadness that had come and gone in waves all day was back with a vengeance. But I didn't dare make a scene, so fragile was our relationship he just might get up, walk off and leave me forever in this Godforsaken place, and then where would I be? So I did the sensible thing and pretended that it was food not love that I wanted; 'Yeah, mine too,' I nodded.

'If we could dump our bags, it'd be much less hassle,' continued Andy. 'We could really have a proper wander round and find somewhere to eat.' He was so matter-of-fact, so oblivious, so couldn't give a shit.

'Yeah,' I agreed, struggling to keep my act together, struggling with the tears in my eyes that were threatening to fall thick and fast, and struggling to prevent the scream that was about to pour forth from my mouth. All I can say is, thank God it was night-time, a black world can hide a multitude of sorrows and sins. Even so, I needed an excuse to get away, be on my own, just for a minute, have a quiet howl, and then collect myself. Start again, with a bright, happy smile.

111

So I made out I was focused on the job in hand, that finding a place to dump our bags was the most important thing in my life. Raising myself from my hard lump of rock, I looked around, and up and down the dark, empty, road. Wandered off, and pretended I'd spotted something interesting across the way. 'Hang on a mo,' I managed to say without choking. And almost jauntily, as if I were skipping, I headed off towards a large clump of trees. As I walked away the tears gushed, like swollen rivers after a tropical storm. Oh, what a blessed relief, as they tumbled and rolled down my cheeks. 'See anything?' I heard Andy shout.

Not a fucking thing. It was dark, and there were that many tears, and I was so broken-hearted, it was hard to see anything beyond my inner grief, but needs must, so with best foot forward I went on a little further, and did spot something! A large wooden board, half-hidden by the trees. At first I couldn't make out what was on the sign but it looked like a cross. Bloody hell! It *was* the sign of the cross. *Are you up there, God? Are you listening to me, after all?* And now I could see there was a footpath, leading to a building, and lights. Quickly, I wiped away the fat, bulbous droplets with the back of my hand and drew a deep breath.

'The Catholic Mission's here, Andy,' I shouted, my quivering voice echoing in the emptiness. Another deep breath followed by a cough, to clear the frog from my throat. 'Think it's worth checking out?'

'Anything's worth checking out,' echoed Andy back, already collecting up the bags and striding over. By the time he reached me I'd managed to knock the sobs on the head and was able to give him a 'we might be in luck' kind of smile.

We followed the path that led to the lights that came from the Mission church. And as we neared the building we could hear singing. There it was, 'Silent Night' again.

'It sounds better in Hausa,' Andy remarked.

Beautiful, more like, African voices filling the African Christmas night air. I was that moved, the hairs on the back of my neck actually tingled. We walked on, up to the mud church with its pointed tin roof. Hovering at the entrance, we could see the place was packed out. There were all types, young and old, rich and poor, people dressed in rags others dressed up to the nines, all of them Nigerians, and all of them here to pay homage to the Baby Jesus. Maybe that's why all of Mubi was deserted, because the whole town were gathered together in this church. A Catholic conversion en masse, in Mass, so to speak.

By now the singing had stopped and all of the congregation were kneeling, heads bowed, silent in prayer. Well, apart from the odd cough and splutter and wailing baby to break the quiet communication that was going on between man and God.

'It's Midnight Mass,' I whispered. 'What do you reckon?'

'You're the Catholic. What do you reckon?'

'We go in,' I said, surprising myself. Mass was, after all, not really my thing.

So we put our bags down by the door (Catholics don't steal, you see, the nuns told us that so it must be true) and stepped inside. Into a candlelit world full of flickers and shadows, and the air thick with the smoky, pungent smell of incense and myrrh. It was quite beautiful, and very, very atmospheric. Quietly, almost on tiptoes, we made our way down the aisle, to the back of the church. And by a statue of Mary and the Child, where small, twinkling candles and sprigs of pink and white bougainvillea lay across and around the Virgin's feet, we knelt down on the cold concrete floor and clasped our hands together. And whilst everyone else there bowed to the ground, Andy included (*What was he praying for? A miracle to happen and I disappear?*) I lifted my head and took in the sights, just so as to distract myself from the sadness within.

At the front of the church, in prime position was the shiny green cloth-covered altar with two large silver candelabras either side, their thick creamy candles alight with dancing flames. Behind this dazzling spectacle was the even brighter tabernacle, a vision of gold and glitz. The priest, a little man with a large balding head, had his back to the congregation and was having a poke around in this holiest of holy cupboards. He was after the Body of Christ that languished in host form in a big silver chalice. Meanwhile, to the left of the altar was a small, crudely made crib. I had to lift my head really high to get a good look at the young girl dressed in white robe and blue veil, sitting beside it. She looked absolutely serene. *Lucky thing*. Her eyes were down, gazing at a tiny baby who lay asleep in her arms. Gently she rocked the little bundle, and when I lifted my head even higher to get a better look, I could see the floor around Mother and child was strewn with red and white flowers, and behind them both, a large statue of the man (God?) himself, the Sacred Heart of Jesus. It was truly a wondrous scene. Made me quite proud to be a Catholic.

A bell rang. Three times. The clear, silvery sound tinkled and hung in the air.

The little Irish priest (don't ask me how I knew, he just had that Irish priest look about him) was now taking Holy Communion. With one voice the congregation began to sing, 'Oh, Come All Ye Faithful', in Hausa, and still warbling, hands clasped, all the adults, and children over the age of seven, stood up and slowly made their way up to the altar rails.

And before I knew it, I was up too. Couldn't help myself.

'Where are you going?' hissed Andy.

'To take communion,' I hissed back, and clambered over his legs. Following the all black worshipers up the aisle, I waited my turn, knelt down at the foot of the altar, stuck my tongue out, Father dipped his hand in the silver chalice and voila! The body of Christ was within.

Back in my pew, I felt very holy. Closed my eyes, hands together and prayed. Not the usual stuff, the usual mantra, sorry God for all my sins, Amen. No, this prayer was much more profound. It came from the heart.

Forgive me for the bad things I have done in my life, dear God. Forgive me for forgetting you and not being a good Catholic girl. Forgive me for not going to confession before taking Communion. Forgive me for only talking to you when I need you. I'll try to make it up to you, I promise. But I do need you now. Please, please listen to my prayer, dear Lord. It's the rebirth of the world tonight. The rebirth of love. Tonight is a celebration of life, not death and the end. So please give me back Andy, sweet Lord, please. Please. Thank you. Amen. And please make sure you let Mum and Dad know I'm all right. And don't forget about Andy, God. Make him love me again. Amen.

The final blessing.

The Irish voice (I told you the priest was Irish) rang out.

'The Mass is ended. Go in peace to love and serve each other as you love and serve the Lord. And,' Father added with a quaint, crooked smile, 'may I wish every one of you a very, very happy Christmas. Amen.'

And a rousing 'Amen' from us all.

And we were all up. From solemn worshippers, the congregation were now in party mood. Oh, the cheery greetings, oh the handshakes and laughter.

HAPPY CHRISTMAS EVERYBODY!

'Come on,' came the command from Andy, 'let's get out of

here.' He pushed me through the throng. 'Happy Christmas, Happy Christmas' people were saying, and we're smiling and nodding and joining in the fun, when all we wanted was to get the hell out. Finally managing to get to our bags, we edged our way through the wide, double doors, and went and sat on the little stone wall that ran round the church.

'Happy Christmas, Janni,' said Andy, in a monotone voice that suggested he didn't really mean it.

'Is it?' I blankly asked.

The joyous mood in the church had got to me. It made me feel a little depressed (as if I wasn't already). It just wasn't right, me sitting close up to Andy, not being able to spontaneously kiss him, hug him, and love him. It just wasn't right.

'Don't start.' Andy shifted himself and casually picked at his thumb.

'Start what?'

'Whatever it is that you're starting.'

'I'm not starting anything,' I said, wishing with all my heart that he'd lean over and bury his face in my neck. 'I just want everything to be alright between us.'

'Oh, for fuck's sake, Janni.' Andy shot me a dark look. 'You know the score. What do you expect?'

'I dunno?' I whispered, feeling utterly wretched. Swallowing hard, I glanced down at my hands, at the Bida brass ring that was still there on my wedding finger, the ring I'd not taken off since the day Andy had put it on. 'Let it be a symbol of our love,' he had said. *Oh God, where had it all gone wrong?*

Sighing, Andy rummaged about in his bag for his fags. Was about to speak – *Fuck off, maybe?*

'Ah, there you both are,' said a thick Irish voice from behind.

We turned. We smiled. We chorused. 'Happy Christmas, Father.'

'And a very happy Christmas to you, too. The name's Father Reilly.'

Hands were shook. We introduced ourselves. We both put on a good show. Father was obviously quite impressed. 'I must say, it gladdens my heart to see a young couple like yerselves attend Midnight Mass. There's a few Europeans here in Mubi, but – well, they don't think it's quite the thing to come to church, even at Christmas,' he trilled, throwing up his hands, and giving us a 'what can you do' kind of expression.

We nodded. Showed we understood what he meant.

'It was a very lovely Mass, Father,' I said.

'Aye, it was,' agreed Andy. 'Very moving.'

'To be sure, to be sure.' Father scratched his freckly, bald head, and happily smiled at the compliment. Then asked: 'Where are you both from?'

We told him.

'On holiday?'

'Yes.'

'Have you anywhere to stay tonight?'

Andy said yes, I said no. Simultaneously.

'You haven't, have you?' Father looked at Andy.

Andy shrugged. 'We'll find somewhere.'

'I doubt it, not at this time of night.' Father tapped his watch, making his point. It was one in the morning. 'You'll not be wanting to tramp the streets of Mubi on Christmas Eve, to be sure.'

'No, really we're fine,' insisted Andy.

But Father wasn't having any of it. There was plenty of room in the Mission house and he'd be delighted to have us stay the night as his guests. And that was that. He wouldn't even let us carry our own bags. 'No, no, Simon will see to them.' And right on cue, from out of the shadows a young bloke, a year or two older than me, bounded over as if he'd been expecting us all along. *Very, very Mary and Joseph.* Picked up our bags and gave us a 'well met good friends' smile. I was certain he was a priest in the making.

'Now, my children,' said the blessed Father Reilly, 'come along.' And he and Simon (the future Father Simon) blazed a trail down the path towards the bright lights of the Mission house. Andy looked at me and I looked at Andy. We shrugged.

'Nothing to lose, I suppose,' was his thoughts on the matter.

I nodded. I was just glad of the offer of a bed.

Thus we followed in the footsteps of the good Father and the blessed Simon. *It was definitely a bit Mary and Joseph.*

'And behold I bring you tidings of great joy'.

The good news was that Father had food in plentiful supply and we who were starving (even I, despite my anguish and sorrow had begun to feel a little hungry again) now ate. Despite the very late hour he sent the more than willing Simon off to the kitchen, and half an hour later we were scoffing baked beans on toast, fried bits of bacon, and a soggy cheese omelette. Delicious. All washed down with a celebratory couple of glasses of beer.

'And behold I bring you tidings that aren't so good.'

The bad news (from my point of view) was Father had seen to it that we had separate rooms. Looking at this arrangement logically, I suppose it wasn't that big a surprise. You can't have two unmarried people committing that most dreadful of sins under God's roof, right next to a real live, sleeping, praying priest, now can you? Nonetheless, it still upset me. Not so much the sleeping apart, it was only for the one night after all. What bothered me was that Andy didn't seem at all bothered, almost grateful in fact. He beamed when Father imparted the news that the two beds in the two spare rooms were ready.

'Now,' said Father Reilly, as we bade him goodnight. 'I shan't be here in the morning as I have to say Mass about twenty miles away. But my steward will be around to make you breakfast. Just ask him when you want it.'

'Thanks,' we both said.

'God Bless,' smiled Father, and he trotted off down the corridor and disappeared through a door.

Simon showed us to our rooms. Gave us the mine host run down, bathroom's here, kitchen, should you need a drink in the night, over there.

'Thanks, Simon,' we both said.

'God Bless,' smiled Simon, and he trotted off and did the disappearing act too.

We stood at opposite doors.

'Night, Janni.' Andy had his hand on the handle.

'Night, Andy.' *Please, please say this is all silly. Please, please tell me that you want nothing more than to spend the night holding me in your arms. Or at least, please, please come over and give me a kiss.* He was turning the handle. 'Andy?'

'What?' His expression was cold and hard.

I couldn't stop myself. 'Spend the night with me, Andy. Please. It is Christmas.'

Oh, God did I sound like a lame and pitiful creature. Were I a dog, they'd be putting me down out of kindness.

Andy shook his head. He screwed up his eyes and twisted his lips. 'Now you listen to me, and get it right, once and for all,' he hissed. He stuck a finger in my chest, and stabbed hard. 'I'm not playing games with you. It's over. Get it?'

And that said, like the priest and the pre-ordained Simon

before him, he turned and disappeared.

Bang shut went his door.

I thought I wouldn't sleep. Plonking myself down on my little wooden bed, and staring at the stars through the window, I wanted to cry.

Actually I did cry. Buckets.

And when I could sob no more, when everything inside had shrivelled up and died, then came those hideous, four fucking horsemen. Bring on Mr Terror, Mr Bewilderment, Mr Loneliness and Mr Despair. Yep, they galloped into my head, and what a load of bastards they were.

'He'll never go back to you,' smirked Mr Terror. *'He doesn't love you anymore. He'll meet someone else and you'll be out in the cold. Forever. Ha. Ha.'*

'You've fucked up again, you silly cow,' laughed Mr Despair. *'You're always fucking up. There's no hope for you. Ever.'*

'So, why do you always get it wrong, hey?' demanded Mr Bewilderment. *'Have you got some fucking problem? Is there something we don't know about?'*

'You're on your own kiddo,' declared Mr Loneliness shaking his head. *'And you'll be on your own for the rest of your life. Who'd want a sad sack of shit like you?'*

See what I mean? Thoughts like this are hardly conducive to getting a good night's sleep. But miracles happen, and I finally stopped beating myself up, because physically I was too tired to think anymore. And as soon as I'd switched the light off, and crawled into my little bed, and tucked the sides of the net in, and put my head on the pillow, my eyes closed. And I was off with the fairies.

The early morning sun peeped in through a small slit in the curtains, its light lying like a piece of golden tinsel across my bed. From somewhere a cock heralded the dawn of a new day. Christmas Day.

'Christmas won't be Christmas without any presents.'

All over the world, everyone will be up, and out of their beds, opening their gift-wrapped goodies. But not me. All over the world everyone will be looking forward to Christmas dinner with their friends and their families, pulling crackers, wearing funny hats, and having a good time. But not me.

I sighed. Watched the dancing lights on my bed, and went over the last few weeks, the last few days. Tried to work out where it had all gone wrong. How, I thought, can you love someone so desperately one minute, and then not be sure you love that same person, another minute.

'The fuck knows,' I said out loud, and slipped out of bed. The concrete floor felt cool under my bare feet, I padded over to the window and pulled back the curtains. What would the world look like today, Christmas Day?

All I could see was the usual dry, leafless bushes, and a baobab with its naked silver branches held aloft as if it was praising the blue, cloudless sky. And beyond the compound, some distance away, there were rocks, large bare, black-grey rocks. And that was basically it. Not what you'd call a typical Christmassy scene.

Sighing, I delved into my overstuffed bag and pulled out my towel, wash bag and yes, I had brought my blue silk kimono. Suitably attired, I opened the door, had a tentative peep, no one about, good, I didn't want to bump into a priest when half-naked, and scurried down to the bathroom. Washed, showered. Returned to my room, and dressed. Put on a long red skirt and a white cheese-cloth top, a touch of eye shadow, not too much, a hint of lipstick, not too much, a smidgen of mascara, not too much, some hoop earrings, not too big, a couple of bangles, not too many, and a simple necklace of cowry shells. And left my hair loose. So I could toss it back, just a little.

Feeling good on the outside made me feel a little better on the inside. I even hummed 'Away in a Manger' as I meandered down the bare walled corridor in search of the kitchen. Through to the sitting room, a room with very little in it, just a big picture of the Pope with his hands clasped in prayer on one wall, and a large, simple wooden cross on the other wall. Four bog-standard uncomfortable easy chairs, a coffee table, and a bookcase stuffed with books. No carpet or mat on the floor and just plain white curtains up at the windows. The dining room, where we'd eaten last night, was much the same. Bare concrete floor, white curtains, a picture of Mother and Child, an empty table and four empty chairs.

I moved on, outside to the kitchen, a small square, mud building standing a little way from the house. Entered it, and encountered a middle-aged man dressed in typical steward uniform, white trousers and white shirt, standing by a wooden table, dissecting a grapefruit with the juice running down and all over his large black hands.

'Good morning, Madam,' he said politely.

Politely, I gave him a good morning back. Asked if it was possible to have a cup of tea.

'No problem, Madam. And –' brandishing a knife and pointing to a segment of grapefruit, '– I make you good breakfast.'

While the good breakfast was being made, I sat with my cup of tea on a step in the sunshine, and lit up a fag. And looked to the hills and pondered on what lay beyond them. And watched a bird fly right across the light of the sun, its wings turning to silver as it did so. I heard children's voices in the distance, and the odd drone of a motorbike passing by. And a door opening and shutting, and the soft tread of shoes walking on concrete. Looked up and saw Andy. Dressed in his old blue jeans and a T-shirt.

'Hi,' I said. Wanting to jump up and kiss him. Instead, I tossed my hair back, just a little.

Curtly he nodded, and planted himself down next to me on the step. Cupped his chin in his hands, he stared out at the grey hills, deep in thought.

'Funny kind of Christmas, isn't it?' I said to the ants as they marched past my feet.

'Yeah, reckon it is,' Andy sighed. He picked up a small twig and began doodling lines and squiggles in the sand.

And that's how it was for the next ten minutes or so. Me following the movements of some ants and Andy drawing weird shapes with a stick.

Not what you'd call very Christmassy.

We were called in for breakfast. The table was now laid, teapot steaming, jug of milk, sugar bowl, two cups and saucers, and two bowls of chopped grapefruit. And a plate full of toast. Plus a jar of marmalade and a dish with some butter.

'Looks good,' commented the Quiet One, sprinkling a blizzard of sugar onto his citrus segments.

'There's an ant,' I pointed out. Two of them actually, small tiny things darting about in the sugar grains. That sorted, and I asked Andy if he'd like tea.

'Wouldn't mind.' And he handed me his cup and saucer.

Duly poured, we commenced with the breakfast. For the next twenty minutes all that could be heard was the chink of cups, the scraping of butter and marmalade on toast, and us munching. I finished first, left Andy plopping another large dollop of the orange stuff on his toast, and went back into the sunshine. Sat on my step, and puffed on a fag. Five minutes later, I heard the scraping of a chair then Andy emerged.

'Want to have a look round Mubi?' he asked, his expression blank, unsmiling, dead formal, like we really didn't know each other that well.

I stubbed out my fag, and said, 'Yeah,' and didn't smile either. The feel good factor I'd felt earlier was definitely on the ebb.

Mubi looked different in daylight. The place was buzzing. It was a typical Nigerian town, a mishmash of mud and corrugated tin edifices, the colourful streets throbbing with music and mayhem. Men sat in doorways flicking the flies, women sashayed around with pots on their heads, dogs sniffed, donkeys brayed, kids gawped; it was all the usual stuff.

Somehow, without planning to, we ended up at the market.

It was a rough square of open stalls selling bolts of bright fabric, tubs of ground manioc, odd bits of cookware and an assortment of vegetables and fruits. All around the open area women squatted in the dirt offering a few meagre items for sale; a handful of peanuts, four eggs, a bunch of leafy greens, a couple of yams.

Children closed in on us, hands outstretched. We ignored them. We weren't in the mood.

We'd said nothing to each other all the way (goes without saying, really). Andy had taken the lead and I'd followed slowly behind. It was sad. So many sights, so many sounds I wanted to share with him. Say, 'Hey, Andy, did you see that fat lady with a hen on her head?' 'God, look at that lovely Fulani blanket.' Point to the dyed skins of animals drying on the ground, comment on the beautiful coloured cloths that hung from a stall. Mention the fact that some Africans were speaking in French. 'Gosh, are we really that close to the French Cameroon?'

But he didn't want to talk, had cut himself off; was in a world of his own.

'Fancy a drink?'

Deaf ears walked on.

Suit yourself. But I felt a little angry and it bubbled deep within.

Stopping by a shack, I bought myself a Coke, thought about it, and bought one for Andy too although he didn't deserve it. By now Andy had planted himself on a large stone under a red flowering tree. I ambled over, plonked myself down in the dirt, handed him the drink, he was lucky it didn't get thrown in his face, especially as there was no word of thanks. I took a sip, another sip. Glugged the warm, fizzy liquid down and afterwards, when it was all gone, wiped my lips with the back of my hand.

Then took a deep breath. I had nothing to lose.

'Andy.' My voice was steady. I looked him straight in the eye. 'We need to sort this out, once and for all?'

The eyes opposite me rolled over and upwards. 'Sort what out, for fuck's sake?' Deliberately, he turned away. Cold-shouldered me; stared at a group of kids playing amongst piles of rubbish in the nearby ditches. God, did his attitude make me very angry.

'Sort what out! What the hell do you think?'

If looks could kill this was the one that would do the job perfectly. Turning, he twisted his face and spat. 'Jesus, woman, I don't know, I can't read your crazy, fucking mind.' Shifting his position, Andy's hands squeezed the neck of the Coke bottle. Perhaps he imagines the bottle's me, I thought. He wants me dead. Whatever, I'd had enough of his shite. His hot and cold running moods, his terminal silences. This worm was for turning.

'Now you listen to me.' A finger was wagged in his face. 'You promised me the world once. Remember?' If he did, he didn't say. All I got was a snarl. I tried another tack. 'Even, even if you don't love me anymore, you could at least be friendly, for God's sake.' Still nothing. It was hopeless. He just turned away and resumed his vigil on the kids in the ditches. But I wasn't done yet. Not by a long chalk. Giving out a long, angry sigh, I spoke to the back of his head. 'You don't see it, do you? I'm a person, someone you once loved. I'm not some flipping toy you can discard and pick up at whim.' I rose up from the dirt and stood in front of him, over him, face down to face. 'I don't know what your problem is, Andy, and I don't know what I've done to deserve this. You're like a woman with a menstrual disorder. Up, down, up, down, take it all out on Janni. Well, do you know something (*even I surprised myself when I said the next bit, but honestly, I was at my wits' end*) I really don't know what I ever saw in you? You're a con. You're a waste of fucking space. Dad said I could do so much better and he was right. I don't need you. I don't even like you. You can go to Hell.'

And there you have it!

The final nail went bang in the coffin. The end. Tears would come later, but right now I really felt like a load had been lifted. Without another word I turned on my heels, took my empty bottle back to the shack, and even managed to have a laugh with the bloke behind the counter. He said I had a very nice smile and wanted to know where I'd bought my pretty coloured lipstick.

'England.'

'Ah, it is good. My wife, she be very happy if she have this colour.'

Well, it was Christmas, and as I'd got two of the same lipsticks in my bag (told you I never travel light) I handed one over, the one that was already half gone.

'Madam, many thanks. My wife be very, very happy with this.' And he wished me a, 'Merry, merry Christmas,' even though the fez on his head told me he was a Muslim.

'And a very, very happy Christmas to you.'

And I smiled, and floated off. And tossed my hair back, just a little. Began to wander round the stalls, said hello to the big fat ladies squatting on the ground; they laughed, showed off their bright koala nut orange teeth and waved at me with their red henna hands. I sniffed the spices, and inspected the mountains of weird looking vegetables; picked up and tried on some bangles, had a nose round the multicoloured cloth stalls; stopped to watch a shoemaker create a lovely pair of sandals out of an old piece of leather; smiled at the little girl who was sitting cross-legged in the dirt weaving a brilliant red blanket.

By the bag stall someone got hold of my hand. A voice in my ear muttered, 'I'm sorry.' I shrugged, was on a roll, wasn't prepared to forgive him. Just yet.

'Actions,' I declared, not even bothering to turn round, 'speak louder than words.'

An hour later, we were having Christmas dinner, turkey, roast potatoes, bread sauce, runner beans, baby carrots, the whole works. Followed by Christmas pudding with brandy butter and thick, lumpy custard. Delicious.

After Andy's grovelling apology, 'I'll make it up to you, I promise,' (see what I mean, where did I stand? the fuck knows?) we'd decided to see if we could find the club in Mubi. But when we asked for directions, a bit like the night before, no one seemed to know where it was. I suppose that figured, we were in the Nigerian part of town and Nigerians don't usually frequent these bastions of colonial society, as well you know. Still, as luck would have it, a MNR Land Rover pulled up outside a shack, the driver was after buying some fags, and Andy legged it over to him, and five minutes later we were getting a lift to the Catering Rest House.

'The club,' said Andy. 'We want the club.'

Mr Driver smiled. 'Yes.' And pointed to the Catering Rest House.

'This will do, Andy,' I said, not bothered. Anywhere would do, I was feeling that happy. 'There might not even be a club in Mubi,' I suggested, though I doubted this, if a bush town like Gombe had a club then a bush town like Mubi would have a club but, like I said, who really cared?

So the Catering Rest House it was. And very nice it was too.

There were a few people in the dining room, all Nigerians, affluent Nigerians, who were out for a Christmas treat. And we joined them, pulled a few homemade crackers, wore silly homemade paper hats, and got well and truly pogged. So much so, that I had to go to the loo and throw some of the dinner back up. It was the first time in ages.

Afterwards, we got another lift from one of our fellow diners back to the Mission. Father Reilly was still out and about, and the future Father Simon wasn't around either. 'They be having celebration time with the Fathers in Zummu,' said the cook-cum-steward when we asked.

So we wrote them a note that said thanks, and wished them both a happy new year. Tipped our man, got our bags, and half an hour later we were back on the road.

I wasn't quite sure where we were heading to, but it didn't matter to me where we were going, what mattered, what really mattered was that Andy and I were just that little bit closer. Very close, in fact. We ambled down the old, dusty road out of Mubi, hand in hand. We were laughing, and talking, it was just like none of the bad stuff had ever happened. Romeo was quite definitely back with his Juliet.

'Fancy a smoke?'

Did I? It had been two days since we'd indulged. Here in the bush, with the grey, black hills all around, and the growing, thickening silence of the late afternoon, it would be nice to get a little bit stoned. So, by a giant anthill, we brushed a small clearing in the sand with our feet, and sat down on our bags. And while Andy did the business I played jacks with the stones, and sang to him. *I love you in the morning/Your hair upon the pillow* – that song. Andy's song.

All was all right with the world.

After our second joint a lorry came by. It stopped.

'Where you go?' hollered the driver from high up in his cab.

'Yola.'

'I go near to this place. You want ride?'

Of course we did. Picking up our bags, we threw them into the back, and hauled ourselves up and sat next to the driver in the front. And as the driver put his foot on the gas Andy turned to me, got hold of my hand and said, with a heart-warming smile, 'Are you okay?'

'Wonderful,' I replied.

Then he kissed me. It was just a kiss on the cheek but it was a kiss all the same. And for the whole of the journey he held me close. I felt better and better. All the sadness of the past just rolled away. This, I said to myself, was what travelling with your man was all about.

Especially as we were now heading for the Mandara Mountains, they looked almost purple in the distance. As we trundled towards them down the deserted bush road, the sun began its descent and just as it hit one of the peaks, it exploded. The aftermath was kaleidoscopic, dazzling, every bit of the sky shimmered and glowed.

There was still a red wash in the silver, grey sky when we reached the driver's destination. The place was just a few mud huts built around a crossroads.

'How far Yola?' Andy asked the driver, as we scrambled out of the lorry and grabbed our bags.

'Not far, sah.'

'How far?'

'Maybe one hundred miles.'

This, for Africa, was just a jaunt.

'Might as well kip here tonight,' Andy suggested. 'Hitch another ride in the morning. What do you reckon?'

'Fine by me,' I said. Everything now was fine by me. In fact, everything was just perfect.

We took a look around. There wasn't much to see apart from mud huts and bush. A man appeared as we approached his palatial little palace. He smiled shyly, offering his hand; others, everyone in the village, about twenty people, quickly gathered and stared.

'He's invited us to dinner,' smiled Andy, after he and the bloke had exchanged a few Hausa words.

Five minutes later we were sitting on two broken bamboo

chairs, around a wood fire with a big, soot-blackened earthenware pot full of food bubbling away on the top. Ten minutes later we were eating gari and rice, washed down with a big plastic mug of (oh, Mother would groan) unfiltered, un-boiled, untreated water. Feeling very native myself, I suddenly jumped up, took over the cook's stone (her seat by the fire) and began to stir whatever was in the blackened cauldron. The locals thought my actions were hilarious, they were pissing themselves with laughter, 'Ayeee', they shouted, 'more, more, more.' I suppose this rather over the top reaction was down to the fact that they'd never seen a white girl go loco before. Come to think of it, this village was so remote they'd probably never seen a white girl, full stop.

An hour or so later, we were strolling hand in hand down a lonely bush road. For some weird reason we just fancied a walk in the dark. The moon was up, the stars were out, and the crickets were having a field day. It was all rather lovely, even my bag didn't feel *quite* that heavy. Half a mile on, and there was another fire burning in a village (does three mud huts make a village?) so we sat round with this lot of locals, and being Christmas Day we entertained them by singing a medley of carols. They loved it! Didn't know the words, obviously, but they soon got a hang of the tunes. A couple of women, and a few of the kids, even got up and danced. They shimmied around in the dust of the compound, their ebony bodies gleaming with perspiration in the silvery, spectral moonlight. And in the midst of all this, a lone drummer began to beat a vigorous tattoo. The night air pulsated. The drumbeat became louder, more insistent, throbbing, as me and the locals pitched in with the carols. Oddly enough, it all felt very Christmassy. Now I'm thinking, as the blaze crackles and the flames light up all our faces, and my lover's next to me squeezing my hand, and we're singing 'Hark the Herald Angels' deep, deep in the bush, well blow me, this is the best Christmas ever!

When we all decided to call it a night, Andy and I headed back up the lonely path, torches blazing, in search of a good place to camp. In the end we decided the side of the road was our best option, less bush meant less creepy crawlies. So we dumped our bags, Andy swept our chosen patch with a brush made of twigs, and we laid out the sleeping bag. Snuggled in, all warm and cosy. Smoked a couple of joints, got a little stoned. Lay on our backs, and looked up at the stars. Suddenly, a swooping streak of light shot through the sky, and fell down to earth.

'Make a wish,' whispers Andy.

'Can I wish for anything?' I whisper back.

He smiles into my smile. 'Anything and it's yours.'

'I want you.' My face fits into his.

'You have me.'

Desire mingles with relief.

'Forever?'

'Forever.' His breath is warm on my cheek, his fingers play with my hair. 'I don't want to lose you, Janni.'

The crickets sing praise in the trees. The moon beams bright in the sky.

'You won't lose me,' I promise. He is my world, him in the middle, me all around. How could he lose me?

'No, but if I did, I'd search the whole of Africa to look for you, Janns.'

I glow at those words.

I was back in my star-studded dream.

But there's always a down side.

Have you ever slept on rough ground? In the bush? Believe me, it's not comfortable. Every which way you turn, there's a stone in your shoulder blade, or a mosquito buzzing in your ear, or something crawling up your arm, or your back is killing you, or your legs have gone numb because you've had to lie in one position all night. Or worse, you need a pee. Then you have to wriggle out of the bag and fumble about in the dark. You don't want to move too far away and do the business because you haven't got any shoes on and you can't see what's where and what's in the bush. On the other hand too close might mean an accidental piss on the makeshift bed and apart from the wet, your sleeping bag will start to smell like a toilet.

Still, we managed to get a few hours of shuteye in the end.

A dozen people were standing around gawping at us when we drifted awake in the soft light of the early morning. Several more had climbed trees to get a better look. This is not what you really want first thing, especially when you're bursting and they're following you into the bush. But the locals meant no harm; in fact they were actually quite helpful. Two of them scurried off and came back with our breakfast, bananas and bread. And this quite substantial meal was swilled down with water that was fresh from the local well.

By eight, we were all packed up and ready to go. By nine, we

127

were on our way to Yola, sitting snuggled up in the back of an old, battered lorry, rolling through one village after another, over narrow bridges of loose planks, banging into ruts and clanking bottom on sudden dips.

After four hours of this, I felt like I'd spent most of my life burning under a hot sky in the back of a truck, but finally we came over a hill and saw the Benue River way down below. It was a beautiful sight. Sun-flecked water, broad, peaceful, cool, a gentle winding thread of murky blue against the dusty, brown landscape. And over on the far side of the river straddling a hillside stood the town of Yola, gateway to the Mambilla Plateau.

We rumbled across an old wooden bridge. Below, and as far as the eye could see, little boats, hollowed-out wood narrow and tilting upwards at both ends, bobbed up and down on the sparkling water, and along the sandy banks fishermen were out with their calabashes bagging and bringing in their catches, whilst their women were all knee-deep in the shallow waters doing the usual scrub, rub, and slap routine. Add to this scrum of human activity small, wet, glistening brown bodies darting in and out of the gleaming liquid-light and you've got quite a scene.

The lorry driver dropped us off at the market place in town and we ambled over to the Peacock Restaurant. It had been recommended to Andy by previous VSOs who'd already blazed the Yola to Mambilla trail. And I could see why. It wasn't as posh as the name might suggest but as far as native eateries go, it was pretty good. Blue and white check cloths (a bit grubby but so what) covered the tables, and we enjoyed a 'plate of coffee' and some dish that was supposed to be an English breakfast, fried eggs with porridge (!), toast and baked beans.

After our brunch we made a few purchases, bought bread, biscuits, a few tins of Heinz Vegetable Salad, some Oxo cubes, bottles of Coke, and then at a leisured pace, made our way down the narrow winding streets to the river, gathering, as always, quite a crowd of hangers-on like tumbleweeds in the wind.

As we neared the giant causeway something smelt fishy. Nearer, and the smell in the air got stronger and more revolting. Even more revolting were the abandoned fish eyes that looked up at us from the sand. 'Yuck!' As one of the beady things got trapped in my open-toed sandal. 'Uggh!' As I went to remove the offending slimy, squidgy eyeball.

Bypassing kids and their mums, stepping over fish scales and fish bones, ignoring vultures ripping dead things apart, we headed towards a small group of fishing boats. One old boy was having a quiet kip in his floating log, and Andy waded over to him. Made a deal, and ten minutes later the both of us, with our man at the helm, were sailing down the Benue River.

I lay back in the boat with one hand trailing in the brown, silken water. This is lovely, I thought. Further away from the hustle and bustle of the crowded banks of Yola and all became quiet, just birdsong and the gentle splash of the boatman's oars to interrupt the silence. From time to time soundless aquatic creatures broke the watery surface, plop the ripples widened, became smooth again as the fish, or whatever it was, disappeared. Elsewhere, dragonflies hovered over the water their wings made shiny by the sun, and kingfishers and other brightly coloured river birds flew down, skimmed the surface, dived, and with their catch sped off to their nests in the banks.

It was so bloody hot Andy took his shirt off.

'You blokes are so lucky,' I said, raising my head and perusing my lovely, lovely man sitting at the other end of the boat. 'I'd love to be able to take my top off.'

'Why don't you, then?'

'Because,' I shot a look at old matey, 'I can't.'

'Och, he won't mind.'

'What do you mean, he won't mind?'

Andy gave me a lazy smile. 'If you hadn't noticed, Janni, most women in this country go about with their tits hanging out.'

'Yeah, but…'

'Yeah, but what?'

'Oh, fuck it.' And like a true free spirit, off came the top. From very clammy to almost cool in one simple move.

'Nice,' Andy said, raising his eyebrow, meaning nice from his point of view, not mine. I smiled, glanced at the boatman, he still had his eye on the job but it did my heart good to know that Andy was taking notice. About bloody time.

And so we sailed on, me and my man, out into the wide, open river. Yola was now in the distance, just a hillside full of tin roofs glinting in the sun. To our left and our right were sandbanks and trees, and isolated villages popping up every now and then along the ridge. We spotted the odd signs of life, a lone fisherman here, a small group of kids or washerwomen there, otherwise it was just birds, fish, dragonflies and us, all in all a perfect combination.

129

'Fancy a swim?'

'A swim?' I looked at the cool, cool water. 'Do you reckon it's safe?'

'Of course it's safe.'

'What about bilharzia?'

'Naw, you only get that when you swim in stagnant water.'

'Then what about hippos?'

'Hippos!?'

'Yeh, hippos.' And I told him Dad's tale.

'Och, there aren't any hippos around here. Come on.'

And Andy was off with his clothes, and into the water. Disappeared, and came bobbing up on the other side of the boat. 'It's lovely,' he gasped, and went under again. Then up, and was splashing about. So I took off my shorts but modestly kept my knickers on, exposed tits are one thing; bare bottoms might be pushing the free spirited fancy just a little too far.

'One, two, three,' I shouted, and jumped in.

Oh, it was beautiful, the sweet feel of the water. Down and up, then I swam over to Andy, gave chase, his crawl to my breaststroke. I didn't stand a chance so he let me catch him, we splished and splashed, then drifted for a while on our backs, both of us carried by the lazy current, the air full of birdsong, the afternoon sun warm on our faces.

'Isn't this romantic?' I murmured to Andy as we floated gently along.

'It's wonderful,' he murmured back, and got hold of my hand. Pulled me to him, took me down, and pushed back my dancing, swirling hair, kissed me as the water flowed and rippled gently over our heads. 'Let's make love,' he whispered, as we came up for breath. We were behind the boat; the boatman had his back to us, was dipping the oars slowly and humming a song to himself. Perfect. We drew close, tangled up our bodies and lost ourselves in the moment.

Until.

'Wallahi, wallahi!! Hankali!!! Hankali!!!'

The stoic boatman, who'd been keeping his eye on the job, had not batted an eyelid for the whole of the trip, was now standing, pointing at something in the water, and yelling at us.

We both stopped in our watery tracks.

'Hey,' Andy shouted back, 'what's the problem?'

'Wallahi!!! Wallahi!!!' Pointing, pointing at a spot just a few feet away from where we were. We looked. On the surface there didn't appear to be anything amiss. No waves, or splashes, or hippopotamus bottoms rising high in the air.

'What's he saying?

'Dunno,' gasped Andy. More screams from the boatman. More finger pointing. We looked wildly around as we doggy paddled in the water. 'Fuck, maybe he's seen a crocodile.'

CROCODILES!!!!

Oh, my God!

Splash, splash, splash. Gasping for breath, hearts hammering on chests we raced up to the boat. Andy heaved himself over but I was still in the water. As hard as I tried I couldn't pull myself up. I'm dangling, I'm screaming. 'Oh, for fuck's sake. Help me, Andy.' And Andy's got hold of my arms, and he's dragging me, and pulling me. My naked boobs are getting squashed as I'm hauled over the side, I can feel the splinters going in as I'm dragged unceremoniously across rough, unvarnished wood. 'Jesus Christ,' as finally I'm lying curled up in the tub of the boat gasping for breath. Gasping but safe; with my legs still intact.

'What the fuck was all that about?'

The boatman was back on his seat. We looked out at the water. There was nothing. Everything calm with not a plop or a ripple, the surface as smooth as glass.

'Hey, man, what was the problem?' Andy asked the question with a gesture, pulled up his shoulders, held up his hands. And repeats it in Hausa.

'Ba komi,' shrugged Mr Boatman. All is okay.

Maybe he was just having a laugh?

Further down the river we came across small islands, deserted tropical hideaways that were like emerald jewels jutting out of the water. Some were the size of pinheads, just a rocky mound with a bush and a tree but others were like mini kingdoms, and had forests and wide, sandy beaches.

'Take your pick,' invited Andy. Certainly we were spoilt for choice. We glided past three or four fair sized gems that all looked perfectly romantic.

'That one,' I said. Maybe because the sand sparkled a little more, maybe because the trees were a little greener, maybe because the water that lapped the edges was a little more blue? Certainly it looked lovely.

Slowly the old boatman steered his floating log up to the

island, nearer and he lowered the paddles, jumped out into rocky shallows and with us still in the boat, heaved it up onto the bank. For an old man he was pretty strong. Andy and I abandoned ship, and back on terra firma our feet sank into warm, yellow sand.

'Here, take the bags,' said Andy, retrieving them from the inner sanctums of the boat. Duly taken, I walked the few yards across the beach and put them both down by the trunk of a gnarled tree, along with the bread and the rest of our food purchases, and while Andy sorted the boatman out paying him the promised nairas, I went and had a bit of an explore. Poked my head first into the little sun-dappled wood, the air full of the sounds of birds and insects, then ran down the beach and picked my way along flat rocks that went into the water, noticing, as I did so, little red butterflies that fluttered and danced in and out of the reeds.

'This is lovely,' I shouted, dipping my toes into the sun-flecked pools where small fishes darted. A bit further on was a large, comfortable looking rock and I waded over to it, plonked myself down and lit up a fag. And felt at peace. Puffing, I watched as a flock of white egrets swooped down into the grasses along the river bank, their long wings flopping lazily. Perused the long-legged lily-trotters as they padded daintily over the vegetation atop the languid waters, listened to the hornbills as they flapped noisily, and in the most ungainly fashion, among the still-rooted trees at the water's edge. Watched as the boatman and Andy gently quibbled over prices, and finally came to an agreement; caught the gleam of a silvery snake as hands were shook, it sparkled and winked in the sun. Saw him laugh; look my way. And butterflies, like the clouds of multicoloured butterflies that hovered over the bright, yellow flowers growing out of the bank, danced in my tummy. The bad times were gone. All was good. My lover was back with me once again.

Andy's long legs kicked through the sand. He picked his way over the rocks and sat down next to me, rolled up a smoke, and together we watched the boatman get into his dugout and sail back down the river. 'Goodbye,' we shouted. 'Na godi.' He turned and gave us a wave.

Finally we were all on our own. The island was ours.

I took the lead. 'Come on,' I shouted gleefully. Stripping off, I ran, splashing into the water and when it was deep enough for me to turn on my back, I floated downstream. Andy followed, pushed through the cool, cool shimmering liquid, it parted in a shining and gentle rise, as he made his way towards me. Light with happiness, I spun myself into his arms, we touched, we kissed, explored each other's bodies. Parted, and we swam back to the beach. Out of the water and we raced through the sand, laughing; I'm running, he's chasing, we're wet, the droplets falling off us like a shower of raindrops on a beautiful spring morning.

'I'm coming to get you.'

'No,' I'm shouting, in a giggly kind of way.

'Got you,' as Andy grabs and pulls me down.

'Be gentle,' I hear myself whisper. He's beside me, with the sun and the sky overhead, and the water tickles our toes.

'I'll be anything you want me to be,' he murmurs. And my whole being, body and soul, is warmed with his flame.

And afterwards.

Well, we slept for a while in blissful contentment, our legs and arms all tangled up, on the beach. When we awoke, the sun was already beginning to fade and the river sparkled silver and red. We ran in the kaleidoscopic water and washed off the sand then hand in hand, still naked, did a full trek round the island. It was so small it took us less than twenty minutes but in that twenty minutes we found on our return, the birds had had dinner on us and left us with nothing. They'd eaten the biscuits and the bread, and Andy, after scrabbling round in his rucksack, now discovered that he'd left the tin opener back in Maiduguri.

'Oh, dear,' I laughed.

'Hungry?'

'Very.'

'Me, too.'

We plonked ourselves down on the sand, and had a think while having a drink from a bottle of Coke.

'The shore isn't too far away,' said Andy.

'The mainland, you mean?'

'Aye,' he nodded, rolling up a spliff.

I looked across, at the deep reflections of trees and rocks that sank into the water on the far side of the river. From here, the sandy bank on the mainland looked quite a distance. 'You're not thinking about swimming over there, are you?'

'Aye, why not,' said Andy, lighting up. 'I could find a village, get some more food.'

'But it's miles away.'

'About a hundred yards, if that.' Andy passed me over the joint.

I took it, and inhaled deeply, and turned my eyes to the up above. The sun had now completely disappeared, and both sky and water was a silvery, charcoal grey.

'But it's getting dark.'

'But we've got to eat, my pretty one,' laughed Andy, leaning over to kiss me. I kissed him back, ruffled his hair, oh it felt so good to touch him again and not have to keep my distance. 'Tell you what, I'll make a fire, and you sit tight. Keep the home fires burning while I get us our dinner.'

Despite my reservations, he might drown, a crocodile might eat him, he might find somebody else and never return, I agreed to this crazy plan. We went and collected wood, a whole stack of branches and twigs, from our forest. A fire was duly made up, and while I sat by its crackling blaze, Andy swam off in the dark.

'Don't be long,' I shouted as he sank into the water.

'I won't be,' he shouted back.

'Take care,' I yelled, as he was swallowed up in the gloom. All that I could hear now was a splashing rhythm, getting fainter and fainter. Then nothing.

Total silence.

Total, utter, bloody silence.

I shivered, partly because the night was cool, partly because I was afraid. Well, anyone would be in the circumstances. Here I was, alone, on an island in the middle of the Benue River. And Andy was out there, somewhere in the dark. I looked around, scanned the night sky that was filling up with stars. *Crocodiles. No, don't think about crocodiles, for God's sake.* I rolled another joint. Lit up, inhaled. The drug hit my brain. Sat closer to the fire. Up above, the moon rising high in the sky, was taken by moving clouds. They looked ominous. It all felt so unreal. I heard movements. Echoes. Sighs. Were they from the spirits of the waters? Or was it the dope that was making my imagination go haywire? Whatever, paranoia had definitely set in. I felt spooked. Bushes were turning into monsters. *There's something coming to get me, I can hear it.* Images were formed. T*here's a man behind that tree, I swear it. That rock isn't a rock. What was that plop? A crocodile? I'll be eaten alive!*

And what if Andy never comes back? No one knows I'm here. How am I going to get myself off this island? What if Andy's dead already? Will I look good in black?

I rolled up a second joint. Sat even closer to the fire, threw on another log. Thud! It crackled and it blazed.

Now my imagination was really going crazy.

'Lord of the Flies'. Piggy's fat little face; his smashed glasses, a dozen small boys on top of him, pummelling him, and kicking him to death. Where was Ralph when I needed him? Oh, shit, the boys had got him too. Was I next on their list? Was that a buzzing sound I hear?

See what I mean? I was going nuts.

Come back, Andy. Oh, please come back. I shouted, heard my voice echo in the empty night. 'An-dy-An-dy.'

Nothing. Hang on a minute! *There's something in the fucking water! Closer. Oh, my God, I can hear heavy breathing! Panting! Grunting! Closer! I can see it! A huge, dark figure, towering, swaying. Oh, my God*!!!!

'Aaaaaagggghhhhh!!!!!'

'Janni.'

It was Andy. He had a fish in his hands.

We cooked the carp, roasted it in the glowing embers of the fire. Andy also managed to bag a tin opener from the fishing village where he'd got the dead aquatic creature, so we had vegetable salad as an accompaniment. Afterwards, we boiled up water from the river in the empty tin receptacle, and stirred in an Oxo cube. It made quite a delicious drink.

When we had drunk and ate our fill, Andy read me his poems as the reflection of the fire flickered on the water's edge. Then we made love. And afterwards studied the stars, Andy told me about Orion, the Plough, and showed me the Seven Sisters. We talked about travelling to India together, getting an old van and painting it in loud, pink and purple colours, with big orange flowers. We plotted the journey, through Europe, Turkey, Persia, Afghanistan, and Pakistan. And afterwards, when in our imaginations we'd finally arrived and were gazing at the Taj Mahal and were weary from the great overland trip, we decided to call it a night and snuggled ourselves down into the sleeping bag. It was cold, very cold by the river and the midges swarmed and bit at us, as did the mosquitoes, but together we were invincible and even when the fire fizzled out, we kept each other warm.

I awoke with the sun on my face. The sound of river life, birds, insects, flying fish, filled the air. Opening my eyes I saw that I was alone. Pushing myself out of the sleeping bag, I looked around, at the tranquil water that shimmered blue and gold, at the trees heavy in shades of emerald and dark green, espied a crab trundle over the mountains of sand, caught a glimpse of a bright red tail as something flew over my head.

Brushing grains of the white stuff off myself, I got to my feet and scanned the shoreline. I couldn't see Andy anywhere. I called him but no answer came. For one awful minute I thought he might have done a runner, events over the past few weeks still made me a little nervy, but his bag was still there, his little, worn poetry book lay beside it, and his old bush hat had been hung on the branch of a tree. They were his most treasured possessions; he'd never leave that lot behind.

Thirsty, I opened the last bottle of Coke, and wrapped my oyster-coloured shawl around me, and headed off down the beach. It was hot, even by the water, even beneath the trees. I kept calling Andy's name, expected to hear his voice ring out but there was nothing. So I sat on a rock, lit up the first fag of the day, and looked out across the water. The river sparkled, the river dazzled, and there in the distance I spotted a boat. And in the boat I spotted a blonde head. Immediately I was up.

'Andy! Andy!' I shouted, and raced down the beach. He waved, and stood up as the boat got nearer and nearer. I noticed the boat was laden with mats, and baskets, and calabash pots. I ran in the water, threw my shawl off, it landed on the sand, and began swimming towards the floating dug-out and my man. 'Where have you been?' I gasped, as I finally reached him and was clinging onto the side of the boat.

'Getting you breakfast, of course,' Andy chuckled. As did the old man at the helm, certainly he gave me the once over, well several once-overs actually, and his toothless face broke into a leering grin. I suppose it wasn't everyday a white girl in her birthday suit swam up to his floating log and showed off all her bits, but such was my happiness I couldn't have cared less. Let him see me, let the whole world see me in my glory, as I swam with the boat in the deep, and rose naked in the shallows.

'So what's for breakfast?' I asked excitedly, as Andy jumped out onto land with his bag of goodies. By now I'd covered my nakedness with my shawl again, didn't want to cause too many palpitations, the boatman might go into heart attack mode. And could I have lived with the guilt?

'Hang on. Hang on,' laughed Andy, 'not so fast. Let me sort old matey out first.' So while he and Mr Mat-carrying man got down to business, the usual stuff, I'll give you fifty kobo and no more, ok make it sixty, I went off and brushed my teeth in the river and had another splash about. And when the old boy and his boat drifted off, I returned and plopped myself down on the sand. Andy delved into his bag.

Out first was a loaf of bread. 'Oohh,' I said.

Next, a small lump of something wrapped up in newspaper. It was like Christmas all over again. Actually, come to think of it, it was still Christmas. Really, I'd lost all track of time. 'What's in there?'

'Duh, duh,' sang Andy, unwrapping the parcel and revealing a white, foul smelling blob.

'What's that?' I pulled a face.

'Cheese. Taste. It's delicious.' And it was.

Next, Andy pulled out a bunch of bananas, then a couple of mangoes, followed closely by four or five guavas. And a packet of Maggi chicken noodle soup. And two lollipops! Yes, two lollipops, two sweets on a stick. 'Bloody hell, Andy, you've surpassed yourself.'

'But wait until you see this.' Out of his bag he pulled out a little brown bottle, no bigger than the size of my thumb. 'For you.' And he gave it to me, and with it came a kiss. A long, drawn out kiss. A kiss that sent every butterfly in my tummy off into a mad, dancing twirl.

'What is it?' I asked finally, when we'd come up for breath.

'Perfume.' And he unscrewed the little tin top.

'Perfume?' Andy put the little bottle up to my nose. A heady mix of jasmine maybe, frangipani perhaps, lotus flowers? Whatever, the sweet, sweet scent smelt gorgeous. I threw my arms around him, intoxicated with the romance of it all.

And so it was, before we had breakfast, we made love in the sand. And after breakfast, we picked up from where we had left off. Then fell fast asleep. Awoke, and had a swim. Crawled back onto the beach, sucked our lollipops, and when the sweet stuff had gone battled with the sticks in our mouths, like a sword fight, as we lay on our tummies.

Then it was finally down to business. Domestic duties. We did a bit of clothes washing. Andy scrubbed his pants and some T-shirts; I did the slap, wham routine with my knickers, and lost a pair as they got caught up in the current. Watched as they floated away on a ripple.

And afterwards? Well, for the rest of the day we did very little,

137

just enjoyed the peace and quiet, and beauty of our island. Swam a bit, lazed in the sun a bit, read a few poems, smoked a few joints, and made love. Several times. As dusk fell, and the sky and the water turned from blue to red, to silver, to grey, and finally dark blue, Andy made up another fire and we feasted on vegetable salad, bread and chicken noodle soup. Then to bed, all cosy and warm. Gentle caresses, a surging, then quiet.

The world outside had ceased to exist.

The next morning we packed up, and waited for a boat to come along. Like buses, there was nothing for ages then three floated by. But they were all going upstream, and we wanted downstream to Yola so we got one of them to give us a lift across to the mainland, and walked the rest of the way.

After our nice and easy couple of days, this sudden exertion was like a slap in the face. One weary mile, after one weary mile, across thick, sandy ground, it was like walking through treacle. And my bag felt so bloody heavy, heavier than it had ever felt before, but I didn't complain because I was doing this for Andy.

In fact, come to think of it, everything I did, I did for Andy. *Everything*.

No one else in the world would have got me to trudge miles through the bush, under a hot noonday sun. I'd have said, 'Bollocks to this, sat down, and demanded emergency transport, or handed my bag over to the other person. Certainly I wouldn't have stayed silent, certainly I'd have complained for the whole of the journey. But with Andy things were different.

It's a strange thing, this thing they call love.

Finally, we came upon civilisation. Well, it was just a few mud huts on the outskirts of Yola town, but after nothing but dried up emptiness, a few mud huts was a welcome relief. Chickens squawked as we made our entrance, goats blatted from every doorway, and the inhabitants, old and young alike, gathered around us like a swarm of flies; a bit scary really, when you haven't seen human beings for ages (well, it felt like ages) to suddenly be in the midst of a mass.

'Andy, if I don't have a drink, I'll die,' I gasped, dropping my bag on the ground and sitting on it. So my man asked for water, and there was a stampede as everyone raced off and came back with calabash bowls filled with the stuff. Gratefully we poured the sweet liquid down our throats, the rest we threw over ourselves. God, it felt good to be drenched. From somewhere another bowl was handed over, this one was filled with curdled milk, a bit like yoghurt; it tasted weird but what the hell?

Refreshed, we ventured forth with a bit more of a spring in our step. Hit town, and made our way through the usual dirty, muddy and rubbish filled streets, towards the market. We planned to eat in style back at the Peacock Restaurant. Then amble over to the lorry park and hitch a lift over the hills and far away.

That was the plan.

But plans change and things didn't quite work out that way.

CHAPTER 5

Yola and the Mambilla Plateau; the end of 1973

The Peacock was almost in our sights. Already I could taste the 'plate of coffee' and porridge and toast. We were walking side by side, holding hands, not talking, didn't need to, we were both on the same wavelength, the last couple of days had made me certain of that.

As we made our weary way up the hill the usual scrum of vehicles passed to and fro, cars, lorries, motorbikes, bicycles, the hooting and the honking, and the clacking and clattering, and the roaring and the rumbling, so loud I could hardly hear my own heavy breathing. Bang! Pop! Something exploded! Up I jumped, ten inches in the air, which was a bit of a difficult thing to do with a cumbersome bag.

'What the hell was that?'

Andy laughed. 'Just an engine backfiring.'

'Baturi, changi, changi.' A little boy with ringworm circles on his head thrust his hand right into my face, nearly poking my eye out.

'Ba changi,' I snapped, pushing him away.

Just then a massive lorry with bags of cement trundled by and whipped up a cloud of dust. I could taste the grit in my mouth.

'Jesus, Andy, I wish we were still on the island.'

'Hang on in there,' he soothed, squeezing my hand. 'We'll be back amongst nature and enjoying the peace and quiet again by tonight.'

'Thank God,' I responded, with a heartfelt sigh. In my mind I was already there, in that place, in that dreamworld of ours. Those magical, those elusive Misty Mountains.

No surprise then that I didn't really take much notice of the Land Rover that pulled up a little way ahead of us; it was just one of the many in our sights. And neither did I pay any heed to the toot, toot, toot, of its horn. It was only when the driver's door swung open and a white bloke stepped out, and shouted, 'Hoi, Andy,' that I gave it my full attention.

'Rich!' Andy shouted back, his face full of smiles. Both blokes zig-zagged their way through the crowds. 'Hey, man, how you doing?'

'I'm doing good, And. You?'

'Yeah, ace. But what the fuck are you doing hanging around Yola?'

'I was here for Christmas.' Rich moved slightly to avoid a collision with a man carrying a box of oranges on his head. 'But I'm heading back to Serti tomorrow. You?'

'Och,' smiled Andy, delighted. 'I'm heading your way too, man. Maybe I can cadge a lift?'

'Sure,' Rich nodded. 'Where're you staying?'

'Well, I hadn't planned on staying anywhere in Yola but I reckon I'll suss out the Forestry Rest House, see if there's a spare bed for the night.'

'Dunno, man.' Rich shook his head, thinking. 'It's quite full at the moment. Lots of bodies dossing around but you could kip on the floor. Or,' he smiled, 'I could lend you my camp bed.'

'Where are you staying, then?' Andy put one of his crudely fashioned cigarettes to his mouth. Rich, who was already smoking, gave him a light.

'At Jenny's, the girlfriend's. There's not much room there either. A load of her teacher friends have hooked up, there's female bodies all over the place.'

'Nice.' Andy smiled, and drew deeply.

'Yeah, nice,' agreed Rich, puffing. 'But noisy.' He scratched his ear; then swatted a fly. 'I'll give you a lift to the rest house if you want. You can suss out the scene there for yourself.'

'Ace, man.' Cigarette smoke floated out of Andy's mouth. He pushed back his blonde hair with his fingers. 'Have you seen Casey on your travels?'

'Yeah,' nodded Rich, sidestepping again to avoid another collision, this time with a guy on a bicycle, 'he passed this way yesterday. He's doing good. You'll probably see him in Serti, he's planning on being there for the New Year.'

'Cool, man.' Andy took another drag. He grinned excitedly. 'Did he tell you I'm heading off to the Cameroon?'

'Wow, man!'

And so it went on… chatter, chatter, chatter…ace, man, cool, man…natter, natter, natter… wow, wow, wow…

Meanwhile, a few feet away from these two buddies who'd so happened to delightfully bump into each other on a busy thoroughfare in Yola town stood me, a total lemon. Almost forgotten. Definitely ignored.

Hanging around, and kicking the dust up with my shoes, I lit up a fag and patiently waited. Waited for Andy to turn around, draw me in, and say, 'Rich, this is Janni, my girlfriend.' But he did nothing of the sort. Instead, for a full ten minutes all I got was a view of his back and a bad attack of the blues. Especially as I wasn't even given a mention in this, his, oh so, animated conversation with Rich. There was nothing about our journey together, our river trip, our days on the island, or our anything. It was I, I, I all the time. I'm doing this; I'm doing that; I've done this; I've done that. *What the fuck? Hey, Andy! Remember me?*

And, when Rich, whoever Rich was (I hated him anyway), finally, oh bless him, just happened to glance over Andy's shoulder (a look of total surprise, oh my goodness, a white girl! where? there!) and ask, 'Who's this?' only then did Andy turn, only then did Andy take note. But there was no warm smile. No open arms. Just an expression. It was one of total indifference.

'Oh, yeah, this is Janni.'

Dismissive. Like I were a casual acquaintance who just happened to be passing by and wasn't welcome. Wasn't wanted. An unpleasant alien from the planet Zorg, or something really horrible the dog had dragged in. I felt like I'd been hit by a tidal wave and was drowning.

We were back to square one.

'Hi,' nodded Rich, giving me the once-over.

I don't think he was that impressed. After three days, or was it four days in the wilderness, I must have looked a mess. No make-up. My lips dry and cracked from hours spent under an African sun (if I slid my tongue along them they felt just like coarse sandpaper), my hair sticking out every which way and resembling a bird's nest, and the rest of me bathed in a ton of sweat, and dust, and whatever else. Fuck, I wanted a hole to open up and swallow me instantly. Either that, or throw myself in the path of a ten ton truck.

'Hi,' I whimpered, feeling utterly, utterly wretched.

Rich, with a quizzical look, glanced at Andy. His brain connecting. He jerked a thumb in my direction. 'Is this…?'

Andy cut him short. 'Come on, Rich, I'm in need of a drink and a bath, man.' Quickly picking up his rucksack Andy moved towards the Land Rover, leaving Rich to work it (me) all out for himself.

And Rich did. Pretty quickly.

He gave me a smile, the kind of pitiful smile you'd give a pathetic cat that's just been fished out of a river, or a condemned man who's about to be fried, or a sad, fucked up girl who's just been thrown out with the rubbish by her so-called boyfriend in full view of the general public. 'Coming?' asked Richard, still with that smile.

Pathetically, I nodded and followed him, with my heavy bag and my even more heavy heart, to the Land Rover. Andy had already made himself comfortable in the front seat. He was nattering away to another bloke, oh horror of horrors, the most handsome bloke I think I'd ever seen; long black, wavy hair, rugged and tanned, the perfect male specimen. This nightmare was going from bad to worse.

'I'm afraid you'll have to sit in the back,' said a somewhat sheepish Richard, opening the rear door and moving towropes, tyres, and several dirty, rusty jerrycans out the way. Mr Handsome twisted around in his seat and perused me as I climbed in amongst the tools and the dirt.

'Hi,' he said smoothly. The accent was French. 'Ow are you doing?'

My cracked lips hurt as I made tremendous efforts to smile. 'Fine, thanks.'

And then Andy turned too. Actually acknowledged me. But only to say,' You've got my zippo.'

'Have I?' I mumbled.

'Yeah, I gave it to you. Remember?'

No, I don't fucking remember, you total out and out bastard. But keeping this thought to myself, I dutifully checked my pockets and my bag and found it nestling amongst the lipsticks and the eye shadow. 'Here.' I leaned over the jerrycans. God, it would have been so easy. Just a flick, that's all it would take.

'Cheers.' He barely gave me a glance.

And so we headed up the road, away from the mayhem and chaos, on towards the more civilised part of town where flowers grew and there was hot and cold running water. And while I sat miserable and wretched in the back, all alone, confused, bewildered, so unable to work any of it out, the three chaps in the front all babbled merrily away, well Rich and Andy did, Mr Handsome was more of the silent, broody type. A bit like me, I supposed?

Sad thoughts overwhelmed me.

Did the last few days mean nothing to him? It can't be possible, surely? We were having such a good time. No, not good. More than good. A beautiful, wonderful time. He told me he was sorry about the way he'd behaved. That he really loved me. Really, really loved me. So why? Now? What the fuck's happening? What the fuck's going on?

'You're from Gombe, aren't you?'

'Sorry?' *Was someone actually speaking to me?*

Richard, driving, turned his head around briefly, and repeated the question; shouted his question because the noise of the engine was loud. And I far away, stuck in the back like an ostracised leper. 'You're from Gombe, aren't you?'

'Yeah, that's right.' *How did he know? Ah, of course, even in the remotest of places, word gets around.*

'You'll know Lizzie then?' Eyes off the road, he glanced quickly back at me again.

Lizzie! 'Yeah, of course I know Lizzie.' *She was once my best friend.*

'She's here.'

Did I hear right? The Land Rover, going over bumps, was making a hell of a noise. 'Sorry. What did you say?'

'I said she's here.'

'Where?'

'Here.' Rich was looking at me through his rear view mirror. 'In Yola. Staying at my girlfriend's house.'

'In Yola? What's she doing in Yola?' Shifting myself slightly, I leaned forward and banged my knee on a car jack.

'On her way back from Mambilla.'

'From Mambilla?' I exclaimed, rubbing my sore bit.

'Yeah, she spent Christmas there. She's going back to Gombe today.'

'Is she?'

And I thought, phew, at least I won't have to face her.

Rich was decelerating, turning left at a crossroads. 'But she might still be around,' he said, changing down into third. 'I don't think her bus goes until four.'

And then I'm thinking, oh the fuck, no. Especially as Andy suddenly jerked his whole self around in his seat. All smiles. He sounded very considerate. 'Y'know, Janni,' he said, rather sweetly, 'it might be an idea to try and catch up with Lizzie. Check with her how it's going for your folks. They might like to see you, you know.'

Meaning?

And my heart nosedived straight into my boots.

I was still praying to God when the Land Rover pulled up outside the Forestry Rest House. *Please, please make it that Lizzie has left already. Please, please don't allow Andy to send me back to Gombe with her. I can't go back there now. You can't let him send me back. Please. Please. Please.*

Doors were opened, bags taken out. I'll give Richard his due he carried mine up to the bottom steps of the veranda. 'I'll shoot round later,' he said to Andy, giving his mate a slap on the back.

'Yeah, cheers, man.' Andy nodded his appreciation.

'And if I see Lizzie...' Rich looked at me, '...I'll tell her you're here. Okay?'

Please, God, don't let their paths cross. 'Yeah, do that,' I said, in as nonchalant a voice as I could muster.

Under a thatched roof where a flock of Laughing Doves chuckled from one of the wooden beams, we waved Rich and Mr Handsome off.

'Cheers,' shouted Andy.

'Thanks,' but no fucking thanks from me.

If we hadn't bumped into Richard it would have been all so different. Of that I was certain. Lunch at the Peacock then we'd have been on our way, just the two of us, tripping the light fantastic on the road to Mambilla. Sharing our dreams and our love. Sharing our smokes and our poems. Gazing up at a star-spangled sky. Drinking chicken noodle soup by the light of a fire. I could go on... Instead, I'd been dropped like a hot potato, *again*, and even worse would probably be back in Gombe by tonight. It was the stuff of all my nightmares.

'Hey,' bellowed a voice from behind.

Jumping slightly, we turned. A man with a big Fulani hat on his head, and an even bigger smile on his moustached face, stood, larger than life, on the top step of the veranda. 'Bruce!' we both shrieked together. Madly, gladly, I rushed up the steps and hugged him, threw myself into his arms. 'Oh God, am I pleased to see you,' I screamed. And I was. Oh, I was, I was, I was. Finally I had a friend in the enemy camp. Maybe there was a God after all.

'Wish I had this effect on all the ladies,' he laughed, as we disentangled ourselves. He gave Andy a friendly punch on the shoulder. 'So? How's it going? I thought I might bump into you two lovebirds at some point, en route to Mambilla. Did you have a good Christmas?'

'Yeah.' Andy threw me a glance. A slightly warmer glance, not

145

so disdainful. 'A bit of a weird fucking Christmas, actually. We spent Christmas Eve night at a priest's house in Mubi.'

'Blimey,' exclaimed Bruce, pushing the ridiculous straw hat back so we could see more of his bespectacled face. 'Didn't think religion was your kind of thing, man.'

'It isn't,' agreed Andy, leaning back against the cool of the wall. 'It was all a bit cosmic though. We hit Mubi late at night and were wandering the streets, trying to find a hotel…'

'A bit like Mary and Joseph,' I butted in. With Bruce on the scene and Rich and Mr Handsome out of the way, I was feeling a little more confident.

'Yeah,' nodded Andy, thoughtfully agreeing even though his eyes were fixed firmly on Bruce. 'We couldn't find anywhere, so we ended up going to Midnight Mass and we just started chatting to the priest afterwards and he invited us to stay.'

'That'll be something to tell the grandkids,' mused Bruce. 'Christmas Eve, no room at the inn and all that.' He shuffled about in his pockets, and brought out a hanky, and with a loud snort, blew his nose. 'So how long did you stay in Mubi?'

'We hitched a lift Christmas Day and headed our way over here,' I said, and looked quickly at Andy. 'Didn't we?'

He nodded, even though there was still a bit of a frost in the air despite the ninety degree temperatures. 'Yeah, we've been spending a few days on the islands.' There was a pause. 'It was okay, wasn't it?' Finally his eyes did a quick sweep in my direction. I got half a smile.

'Mmm,' I murmured, relieved, relaxing once again into my boots. Acknowledged at last. That was something. But I was still going to have to play this one by ear. It could all change again in another five minutes. 'What about you, Bruce?' I turned my attention on him, reckoning it was a sensible game plan. 'Did you have a nice Christmas?'

Bruce, his hands deep in his pockets, drew them out now, and smoothed his moustache. 'It was okay. I stayed in Maiduguri until Boxing Day. Buggy went totally over the top, as you'd expect.' Andy and I laughed. 'I'm now heading off to Mambilla for the New Year, and then onto Baissa for a week or two afterwards.' Bruce helped himself to Andy's baccy tin, lying on top of his rucksack, and rolled himself a cigarette. Andy was already smoking. Since neither had offered me one, I got my pack out of my bag. 'How are you two getting to Mambilla?' he asked cheerfully, licking the Rizla. 'I hear

146

Rich is here in Yola and is heading back that way himself tomorrow.'

A tendril of smoke curled out between Andy's fingers. 'Yeah,' he nodded. 'It was Rich who just dropped us off.'

'Are you two hitching a lift with him?'

There followed a heartbeat of silence. Nervously I lit up a fag.

Andy, with his back still against the wall, shifted one foot and crossed it over the other. He looked straight at Bruce. 'Yeah.' It was a faint yeah. The sort of yeah that meant 'don't bank on it meaning a yes'. 'What about you?'

'Well,' smiled Bruce, oblivious to the weird vibes that were coursing the air waves under the thatched eaves of the rest house, 'if he's taking you two, I'm sure he'll have room for another.'

'It'll be cool, man,' said Andy, making a move. With his rucksack he headed for the French doors and the inside of the house.

Following suit, I picked up my cumbersome bag. 'I need a bath,' I sighed. *And a total overhaul. I looked the pits.*

'No hot water, I'm afraid, at the moment,' stated Bruce, one step behind. 'No electricity, you see, but it might be back on later, by five or six.'

C'est la vie. Welcome to my world where it's always shit.

'Any chance of a spare bed?' Andy asked Bruce, dumping his bag in the large main room that was cool and white. And was full to brimming with other people's rucksacks and travelling paraphernalia, like a map here, a rolled up sleeping bag there, and what looked like a canvas ground sheet somewhere in the middle. I moved a couple of books and a pair of khaki shorts off one of the three easy chairs and plopped myself in it. Stubbing out my cigarette in an already full ash and fag ridden saucer, I rummaged about in my bag and lit up another.

'Not sure, mate,' Bruce replied, perching down on the armrest of another chair, 'I only arrived myself, about twenty minutes ago. There's no one around at the moment, only the houseboy and he doesn't know much really, only that there's no electricity, but all the beds in the rooms look like they're occupied.' Bruce looked down at the floor space, or rather lack of floor space. He gave a good-natured shrug. 'I suppose we could doss down here, if the worse comes to the worse.'

'Suppose we could,' agreed Andy. He had chucked a sleeping bag off one of the seats and had sat himself down. His head was tilted back. His blue eyes had a faraway quality, like someone in the

147

process of trying to figure out what to do about something that made him unhappy.

It made me nervous.

'Are you hungry?' he asked suddenly, looking at me. Really looking at me. Deep, deep, and even deeper. I couldn't tell if he was being friendly, or what? His voice didn't sound very warm. And there was no smile to light up his piercing eyes.

'A little,' I mumbled, rubbing a finger across my sore lips. They were so dry; bits of skin were flaking off like a blizzard in a snowstorm.

'I am,' said Bruce, patting his tum. 'Fucking starving, haven't eaten anything since six this morning, and that was just a bread roll that I managed to grab off a tin tray in the lorry park at Ngala.'

'We could go to the Peacock,' Andy suggested, straightening himself up. 'What do you reckon?' He posed the question to both of us.

The wind was knocked out of my soul.

He had an ulterior fucking motive. The Peacock was right next to the lorry park. If we bumped into Lizzie I'd be herded onto that Gombe bound bus in a blink of an eye.

'Suits me, even though I don't know where it is,' shrugged Bruce.

Quickly I jumped in. 'It's in town, near the market, Bruce. But we haven't got transport, have we, and it's miles away.' I shot a look at Andy, stretching, arched back, hands behind his head, and affecting an expression of detached, benign interest; he was a picture of innocence. 'We'd never be able to walk it,' I added emphatically, to further my point.

'We could always go in the mini-moke,' suggested Bruce, with a rather smug smile. Pleased that he could be of some help and solve the dilemma.

'What mini-moke?' Shock horror from me.

Andy was already up and out of his chair. 'Where?'

'The one out there.'

We were all up now, and all poking our heads out of the French doors. Yes, indeed, there was a mini-moke parked up by a tree in the compound, a bright orange one. Funny how we could have missed it. Must have had other things on our minds.

'The keys are hanging up, over here.' Bruce pointed to a little bunch, on a hook. 'I was going to use the vehicle myself, anyway. It's Forestry.'

'Well, that's all right then.' Enthusiastically Andy clapped his hands. 'Let's go, gang,' he said to one and all and was about to march out of the door, but stopped before he had his foot over the threshold. He returned to his rucksack, and lifted it up, flinging the straps over his shoulders. 'Better take our stuff,' he smoothly explained, gesturing to my bag. 'We don't want to leave them here while we're out. Just in case.'

Just in fucking case! You complete and utter bastard!

I would have protested in the strongest of terms, 'What a stupid idea, Andy. Who would possibly want to nick my bag of glad rags?' but Bruce was already slinging his rucksack on his back, and acknowledging that Andy had a very good point. 'I've got all my worldly possessions in this,' he proudly stated. 'I don't want some thieving bastard pinching any of it.'

So that was that. We all piled out with our loads, and I miserably wedged myself in the middle of the two-seater, in between the boys, with my bag, and Bruce's and Andy's stuffed in the limited space in the back, and off we went. Back down the same road we'd only just driven up, bump, bump, bump.

And I'm feeling a little bit wretched. And a little bit concerned. My life right now was just full of unpleasant surprises.

And there was one right there, as soon as we entered the gingham-clad tabled restaurant. Lizzie! Yep, it just got better and better.

'Bloody hell,' were her first words. She'd just plopped a yam in her mouth, and it nearly fell out when she saw me. 'Bloody hell,' were also her second lot of words, I really think she was quite taken aback.

Then she smiled. Grinned. Oh, it was a warm, friendly grin. The kind of grin that touched the cold cockles of my heart. 'You look bloody awful,' she cried, as she sprung out of her chair and wrapped herself around me.

'Thanks,' I retorted, hugging her, squeezing her. Oh, it felt so good to be back with my friend.

'Are you ok?' she asked, when finally we had all sat down. She still had a hold of my hand.

'Yeah, I'm fine.' I gave a sort of laugh. And hoped it was convincing.

'Are you sure?'

'Yeah, of course I'm sure, silly.' I puffed on my fag, and blew. 'Why do you ask?'

149

'Because,' Lizzie said, releasing her hand and fluttering it over the table to clear the smoke, 'I've never seen you look such a mess. You look like you've spent a week on a pig farm. Sleeping with the bloody things.' And turning to Andy, who'd said very little up to now, she asked rather brusquely, 'Are you looking after her properly? If you aren't you've got me to contend with, you know.'

She was only joking but I could tell Andy was a little bit flustered. In fact he'd been out of sorts from the moment we'd stepped into the Peacock. Not so cocky, not so in charge.

It made a change, you see, to have *my* friends around me. Actually, I didn't know the two girls Lizzie was with that well, they were from Bauchi (remember the awful party?) but Andy didn't know them at all. And Bruce was my friend, my very good friend. We'd spent quality time together on that lonely bush road from Damaturu to Maiduguri. So basically it was I who was surrounded by pals, and Andy was pretty much all on his own. Not that I wanted it this way, of course. More than anything I yearned for the good old days, when I was the most important person in Andy's world and it was me and him up against everybody else. But there you go. Times change. Needs must.

'Yeah, I'm looking after her fine.' And, bloody hell, the next thing he did was to reach out and push the hair (bird's nest) back off my face. And then he gave me one of his wonderful, gentle, butterfly fluttering smiles. Like I said, my life was just full of surprises. And he could hardly send me back to Gombe after that. Especially as Lizzie was enthralled by Mambilla, and kept telling us how beautiful it was, and how every expatriate in Nigeria should make time to explore this most fascinating part of the country. 'You'll love it, Janni,' she beamed. 'You'll really love it. It's one of the most gorgeous spots on planet earth.'

And so it was that we had a rather pleasant little meal in the Peacock Restaurant. We ate our fill and even cracked open a few bottles of beer, belated season greetings and early New Year celebrations with old friends, all who would be passing like ships in the night.

'Are Mum and Dad ok?' I asked when the talk had finally moved on to other things; the boys were knee-deep in conversation with the Bauchi girls, a heated debate about British Trade Union membership, so this was my chance. Lizzie hadn't mentioned Mum and Dad, as yet. I suppose she was waiting for me to broach the subject because it was a difficult one. Leaving parents the way I'd left mine was not something that just popped up in a conversation, although that was what I was doing right now. Trying to play it down.

Lizzie considered the question. 'Well,' she said, frowning a little. 'They're worried, Janni. Very worried, they care about you a great deal but,' and she smiled now, 'they're coping pretty well. Nothing out of the ordinary going on. And they'll be over the moon when I tell them I saw you.'

I chewed on my lip, my sore lip that felt all dry and chapped. 'Give them my love, won't you? Tell them I'm really okay.'

Lizzie squeezed my arm. 'You can bet on it.'

I twiddled with the Bida brass ring on my finger. 'Thanks, Lizzie. And I'm sorry, y'know…'

'For what?'

'You know what.'

'Yeah, I know what. And you know what?'

'What?'

'It's okay.'

Well, it was far from okay. There again, it was better than it had been. At least Lizzie and I were friends again, and that counted for much. And my parents appeared to be coping, I'm sure Lizzie would have told me if they weren't. Plus, she'd be letting them know I was still vertical and not lying somewhere in the bush, dead in a ditch. That would bring them some comfort.

On the Andy front, I still wasn't sure. Like I said, I'd be playing this one by ear. But at least I had a reprieve, Mambilla bound, and there was hope yet.

Anyway, we said our goodbyes to the girls, they had a bus to catch, and we piled back into the mini-moke with all our bags. 'Back to the rest house?' asked Andy, with his hand on the steering wheel. Not to me, to Bruce. In fact, as soon as Lizzie had disappeared, Andy was back to his old, cold ways. I might as well have been invisible; he looked straight through me when he asked the question.

My innards sunk to my feet.

Bruce, happily oblivious, put his hands behind his head and squinted in the sunshine. 'Mind if we stop by the market, I fancy some oranges.'

I heard Andy draw a deep breath. 'Sure.' He started the engine.

And so we headed off to the chaos of the market, hooting and honking down the dusty streets clogged up with people and traffic, while we slowly cooked in the heat. Finally, we pulled up alongside another Land Rover. Fuck, it was Richard and his mate. And they'd seen us. 'Hey, you lot! Over here.'

So over we went, me still looking an utter, utter mess, and Andy's mood getting darker and darker by the second. *What was with this guy?* As we all wandered round the stalls, picking up and inspecting tomatoes and oranges, even Bruce noticed something was amiss. Andy walked two paces in front of me all the time, and talked to everyone else except me.

'Is everything okay with you and Andy?'

Bruce and I were sussing out how ripe the mangoes were. They felt very squidgey. 'Yeah,' I replied brightly, even though there was a howling inside. 'Of course.'

Bruce shrugged. 'Is Andy okay, then?'

'What do you mean?'

'Well, look at him. He looks really pissed off.'

So I looked in the direction of where Bruce was pointing. Andy was sitting slumped under a rather large cotton tree, back up against the trunk, smoking a cigarette, his eyes staring into space. Not that there was a lot of space here, African markets are one of the most filled up places in the world, but Andy didn't appear to be noticing anything of what was going on. It was like he'd gone away in his head. I'm not sure where, but I kind of reckoned I wasn't there with him. And it hurt.

'I think he's just tired, Bruce. We both are,' I explained, hoping my upbeat tone sounded relatively sincere.

'Yeah, travelling gets to you like that,' agreed Bruce. But I don't think he was *that* convinced and might have pursued the subject if Richard hadn't just then bounded over, his arms full of juicy fruits, and his hand holding a half-eaten banana.

'Fancy a swim in the river, you lot?'

'Umm,' ummed Bruce, pondering the question.

I shrugged, self-consciously rubbing (and hiding) my sore little lips. But Richard wasn't really interested in me, anyway. He was after Andy. 'Where is he?' Bruce pointed in the direction of the rather large cotton tree where slumped my (?) man. 'Hoi, Andy,' Rich yelled. 'Get off your fat arse and come for a swim in the river.'

Andy, on another planet, returned to earth.

Slowly, like an old man with the weight of the world on his shoulders (was I really that heavy?) he pushed himself up from his root, and bypassing the ragtag assortment of Africans, came over. 'No, man,' he said wearily, with a shake of his head, 'I'm fucked. I just need a bath and a kip.'

'Suit yourself.' Rich devoured the end bit of the banana and chucked the skin. 'We'll see you later then, maybe at the club?'

So that was that.

Rich went off in search of Mr Handsome and we headed back to the rest house. And for the whole of the ten minute journey we none of us spoke. Well, Bruce tried to make conversation but Andy and I were pretty unresponsive. So he gave up the ghost, and ate an orange instead.

The bad news was that all the beds were bagged and we'd be spending the night on the hard concrete floor. The good news was the electricity was back on. Immediately Andy went off and ran himself a bath (see, he didn't even do the gentlemanly thing and let me go first), while I whiled away my time sitting in the sitting room with Bruce and the four other guys who'd turned up while we were out. I'd never met any of them before. They came from various places, all of them on their way back from Mambilla, and all of them quite dishy. But I was so aware of how awful I must have looked. I couldn't even toss my hair back it was that dry and sticky. And inside, I was all tied up in knots. So I didn't say much, just sat quietly in a chair, and pretended I was reading the Hobbit.

After half an hour Andy emerged, all fresh and smelling like a daisy. 'The bath's yours,' he said to me, his eyes avoiding mine. 'I've left the water in.'

How nice was that. Obviously he'd used up all the hot.

'Cheers,' I said. Fuck you, you bastard, I thought.

Lugging my dirty, great bag behind me, I headed down the corridor, and through a bedroom, bloody hell, there was a naked bloke lying fast asleep on the bed. Not wanting to wake him, it would have been a bit embarrassing, I tiptoed the rest of the way to the bathroom, to the bath filled to the brim with brown, dirty water. But did I care? Not a bit of it. I was off with the clothes and in it before you could say Jack Robinson.

Oh, it was lovely. Let the warm liquid (tepid liquid, really) slide over me as I sunk lower and lower, down and down, until it was just above my chin. And there I stayed until the water was almost cold. Only then did I wash all my bits, scrubbed and lathered, sponged and flannelled my body until it shone like glass; attacked my lips so that every bit of dry skin came off and were floating little pieces of white stuff on the water. Plunged my head under, up again, smothered my scalp in shampoo so I looked like I was wearing a fluffy white hat. Rub, rub, rub. Harder, harder. Get rid of every bit of shite, sand, dust, that was living and had made a home in my hair. Back down. Up again. Down. Up. More shampoo, even more than the last time. Now I looked like I was wearing an albino Busby. Scrub, scrub, scrub. Get the little fuckers out. And then back down again. Up again. Down again. And up, up, up.

And out of the bath. I looked down at the water. It was black. With grey suds floating on top. 'Yuck,' I said, and pulled out the plug.

Half an hour later I was back in the sitting room.

I knew I looked good. Fantastic, actually. Underneath that grime was a very pretty, golden-skinned girl. My hair, still a bit damp, shone like the sun, and there were ringlets, loads of them, running right down my back. And my eyes were touched with blue, just a hint, a little bit of eye shadow, and a little bit of blue-black mascara. And I had baby soft lips, painted a pretty coral pink. And silver hoop earrings, and silver and red bangles, loads of them up both my arms. And rings on my fingers and rings on my toes (the right foot, of course, I didn't want to draw too much attention to the left, for obvious reasons). And I wore my beautiful, my feminine, my lovely red gypsy skirt, it swished and it swirled as I walked into the room. And I threw back my hair, just a little, and played with the beads that hung round my neck. And let the strap on my gypsy-style top slip down a little, so my shoulders and my bosoms got a little more of an airing. God, did I feel bloody good!

'Wow,' exclaimed Bruce. 'That's a bit of a transformation.'

'Well,' I said modestly, 'I gave it my best shot.'

One of the blokes, Chris, asked if I wanted his chair. I graciously accepted (it was about time I was treated like a lady). 'Cheers,' I said, and dived in, and curled myself up. Like a cool, cat queen. Purring. Chris couldn't take his eyes off me, I think he got a whiff of the perfume, frangipani was it, mixed with jasmine, just a little dab behind the ears, and on the back of the wrists, and in that little space between the bosoms.

And the others, well they were equally smitten, all of them, including the naked bloke who was now up and obviously dressed, ogling and grinning sheepishly, they were putty in my hands. 'Can I get you a drink?' 'Fancy a smoke?' 'Do you want the fan on?' 'Let me peel you an orange.'

As for Andy?

154

Well, he was trying to be cool about it, like me looking glam was no big a deal. He rolled a joint, stayed focused on the job, acted as if he didn't care. Lit up, puffed and blew smoke rings in the air. But I could see him watching me out of the corner of his eye.

Suddenly, out of the blue, he jumped up, and got hold of my hand. 'The Catering Rest House is just down the road. Fancy a drink?'

Did I?

'Come on,' I said, with a toss of my head. And I left a trail of perfume in the air.

In the stillness of the evening, we meandered our way down the quiet road. Under a canopy of trees, passing neat little bungalows with their veranda lights already switched on, listening to the murmur of distant voices mixed in with the noise of the crickets. I so wanted to ask Andy what it was that was wrong, almost blurted it out feeling the words well up inside me, but right now wasn't the time. I didn't want to spoil the moment. He had a hold of my hand, our bodies brushed up against each other, and we were close. It was just like before when we were happy and easy together. *Please, God, may it last.*

Reaching the Catering Rest House, we trotted up the steps, two at a time. Inside, Andy was asked to sign the visitors' book. He scribbled us in as Mr and Mrs. My heart missed a beat. We headed for the bar. It was empty. Perfect. Plonking ourselves down in two comfy chairs, we ordered drinks. Andy got out the fags. We lit up, sat back, and perused each other. 'You look wonderful tonight,' he said, finally.

'Do I?'

'Aye.' And he nodded his head.

The steward arrived, and drinks were put on the table. We leaned over at exactly the same time, and picked up our glasses.

'Here's to you,' Andy murmured. And put his drink to his lips.

'And you,' said I, and took a sip from mine.

And then we talked. About little things and big things but not about things that hurt. We went back to India, Nepal, and agreed how romantic it would be. Travelled on into the Orient; the mysterious Far East. 'But you must get a proper rucksack,' he laughed. 'You can't go round lugging that old bag of yours around forever, you know.'

I couldn't disagree.

Then our journey took us to Scotland, to the little village, to

155

the little stone house where his family lived. He said he'd take me fishing; show me the place where he caught his first fish. 'I was only five at the time, and it was a really big deal. But what I actually caught was just a small tiddler.'

'Ah, well, better than frog spawn, I suppose.'

'Aye, I reckon you're right there.'

We were in the Cairngorms, skiing down a snowy, mountainous slope, when Bruce turned up. 'Sorry about bothering you, guys,' he said, striding over and throwing himself into the next empty chair, 'but I thought I'd just let you know we've been given the offer to sleep round Baz's tonight.'

'Who's Baz?' I asked.

'Forestry,' they both trilled. Might have known.

'I thought he was in Mambilla.' Andy reached for his drink.

'He is. But he left the keys to his house with Si.'

'Who's Si? No, don't tell me. Let me guess. Forestry?'

'No. Teacher. At the secondary school here in Yola,' Bruce smiled. 'Anyway, Si came by a little while after you left to check who was around. When he heard that we hadn't got a bed he offered us Baz's house. Said he'd meet me at the club at around eight for a drink, and give me the keys then. What do you reckon?'

'Great,' grinned Andy. And looking at me, he said with a nudge, nudge, wink, wink, 'Just think. A proper bed tonight. What a treat.'

We ate a solitary dinner, the three of us, in the Catering Rest House Restaurant, under the clunk, clunk of a slow moving fan, watched on by a lone steward ready to serve us, with an old, tin tray always clutched in his hands. And just like the Catering Rest House in Gombe, it was groundnut ingredients all round, in the soup, in the stew, and in the pudding. We also got a little bowl with our pre-dinner drinks. God, what would our shit look like in the morning?

After we'd eaten our fill, and I'd done the business, we headed off to the club. We didn't have far to walk, in fact it was just round the corner, a squat little building that sat on top of a hill (a bit like Gombe Club) with magnificent views of the river way down below (not at all like Gombe Club).

And what a strange place it was.

We stepped into a small room with just a bar. No stools, no comfy chairs, and no marked, scratched coffee tables.

'Evening, Sahs, Madame,' said the barman, polishing a glass with a very grey, grubby cloth.

156

'Evening,' we said. 'Where is everyone?' Quite a few Land Rovers and bikes were parked up outside. They had to belong to someone.

'They be on da veranda, Madam, Sahs.' And the barman abandoned his chore, and kindly led the way.

Out the back was a very long table. And around this very long table sat a bunch of old colonials, thirteen of them, all blokes, all with moustaches and beards, not one hairless face amongst them. It was very surreal. Like Da' Vinci's 'The Last Supper' gone totally wrong.

We introduced ourselves.

'Mind if we join you?' Out of politeness, of course, there was nowhere else to sit. 'Not at all. Not at all.' They were delighted. Hands were shook, chairs moved to make space, and, 'What would you young people like to drink?'

'Beer,' we chirped.

'Smoke?'

'Cheers.'

Matches were struck, sixteen cigarettes lit, a blanket of thick smog settled over the table.

'You're Tony's daughter,' piped up one old boy. His walrus moustache was covered in foam, as was the hairs that dangled long and wild from his nostrils. 'I can tell. You look just like your Mum.'

'By, gum, so you are,' exclaimed another whose eyebrows were as big, if not bigger, as the white bushy beard that hung from his chin. 'I knew you, you know, when you were knee-high to a grasshopper.'

As they all did. Every one of them knew my Mum and Dad. And every one of them knew me when I was on a par with an insect that likes to hop around in the grass. They all had a story to tell. Christmas Day 1959, how I screamed when Santa Claus arrived on a camel. Easter Sunday 1958, ate too much curry sauce and was sick on the floor of the club. Summer 1957, jumping on the bed, went flying and landed nose first. It was a race against time; they had to get me to the doctor's. The nearest one's in Bauchi, a hundred miles away. '...of course, the roads aren't like they are today. Your Mum and Dad were panicking... And how the devil are they? What's that lovely Mother of yours up to?' '...did you know your father and I fished in that river over there, in the fifties... the good old days.' '...did he tell you the one about the hippo?'

Oh, for fuck's sake, get me out of here.

157

Half an hour and more mind numbing stories later, Si rolled up with the keys. It was a longed for deviation. Everyone around the table moved up a bit, he was given a chair. More drinks were ordered. More drinks were drunk. More smoke billowed and gathered in the warm, hazy air.

And then Richard and Mr Handsome put in an appearance some ten minutes later. With them was Jenny the girlfriend, and four of her pals. Like musical chairs, we all moved up one, two, three, four seats, made spaces, so they could sit down. And we all went round the table introducing one another.

There was Brenda. 'Hello.' She was fat.

And Fiona. 'Hi.' With two double chins.

And Stella and Louise. 'Hi, there.' Both had fallen from the Ugly Tree.

Jenny wasn't much to write home about, either. She wore glasses and had a rather big nose.

In truth, I was the belle of the ball. Richard and Mr Handsome (Jean-Claude, actually) did a double take when their eyes fell on me.

It isn't?

Yep, it fucking well is.

Final arrangements had been made, Richard and his sidekick, Jean Claude, would pick us up from Baz's at nine o'clock sharp(ish) tomorrow morning. Si gave us a lift to our pad for the night, stopping off at the Forestry Rest House to pick up our bags and stuff on the way.

'Cheers, Si,' as we stumbled out of the Land Rover, having had one too many beers.

'Have a Happy New Year,' he shouted, before putting his foot on the gas.

We dragged our bags up the gravel path to the house, a small concrete box with obligatory veranda, and little else. But it was built on a hill, and from where we were standing we could see the river way down below, a ribbon of black sparkling water that gurgled in the dark.

We moved on up the veranda steps. Andy fumbled with the keys; it took him about five minutes to open the door. We all giggled.

Finally, the door belched open. Or it might have been one of the boys.

We entered a dark, dark place; it smelt faintly of paraffin oil, cigarettes and mothballs.

'No lights,' I declared, finding and flicking the switch in the sitting room a couple of times.

Bang! Clatter! 'Shit, shit, shit,' as Bruce went bump in the night.

'Are you alright?' I giggled. I could hardly see a thing.

'Think so.' More disturbed furniture noises followed. 'Andy, for fuck sake, man, get us a light.'

'Hang on.' Click, and voila, the Zippo ignited. The small tongue of fire a beacon.

All of us tried to get our bearings in this shadowy world. Not an easy thing to do, especially when drunk. But Andy, with the small pool of light, managed to locate the kitchen. A switch flicked. Nothing.

'Electricity must be off again,' we heard him call out.

Then we heard drawers being opened, and the sound of cupboards being searched. 'Found some,' came the triumphant cry.

'What?' By now I'd managed to locate a chair, and was slumped.

'Candles.' Andy appeared, like a choirboy with two already alight in both his hands. 'There's more. Come on. Let's get this place sorted.'

Using whatever we could find (saucers, plates, mugs), we lit the twenty or so candles and set them up around the room. Instantly, orange winged moths flew in through the open front door, they danced round the tiny flames like a troupe of fairy ballerinas. And the flickering lights made what was really quite a dreary place, a typical bloke's pad with very little in it, just a couple of easy chairs, a coffee table, a scattering of books, tapes, records and a record player, look really cosy. So cosy, we all had to sit down and partake of a joint. As you do.

'This is the life,' mused Andy. Taking a drag, he passed the spliff on to me. We were sprawled on the floor, the three of us, all tangled up, it was difficult to tell where we individually began or finished.

Drawing the smoke deep in my lungs, it hit the spot. I kept it there for as long as I could. My head whirled, my body floated. I sighed, a contented kind of sigh, as the grey stuff poured out of my mouth.

Andy shifted himself, propped his head up with his hand, and gazed expectantly at me. 'What are you thinking about?' he murmured. He was gently stroking the curve of my shoulder; the sensation touched every part of me, body and mind. We smiled at each other. The glow of the candles made him look golden. I wanted to dig deep and bury myself in his soul.

'Umm?' I said, considering the question, trying to find the right words. Perfect peace. No, that wasn't enough to explain how I felt at this moment. I had a vision of profound contentment, of love and fulfilment, of being so deeply in harmony with my world. What had gone wrong, what had happened, all of it was totally and utterly forgotten.

I took another drag. One more puff for the brain.

In our triangle, the two boys were looking at me.

It had gone. For one split second the words that summed up everything, how I felt, what I meant, had been there, but now they were gone. So I came out with something crass. 'We belong together, don't we?' I said to them both.

'What?' Bruce snorted. 'Isn't that a song?'

'A song?'

'Yeah,' nodded Andy. 'Pinkie and Perky.' And they both went into piggy mode, grunt, grunt, snort, snort, ending up with all of us rolling around on the floor, laughing, laughing, on and on, until our stomachs really, really ached.

Twenty minutes later, and now moderately calm, we went off in search of the bedrooms. Candles lit the way. Mosquitoes buzzed around our heads. Creeping down the shadowy corridor, there was a door right at the far end, and one, halfway down, to our left. 'The bathroom,' said Andy, opening the latter. A moth flew down from the ceiling and danced round the candle's flickering flame.

'Phaw. It smells a bit pissy in here,' the comment from me. And we could see why. There was a wad of mushy toilet paper in the bowl, the seat was up, and there were congealed, yellow blobs all round the rim. Elsewhere, a lizard had made itself at home in the grime stained bath, its beady eye on the hand-sized spider that was crawling along one of the rusted, drip, drip, dripping, taps. 'I don't think I'll be having a bath in here,' I declared, my noise wrinkling.

We moved on, Bruce hung back. We heard the sound of urine hitting the inside of the paper-filled bowl.

The other door led to the bedroom. 'Is that it?' asked Andy, as we stood in the shadows. The dim pool of light revealed just one single bed in a room with nothing else.

'There's another door,' Bruce pointed out, having sidled up

behind us; he was still doing up the buttons on his flies.

Indeed there was. The second bedroom lay beyond it.

'This'll do us,' said my man. A large double bed, with net, took up most of the space.

With our sleeping arrangements now sorted, we returned to the sitting room and made ourselves black coffees as there wasn't any tinned milk, and after another shared joint, we all called it a night.

The sleeping bag was thrown over the bed, and we undressed. 'What's that noise,' I asked, as I pulled off my top.

'What noise?' Andy was sitting on the edge of the lumpy mattress, untying his desert boot laces.

'Shush,' I whispered.

There it was again. Scuffling, scampering, like the patter of a hundred tiny feet.

With one shoe off and one shoe on, Andy went over to the far end wall, and bent down and listened. Amidst the pitter-patter there were several scratches, and several squeaks. He looked up and laughed. 'Rats, I reckon.'

My hand flew to my mouth. 'Ughhh!'

I could picture them, horrible, nasty black, hairy things with pointed noses, sharp yellow goofy teeth, and long, long, revolting pink tails, all in that wall, scrambling over each other, darting and squeaking, scampering and shitting just a few feet away. And what if they decided to pay us a visit? Had an overwhelming desire to crawl up the bedpost and share our sheet and our sleeping bag?

'Ughhh,' I screamed again.

'Hey, don't worry.' Andy came over; with a warm smile and an easy manner he opened his arms, drew me close and kissed me. 'They won't bother us if we don't bother them.'

'Are you sure?' Although already I was feeling safe in his arms. Nothing, not even a colony of rats nesting just inches away, scared me when he held me like this. I felt so – oh, how did I feel? 'I love you,' I whispered.

He didn't answer but he led me to the bed. And everything else disappeared.

It was just the two of us, drifting, with the rest of the world falling away, everyone and everything in it, even rats, because nothing else mattered at all.

We left old Yola town the next morning, destination Serti.

Despite clogged-up heads from too many beers, all three of us were up, dressed, and ready to rock and roll by nine. Richard, with Jean-Claude the hunk sitting beside him, bumped down the driveway dead on the dot, in an old army lorry.

'Hey, man, where did you get this,' asked Andy, impressed.

'Inherited it,' explained Richard. 'Probably abandoned during the Biafran War and no one ever reclaimed it. The guys on the reserve have been using it for the past seven years or so. It's good for carting animals about. I've even had a baby elephant sitting in the back.'

I didn't doubt it. As we piled in ourselves, and sat alongside Richard's cook and his loads, there was certainly a strong waft of odour de beast. But it wasn't an awful smell; in fact it reminded me of Smokey's stable: that lovely aromatic mix, sweet hay and horse manure. There's nothing quite like it.

And so we set off. Bump, bump up the road.

As luck would have it I managed to bag the armchair, one of a few pieces of furniture Richard was taking back to his place in Serti (maybe someone in Yola was going back to the UK and had had a house clearance sale) so mine was a bit more of a comfortable ride than Andy, Bruce and the cook's who all had to put up with a two hundred mile journey through the bush sitting on top of a load of hard, wooden boxes. Still, it made up for yesterday's performance when I'd been relegated to the back and had to endure jerrycans, tyres and Spartan discomfort while Andy had the luxury of a soft plastic seat.

'Why,' I asked, as we headed up the drive, away from Baz's house, 'does Richard cart elephants about?'

'Because,' explained Andy, 'Richard's a game warden.'

That made sense. Certainly he looked the type, rugged and handsome. I could see him stalking a lion in the grass with a double-barrelled shotgun.

And so we rolled on. Well, actually, rolled is a bit inapt, we more bumped, and toppled, and bounced, as the lorry went down holes and up mounds along the red-coloured bush roads. Our heads began to get used to the bangs as we flew out of seats and landed on each other. But we laughed, and we sang, and enjoyed every moment because there's nothing quite as exciting as wilderness travelling. Especially when you're part of a gang.

On the scenic front, this was definitely out of Africa: a world of bare, ridged hills and dry, dry bush baking under a white-hot sun. Small villages of red mud and brown straw popped up along the way, all much the same but each one different. Meaning, there might be a dozen huts in one hacked clearing of the bush, and half a dozen in another. We'd stop sometimes, to buy a drink, or some (dog?) meat on sticks, and then we'd move on, eating up the miles, further and further, heading south.

In a little village called Beli we pulled up to have mid-afternoon tea. With a market and a single petrol pump, Beli was a substantial place. We sat in a zanna-mat hut drinking yoghurt from calabash bowls along with large plastic mugs filled with a sweet, sickly liquid, as the whole village looked on. And what a strange bunch they were, especially the women. Like the duck-billed lot back in the plateau region near Jos, they were naked bar a circle of leaves round their privates; their hair was shorn, and they had holes in their earlobes big enough for me to put my fist through. And whilst they sat smiling and giggling in the dirt by their baskets of fruit, or nuts, or rotten smelling meat, with small and not so small babies sucking at their limp hanging breasts, they all puffed madly away on clay pipes. And whatever it was they were smoking, I could definitely smell dope or something similar in the air.

'Hemp,' explained Richard when I asked. 'It's their custom. Much of what we smoke is also grown around here.' No wonder they all looked pie-eyed and happy.

On the road again, but always stopping somewhere for something, even if it just happened to be a pee. In one nameless village, I held a baby in my arms. The mother had simply handed it over to me, like a gift. I explained I couldn't keep it, and she laughed, and I laughed (nervously) but I held on to the little thing for the duration of our stay.

Actually, I was trying, really to drop a subtle hint to my man. And my 'ooohing' and 'aaahing' paid off. Andy came up close to 'surrogate' mother and child, and whispered, so no one else could hear, 'Suits you. Reckon you'd make a wonderful mum.'

My stomach did a flip.

Once, a long time ago, well it seemed a long time ago so much water had now passed under the bridge, Andy had talked about us having a baby together. It was the night he asked me to come to Mambilla with him. Remember? 'Come away with me, Janni, come away.' I'd said yes, and in the joy of the moment we ended up flying to the moon. Afterwards, lying there, breathless and sticky, he'd turned and murmured, 'I hope I'm right, I hope it's happened.'

'What?' I whispered, not understanding.

163

He placed his hand on my belly. 'Just now, I felt as if a child, our child, was conceived. Do you know what I mean?' I nodded, felt a warm rush race through my body. It's the most romantic thing any man can say to a woman. Like climbing into each other's souls.

Sadly my period came a few days later but from then on, even though I'd not thought about babies before, I so wanted to have a love child with Andy. It was the ultimate hippie accessory. The consequences, too young, sleepless nights, nappies, teething problems, tantrums, meant little to me. Our love, our dreams, our hopes, whatever, would see us through.

And then 'something kinda died.' Everything shattered by those three little words; until today, holding the little brown package in my arms, him whispering those words. No wonder my stomach did a flip.

Maybe there was a God, after all.

In another village, we all sat under a big, silver baobab and had several smokes. Whether it was because the heat was getting to me, or the long journey was taking its toll, the drug really addled my brain, more so than usual. Suddenly I needed to be on my own. So I got up, and took a stroll.

'Where are you going,' I heard Andy call out.

I didn't even bother to turn around. 'Nowhere,' I answered, my voice echoing in the emptiness. I walked on, with the sun bright in my eyes and the perspiration dripping down my back, down a henna coloured road, away from the squawking chickens, the blatting goats, the children giggling in the dust, the red mud and brown thatched huts, and the boys under the tree. Finally, I plopped myself on a black, granite stone. And sat there, alone, perusing the view. The village, the huts clustered together so tightly. If I squinted the whole place disappeared, it just melted into the background, and there was nothing but silent savannah. Red, brown and yellow. Endless. All around. And the distant mountains that rose above this wilderness world, volcanic, I could almost hear them explode.

A movement, far in front of me, caught my attention.

An albino came into view, a Fulani girl, tall, and beautiful and white. She was balancing a large pan on her head, piled high with plantains. She walked unhurriedly, sedately.

I was mesmerised.

My eyes followed her into the papery bush as she sashayed alongside her black companions. Against them she looked almost transparent, opaque, and not real. It was all rather strange.

164

Especially as I began to think that maybe she was me. I had an overwhelming desire to jump up and chase after her, take the pot off her head and put it on mine. Then walk away into the bush. But of course I didn't, instead I watched the graceful sway of her body as she disappeared into the tall, yellow grasses.

Funny thing, I felt like I'd disappeared too.

On the road again. Bump, bounce, and topple. It was hot, it was sticky, the journey seemed never ending but at long last, at around five in the evening, when I'd given up all hope of ever being stationary again, we arrived at Serti, the place where Richard lived.

Serti was lovely. A little town with cloud covered mountains in the distance that I imagined were straight out of 'Lord of the Rings'. Everywhere was strikingly green, a luscious green, trees and grasses, with colourful flowers popping up all over the place. Very pleasing to the eye after the dry, arid landscape of the north.

Pulling up outside Richard's house, we all clambered out of the army truck. A dishevelled, tired, weary group of travellers were we. Even so, I couldn't help but admire the lovely dwelling place that was Richard's home and our home for the night. Stone steps lead up to a wide veranda that ran the whole way round the white, thatched bungalow. Bougainvillea poured out and down from the roof, touched the ground and curled back on itself so you could hardly see the building for white, pink, and mauve flowers. Elsewhere, fruit trees grew in abundance, lemon, lime, grapefruit, mangoes, oranges, and whatever else might tickle your fancy. No wonder Richard looked so bloody rugged with all this vitamin C at his disposal. And the view from the front of his house was amazing. Nothing but a carpet of green, mile upon mile, that carried on up into the mist covered purple-blue mountains.

Pulling myself away from the view, I lugged my bag up the stone steps. Out on the veranda, tables and chairs had been invitingly set up beneath the cascading show of creepers and flowers, and two blokes and a girl dressed in red were enjoying late afternoon tea.

'Anne,' I screamed, as the crimson vision jumped up and met me halfway on the steps.

'I thought it was you,' she grinned, giving me an almighty big hug. 'Amy kept saying you'd probably be arriving any day now, and here you are. Brilliant.' Getting hold of the other handle on the bag, Anne helped me with it up the last couple of steps. Both of us blabbing away.

165

'Amy's here. How fantastic. Where is she?'

'Having a kip. You know how she is. How was your Christmas?'

'Amazing. Yours?'

'Ace. Christmas's will never be the same again. Where's Andy?'

'Over there by the truck. Helping Richard with his loads.'

'Is that Bruce with him?'

'It most certainly is.'

'And who's that other luscious guy?'

'Jean-Claude.'

'God, what a specimen.'

'Isn't he just. French, you know.'

'Looks it. Has he a girlfriend?'

'Couldn't tell you, only met him yesterday.'

'Well, he'll certainly liven the place up. You must introduce me.'

By now Anne was back in her seat and I'd fallen into the nearest empty chair.

'Tea?' asked one of the blokes, already pouring brown liquid into a white enamel mug.

'Love one,' I said. And for the next half hour, while Andy and the others carried loads and were busy, me and Anne and the two guys, who I'd never met before, sat out on the veranda and supped tea and ate biscuits, while pondering on the state of the African nation, as only expats know how.

It was most civilised.

Later, Amy joined us, then my lot, and a couple more folk from Maiduguri strolled out on to the veranda. It was quite a reunion. I would have stayed in my chair for the rest of the evening, it was so lovely out here, all of us swapping intrepid stories as the day drew to a close, but my body was stinking dirty. And it was imperative I look my best. So I made enquiries. 'Any chance I can have a wash, Richard?'

'Yeah, course. Follow me.' So I followed him, lugging the old bag along. Through the light, airy sitting room with its wide open windows and wide open doors that gave passage for the early evening sun to pour in, and where animal heads hung from the walls, as did a picture of Elizabeth our Queen; down some steps and into the dining room, I could hear the tick-tick of a clock, on past the shelves of books and table and chairs, down more steps, along a corridor and back out into sunshine and on towards a clump of trees.

166

To a little edifice construed from wood and matting. No roof, no door, just a brightly-coloured cloth over the entrance swaying gently in the breeze.

'No hot,' I'm afraid,' declared Richard, holding aside the flimsy partition that acted as a barrier between the outside world and a person's nakedness. Stepping into my outdoor bathroom I was given the low down on the best way to go about it. 'Tap. Turn on. Water from shower, here. Bucket, should you need it. Soap and flannel, if you want it. Good luck.' And that said he left me to it.

Apart from the goose bumps it was all rather lovely. I stood beneath the rustling orange trees with ice-cold water sprinkling over me while up above, birds flew high in the silver sky. And there was more of the same to come. As I stepped out of my open-air washroom, ready to head back to the veranda, to the others, to my cup of tea and my fags, I got caught up with the sunset.

Actually, it was Anne's red dress I noticed first. She was taking an evening stroll, was in quiet contemplation as she walked down the empty road that lay beyond Richard's house. Her red dress glowed in the thickening light and made her stand out from the hills in the distance. I watched her as if dreaming, the whole scene, mountains, the sun going down, the bright-coloured earth, the emerald green grasses, and her vivid red dress. It was totally mind blowing.

So I sat on a ladder that rested up against the water tank by the side of the house, and there on my own, in the stillness of the evening, I watched the sun die. Smoking a joint that I had found in my bag heightened the experience. To be right here, right now, so peaceful, so undisturbed.

Perfect.

I didn't hear a thing. It was only when I happened to turn away from the mountains, from the burning planet for a moment, that I realised I wasn't entirely on my own. Jean-Claude sat nearby, on a step, his head back against the white painted mud wall, and in his hand he had a pen and a little notebook. My eyes zoomed in on him. My God, what a handsome bloke he was. A vision of total beauty. I watched him write a few words, I watched him return to the mountains and the orange ball in the sky. And then I coughed. Quite deliberately coughed.

From across a wilderness space, between my ladder and his step, our eyes met. Lingered. We smiled. My heart lurched. I was totally caught out by the intensity of the moment.

A voice from somewhere shouted out, 'What are you writing about, Jean-Claude?'

He replied. 'Just words, so I can get into the mood of the sunset.' But he never dropped his gaze. And neither did I.

Then the spell broke. You can imagine how I felt when Andy suddenly materialised. He came up from behind and made me jump. 'There you are. I was wondering where you'd got to.' Moving over, he joined me on the ladder, offered me another smoke. 'Cheers.' I took a puff, and looked quickly over to where Jean-Claude was sitting. He'd gone. There was nothing but an empty space on a step, and the after glow to remind me of him.

Andy kissed me. 'You look beautiful dressed in sunset,' he murmured.

In body and spirit, I was back with my man once again.

There were twelve of us for supper that night. We all sat in the sitting room amongst tilly lamps and candles, eating curry and rice (courtesy of the travel weary cook) on our laps. Anne had a book of poems with her, she's an English teacher so that figured, and when she'd finished her meal she gave us a recital.

Everyone, because we were all a little stoned, and all a little chilled, got into the mood. Jean-Claude (that gorgeous, beautiful man who I occasionally maintained eye contact with just for the sheer adrenalin pack that it punched) picked up a guitar and began to gently strum along with Anne as she wafted on about Kublai Khan, lonely clouds, churchyards and the like. Someone else joined in with a mouth organ, whilst another tapped a soft accompanying beat on a bongo. More joints were rolled and passed round. Incense was burnt. Moths bumped against the glass of the lamps. Crickets hummed. A bat flitted in. Orange and lemon trees stirred in the breeze. It was all very mellow, and very bohemian.

After Anne, Andy followed with his Robert Burns' poems. I was hoping he'd read my favourite, the Red, Red, Rose one, but he didn't. There again, he did give us a wonderful rendition of 'Anna', my next favourite, and a few times he looked straight at me as he delivered his lines in that soft, Scottish, melt in the mouth, beautiful voice. Not to be entirely outdone, I scrabbled about in my bag and pulled out Hemmingway's book, 'The Snows of Kilimanjaro'. Having never read it, bar the first page, I'd no idea what the story was about. But it soon became apparent. In a hushed room, with a guitar, drum, and mouth organ playing quietly in the background, and Andy lying on the floor with his head in my lap, his eyes to the ceiling, the smoke drifting out of his mouth, I began to realise I was reading about a couple that resembled the two of us; a conflict of love and hate between a man and a woman. Bloody hell! It all sounded so familiar. And how much of it was Andy taking in? I glanced down. It was difficult to tell. But there was an odd look in his eyes.

Then I remembered. 'A girl like you would appreciate a book like this.' To this day, I still didn't know what he meant by this turn of phrase. I'd actually never asked. Maybe he'd had some premonition? Or maybe not?

I didn't finish reading the story. It had been a long day and a long journey. I was that tired. Page twenty and I closed the book, and my eyes, and drifted off while the music gently played on. Falling into a deep, deep dreamless sleep. Someone put a blanket over me, and a cushion under my head, probably Andy. He also pulled out his sleeping bag and curled up beside me.

And that's how it was, the both of us, on that floor, until the morning.

It was time to move on.

Amy, Anne and some of the crew, including Jean-Claude (shame), were going to Baissa, a forest reserve in the Mambilla foothills, to celebrate the New Year, whilst me, Andy and Bruce were heading upwards onto the plateau itself. Richard was to take us as far as Masai-Mari, the first town on the tabletop mountain, and then we were going to make our own way to Gembu where a Canadian volunteer friend of Andy and Bruce's lived a solitary life high up near the Cameroonian border. And afterwards, having seen the New Year in with new (and old) acquaintances me and my man were going to push on over the hills and far away, over the border. How exciting was that!

So we said our goodbyes. It was kisses from the girls, handshakes from the boys. 'Happy New Year to you all. See you back in Maiduguri,' shouted Anne and Amy, as they crunched their way down the stony driveway, their arms waving madly, and their heads hanging out of the Land Rover driven by Jean-Claude, the hunk. Funny thing, I never did find out what the guy did, why he was here in Nigeria and where he was based. But I did get a hug from him that was kind of nice, especially as we did it in front of Andy.

Anyway, once that lot were packed off, it was time for us to

169

gather our stuff and make a move. So we piled into yet another vehicle, a two-seater Land Rover with open-back wagon. Andy and I took to the rear whilst Bruce and Richard sat in the front.

'Goodbye,' I shouted to the cook, who was there on the veranda, waving. Glad to see the back of us, probably. Preparing twelve dinners and twelve breakfasts, and endless cups of tea and coffee, is a little much, especially straight after a two hundred mile journey.

And so we went bump, bump down, or rather bump, bump up another bush road. Out of Serti, we headed straight for the mountains.

For the first twenty miles we were surrounded by flowery meadows, acres and acres of yellow, dewy grass sprinkled with every imaginable colour under a honey-hued sun. A golden world, as if King Midas had personally touched every petal, every leaf and every blade. It was absolutely lovely.

Africa it was not. 'More like England on a warm summer's day,' I exclaimed, standing up in the Land Rover to get a better view.

Insects hummed, and butterflies danced. In and out of the long grasses and wild flowers they hovered and fluttered while the blue, blue sky was filled with the sound of birds, wagtails and swifts, hornbills and swallows.

Not that I knew the names of any of the birds, of course, but my man did and took great pleasure in informing me what was what. 'See the tail bobbing on that one over there? That tells you that it's a Yellow Wagtail.' And which was which. 'The long curved wings on that little bird. See? That's a Little African Swift. While that one there, is a common Palm Swift. Their tails are forked.'

'Oh,' I cried, craning my neck and leaning back, not wanting to miss a thing.

'Careful!' shouted Andy, as we flew over a crater. Too late, I was down. 'Here, give me your hand.' Back on my feet, he positioned himself behind me, held me steady with his arms, his hands gripping the side of the Land Rover. 'OK?' he asked from somewhere up above.

'Yeah,' I shouted, and my little word got carried away on the wind. But I was more than okay. Exhilarated best sums up how I felt.

And so, in this blissful state, we trundled along. We waved at a little girl, who with her mum, was walking alongside the road with a calabash pot on her head. Shouted hello to the old man who slowly followed behind, with a bundle of wood strapped to his back; perused a herd of goats as they skipped and gambolled in and out of the flowered grasses. 'Look,' cried Andy, pointing high up above. 'A Kite. Over our heads.'

I looked up, expecting to see a balloon like thing on a string. There was nothing except blue sky and birds. 'Where?'

'There. A Black-shouldered Kite. Amazing.' Well, to me of course, it was just a bird. Although it did appear to be standing on its tail in the air, which I suppose made it a little bit different from the rest. 'It's hovering,' explained Andy. 'Ready to go in for the kill.' And just as he said that, it swooped. One second in the long grass. And up again. With a lizard firmly gripped in its claws as it soared high into the air, and winged its way towards the purple-blue mountains.

Going in the same direction, but land bound, we went at a much slower pace. Nonetheless, it wasn't long before we too started to make our ascent. The road began to wind, and twist and turn, higher and higher, sheer drops on either side, between forests and valleys, it really was like being in another part of the world, the Alps or the Dolomites or the Spanish Pyrenees. Small rivers ran, coiling their way in and out of the hills, and streams trickled down the slopes. And everywhere, green grasses gently swayed in the breeze, as did a carpet of beautiful mauve flowers.

We stopped halfway for a smoke, sat on a rock and perused. Way down below a river flowed, meandering its way through the rocks and the valleys, on a journey to some distant place that I knew I would never visit. In the silence, we heard a drone. Far above us an aeroplane crossed the sky. We all looked up, shielded our eyes from the glare of the sun; followed the vapour trail, a long pale line of smoke in an otherwise cloudless sky. 'Funny to be in the middle of nowhere and see something like that,' mused Bruce. 'There's probably a hundred people up there, reading, having chicken and chips and a glass of wine with their dinner, and at the same time we're down here surrounded by all this, a million miles from civilisation. Weird, isn't it?'

'I wonder if anyone of them can see us?' I asked.

Andy laughed. 'Shall we give them a wave?'

So we waved. We all stood up on our rock, shouting and flapping our arms about, four little dots on the ground making contact with the great silver bird in the sky.

Talk about silly!

We reached Masai-Mari just in time for lunch. It was another pretty place. Set in the middle of woodland, it stood way up on the plateau, surrounded by soft, rolling hills, with one very large peak that loomed high above the others.

We met up with Graham, a VSO lad (Forestry, of course) who was based here in the town. Actually he was the only white bloke in the vicinity. He seemed nice enough, and my three travelling companions knew him well. In fact, they were all very old friends. So much so, that I began to feel a little left out.

Actually that's an understatement. I felt positively ostracised.

Let me explain.

We'd all trooped into Graham's sweet little mud-thatched house, it was cool, a welcome relief, believe me, the fan was on, the chairs were reasonably comfy, and he'd offered us all a beer. That was fine, there's nothing like a cold beer on a hot day, especially when you've been on a rather long journey.

So far so good.

'Where are you from?' asked mine host, as he lit up a fag.

I laughed, and looked at Andy who was too focused on rolling up a joint to pay any attention to me. 'Well,' I said, 'it's a bit of a long story.' And was about to tell him the tale when Andy, who had obviously been listening, piped up.

'She's from Gombe.'

True, of course, but it was the way Andy said it. The tone wasn't right. And anyway, who's she? The cat's fucking Mother.

'Ah, Gombe,' continued mine host. 'What do you do there?'

I was about to say, actually I don't really live in Gombe, I live in Maiduguri with Andy, but again my man got in first. Very quickly.

'Janni's just left school. She's spending a year with her parents.' His eyes focused on me. 'Aren't you?'

Am I?

'Oh,' nodded Graham, quite obviously unimpressed. A schoolgirl, living with her parents; not exactly what you'd call exciting. Blimey, she must be as green as the grass in the hills.

In truth, I really couldn't have given a fuck what Graham thought about me (in normal circumstances of course, I would, but we're talking about untypical times here), what bothered me was what Andy was thinking. His sudden change in manner suggested he was reverting to type alien. By that, I don't mean total blank out,

172

but there was a sudden cold chill in the air that didn't just come from the fan.

'Can I use your loo?'

Having sat through ten minutes of masculine chit-chat, I decided my best plan of action was to go check out the visage. A bit of hair makeover, lipstick restoration, and eyeshadow renovation never goes amiss, as well you know.

'Sure,' said Graham, not getting up. 'Go out the front door and round the back of the house. You'll find it there.'

'Thanks.'

So I trotted off, out of the front door and straight to the Land Rover. Retrieved my cumbersome bag and had a root around. Found what I was looking for, my make-up, and headed to the back of the house where I encountered a pig. A big, fat, hairy pig. It was lying in a pool of mud, on its side, not moving, like it was dead.

'Blimey!'

I steered my way quietly round the bulbous creature so as not to disturb it. Too late, it had heard me. There was a snort, and the animal opened a white-pinkish eye, raised its head and looked straight at me.

'Hello, little pig,' I said, somewhat nervously. It answered by way of a grunt. And then thankfully went back to its daydreams. Quickly, I legged it to the toilet. It was just a hole in the floor with three mud walls, a thatched roof, and a mat over the entrance. No mirror, no hand basin, but a full bucket of water was provided should you need to wash your hands. Which you would, even if you were usually quite lazy about such things, because there wasn't even any loo paper, just torn up squares of old New Nigerian newspapers hanging from a looped wire on one of the walls.

I sighed, and did the business as I squatted. Then gingerly, using General Gowon's smiling face, wiped my bum. A quick hand plunge in the bucket completed the process. Next, I got on with the major renovation job. Being an inventive little soul, I poured the rest of the water in the bucket down the hole, and then turned it upside down and used it as a stool. Perching my little compact case, with mini mirror, on top of the squares of newspaper, I managed to work on my face. So small was my mirror, I had to do each bit by piecemeal, and even at the end it was difficult to judge how the overall look was, and I was still not too sure about my hair. So I plaited it and tied it up in a bun with a few seductive tendrils escaping down.

Back outside, the pig was still basking in the sun and had been joined by a couple of chickens that were having a fine time flapping about in the mud.

'Hello,' I said again. All three creatures ignored me but a scraggy old cat with half an ear, came from out of nowhere and rubbed itself up against my leg. There were several ticks, big fat black bulbous things they were, on its back, and I could definitely see a rather large colony of fleas having a hop and a jump about in the bald bits of its fur. 'Meow,' meowed the pussycat, as it brushed up against me. 'Yuck,' said I, and legged it across the yard as fast as I could.

Back in the sitting room there was nobody there, just a load of empty beer bottles and a couple of full ashtrays. I checked outside again. The houseboy was hanging some washing on a line that was strung between two wooden posts. 'Have you seen the Masters?' I asked.

He nodded. Pointed a finger. 'They be go there.'

'Where?' I couldn't see them.

'They be go down that road.'

I was baffled. 'Do you mean they went for a walk?'

'That be right, Madame. They done go for the town.'

What a load of fucking bastards. How long had I been in that loo? Ten minutes? Fifteen minutes? Twenty minutes max. In the meantime they'd taken it upon themselves to go for a walk. Without me!

See what I mean? Utterly ostracised.

'Thanks,' I said curtly, wanting to pull all the clean bits of linen off the line and give them to the pig for his dinner. And what was it with Andy? First, he gives me the cold shoulder when we meet up with Richard. Then it follows with Graham. Was I such an embarrassment?

The fuck knows, I said to myself, and with hurting heart headed off in hot pursuit.

Down winding streets, past ramshackle mud houses, greeting astonished townsfolk as I passed them by. 'Oh, piss off,' was what I really wanted to say. I was in no mood for pleasantries but was in alien territory, I needed as many friends as I could get right now. So I smiled as they all followed me and didn't even kick the chickens or the goats when they got in my way. Onwards and upwards I went, through the market, everyone stopped and stared. 'Have you seen four white blokes?' I asked. Nobody understood a word, they didn't

174

even speak Hausa, but they all wanted to go where I was going and dropped their chores, abandoned their wares, and like the Pied Piper of Hamelin, I led the way. Out of the village, down a narrow path fringed with green grass and small purple flowers, across a stream via a log, and a little further on we were walking in woods. Multi-coloured butterflies hovered over shrubs thick with bright yellow blooms while long-legged insects crawled and hopped about in the emerald grass. Cicadas whirred endlessly and invisible birds sang from the trees. And above me the sun shone through the roof of the forest. All very lovely but I was on a mission, not a nature walk.

'Oh, fuck it,' I said, after ten minutes of useless ambling. The blokes were nowhere to be seen. So I turned round and gave up the chase.

Back at Graham's house, as I turned into his compound, I could smell fried liver and onions. 'There you are!' Bruce sat sipping a beer out on the veranda.

'Where've you all been?' I exclaimed, totally pissed off. The sweat was pouring off me and I was parched.

Bruce looked surprised. 'We went looking for you.'

'What do you mean you went looking for me? I was in the toilet.'

'But you were ages, Janni. We all thought you'd gone for a walk.'

Plopping myself down on the step, I flicked away a fly. 'Really?' I exclaimed, with wide-open eyes. 'You really, including Andy, thought I'd gone on my own for a walk?'

'Really,' nodded Bruce. 'Especially Andy. He was worried about you.'

Slightly appeased, I looked around. 'Where is he, anyway?'

'Andy? He's helping with the dinner.'

'Liver and onions?'

'Smells like it.'

I smiled. 'Give us a fag, Bruce.'

Well, we ate our liver and onions, with fresh local bread, followed by coffee. And Andy was back to being nice to me again, so, all in all, I put the whole debacle down to a bad case of the jitters. It's a travelling thing, you see. Makes you a little bit unsettled at times so you take it out on your nearest and dearest.

Anyway, it was time to move on. As luck would have it, a lorry belonging to Forestry was going up to Gembu that very afternoon, so it was goodbye Graham and goodbye Richard, and off

175

we three went to catch our next mode of transport. Bruce sat in the open-back this time, Andy and I in the front with the driver. Out of Masai-Mari, climbing for a few more miles, and then we hit the plateau proper.

It was wild, wonderful country, undulating hills, as waves on a sea, and totally empty. For ages we saw nothing, not a tree, not a bush, not a village, not an animal or a person. Just hills. They curled up on themselves, disappeared into the blue-grey sky, and re-appeared again at the turn of a bend. Amazing.

Twenty miles on, Bruce shouted, 'Wow.' From the back, he tapped on the rear window. 'Look over there.'

We looked. A pure white, wild mountain pony stood majestically on the crest of a distant hill. Like a king looking down on his subjects, it watched us for a while, so proud, head held high, not moving. Then, as a creature in one of my fantasy dreams it raised its magnificent tail and with indescribable grace, thundered down the slopes. This was Pegasus flying; his hoofs barely touched the surface, over the grass and the flora, his mane blowing like wings in the wind. What a magical sight.

The rest of the journey we drove through high plains filled with frolicking baboons and herds of cattle. Dust hung in the air coating us. A cool breeze repelled the worst of the flies that were always there, buzzing around.

Late afternoon we arrived in a small town called Ngorogi. Like all the other habitations on the plateau, it was just an isolated cluster of ramshackle, mud buildings running up and down and along some higgledy-piggledy streets in amongst the wilderness. Pete lived here, another of Bruce and Andy's Forestry buddies, and as we were all in desperate need of a piddle and a thirst-quenching drink Andy suggested we stop by his house. Bruce and I didn't need much persuading so the driver was given directions. Turning off the main (the only) road through the town, we took a right and headed up a single-track lane, winding our way along it for about half a mile. Turned a corner, round a hill, and there it was, Pete's little abode.

First impressions were deceptive.

Out of the lorry, we kicked and stretched our legs about a bit, and admired the panorama. 'Wow,' I sighed, 'wish I lived somewhere like this. What a view.'

Yes, what a view. Overlooking the picturesque mud and thatched village way down below, with the plateau before us, an unbelievable, seemingly unbroken expanse of soft green stretched as

176

far as the eye could see. I felt I'd reached the world's end. That like the early explorers believed, if we stepped over the distant horizon, we'd be tipped over and hurled into the vastness of space.

'Look,' said Bruce, pointing to the sky above. We looked. An eagle soared, so far away, it was like a fragment of paper drifting in the wind. From behind, a pair of swallows flashed past, twittering excitedly. A moment there, then gone, just a shimmering blur of blue in the sunlit heavens.

Certainly, this house was in a dream location. And even though the building itself was a bit characterless, a fairly modern square, breezeblock construction with corrugated tin roof, someone at some time had planted rose bushes all along its front, a riot of red, pink and white flowers that tumbled over and up and along the wide veranda. They made for a very pretty façade.

Meandering up a stone-flagged path, every crack crammed thick with tiny mauve flowers, we made our way towards the house of Pete. Closer; and it didn't look quite so inviting. Behind the rose bushes the four large front windows, and the glass panes on the French doors, were filthy, covered in cobwebs and grime. I reckoned, even from here, that there was no way anyone on the inside could peruse the beautiful view outside, the thick, cloying dirt were like blackout curtains. Plus there was rubbish strewn all over the veranda, old fag packets, empty beer bottles, discarded newspapers, it was like someone had gone whoosh(!) with a full dustbin and chucked out all the garbage. It was everywhere. As were the flies and the bluebottles, buzzing and zizzing over and on deep piles of bat droppings and decaying waste. My God, I thought, what kind of bloke lives here? I half expected a wild, demented hermit in rags with long fingernails and a tangled mess of hair, to suddenly appear on the veranda holding a double-barrelled shotgun aimed straight at us. 'Get ye gone', he'd snarl, and we'd be fleeing as bullets pinged and whizzed round our legs. But no such thing happened.

In fact nothing happened, we mounted the veranda steps and apart from the tread of three pairs of feet and Bruce farting, the place was deathly quiet.

'Is this Pete bloke here?' I asked.

Andy shook his head, pulled his cigarettes out of his pocket and lit one. 'No, he's away in Jos. But he did say for us to make ourselves at home if any of us were ever passing this way.'

Wow! Unstinting in his generosity, this Pete guy certainly

knew how to roll out the red carpet. By now, we were all knee-deep in the refuse and litter, stepping over lizards, insects and spiders. Andy, being a sporty type, kicked an empty baked bean tin across to Bruce, who kicked it back, another strike from Andy and it clattered along the debris-strewn concrete, ending up in one of the red-flowered rose bushes. Bruce laughed. 'I bet that'll still be there in a year's time.'

'And the rest,' chuckled Andy, who was now peering through the grimy windows. 'If you think it's bad out here, come and take a look at the inside.' Opening the unlocked French door (it figured, who'd want to steal anything from this place?) I was ushered through into a room devoid of sunlight. A crypt-like stillness hung in the air. As did the smell, a mix of mould and wood smoke which, funny as it may seem, was not entirely unpleasant. From the windows, great strings of cobwebs hung like lace curtains, and like fishing nets from the rafters. As for the furniture, or what few bits there were? Well, what can I say? I'm not averse to the odd sprinkling of dust (ask my Mother, she'll tell you) but Pete's house made Miss Haversham's place look like it had just had a bloody good spring clean. Inside, there were more powdery particles than you would get in a Saharan sandstorm, the furniture, the books, everything was thick with the stuff, you could draw the most amazing masterpieces if you put your mind (and finger) to it, on the table, the chairs, the floor, even the walls looked like they had a bad case of dandruff.

But it wasn't just the dust, or the black-patterned marks on the ceilings, or the cobwebs, it was the mess. Think rubbish on the veranda and multiply by a hundred. That sums up the interior. It was if a cataclysmic tornado had swept through the house.

'God,' I said, disgusted, 'how can anyone live here? It's awful. This Pete must be a right smelly, horrible bastard.'

That comment didn't go down very well. Andy shot me one of his funny looks. 'You can't go round saying things like that. You've never met him. He's a good friend of mine, and a real ace bloke. One of the best.' That said, and Pete's knight errant removed a load of junk off one of the scabby, old chairs. 'I've seen worse, believe me,' as he plopped himself down. Instantly, up went a thousand particles, into the air they billowed and mushroomed like the fallout from an atomic bomb.

Standing by the door, I perused the cloud. 'You were saying.'

Andy coughed, several times. Loyal to the end. 'Och, a lot of the dust is just soot from the fireplace over there.' He indicated to the black, black hole that was chocker-block with ash and assorted debris. 'And...' making his final point '...Pete's not keen on exploiting the black man, so he won't have a boy or a cook, which means he does all the housework himself.'

'I can see he's kept busy then,' I muttered, a tad sarcastically.

Andy didn't answer; turning an imaginary knob he switched me off and began picking up books, reading the titles, flicking through pages. Then he moved onto a load of tapes scattered and stacked on a very marked, very scratched coffee table. Selecting one, he headed over to the cassette recorder sitting in a pile of dust on a bookcase that was filled with rubbish and literary works. There, he put in, and flicked, and clicked. Curved Dare. Strange, haunting music, very apt, enough to send shivers down anyone's back.

I left Andy rolling up a joint and went off in search of the toilet, wandering down the bare, gloomy corridor, and met Bruce coming in the opposite direction. 'It's fucking diabolical,' he grimaced. 'Believe me, you don't want to go in there.'

I shrugged. 'Needs must, Bruce,' and bravely went forth, into a malodorous, maggot-crawling, unhallowed privy. 'Oh, Jesus.' I straddled and piddled straight onto the vile, contaminated floor, unable, refusing, to go one step further and do the more conventional thing in a porcelain bowl that was filthy.

Back in the sitting room (if you could call it that) I gingerly cleared a space for myself on one of the chairs, and sat down. Curved Dare was still blasting out its weird mix of strange, ghostly melodies, and after partaking of the weed I felt truly bombed, and truly freaked. If Andy and Bruce hadn't been with me there was no way I'd have stayed in this creepy place on my own. Every now and then I'd catch a glimpse of Miss Haversham staring at me, she was watching my every move; I could feel her dead eyes piercing into my thoughts. And the Bogey Man was in on the act too, ready to jump out of the fireplace, rip my brain out and gobble the grey matter all up for breakfast (or tea, rather, as it was late afternoon). I wanted to run out of the house, down the stone steps, into the sunlight, and fly away with the eagles. But I didn't. Instead, I partook of another joint and made myself even more paranoid. As you do.

'Anyone for tea?' Bruce, who'd been having a poke around the black, sooty, squalid kitchen, popped his head round the door. 'I've found three quite cleanish cups, so what do you say?' I could barely speak but managed a nod. Andy, sitting cross-legged on the floor, beating his hands on a book in rhythm to the music, mumbled that, 'Aye,' he was up for a cuppa, too.

While waiting for the old pot to boil on top of the wood burning stove (the whole process from lighting to pouring took almost half an hour) Andy, who was pretty much out of it himself, dragged me off for a walk round the compound.

It felt good to be back in the sunshine. Instantly the gloomy thoughts flew away with the red-winged butterflies, a never-ending, rolling wave of them, over the guava bushes they went, heading for wherever, beyond the hills, the forests, the savannahs and the sand dunes.

We wandered round to the back of the house where a small herd of village goats were dining on the hibiscus. Their minders, three little boys each with one little stick, squatted in the cropped grass under the shade of a cotton tree. They smiled and giggled, and we smiled and giggled back. Then we continued on our way, back to the front, and sat on a steep outcrop overlooking the plateau, perusing the magnificent vista before us, listening to the silence, taking in the scent of dust and dung and wild, African flowers.

I could sit here forever, I thought. Andy and I with the sky and the hills; it was the perfect combination.

'Tea's ready,' hollered Bruce from the veranda.

I didn't want to move. Certainly I didn't want to go back into that horrible house. But Andy was pulling me. 'Come on. We'll drink up and then be on our way.'

So we retraced our footsteps, along the stony path, and up the steps, gingerly avoiding the debris.

'Here.' Andy was plucking a single red rose from off the tumbling bush that formed a thick arch over the veranda. He smiled. 'For my love.'

And gently he tucked the sweet smelling flower into the wild curls of my hair.

After swigging our tea, a much needed thirst quencher, we were on our way again. Thank God. As we zig-zagged down the hill, I made a vow to myself that I'd never darken that doorstep again. Pete might be a good bloke, an ace bloke, but his house was a singularly horrible place and I was glad that we'd left it behind.

Andy and I were in the back of the lorry now, Bruce lorded it in the front with the driver. As there were no seats the both of us had to stand for pretty much the whole of the time, and it soon became obvious why Bruce had had no qualms when we suggested we do a swap. It was really difficult keeping ourselves upright, what with the bumps and the lumps, especially when the jerry can toppled and leaked all over the floor, making it very slippery. Still, we hung on and clung on to the sides of the lorry, and somehow managed to keep vertical. And whatever were our discomforts, the world around us made the difficult journey worthwhile.

At this hour of the day the sun had already dipped out of sight. The colour of the sky was changing from red to purple; up here on the plateau darkness came quickly.

As the lessening light hung over the plains, and shadows settled over the valleys, cattle made their way home, herds of them lolloping down the grassy mounds, their bells tinkling, their minders, little boys with big sticks, calling out in the vast emptiness, as they ran and tried to keep up with their charges.

Now and then we would pass through a small mountain village with streets lined with trees, and their thatched and mud houses and compounds looking neat, clean and very well kept.

Fires were lit as night came, soon the rolling hills were dotted with twinkling lights that made it seem like all the stars in the sky had fallen to earth. Except when you looked up, they were still there, the Plough, the Bear, shining away while a white moon sailed over and took its place in amongst them. If it wasn't for the oil leak, and us slipping and sliding, I reckon this was the best bit of our journey so far.

We reached the small town of Gembu at around eight. The plan was we head for Steve's place, the Canadian volunteer who was yet another Forester. Certainly Gembu was full of trees, tall, pine like ones all along the side of the road and climbing up the slopes. If you sniffed, there was definitely an Alpine waft in the air.

We drove through the town. It was a tidy little place. There was none of the squalor, or the rubbish, or the penetrating stench of vaporizing urine and human excreta as you would expect to find in the rest of urban Nigeria. I'd have been quite happy to live here myself.

We stopped briefly and purchased more dog meat on sticks, and some warm, sticky buns, and partook of a couple of beers, sitting on a rickety wooden bench outside a small bar, with mud walls and mud floors, plus the usual gawpers crowding around us, amazed at our presence in their neck of the African wilderness.

Then we hit the road again for the last part of our journey.

Out of the town, we were now going down a very steep track, and I mean steep, the lorry was all but standing on its nose, and Andy and I having a whale of a time in the back, what with the oil and our vertical vehicle. Still, at last Steve's house all lit up like a small lantern in the sky, came into view a hundred or so yards away up a hill. Naturally, we were expecting door to door service but we hadn't even begun the climb when the driver suddenly braked. Andy and I shot forward and almost flew out the back of the lorry.

We yelled out various swear words, as we picked ourselves up.

Switching off the engine, the driver opened his door and got out. Bruce did the same.

'Hey,' shouted Andy, 'why's he stopped here?'

'He claims he can't go any further,' said Bruce, shrugging.

The headlights were still on, and the three of us peered down the road. Ahead we could see the silhouettes of far away crags but there weren't any obstacles blocking our immediate path, the way forward looked pretty clear.'

'Hey, why you no go further?' bawled Andy, as our driver disappeared into a clump of bushes and let loose a torrent that sounded like raindrops on leaves.

'No can go more,' explained our man, meandering his way back with a fag in his hand. 'The road done stop here.'

'What you mean?' Andy jumped out of the lorry, and went off to inspect, unconvinced. He followed the beam of the headlights to their end and then was swallowed up in the dark. 'Oh, fuck,' came the shrill cry. 'Oh, Jesus Christ!'

'What,' I shouted. But Andy didn't answer. There was just an empty silence that hung dangerously in the air. 'My God, something's happened to Andy.'

I was out of that lorry and off, with Bruce close behind, hurtling head on down the strip of light and into the blackness. Along with my legs, my mind was racing. Lord knows what we'd find. A pride of lions? A pack of hyenas? He's been bitten by a bloody snake. Oh, my God, how will I cope? I've never seen a dead body of a loved one before.

'Take it easy, both of you, there's a bit of a drop there, just in front of you,' a smooth voice said in the dark.

'What!' we screamed, stopping that instant.

Readjusting our eyes, we could just make out Andy. He was sitting down, swinging his legs, smoking a fag. Meanwhile a huge

African moon was edging its way from behind the silhouette of hills, bathing us, and the world, in a silvery light as if a celestial being had just flicked on a switch.

'Fucking hell!' Bruce screamed.

'Oh, my God,' I cried.

And more of the same.

We were inches from space. Standing on the edge of a cliff. One step further and we'd be flying. The fires burning in the village below us looked to be a long, long way away. Several hundred feet to be exact.

'Mmm,' muttered Bruce, staring down at the void. 'I see what the driver meant.'

CHAPTER 6

New Year's Eve 1973

We made our weary way up the steep little path. Crickets whirred, as always, bats flitted, nocturnal birds cooed, and there was a weird trilling sound coming from somewhere high up in the trees.

'Frogs,' answered Andy, when I asked.

'What? Frogs? Up there?' *How very strange.*

Finally reaching the bottom veranda step, the boys, who were ahead of me by several paces, sat and patiently waited as I huffed and I puffed and lugged my old bag up the slope. God, it truly seemed to get heavier and heavier. And for the first time in my life I wished I didn't smoke. Until, of course, I reached the top. My first words, after I got my breath back, were, 'Bloody hell, I could do with a fag.'

Above us, up eight or so steps and across the large wood-slatted veranda, there was a pool of light coming from an open door and we could hear the murmur of voices from inside the house. Those inside must have heard our dulcet tones too because someone appeared on the top step and blasted us with a torch beam.

'Hey! Andy. Bruce. I figured it might be you,' came a cheerful Canadian drawl. 'Get your goddamn arses up here.'

We duly obeyed. As I clambered up the wooden steps, still last in the line, I did wonder if Andy would go all moody again and do his 'I'm ignoring you, Janni' party trick but my worries were quickly dispelled when I reached the top. Having shook hands with his mate and shared a few pleasantries, Andy pulled me close and said, rather proudly, 'Steve, I'd like you to meet my wee lassie, Janni.'

'Hi,' we both smiled, taking each other in. Steve seemed nice. A handsome kind of guy in a Canadian lumberjack kind of way, tall, about six foot three, tartan shirt, blue jeans, desert boots, and brown wavy hair. And very muscular, the lumps on the top of his arms were bursting out of his shirtsleeves.

'I kinda reckon you must be the famous little Gombe lady I've heard a lot about already,' twinkled Steve, waving a mosquito away from the side of his head with his torch.

I looked at him, pleasantly surprised. 'You've heard of me? Blimey.'

Steve chuckled. 'The bush telegraph is kinda an amazing thing, don't you think?'

'Yeah,' I agreed, wrinkling my nose slightly, considering the news of my fame. 'Who was it that told you about me?' One of my million admirers.

'Lizzie. She was here for Christmas.'

A little deflated, I managed a laugh. 'Good or bad?'

Steve, being a very nice bloke, picked up my bag. 'A bit of both, honey.' And winked. 'Come on you guys,' he said to us all. Then lead the way into his dear little house.

It was lovely.

Warm and cosy. With a big open fireplace, and the room pungent with the sweet smell of burning pine logs as they crackled away (it gets pretty chilly high up on the plateau at night). Lit hurricane lamps hung from the ceiling, and there were four large, comfy looking chairs covered in bright, handmade native blankets. Along the mantelpiece Christmas cards jostled for place, loads of them, snowmen, robins, holly et al, and tinsel and baubles festooned around the walls.

What a difference from Pete's house. I felt like I'd stumbled upon a log cabin tucked away in the mountains. That if I went and looked back outside, there might be snow on the slopes, and a twirl of white flakes falling through the pines. The African savannah seemed a long way away and I could see why so many people wanted to spend their Christmas's here. It was just perfect.

And to prove my point, there were two other visitors aside from us this very night. They were sitting around a long wooden table at the far end of the room, eating their dinner, meat casserole served with rice and peas. Putting down knives and forks, and wiping their mouths with paper napkins, they stood up as we made our entrance. Steve introduced us. Sarah and Sue from Kano. It was more handshakes all round.

'Pleased to meet you,' I said, smiling, even though I wasn't really. They looked so incredibly boring; everything about them, their clothes, hairstyles, the way they both pushed back their tortoiseshell glasses, screamed bland, bland, bland.

Still, at least I wasn't up against any female competition.

'Don't let your dinner get cold on account of us,' said Bruce magnanimously, pulling up a chair and sitting himself down at an

185

empty space at the table.

'If you're sure,' said the taller of the two, apologetically.

'You won't think us rude,' said the smaller of the two, apologetically.

We assured them we were and we wouldn't.

Happily, the girls sat back in their seats and returned to their meal. Andy and I planted ourselves either side of Bruce. 'Do you two mind sleeping in the office?' Steve asked, still with my bag in his clutches.

'No, doesn't bother me,' shrugged Andy. 'A bed's a bed.'

'No it isn't,' laughed Steve. 'You'll be sleeping on the floor.' He looked at me. 'Is that okay with you?'

Anything was okay with me as long as Andy was close by my side. I nodded. 'Yeah, that's fine.'

'Great.' Steve hauled Andy's massive rucksack with his free hand, and trundled off, out of a back door with both our bags.

The girls were still eating.

'Were you here for Christmas?' I asked, not because I was interested in their festivity arrangements, it was just that I couldn't think of anything better to say.

No, they said, pushing back their tortoiseshell specs in a synchronised movement, they'd spent the Yuletide in Baissa. 'We only got here today ourselves,' tittered Sarah. Or was it Sue?

'Did you have a good journey down?' enquired Bruce, lighting up.

An expression of horror, like someone had died, came over the girls' faces. And the specs went back that far they almost turned into Alice bands.

'Er… would you mind?'

'Mind what?' smiled Bruce, as he blew out a smoke ring.

Both girls had another stab at their glassy eyes. Gave a tremulous glance at the wispy circle hovering over Bruce like a halo. 'Not smoking,' squeaked Sue, her cheeks a little flushed.

'Just while we're eating,' explained Sarah, quite beetroot herself.

Bruce raised an eye. Perused the fag in his hand. 'Oh, sorry.' He smiled pleasantly. 'Didn't think,' and went off in search of an ashtray.

Meanwhile, our host had returned.

'Are you guys hungry?'

Andy, stifling a yawn, shook his head. 'No, cheers, we had

something in town before we got here.'

'Shame, there's plenty of casserole left. What about you two?' He glanced at me and Bruce, lifting the lid off an earthenware pot that sat on the table, and gave what was in it a stir as way of enticement. It worked. The stew smelt and looked bloody delicious. For a brief second I thought about asking where the toilets were, so I could puke up my earlier meal and commence with the feasting all over again. But I fought off the temptation, too bloody tired for all that malarkey. 'No thanks,' I said, slapping a mosquito off the back of my arm. I had to wipe the bug's corpse off my hand, using my trousers.

'Me neither.' Bruce patted his stomach, and chuckled. 'I've got half a dog in here and I reckon that'll do me for the night.'

The two girls blanched. I caught Andy's eye. We smirked.

'Well, if you're sure.' Steve swept up the pot, and an empty plate, his, he'd already finished eating before we'd arrived. 'Can I get you guys a drink then?' It was beers all round, well for the three of us; the girls were silently nibbling their dinner, a little green around the gills, and were slow to put in their order. Still coming to terms with Bruce's rather unsavoury revelation that he ate dogs, I supposed. 'What about you girls? Fancy a beer?' Steve smiled at them both.

They passed. 'Just water will do, thanks,' said Sarah, chewing slowly, and covering her mouth delicately with her hand.

'Sure?' She nodded.

He looked at Sue.

'Water will do for me, too.'

'Sure?'

'Absolutely.'

Steve disappeared. We heard the familiar clatter of a plate being dumped in a sink, a fridge being opened, and the clunk, chink sound of glass bottles. The girls carried on eating, determined to clear their platters clean, despite everything. I suspect it had something to do with Africa, and famine, and a social conscience? They seemed the sort.

Andy got up from the table and lazily ambled over to Bruce who was warming himself in front of the fire. The two boys murmured amongst themselves, checking out and flicking through the books on the bookshelves. I tilted my chair back and had a stretch, and observed a fat rhino beetle droning around Sarah's head, too weary to do anything else.

Back in the room, Steve put the beers down on the table, disappeared again, and reappeared with a jug of water, some glasses, and a bottle opener. Off came the caps, Andy and Bruce wandered back to the table and sat down, the girls poured themselves each a tumbler full of water, and they daintily sipped while we swigged from the bottles.

I smiled at the taller one of the two girls.

'What do you do in Kano, Sarah?'

'Teach.'

'Fancy that. What subjects?'

'English and Sciences.'

'Interesting.'

All round nicotine withdrawal had set in. The three of us were fidgeting, I with the pepper pot, Andy with a napkin, and Bruce removing wax from his ear.

'Do you teach as well, Sue?'

'I do.'

'What?'

'Maths and PE.'

An artificial beam shot her way. 'Not my favourite subjects, I must admit.' I straightened my rounded, aching shoulders and went back to my fiddle with the pepper pot. Steve and the boys chattered on about absent friends they all knew.

Finally the last pea was swallowed, the one remaining grain of rice gone, the plates taken back into the kitchen.

'Do you mind if we smoke, now?' I looked sweetly at both girls.

'No, do,' chirped Sarah, fluttering her hand, already preparing herself for the inevitable smoke swirl.

'Please go ahead,' nodded Sue, coughing a little, placing a delicate fist over her mouth.

Gratefully, and with much pomp and ceremony, the fags came out and matches were struck. And in a haze of smoke, I continued to make polite conversation, as you do.

'How long have you been in Nigeria, Sarah?'

'Six months.'

'Like it?'

'Love it.'

'And, what do you do, Janni?' Sue, who was filling up her glass with more water, smiled at me pleasantly.

I shot a look at Andy. He was deep in conversation with the

boys, something about Scottish footballers being better players than English ones. Bruce, it seemed, wasn't that convinced. He was laughing, a snorting sort of laugh. I turned back to the girls.

'Nothing, really.'

The girls looked bemused. I explained – kept the story simple. Eighteen. Gap year. Met Andy. Travelling around.

'And what are your plans at the end of all this, Janni?' Sarah took a sip from her glass.

I lifted up my bottle, and had a swig. 'Plans? Difficult to say.' And diverted the subject. 'Have you two been to Maiduguri?'

They hadn't. But they had heard it was a veritable oasis. 'Lots of tree planting, I hear,' piped up Sue.

'I gather they make the place look very pretty,' added Sarah.

I nodded. 'They most certainly do.'

And that's how it was for the next fifteen minutes or so, me and the girls blabbering on about scenic things, Andy, Bruce and Steve in animated discussion about boring old football.

It was all pretty tame until Andy got out his dope tin and commenced with the ritual. The girls observed, and seemed a little perplexed, a little unsure. Then something connected. Sue put one hand to her throat as if she was about to strangle herself. Sarah, wide-eyed and horrified, pushed back her tortoiseshell glasses and shot a 'oh, my God' look at her friend.

The boys and I pretended not to notice.

The joint went round the table.

My turn, I took a deep, deep puff, expelled the smoke, and took another. An invisible wave washed over my brain and the feeling was good. One more drag and with a gleam of mischief, I passed it to Sarah. Her eyes popped out and practically bounced off her specs.

'I don't, thanks,' she said aghast, with an emphatic wave of her hands and an emphatic shake of her head.

'Sure?'

'Absolutely.'

I leant across to her mate, enticingly waved the smouldering scrap of weed in front of the large glasses. 'Gosh, no,' she practically screamed. 'Oh, gosh, no.'

'Sure?'

'Certain.'

See what I mean? They were a couple of drips.

Still, the boys and I got nicely stuck in.

189

All life's niggles and stresses were washed away on a tide of alcohol. Either that or they disappeared in a puff of grey smoke.

Steve put on a tape. 'Stairway to Heaven.'

Perfect.

I got up from the table and ambled over to one of the comfy chairs and threw myself in it. Andy moved to the fireplace, selected a log from the stack, chucked it on then settled into the chair next to mine. We watched as the flames burst into life once more and appeared to dance in rhythm to the music.

I don't remember the girls saying goodnight. One minute they were there, the next they were gone. Meanwhile we carried on celebrating the eve before New Year's Eve well into the night. More beer was drunk and more joints were rolled. A rosy haze settled over us all.

But over me and Andy especially.

Lying back against the brightly coloured blankets, the tilly lamps twinkling away, the fire crackling and warming our toes, the music lulling us into a dreamy existence.

Talking with Bruce and Steve but not really talking, not really listening, our eyes on each other, as if the only people in the whole wide world were the two of us, in this room.

An inexplicable feeling of contentment, of serenity, settled over me.

This, I thought, is how it should always be.

Especially when Andy got up, saying, 'I'll be back in a mo,' and headed out of the house, returning with his little book of poems some minutes later. Settling himself down on the floor, legs crossed, up close so I could touch and caress him, he read to me, verse upon verse, lingering over a line that meant something special, '.....*and I will love thee still, my dear, 'till all the seas gang dry'*, smiling, that, oh so, sensual smile. There was a quickening of the pulse, and the butterflies in my tummy went wild.

I loved him, I realised, more than ever, if that was at all possible.

Finally, Andy closed up his book, chucked the butt of his cigarette into the dying embers, took hold of my hand, and whispered, 'Let's go to bed.'

Our arms filled with cushions, we left the boys still drinking, still smoking, and headed off, nay staggered off, to Steve's office, a little building just below the main house. Before we'd even thrown the sleeping bag over our makeshift mattress, before we'd even

190

undressed, in the light of the hurricane lamp, we were away, way, way above this planet in a place of our very own making.

The stuff of my dreams.

Until afterwards, lying together on the floor, and I in his arms thinking niggardly thoughts. Out of the darkness they suddenly came.

How could that be? Everything was perfect.

Wasn't it?

'Andy,' I whispered. My mind swirling in alcohol and my brain clogged up with dope.

'What?' he murmured, half awake, his face buried deep in a bright red and brown, striped cushion.

'We will always be together, you and me, won't we?'

He moved his head, ever so slightly. 'Och, Janni what a question.'

But suddenly I'm scared. Memories of recent times all flooded back, the threats threatening to drown me. 'We will, won't we?'

Quietly he groaned. 'Go to sleep.'

But I needed to know and gently I shook him. 'Will we?'

He opened a blue eye. The moon outside beamed through, a shaft of light from window to face. He looked at me for a second. The eye closed.

'Night, night,' was all that he said.

I awoke early. By my watch it was not yet six. Andy was still sleeping, on his back, golden hair spread over the pillow like the storm in the song.

My head all fuzzy, I needed fresh air, a drink, and a fag. Slipping out of bed, I silently dressed, and made my way out of the little building, across the path to the back of the house. Up the steps, into the quiet sitting room, last night's celebrations, empty bottles and full ashtrays, still on the table and on the floor. There was no sign of Steve's houseboy. Perhaps Steve was like Pete and didn't have one. Anyway, who cared?

On I went. Through into the kitchen, lit the primus stove, filled the kettle with water from the filter, and had my first fag of the day. Smoked, and searched round for the coffee jar, found it in one of the cupboards, spooned some into a mug, added two lumps of sugar, located the milk jug in a rickety old paraffin fridge that stood in the corner, and carried on puffing while waiting for the kettle to boil.

A lizard with a bright orange head shot out from under the

wooden workbench, it scuttled along the floor, stopped abruptly and looked over its shoulder, up, down, up down, doing manic press-ups while watching me, watching it. Then it was off again, across the wooden flooring, and out through a crack under the door.

Five minutes later I was on the veranda.

Sitting in a deckchair, coffee by my side, smoking my second cigarette. The dawn chorus had already warmed up, from every tree birds whistled and called to each other and the branches and leaves stirred in the still of the air, as they flew and flitted about. One came down, a sunbird, I think, and perched on a flowering shrub that grew up by the side of the house, its long, curved beak buried in the pink fragrance. It sipped deeply of the nectar and paid no attention to me, but then I coughed, as you do in the morning, and instantly it vanished in a blur of emerald and purple feathers.

I leant back in my chair and perused the vista before me. From here I could see the plateau, unbroken, infinite. The mists were already clearing and the morning sun, like a round bowl of melted honey, peeped over the edge of the escarpment. From somewhere far away, the crackled call of a village rooster echoed faintly.

I shivered. At this time of day it was still very cool. I went inside, pulled one of the blankets from off one of the chairs, and put it around me. And returned to my seat to smoke and drink and watch and think.

Random thoughts.

About me and about Andy. About me *and* Andy. Together forever? Or what? And my parents? Okay or not? You see, even in the most amazing places, in the most beautiful settings, I was still getting bogged down with my regular hang-ups.

Lost in my internal mishmash, a movement from behind made me jump. I turned my head. Andy stood with a bowl in his one hand and a cup of coffee in his other.

I smiled. 'Morning,' I said brightly, and moved forward in my chair, expectant, waiting for his warm, loving embrace.

But there was no kiss, no hug, no sharing of tender words, nothing to indicate that we two people had spent the previous night in and out of each other's souls. Andy didn't even smile. He had that look about him again. Unreachable. Distant.

I pretended not to notice.

'Beautiful, isn't it?' Throwing the blanket off me, I got out of my chair and swept my arms at all that was before us.

'Aye,' he nodded, not really looking at anything very much,

and that included me. Instead he plopped himself down on a campstool, placed his coffee mug on the floor, and absent-mindedly began spooning cornflakes into his mouth.

'Sleep alright?' I asked, in an effort to get him talking.

He shrugged. 'Not bad.'

'How's your head? Mine's a bit rough, I can tell you.' And laughed, as if what I was saying was a jolly old thing.

Andy shrugged again. 'I feel okay.' That said he placed his bowl on the floor and lifted his mug of coffee to his mouth. Silently, moodily, he sipped, and stared out into the distance.

My centre dropped out of me and fell away, my composure evaporated into the early morning mists.

It was going to be another one of those days.

Totally pissed off, I made my exit, couldn't be arsed to throw myself at his merciless feet, and headed back into the house and to the kitchen where I found Sarah and Sue making porridge. One was stirring, the other was pouring in the milk.

'Hi,' I smiled, trying to sound bright. The last thing I wanted was to have these two muffins picking up on my despair and feeling sorry for me.

'Morning,' they trilled.

'That looks good,' I commented. Sarah had set the milk jug down and was now dolloping a tablespoon of golden syrup into the mush. Sue carried on stirring.

'Want some?' one of them asked.

I thought about it. Porridge or cornflakes? Decisions, decisions. 'Yeah, don't mind if I do.'

Three bowls were duly taken out of the cupboard, set out in a neat line, a final stir, the ladle sought, and et voila, the porridge went from pan into bowls. A steaming trio of oats and syrup and milk.

'I've made a pot of tea. Fancy a cup?' Sue asked, giving a teaspoon a wipe with a dish towel.

'Cheers. A cup of tea would be lovely.' I picked up my bowl. Fuck, it was hot. Quickly I put it down. Sue used her towel and Sarah found a tray. Very cleverly, hot bowls were placed on tray via the cloth. Tea was poured, mugs and a saucer of sugar lumps went alongside the porridge, three large spoons taken out of the cutlery drawer, and that was it. Breakfast was ready.

'Come on,' smiled Mother Sarah, picking up the full to overloaded wooden palette, and Sue and I followed.

We sat at the table, but first we cleared it of last night's debris, me emptying the ashtrays, Sue removing the glasses and bottles, and Sarah wiping down. Then we tucked in.

'This is delicious,' I said, plopping a spoonful of porridge into my mouth. And it was, sweet, and gooey, and warm. I glanced over at Andy who was still out on the veranda, doing what I had been doing half an hour earlier, smoking and drinking and watching and thinking. About what? Oh, the fuck knows.

'So,' I took a sip of my tea, 'what plans have you two got for today?' I said this loudly, hoping to stir Andy into action, hoping he would turn around and draw himself in. It was pointless. He was only a door and half a veranda away but he might as well have been on the other side of the planet. Deliberately he kept his back to us, deliberately he ignored us.

Not today. Not again. Please.

Sarah was trilling away, something about having decided to catch the Forestry lorry and spending tonight in Serti. '...tomorrow we'll head back for Yola and then make our way to Gombe, and then Kano. We're due back at school on the sixth.'

'Gombe?' I dragged my eyes away from Andy's back. 'You're going to Gombe, did you say?'

They both nodded. 'Yes, we've a good friend who lives there. Ian. You probably know him.' That figured, 'born agains', of course. Now it all really made sense.

I smiled, despite the moaning inside. 'Yeah, sure I know Ian.' I took another mouthful of porridge. 'And Pru.'

Well, you'd think the girls had just had an orgasm!

Delightedly they wiggled in their chairs, beaming, clapping, oh, what pure, utter joy! 'Pru. Gosh, you know Pru. Isn't she lovely? Such a warm human being,' gushed Sue.

'She certainly is,' I agreed, meaning it.

'And how wonderful that she and Ian are getting married,' Sarah chirped. 'You couldn't get two people more suited.'

'Absolutely,' I agreed, meaning it. Definitely meaning it. I spooned in another dollop of porridge. 'Actually, you couldn't do me a favour, could you, you two?' I looked at them both.

'Sure,' they said, before I'd even told them what it was. As a friend of Pru and Ian's they were obviously willing to do anything I asked. Last night's drinking and drugging now a thing of the past.

'Well,' I warmed my hands around my tea cup, 'if you're going through Gombe you wouldn't mind passing on a note to my Mum and Dad, would you?'

'Oh, of course not,' they beamed.

I took a sip. 'You could give it to Ian. He'll make sure it gets to them.'

'No, no.' Sarah smiled, fluttering her hands, as if waving away invisible smoke. 'We'll give it to your parents in person. We'd be delighted.'

That wasn't a bad idea. Two drips like them, marching up to my house, sitting down with my parents, assuring Mum and Dad that I was perfectly alright, was just the thing to appease my guilt and please the mater and pater. 'What a nice couple of girls,' Mum would say. And Dad couldn't disagree. 'If she's hanging around with people like them, then we've got absolutely nothing to worry about.'

See what I mean?

So off I went in search of pen and paper. I didn't have too far to look; there was a pad and biro staring at me from a bookshelf. Hastily I scribbled my note.

Darling Mum and Dad.

Yes, I'm still alive and having a fantastic time!!!!! I'm here in Mambilla and it's beautiful. Saw a lovely horse yesterday, Dad (he'd like that), *a wild mountain pony, amazing! Reminded me of Smokey. We're spending New Year here in Gembu and then moving onto the Cameroon the day after tomorrow. Andy's well and sends his love. I hope you're both fine, and did you have a good Christmas? And did Lizzie tell you she saw me in Yola? It was lovely to see her again.*

Anyway, must dash as the two girls, Sarah and Sue, are off now (aren't they nice girls?) and will be giving you this note.

Happy New Year – and lots, and lots of love and kisses – Jannixxxxxxxxx

That done, I folded the paper, hunted round for an envelope, found one (already used from the waste paper bin), popped the note in, tucked the flap, scribbled out 'T*o Steve'*, put *'To Mum and Dad'*, and handed the completed article over to the girls. A job well done!

Meanwhile, Andy had wandered back into in the house.

As had Bruce and Steve.

'Morning, girls,' chirped our host, rubbing his sleep-filled eyes. 'See you've found the breakfast stuff. Good.' Blearily he turned to Bruce. 'Name your poison. Coffee? Tea?'

Looking decidedly nauseous, Bruce muttered, 'Coffee,' and emitted a burp. Throwing himself into one of the comfy chairs – now minus the cushions, so not comfy at all – he gingerly lit up a fag, while Steve went off to do the business with the kettle. 'Man, my head hurts,' groaned Bruce, taking off his glasses and massaging his temples.

'I've got some aspirin,' announced Sue, rummaging about in her handbag.

'I'll get you a glass of water,' said Sarah, and she was up from the table and off to the tap in the kitchen.

'Hey, VIP treatment, Brucie baby,' chuckled Andy. He drew out a dining-table chair and sat himself down, putting his feet up on the one opposite. He was smiling – not directly at me but it was still a good sign. The black mood must have passed. 'Mind if I smoke?' he asked Sue as she did her Florence Nightingale bit with the tablets. A flicker of a frown came up on Sue's face. Andy leaned in, a mock, innocent expression on his. 'Just ordinary cigarettes,' he laughed, glancing at me with a twinkle in his eye. Semi-reassured, Sue, being a benevolent Christian girl, gave the okay. Andy got out his tin and began to fashion a roll-up. 'Want one?'

He was looking directly at me now. Warmth had replaced cold. Relieved, I tipped back my chair, holding my tea as if for balance. 'Yeah, please.' Adding, for conversation sake, to keep our new-found communication rolling, 'Did you know the girls are going through Gombe on their way back to Kano?'

'Oh, yeah.' Andy licked the gummy bit on the Rizla, pressed it down, and passed the finished product over. At the same time Sarah reappeared with a glass of water and handed it to Bruce.

'Cheers,' he said grimly, his expression pained; sweeping up both tablets, they and the water were chucked down his throat. Another burp followed.

'I've written Mum and Dad a letter,' I continued, lighting up. A puff; a cloud of smoke floated out of my mouth. Sue, across the table, coughed absently. Sarah waved a hand. Andy was now rolling himself a cigarette. Focused on the job, he didn't respond to my tit-bit of news.

I took another puff.

Steve emerged from out of the kitchen carrying the large wooden tray loaded up with mugs, a pot of coffee, milk, sugar, a plate with a pile of toast, some marmalade in a jar and a dish full of butter.

'Hey,' he drawled, setting the whole lot down, 'get your teeth into this, Bruce. It'll make you feel a whole lot better.' Bruce declined and just went for the coffee. He was still looking very green around the gills.

I took another drag. And continued with my tale. 'Sarah and Sue have said they'll hand deliver the letter to Mum and Dad, Andy.'

A moment of silence.

Andy drew deeply.

The girls had now moved away from the smoke and were across the room, in comfy the chairs, still minus the cushions of course, so they were actually sitting on hard, wooden bases. 'It'll be a pleasure,' chirped up Sue. 'If your parents are anything like mine, they'll be thrilled to hear you're doing okay.'

Sarah nodded. 'My parents were totally freaked when I told them I was coming out to Africa.' She gave an empathic sigh. 'It's understandable. But I write to them every week, sometimes twice, and that keeps them happy.' She shifted in her chair, trying to get comfy. 'So, when was the last time you saw your parents, Janni?'

'The last time?' I echoed hollowly, waving away a non-existent insect. 'Um…'

Andy interrupted. He was looking over at the girls. 'So, when are you leaving?'

'Today.'

'Today.' Thoughtfully Andy nodded, picked up his coffee cup and took a sip. Put it down, spooned in a lump of sugar and stirred the brown liquid absently.

Oh, God what was he thinking? Nervously I drew on my fag, and internally kicked myself for having even mentioned the bloody subject.

'Anyone for more coffee?' asked Steve, happily oblivious, as he bit into toast. The thick orange marmalade oozed over the side and plopped onto the table. Bruce eyed the splodge and gingerly got up from out of his chair.

'I think I need the toilet,' he belched, and made a quick exit.

I felt pretty sick myself. Me and my bloody big mouth.

But then Andy suddenly laughed. 'That'll teach the poor fucker.' The clouds that were threatening dispersed. He handed his cup over to Steve who was pouring. 'I'll have another one.' Steve obliged. Picking up the milk jug, Andy dribbled in a bit of milk and added two lumps of sugar. 'So,' he turned to me, and there was a smile on his face as he stirred, 'how's about me and my wee lassie going for an explore? Take the high road up into the hills and see what we can find.'

Instantly my body relaxed. 'Yeah, I'd love to,' I grinned, jumping up.

We were in for a nice easy day, after all.

Before we left, Steve suggested steak and kidney pie for lunch so Andy and I volunteered to go and buy the offal in town.

We were a happy twosome as we made our way down the wooded slope to the main road we'd travelled along the night before. Above us cotton-wool clouds drifted lazily across the blue of the sky, and a gentle breeze ruffled the feathery pine leaves as we ambled hand in hand in amongst squares of shimmering sunlight.

'Look!' Andy pointed to a little group of black and grey striped mongooses who were having a bit of a game around a tree trunk. When they saw us they scampered away, but not too far, just enough distance between them and us to feel safe, then they stood up on their hind legs and stared in astonishment. 'What sweet little things,' I laughingly cooed.

'Yeah,' Andy agreed. 'They are, until...' he chuckled, '...they bite you.'

I giggled, looked at him coyly. 'Why would they want to bite me?'

'Because...' Andy swung me around, hands on shoulders he nuzzled his face in my neck, and nibbled, '...you taste so very, very sweet.'

'And so do you,' and I nibbled him back.

We were still laughing, still playing around with each other when we reached the grassy mound where, a few feet below, was the road.

Andy jumped down. 'Come on.' He had his arms open wide. I came and he caught me. We kissed while a pepper-bird warbled cheerfully from a branch in a tree. It was a deep kind of kiss, the kind of kiss that fizzled through us both, and lingered even when our lips had parted.

The kiss still glowed as we ran up the road. We were singing now, a medley of songs at the top of our voices. They were pretty daft songs, the ones we'd never dare sing anywhere else.

'There was a soldier/A Scottish soldier...' And, 'My Bonny lies over the ocean/My bonny lies over the sea...' And, 'Jean, Jean the girl from Aberdeen...'

See what I mean?

The kiss still tingled as we huffed and we panted our way to the top of a hill, the one that loomed high over the small town of Gembu.

Andy, of course, was first to reach the summit.

'Come on, come on.' Andy stood on a large, grey rock and clapped his hands. He was grinning from ear to ear. 'You can do it. You can do it. Just one more step.' Exhausted, I reached him, and collapsed, on the warm stone mound, my head resting on his desert-booted feet. 'Fuck,' I groaned, sweat trickling, 'you sound just like my gym teacher.'

Andy bent down, lifted me up, his hands moved back through my thick mane of hair. 'But does your gym teacher kiss you like this?' Pulling me gently, nose next to nose, mouth onto mouth, we melted into each other, wound around one another, and smiled.

My eyes glistened. 'I love you,' I said.

There was a pause. It hung in the still of the air.

I said the words again. 'I love you so very, very much, Andy.'

Andy closed his eyes.

A heart beat.

He opened them again. Gently he smiled. 'Show me how much,' he whispered, pulling me down.

On top of the world, and we soared even higher, flying with the eagles like two fragments drifting in the wind.

Afterwards, we rested a while on our grassy knoll, up close, arms around each other, the sun warm on our backs, looking through half-closed eyes at the beauty and wildness of Africa.

It was a brief moment in time, but one I would remember forever.

In the still heat of the day, we clambered back down the hill and ambled our way into town. It looked even prettier in daylight. Purple bushes of bougainvillea grew wild amongst the mud-thatched buildings, along with bananas and plantains and other green, leafy plants. Healthy looking urchins played on the vehicle free streets, playing chase with the goats and the chickens.

Of course, as we walked, we met the usual suspects. There were the old men with cracked, wizened faces taking it easy under a tree, a young lad squatting by the roadside having a much needed pee, and women in bright cloths balancing calabash pots filled with fruits and vegetables on their heads. Others were carrying their produce on their backs by way of a large, straw-woven basket that had shoulder straps just like a rucksack.

'Blimey,' I commented, 'that's a clever way of carting your loads about, isn't it?'

Andy agreed. 'Aye, reckon it is. You could do with something like that, couldn't you, better than that bloody old bag of yours.'

My face broke into smiles. 'Cor, yeah. What a brilliant idea.' No more lugging, no more huffing and puffing. The ultimate accessory. A basket-weave backpack.

'Come on.' Andy got hold of my hand. 'Let's go and find you one.'

We headed off to the market place, it was where we were going anyway to buy the meat, but steak and kidney was no longer a priority. My bag was a must have and we immediately spotted a pile of them stacked up against a mud wall, next to a chaotic display of earthenware pots, calabash bowls and other native kitchen paraphernalia.

I was over like a shot.

'Nowa nowa?' I pointed to the baskets. Smiled, and waited expectantly.

The village mammy who sat in the dirt alongside her wares stared at me, bewilderment spread across her shiny, black face. She shook her head and scratched one of her low-hanging bosoms.

'Nowa, nowa?' I asked again, stepping over her feet, and tapping a finger on the nearest basket.

Instead of responding, instead of saying, 'That'll be five kobo, m'dear,' she turned her attention to the large crowd that, as always, had gathered round, and babbled unintelligibly to them. They laughed. So did she; her orange teeth like a bright, dental sunset in a hallucinogenic dream.

'How much you silly cow?' I said, now in English, mild irritation made worse by the flies and the heat. A trickle of sweat ran from under my left breast and made its way to my waist, and there was a large damp spot at the top of the crack of my bottom.

The mammy was still ranting and babbling. The crowd were all falling about, hysterical. Whatever my discomfort, the villagers were having a field day.

I threw my hands in the air. 'Oh, for fuck's sake, Andy.'

'She doesn't understand you,' explained Andy, laughing too. 'Y'know they don't speak Hausa round here.' He stepped forward, picked up one of the nearest baskets.

Quickly I jumped in. 'I don't want that one,' I protested. 'I want that one.' The biggest one; the one with acres and acres of room. It was right on the top of the pile. Andy had to reach up, on tiptoes, and balance himself on one leg. With bated breath, we all watched as he stretched out his arm, nearly, nearly, oh God, as one or two wobbled threatening to bring the whole lot, about thirty baskets, crashing down.

'Well done, Andy,' I screamed out in delight, as my man completed his mission, the basket mountain still as steady as a rock, and my basket clutched in his hand.

He showed it to the woman, put his other hand in his pocket and pulled out some coins.

'Ah,' nodded the women, a big orange grin on her face. The penny, or rather the kobo, had dropped. Inspecting the money, she counted it, and shook her head. The smile vanished, and she folded her enormous black arms.

'She wants more, Andy.'

'She's not getting anymore,' Andy retorted, a tad miffed. 'There's over one naira here, and I'm not paying anymore for a stupid basket.'

'I've got money,' I replied, digging deep into my pocket. No way was I going to go away empty handed. But Andy had already grabbed my arm.

'Come on.'

'Andy…'

'For fuck's sake, how long have you lived in this country?' He was pulling me. 'Trust me, this'll work.'

'Oh,' I stupidly replied, now getting the gist.

'No thanks,' we both said to the mammy, and turning our backs, we both pushed through the throng.

'Babble babble babble,' she screamed.

'Walk on,' ordered Andy.

We walked on. A hand grabbed me. A basket was shoved into my face. The mammy pointed to the coins still in Andy's hand. 'I think we have a deal,' he said smugly.

We certainly did. The basket was mine.

The steak and kidney had been bought from the usual fly-ridden meat stall, wrapped in a hundred sheets of newspaper so the blood didn't seep out and stain my brand new shiny basket. Some fruit, bananas, a couple of pomegranates, a handful of guavas, were added. I carried my shopping on my back just like the locals. And they loved it, laughing and pointing, especially the ladies who thought it were great that I was one of them.

Ambling our way back to Steve's, we held hands, our feet crunching on dried twigs as we climbed up the hill. It was cooler up here, the air balmy and warm, the light clear as honey, slanting through trees.

We found Bruce having a quiet moment on the veranda, his big Fulani hat pulled over his face, gentle snores wafting their way out from somewhere beneath the matted rim. 'Don't,' I said, laughing. Andy was leaning over Bruce, hand at the ready.

'What the fuck!' screamed Bruce, eyes bolting wide open.

He was up and out of his chair.

'Hey, man, stay cool. It's only us,' soothed Andy, as the terrified man desperately looked around for his glasses. He was, you see, as blind as a bat.

I found the specs lying at the back of his chair. 'Here.' Carefully I placed them in his hand.

'Cheers,' grumbled Bruce, and put them on. Wanting a cigarette, he removed a crushed pack from his trouser pocket. He gave me one, Andy declined; Bruce felt his shirt pocket for a match. A strike and a flair; we both lit up and puffed.

'Where's the girls and Steve?' I asked, peeping into the sitting room where there was no sign of life, only coolness and quiet. Bruce was back in his chair. Andy plonked himself in another and was rolling a joint. I walked across the veranda, removed my basket and sat myself down.

'Steve's taken them to the lorry park,' answered Bruce, exhaling smoke. He was back to his calm, good-natured self.

'They've gone already?'

'Yeah.'

'We didn't even say goodbye.' Not that I cared.

'Like ships in the night,' mused Andy, flicking open his Zippo, and putting spliff to the flame.

'Where'd you get the basket?' asked Bruce, with a yawn, as I retrieved a banana from its inner sanctums, and began peeling.

I grinned. 'Great, isn't it? Andy bought it for me in the market. All the women have one round here. I'm going to throw away my bag and use it as a rucksack, what do you reckon?'

'Anything, Janni,' stated Bruce, smoke rolling out of his mouth, smiling, 'is better than that worn out old bag of yours, wouldn't you say?'

Happily I nodded. And took a bite of banana.

I ended up preparing lunch all by myself.

Steve, who'd returned from dropping the girls off at the lorry park, didn't come back entirely empty handed. In the back of his Land Rover was a bath. He'd got four of his Nigerian lackeys to bring the enamel tub up the steep, little path and with much ceremony, and a hell of a lot of sweat, they plonked it down on the veranda.

'You guys couldn't do an old friend a favour?' asked Steve, pushing back his bush hat and wiping down his liquid brow with the back of his hand. The favour being that Andy and Bruce help him plumb in the bath. 'Just think,' enthused Steve, as way of encouragement, 'tonight, instead of a cold shower, we can all have a hot soak.' Meaning, we'd have to heat up water in the pans first. But there you have it. In the bush you go with the flow.

'Leave dinner to me,' I confidently declared, as the boys, armed with toolbox and plumbing stuff, followed the four local lads who were now lugging the bath along the veranda and around to the back of the house. Mimicking Jonathon's little African hum, I trotted merrily off to the kitchen with my well wrapped up goodies in my hand. Tentatively I began undoing the stained and bloodied newspaper.

'Yuck, yuck, yuck.'

The smell was foul, and the meat quite revolting. A big slab of red-black flesh complete with gristle and bone and grey ugly fat. And the kidneys? Oh, my God the kidneys, just touching them was enough to make me squirm and want to puke on the spot. If I hadn't been so keen to impress the boys, Andy especially, I'd have chucked all of it out with the rubbish and made everyone beans on toast.

But no, a girl has to do what a girl has to do.

And so it was on with the job.

If only Dad could see me now, I said to myself, as I hacked and slashed and sawed my way through the slimy, fibrous, gristly, dismembered animal part. And my Mum, and Jonathon; they'd all be surprised. Despite Miss Carbunkle's Hostess Cookery classes and my 'O' level in Domestic Science, I don't think any of them had ever seen me prepare a whole meal before. This was definitely a first.

Half an hour later the dreadful deed was done, a pile of offal and a gargantuan heap of dead yuck sat on the chopping board. Blood was everywhere, on my hands, all down my T-shirt, on the floor, up the walls, and right through the kitchen. It was like there'd been a massacre.

'Right.' My eyes did a wander. 'Let's look for a cookbook.'

There was none, I searched everywhere, the cupboards, the drawers; I even had a poke about in the sitting room amongst the bookshelves.

I sighed, and lit up a fag.

And had another one before I got on with the next part of the job – making pastry.

I had a devil of a time rolling it out, it kept splitting and sticking and falling apart.

'Oh, fuck it,' I shouted, and threw down the empty beer bottle that doubled as a rolling pin, and went off to roll myself a joint.

Fifteen minutes later, and more at one with the world, I happily chucked the meaty morsels into a bowl and then went to light the oven. Problem was, it was a wood-burning stove and there wasn't any wood.

Fear not.

Off I floated to the sitting room where a stack of timber awaited me by the open fireplace. Back in the kitchen I shoved an armful in, emptied the wastepaper basket on top, and struck the match. Perfect, I soon had one hell of a fire, especially when I sprinkled a bit of Andy's lighter fluid for good measure.

With the oven now heating happily up, I refocused my attention on the pie. Tears poured down my face as I chopped up three or four onions. They were thrown over the meat, and with a big wooden spoon I gave the raw mix a stir, adding pepper and salt.

'What else?' I looked around. Gravy. 'How the hell do you make gravy?' I couldn't find anything that said 'gravy making ingredients' but I did find two tins of oxtail soup. Perfect. I poured the lot over the meat and the onions. And then did a Plasticine job with the pastry, you know like you do when you're two or three, make weird shapes and pretend it's real dinner.

And so the finished pie went in the oven. I peeled some potatoes and put them in a pot on the top. Even if I say it myself, Fanny Cradock couldn't have done a better job.

Or so I thought.

The boys were very sweet.

'This is good,' smiled Steve, chewing like he'd got a mouthful of rubber tyre.

'The gravy tastes nice,' nodded Andy, sawing through a bullet-hard potato that jumped across his plate and did an incredible double-bounce off the table.

'I'm rather prone to a nice, crispy crust,' was the comment from Bruce. He was munching into a piece of pastry that was as black as the ace of spades. Bits were all around his mouth. It looked as if he'd been eating charcoal.

'It's horrible,' I miserably muttered, putting down knife and fork and pushing my plate away.

'No,' exclaimed the boys, altogether. But I could tell they were lying.

'Look.' I pulled a martyred face. 'You really don't have to eat it.'

There was a collective sigh of relief.

'Actually, I wasn't that hungry,' admitted Bruce.

'Yeah, me neither,' agreed Andy.

Up jumped Steve, full of the joys. He beamed a grin at me. 'Tell you what, Janni, let's save it. I'll put it all in the fridge and we can help ourselves when we want.' He swept a look at Bruce and Andy. 'Whattya say, guys?'

That idea went down a treat.

Ten minutes later we were all tucking into baked beans on toast.

Andy put down the book he was reading. Or was pretending to read. He straightened his rounded back, and pushed himself out of his deckchair and padded my way. 'Coming for a walk, Janni?'

I looked up into his blue, glittering, hard to read eyes.

'We can go up the hill and watch the sunset,' he suggested, his lips stretching in the direction of a smile. 'Say goodbye to the old, and say hello to the new. What do you reckon?'

Despite the warmth of the late afternoon sun, my whole body froze.

His words were an ominous sign.

Let me explain.

We were all out on the veranda, the four of us, where we'd spent the last part of the afternoon smoking, drinking tea, Andy and Bruce reading books, me penning some poems, and Steve strumming away on his guitar. On the outside, a very chilled out scene but for me personally I was experiencing fresh turmoil, mid-afternoon, and the centre of my world had dropped away.

As you know, it had been a very pleasant morning, the walk into town, Andy buying me my basket; even my diabolical attempts at cooking and the end result didn't dampen my spirits. I mean, who really gives a fuck?

Anyway, after lunch, after our beans on toast, we all got up from the table and, being a well brought up lady, I immediately began clearing away the dishes.

'Sit down, Janni.' Andy took the plates I had in my hand off me. He was smiling. 'You cooked, so we'll wash up.' He looked to his mates. 'Isn't that right?'

'Sure,' nodded Steve, gathering up water jug and glasses. Bruce, already back from the kitchen, had a damp dishcloth in his hand. He began wiping the table, scooping up the charred remains of the pastry and some hard, lumpy bits of potato.

Naturally, I wasn't going to argue the toss, I was sick of the kitchen and had left it in a terrible mess. 'Suits me,' I said, happily picking up my fags. 'You'll find me out on the veranda. Oh, and by the way...' I tossed my hair back, just a little, '...make mine a tea. Milk and one sugar.'

'Your wish is our command,' grinned Steve. Andy and Bruce were already gone: I could hear their light-hearted banter above the clatter of cutlery and plates and the clunk-clunk sound of water hitting the insides of the heavy metal kettle.

'Cheers,' I said to Steve, and left them to it.

Wandering out to the veranda, I pulled a deckchair from out of the shadows and placed it in a bright sunlit spot, and there I languished in the yellow heat of the noon.

I must have dozed off.

Stirring, I rubbed my eyes and looked around. I was still on my own, well except for a steady stream of butterflies, small yellow ones, fluttering over a bush just a few feet away. Checking my watch I realised I'd been asleep for more than an hour, so where were the boys? Admittedly I'd made a real pig's meal of the kitchen but surely they wouldn't still be clearing up?

Off I went to check.

I could hear the murmur of their voices as I stepped through the French doors into the cool of the sitting room, a dialectic mix of broad Yorkshire, soft Scottish, and twangy Canadian.

'Man, it's doing my fucking head in,' I heard Andy say. 'I just don't know what to do. I've tried every which way but the message still doesn't penetrate.'

And I thought: What's doing his head in? as I quietly padded across the floor, over to the dope tin that was on the small coffee table. I fancied rolling up a joint and putting on a tape, something like Dylan seemed very apt.

'It's a difficult business,' drawled Steve. 'But you've got to stick with your decision, man. The longer it goes on the harder it'll get.'

I picked up the dope tin.

'Aye, I know,' groaned Andy. 'But it's already a fucking mess.'

Off came the lid. No Rizlas. I took a look around.

'I think you should have stuck to your guns right from the beginning,' Bruce was saying. I heard the fridge door open, then close. There were rustle sounds, the crack of the ice tray and then the dropping of one, two, three, four, in a glass.

A packet of papers lay on the seat of one of the chairs. I went over and claimed it. Bruce was still talking. 'Like Steve says, if you had it wouldn't be so hard now. You'd both be over it, maybe, by now.'

I stopped in my tracks. My heart flew to my mouth.

'Naw, man, not her.' Glasses chinked. Water from taps poured. The fridge door opened again. 'Janni's too fucking intense, and so fucking immature, believe me. There'd never been a right time with her. Man, I was crazy getting involved in the first place. But fuck it, I've made my decision and this time I'm really sticking to it–'

The fridge door banged shut.

The tin fell out of my hands.

Bang! Clatter!

Dried bits of grass were everywhere.

I didn't move. Couldn't move. My legs had turned into hard, granite stone.

The talking stopped. A moment of silence, then they all appeared from out of the kitchen, first was Steve, then Bruce, and Andy behind.

I didn't dare look into his beautiful blue eyes.

'Hey,' smiled Steve, appraising the scene. 'Thought you were still asleep.'

'I… I just woke up,' I stammered, struggling in my nightmare.

They'd been talking about me. About me!!!! My mind went pinging back to yesterday. In Masai Mari, when the boys had left me in the toilet, had gone off together. 'He's cooking liver and onions,' Bruce had said, on my return. So, I went off to the kitchen, heard the murmur of their voices, Graham, Richard and Andy's. I appeared at the door. Deathly silence – Andy cut off in mid-sentence – 'she's getting on my…' and then the voice trails away into nothing. Uneasy glances. Subject changed. 'Hi, how're you doing?' 'Where'd you get to?' 'Och, no, we looked but couldn't find you.'

They'd been talking about me then. And they were talking about me now.

'She's too fucking immature. She's too fucking intense.'

'I was crazy to have got involved in the first place.'

'I've made my decision...my decision...my decision...'

'Need a hand?'

I was on my knees now, trying to pick up the pieces. A symbolic gesture, if ever there was one. 'No, no,' I managed to say, and was grateful that my hair hid my face. But Bruce was already beside me. 'Butterfingers,' he joked, scraping and scooping up a large dollop to put back in the tin.

'Yeah,' I muttered, hardly daring to speak, my throat felt that constricted. With slow movements, I carried on picking up every little piece from the floor.

'That'll do,' said Bruce kindly, replacing the lid. 'There's still plenty more where that came from.' He stood up. 'We'll sweep up the rest.'

I didn't want to leave the spot, didn't want to get up off my knees, gathering up specks of dope from off the floor was quite comforting; I could have done it for the rest of my life.

But Steve now had a cup in his hand. Two actually. 'Come on, Janni, tea's up. And bring the tin, Bruce.'

They all headed out to the veranda. Still on the floor, I peeped through a curtain of hair. Andy was leaning over the balustrade, smoking and perusing the view.

'Janni,' shouted Steve. 'How many sugars did you say?'

'One.' My voice squeaked.

I got up, made a thing of brushing myself down, although I couldn't have given a shit about what state my trousers were in, who gives a toss about dust and fluff when your heart's just been ripped out and shred into small, little pieces.

'You okay?' asked Bruce, ambling back in, picking up the Rizlas from off their spot on the chair. He seemed a little concerned, was looking at me in a funny kind of way.

Ha! Ha!

Did he guess I was hurting? Did he know I'd heard what had been said?

Well, fuck him anyway.

I hated him. I hated them all. Andy especially.

208

I beamed artificially. 'Yeah, I'm fine.' I tossed back my hair. 'Why?'

Relief etched on his face. Bruce smiled. 'Nothing, really.'

He wandered back out to the veranda. Internally sick and outwardly silent, I followed.

'There you are,' chuckled Steve, handing me a hot, steaming cuppa. 'I was just about to organise a search party.'

Ha! Ha! How hilarious.

'Thanks.' My voice suspended, hanging by an invisible thread.

I sat down. I placed my cup on the floor. I looked out at the yawning, melting, shifting landscape.

'Smoke?'

'Cheers.' Carefully I pushed myself up. Carefully, like walking a tightrope, one slip and I'd fall, I went over to Steve, my hand steady, the joint took, and retracing my steps, I carefully sat back in my chair.

The dope hit my mind and made me dizzy.

I closed my eyes; tried to fight off the tidal wave of grief that was drowning me.

Opened my eyes.

Andy, my world. My galaxy. My universe.

He still had his back to me, was still contemplating the vista before him. I wanted to throw myself in his arms and beg for forgiveness, anything he wanted I would do, or be. Instead, I took another drag and leant over the side of my chair to pick up my tea. I startled two fat bluebottles who were copulating on the rim of the cup, and they fell into the brown, milky liquid. Revolted, I pushed saucer and cup as far away from me as I could. And went back to my puffing, smoking until the bitter end, although the bitter end had already been reached.

By now, Steve had gone inside and returned with his guitar. Quietly, he hummed as he played. Bruce picked up his book, found his page, and was reading. Andy stayed at his post, said not a word, to me, or to the others. He didn't need to. He'd said it all, already.

'I've made my decision...my decision...my decision...my decision...

I'm sticking with my decision...my decision...my decision... my decision...

She's too fucking intense...intense...intense...intense...

She's too fucking immature... immature... immature...

I was crazy to have got involved... involved... involved...'

209

I lay back in my chair and studied the clouds as they galloped across the blue, African sky, and wished I were them, and could just float away. How lovely to snuggle up in their cotton wool softness. To drift and disappear into nothingness.

To dream. To dream. To dream.

I'll send you all my dreams, every day in a le-tter... Steve was singing.

Darling I promise you this...

A shadow blotted out the light. Was it the darkness in my soul? No. It was Andy.

A heavy beat, beat, beat, of my heart.

'Here.' He handed me over another joint. It was just what was needed.

'Cheers.'

Our eyes met and we half-smiled at each other. It was something. But it was nothing. I knew it was nothing. Andy returned to his post. The music played on.

A shaft of afternoon sunshine, dust-laden, speared through the quiet shade of the veranda, settling on a bush and a busy, little bird, illuminating its feathers so they turned into every colour of a fantasy rainbow.

'You haven't got a notepad, or some paper, have you?'

Steve, to whom I'd directed the question, stopped strumming, and nodded. 'Look in my desk, I've got several notepads. Help yourself.'

So I did. And returned to my spot, and began scratching out a poem. Writing my way out of the darkness; easing my pain with the end of a pen.

And tomorrow
Shall I see you?
What shall I do?
And how shall you answer?
Will it hurt me?
And shall I stay sane?

So on, and so on and so on...

I wrote many poems that afternoon. From time to time I'd glance up, look Andy's way. He was sitting in a chair now. He'd left his post and I'd not heard him. Quietly he'd wandered back into the house, down to the office, scrabbled for his book in his bag, wandered back, and was reading.

Or was pretending to read.

More often than not I'd find him watching me; he'd be studying me intensely. Making eye contact with him, he'd give me a half smile and then return to his page. A page that never turned. And I'd watch him. I'd watch him intensely. Watching him mulling over something he already knew but couldn't figure out what to do about it. Terrified about what it might be, I'd dive back into my writing and lose myself in my poems.

And then out of the blue he asked me if I wanted to go for a walk with him and see the sunset.

I'd just written a poem about something like that.

...He said, 'Come.'
I gave him my hand and followed the clouds
To the sun,
Where we slept...

In a daze, I picked up my fags and my matches and shoved them in my pocket. Andy popped a couple of readymade joints in his.

'See you later, guys,' called out Steve, in-between songs, as we made our way down the steps. He was smiling. It was just another day for him. Why should he care?

...'Don't let those tears fall,' he said
Catching them in his hands.
'I'll stay with you.'
So I laughed and sang him a song...

'Say goodbye to the last sun of 1973 for me,' shouted Bruce, on his way to take a bath, a cold one, because he couldn't be bothered to boil up the water.

...But he'd gone before I'd finished
And left me just the tears.
'Goodbye,' an echo, far away,
'I'm leaving for the stars
And can't return.'
So I went and slept in the rain...

Andy took hold of my hand. Together we walked down the steps.

I felt I was being lead to my execution.

We didn't say much as we made our way up the slope, in fact we said nothing. But a song was going around and around in my head. *I don't want to say goodbye for the summer/but I'll fill the emptiness...* How?

The slope began to get steeper, we ascended higher and higher, the pine trees disappeared, the vegetation thinned, we were climbing over soft grass and hard granite. We reached the very top.

Around us, beneath us, was a panorama of mountain and valley, of bare rock and grass, a wilderness world under a vast cathedral of sky that was changing and moving, making patterns and colours, as if a celestial artist was up there painting a gigantic picture using every medium known to nature and man.

I found a smooth, low boulder and sat on it.

To the west the sun, a huge red ball of fire, was sinking. Lower, and lower, behind distant hills. Flights of swallows darted and flickered high in the evening sky, their wings like pointed arrows.

Would one slice through the air, and make its way to my heart?

Andy slid down and rested his back against another rock, shaped like a giant tortoise. A light breeze whispered gently and stirred up the grasses and tickled his halo of golden hair. He dug deep into his pocket and pulled out a joint.

'Here,' he said, and chucked it over. The breath of the mountains picked it up and for a moment it danced hither and thither and then dropped just a few inches away from my feet. I leant over and retrieved it. Putting the spliff to my mouth I pulled out my matches, and with my hand protected the flare from the wind.

Several feet away, Andy lit his.

Together, in our separate worlds, in our own private space, with our own personal thoughts, and our very own joints, we watched the sun, the last sun of 1973 die in a majestic calmness. It edged its way under the rim, sinking lower and lower... and lower... and lower...

From the corner of my eye, I saw Andy get something out of his back jeans pocket.

A small flash of pink. His little anthology.

The quiet wind carried his voice to the stars.

'But pleasures are like poppies spread
You pluck the flower, the bloom is shed.'

A deep howl from within.

The sun, orange and round like an incandescent coin, moved lower and lower...

'Or like the snow, falls in the river, a moment white then...'

A pause.

Watching the sun. The last one. The last one together.

'...melts forever.'

As the sun disappeared.

A rippling, roseate of colour lit up the heavens.

I watched as Andy pushed himself up, brushed himself down, and like the sun he too disappeared – behind the tortoise-shaped rock.

'Where are you going?' I screamed.

No answer came.

On my feet, I ran over and around the other side, expecting to find him hiding. He wasn't. Scanning, I yelled out his name.

'And-y. And-y.'

My voice echoed in the emptiness and was picked up by the wind. Shit! What was he playing at? Had he fallen? But on this side the slope was round and rolling, there were no immediate drops or crevices to surprise me or him.

'And-y. And-y,' I called again.

Nothing. Just whispers and a tinkle of bells.

Where the fuck was Andy?

I climbed back up to the top of the slope and rested awhile against the tortoise. My insides felt jumbled and dark.

'Ping-g-g!'

From behind.

I turned.

Andy was watching me from behind another rock. How long had he been there? I wanted to say something but didn't know what. So I just stood and stared.

'Ping-g-g.'

Andy, his arm raised, aimed and fired again from an imaginary pistol. The bullet hit bulls-eye; it went straight to my heart.

'Got you,' he yelled, and dived for cover. Scrambling over stones and grass I headed towards him, and saw a figure run away down the slope. He reminded me of a mountain boy with his goats, skipping, jumping, and leaping.

I gave chase.

If I hadn't felt so wretched with pain, the game would have been fun, the two of us prancing around the top of a mountain under a giant moon that was edging her way up over the black silhouettes of the crags. But as it was, the whole thing was horrible. Andy wouldn't let me catch him.

He bounced from one rock to another, and never looked back. Finally, when I was so exhausted I thought I might have to stop and

213

die alone on the mountain, I saw him take refuge in a cow pen. With beating heart and panting breath, I followed, and threw myself down on the dung-filled floor. I couldn't have cared less.

He sat with his back against the rough wall. Legs stretched out, golden hairs glistening. Puffing, he watched me through half-closed eyes. I was reminded of that moment, at Yankari, when the switch flicked on.

Now it was off.

The circle complete.

'Why are you doing this to me?' I finally whimpered, having lain there for a while listening to the dull, heavy silence, louder than my own heavy breathing.

He gave me no answer. He just stared at the walls.

'Andy, for fuck's sake. Talk to me. Please.'

In the semi-darkness I saw him push himself up. He went to the opening and looked up to the heavens, staring through space and time towards distant galaxies.

Quickly, I rose to my feet. 'Please, Andy.' I touched his shoulder. He brushed me away. 'I care about you so much,' I blubbered, the tears tumbling and splashing their way down my cheeks.

'Jesus!' he exclaimed to a far away sky.

'Why,' I screamed, my feet stamping hard into the cow shit, 'are you doing this to me?'

He tossed me a sneer.

'If you don't know now, you never will,' he muttered through gritted teeth. And that said, he walked out of the door and began his descent. Blindly I followed. Darkness had truly fallen, and I'm not just talking about night.

Somehow, we managed to make it down the mountain, me stumbling, and crying, Andy silent, making big strides to keep the distance between us as permanent as possible.

Back at the house, Andy joined the others in the sitting room. I went to the darkest corner of the veranda. In a huddle, all alone. Somewhere far away, I heard movements, footsteps, someone puffing and panting.

A torch beam.

Graham appeared on the veranda. He didn't see me. He walked across the terrace. He must have driven from Masai-Mari, for the New Year celebrations.

What little was left of my being, sank even further. One more enemy to add to the camp.

In my corner of Hell, I fumbled about for a cigarette. The packet was empty. I chucked it and it fell into shadowy bushes; there was a flutter of wings, followed by a loud squawk. Whatever I'd frightened, flew away.

God! I needed a fag.

And Andy.

Heartless bastard leaving me out here on my own.

I could hear their voices, his voice, murmurs, and wondered what it was he was saying.

'The deed is done, guys. The deed is well and truly fucking done.'

I tried to listen, tried to pick up some of the words but the whirr of the crickets were too loud, and I too far away from the door and the window. But I heard the familiar laugh and it pierced like a dagger. Tears of pain and fury spurted, hot, they poured uncontrollably down my face.

I ached with grief.

Footsteps again.

A towering figure emerged from the cosy interior. Saw me in the shadows, came over. At long last, someone to share my icy, Siberian winter in far away Africa.

'Hey.' It was Bruce, concerned, kind. He knelt down, and took hold of my hand. I couldn't speak. I just buried my face in his chest.

'Whatever it is, it'll be alright,' soothed Bruce, rocking me, and holding me.

'No, it won't,' I managed to say, in between sobs.

'What won't?'

'Andy.'

Silence. A telling silence. It explained everything without having to say the words.

I lifted my head and looked up at Bruce's face, half in and out of the shadows. 'Why's he doing this to me, Bruce? What have I done?'

I felt Bruce's shrug, and heard the deep sigh.

Another silence.

'Please tell me, Bruce,' I sniffed, and looked at his dark form enquiringly. My lip quivered. A blob dropped from my nose. Tears hung on my lashes. 'Please tell me, Bruce.' Another blob. It plopped on my hand. 'Please.'

'Nothing, I'm sure,' he said quietly, but he knew I knew he was lying.

'But something's gone wrong.' A knot closed my throat, and more tears swelled my eyes. 'We were so bloody happy, Bruce. So in love.'

'I know.'

'Then what's gone wrong? I just don't understand. Tell me Bruce?' I pushed myself back in the chair, and brushed a hand across my wet, sticky face, not really giving a shit about the snot that bubbled large from my nose. And if Bruce did, he didn't say, but he did let go of my hand and pulled a pack of cigarettes from out of his pocket. He lit one, gave it to me, and lit another. I took a drag, blew out the smoke in a slow cloud, and watched as a breath of warm air whisked it away.

The nicotine hit made me feel a little calmer. Just a little. I sighed. 'What am I going to do, Bruce?'

'Well, you can't stay out here all night,' he said, after giving my question some consideration, and taking several deep puffs.

'No, that's not what I meant,' I tutted and sniffed. 'I mean, what am I going to do about Andy? About him and me?' I took another drag. 'One minute we're up, and he's all over me, the next he's an absolute bastard. I can't work it out, Bruce, and it's doing my head in. 'What –' I took another long, long, draw on my fag, '– does he want?'

Bruce pondered. Like me, he smoked with intensity. He scratched his head. Mosquitoes buzzed round. He flicked them away. It was useless. They kept coming back. Eventually, he said, 'I don't think Andy really knows what he wants…'

I interjected. 'How do you mean?'

Bruce shrugged his big shoulders, took a last puff, and stubbed out his fag with his foot. Placing both hands on my bent up knees, he faced me, his glasses glinting. 'Look, Janni, Andy's a good bloke and I don't believe he means to hurt you.'

'Huh,' I snorted. But it wasn't a loud snort. Just a whimper, really.

Bruce continued. 'You've just got to give him some space, I reckon.'

'How?' I asked, my voice all a-quiver.

Bruce shook his head. 'I don't know, Janni.' Shrugged his big shoulders again. 'You'll have to work that one out for yourself.'

'But you talk. He tells you things…'

216

'Not really.'

'But I heard you all. In the kitchen...'

A big, fat rhino beetle droned in on us. It landed in my hair. Got tangled up. Buzz buzz buzz. Bruce plucked it out, chucked it. It went hurtling into the wall, and plummeted to the ground on its back. Slightly dazed, and with some effort, the beetle managed to turn itself over and stagger away.

'Look, Janni' said Bruce, not unkindly, pushing himself up from the floor, as if taking a cue from the beetle. 'It's Andy not me who you should be having this conversation with, pet, and he's in there.' He gestured to the pool of light and the open door. 'Shall I get him to come out and talk with you?'

'He won't talk to me, Bruce.' I sniffed. 'He's ignoring me.' I shrugged. 'What's the point?'

'There's always a point. Give him time to thaw out. Come on.' He got hold of both my hands and began pulling me up. 'Get yourself sorted, and put that pretty smile back on your face, and let's go and celebrate the New Year. What do you say?'

Back on my feet, I felt a bit unsteady, like I'd spent the whole day on the piss. 'Yeah, okay,' I mumbled, still holding onto Bruce. 'But...'

'But what?'

'Do you really think Andy means what he said? That he was crazy to have got involved with me? And am I really intense and immature?'

'Oh, Janni.' He enfolded me in his arms, held me tight. I got a whiff of sweat mixed with cheap carbolic soap. 'People say things they don't really mean when they're angry,' he said, his voice from somewhere up above. 'Don't take it to heart.'

'But am I, Bruce?' I insisted. It came out quite muffled; my mouth was pressed to his chest.

Bruce chuckled. He let go and smiled down at me. 'Right now? Yes. A definite yes. So chill. Get your arse in gear and be cool.' He gave me a gentle push. 'Go on.'

I moved slowly. 'See you in a bit, yeah,' I said, over my shoulder. He was watching me, a big hunk of a guy half in, half out of the shadows. His glasses glinted, and made it look like his face was an owl.

I made a detour, round the back of the house, heading for the office, and my make-up bag, using the moon as a torch. Safely

217

ensconced, I lit the hurricane lamp in the room and began to patch up my face. Not that I was really that bothered about how I looked anymore, there was no point, as beautiful and as slim as I'd tried to make myself be, it just hadn't worked.

The man I wanted didn't want me.

And holding on to that dreadful, dreadful thought, I lay down on our sleeping bag and stared at the ceiling, immobilised again, with sadness and longing.

Half an hour later I was back to slapping on the mascara and smearing on the lipstick, I even brushed my hair, and paid a quick visit to the bathroom where I splashed myself with cold water in the new bath, as way of a wash. It certainly made me feel a little bit better, especially as I'd now worked out that tomorrow was, after all another day.

Another year, in fact, a New Year, and anything could happen. Andy just might see the error of his ways and make a New Year resolution. No more Mr Bad Guy, be good to Janni.

So, it was with a little more spring in my step, I made my way back to the house. Taking a deep, deep breathe with head held high and with a tummy full of knots, I walked through the French doors and into the room.

The four boys were sitting around the table, playing cards, Crosby, Stills and Nash crooning in the background, the smell of dope hanging thick in the air and mingling with wood smoke and whisky.

For a moment or two, a silence came from the table, a horrible silence. I wanted to turn around and run. Either that, or throw myself at Andy's feet and beg for mercy.

But the moment passed.

'Hey, good to see ya,' drawled Steve, sounding genuine. He smiled, and patted the empty chair next to his.

Nervously I made my way over. Graham said hello. I helloed him back. Bruce passed me his joint. I took it, and glanced over at Andy. He nodded at me, as if from a great distance. I nodded back, and felt the knots magnify and bunch up. 'What are you playing?' I asked, turning swiftly to Steve.

'Bridge. Do you play?'

I smiled a painful smile, pushing my cheeks off to each side to allow it, and sat down. 'Yeah, I do actually. There's a group of us who play it all the time in Gombe.'

Steve beamed. A cloud of cigarette smoke floated by. 'No kidding.'

I laughed, or rather, I pretended to laugh. 'There's nothing else to do in Gombe, you see. It's such a fucking, boring place so we play it every day. Helps pass the time.'

Steve nodded in comprehension. 'Yeah, I know what you mean. But you guys are lucky, usually there's only one of me here so I end up playing solitaire.' He slapped at an insect that had crawled up his bare arm. Squashed; and then flicked it away.

'Or wanking,' smirked Graham, taking a sip from a glass that was full with whisky. Everyone laughed. Even Steve thought what he said was funny.

I didn't. But something that sounded like I did fell out of my mouth.

'Yeah, yeah, yeah,' grinned Steve, reaching for his drink, totally unabashed. 'That game's pretty handy for a solitary guy.'

More laughs.

'Which reminds me,' he took a swig and slapped his deck of cards down on the table. 'It's New Year's Eve, guys, so, come on, what are our plans?'

Andy leant back, put his arms behind his head, and his feet up on one of the empty chairs. He shrugged. 'What's there to celebrate?'

Whoosh, went the arrow. Straight to my heart.

'Oh, come on, man,' laughed Steve, shattering the tension into a thousand invisible particles, 'it's fucking New Year's Eve.'

'Yeah, come on,' said Graham, scraping back his chair, and knocking back the last of the whisky. 'Let's go and hit town.'

Bruce nodded appreciatively. 'Sounds good to me.' He finished off his drink and set the glass down. 'Andy?'

Andy looked doubtful, but stood. 'Yeah, count me in,' he said, stubbing out his fag.

'Janni?'

I was playing with the Bida brass ring on my finger. I felt so sick; so alone. Like an alien: a visiting, unwelcome thing. I looked up at Bruce, doleful eyes and a shake of my head. Be the martyr, suffer, and make them all suffer too. 'I don't think so, Bruce,' I mumbled sadly.

But he was having none of it. Neither was Steve. They were pulling me up by my arms.

Everyone was getting ready, meaning tins of baccy were pocketed, matches and lighters grabbed. It *was* New Year's Eve, after all. Somehow I managed to get my act together, pick up my bag, and follow the others. I was reminded of another time, another world, when four lads and a girl all went off for a walk in the dark.

Andy and Graham led the torchlit procession down the slope. A white moon sailed over the horizon. At the bottom of the hill, we took the road, the same road that only seven, eight hours ago – again, it seemed like another lifetime, another planet – Andy and I had walked, happy and laughing, together, hand in hand.

The heat of the day was fading, though it was still warm. We walked slowly, over dry heaps of twigs and crispy, crunchy leaves, avoiding potholes, and whilst Steve caught up with Andy and Graham, Bruce and I lagged behind. Neither of us spoke. There was nothing to say. I suppose he just stayed with me out of kindness.

In town, we headed for the bar, the only bar, the usual low-roofed, mud and wattle pile, grandly called The Royal Palace Hotel. It was pretty packed out, all the local population who liked a good time, were here to celebrate the New Year. Somewhere over in the corner of the capacious room a gramophone was scratching a rendering of African high life music and men and women were dancing, shuffling round the floor; the young girls' hip movements graceful, fluid and erotically teasing.

'Man, there's something about African girls that really get my balls moving,' I heard Graham say to Andy, as we all pushed our way through the throng. Andy's response was lost to me, there was too much noise, but I reckon he probably didn't disagree.

We all sat at a rough plank table, me next to Bruce, Andy right at the end, as far away from me as he possibly could.

My insides were screaming.

'Beers?' Steve had bagged his seat but was standing up, ready to take orders. He swept all four of us with an optimistic, merry look.

'See if there's a jug of the local brew,' suggested Graham, eyeing up one of the girls as she provocatively wiggled her bum directly at him.

'That okay with you, guys?'

We all nodded our heads.

Steve made his way through the crowd, greeting all of them with easy familiarity, and gave his order to a smiling, happy lady who was a veritable mountain of rotund black flesh. Like his fellow Canadian back in Gombe, he was obviously a regular of whorehouse establishments. Maybe all the blokes were, every white man in Africa (except my Dad, of course) and I just didn't know.

Meanwhile Graham was already up, and was dancing. Cavorting among the girls, slapping bottoms and whispering God knows what scandalous things in their ears. And they loved it, giggling and shrieking. More of them appeared out of the cracks in the wall, and began shuffling around Graham.

'He's up for a promise,' joked Bruce, trying to make light of a heavy situation.

'Gang bang, more like,' chuckled Andy, tapping his feet to the beat. A girl, a very pretty girl, touched his shoulder.

'Dancing?' she enquired.

Andy smiled, my heart turned, he considered the idea. I felt sick.

He shook his head. 'Naw, maybe later.'

Unperturbed, she gave him a brilliant 'I'll get you in the sack for a shag' grin (not over my dead body), and moved on to Bruce.

'Go on,' encouraged Andy, laughing, as Bruce's face shone red with embarrassment, 'it might be the only chance you ever get.'

Cruel bastard.

Bruce went even pinker, in amongst the hurricane lamps he shone like a beacon on heat. 'No, no,' he protested but the girl, giggling, now had a hold of his hand.

'Yeah, go on, man,' grinned Andy, getting into the spirit of it all. 'Fuck, what have you got to lose, Brucie baby.' He laughed out loud at his joke.

'Go on, man,' cajoled Steve, who had now returned with the drinks. He set the tin tray down; there was a big jug with thick, floury goo, and five dirty glasses. 'Have this first.' He poured Bruce out a cup of poison. 'This'll get you going.'

The girl still had hold of Bruce's hand, she was pulling, trying to get him up, he was mildly protesting. 'No...I don't...no..really...' She laughed, freed her hand and picked up the glass, and making funny clicking sounds, as if soothing a baby, she put the drink to his lips.

'Come on, man,' enthused Andy. 'Fucking go for it.'

And go for it he did. He let her pour the stuff down his throat, gagged once or twice, but not unduly, and then got up and let the girl pull him along the floor to an empty space where they began to dance. She wiggled her hips teasingly, and Bruce, with exaggerated concentration, bobbed up and down on the spot.

Meanwhile, back at the plank table Steve had already chucked down two glasses of goo and was now ready for a bit of fun himself.

A remarkably attractive little thing in colourful print skirt, and a garish slash of lipstick across her dusky features, had homed in on the kill. She whispered something to Steve and took his hand. They edged away from the table and began to move to the music, their arms around each other's waists, casually intimate.

Andy and I remained at the table. When Steve left, he had looked at me for one disdainful second then deliberately he turned his back; smoking, drinking, watching the others; watching everybody except me!

But I watched him, studied the gold of his hair, the silver snake on his arm, suffused with emotion, with longing. Was it only a month ago? – Andy would have been the first up, would have taken me in his arms and danced with me all through the night. Would have looked in my eyes and whispered and teased me, words of love, of erotic promises, the things we'd do together, later, when we were alone in our bed.

Now, there was just silence and withdrawal. Our Christmas jaunt should have been idyllic, but sitting here, all cramped up, I couldn't breath. Tears sprang to my eyes. I let them quietly fall.

Bruce was back, just for a second, to refill his cup, have a swig, and return to his girl. 'Bloody hell,' he gasped, his face glowing, as he banged down the now empty glass and smacked his lips with relish. 'She's a fucking mover, Andy, me old buddy.'

His old buddy said something mildly encouraging, smiled. 'Go for it, man. Take it easy but take it,' although Bruce no longer needed any inducement from any of us, he was well on his way.

And so the music throbbed on. Dancers shimmied around. In the dust, sixty or so ebony bodies and three pale ones gleaming with perspiration, in the light of the hurricane lamps; and the air thick with the smell of sweat, cigarette smoke and warm beer. And Andy and I, in amongst it all, but so far away.

'Drink?'

Andy had got up out of his seat, and was looking at me. Was looking at me!?

And me a nonentity.

Bloody hell!

'Um...' I looked at my glass, still full, the poison within, untouched. I swallowed. It hurt. '...I wouldn't mind a beer.'

Coldly he nodded, and marched over to the bar and ordered two bottles. I settled back in my chair, scratched at the dried tears that had probably left a stain on my face, and stared at a couple of moths dancing around a hurricane lamp tied to a rafter by string above me. Oh, how I wished it was just the two of us again, and we were them, twirling in lamplight, flying together.

Andy was back.

He banged down my bottle, and took a long, drawn out swig from his. I didn't touch mine. Instead I lit up a cigarette, and dared myself to open my mouth.

'Andy...' I leant over, trying to smile, to defuse. 'Would you like to dance?'

Andy rolled his eyes back, and gave a smirk, that was filled with sarcasm. 'I don't think so,' he said.

My insides felt hollow. Andy, as cold as the air was warm, turned the other way. He lifted his bottle and drank. And I, in pieces, abandoned, sat there, my head filled with dread.

Graham returned for a quick drink and a fag. 'Fuck me, man.' His face full of smiles and droplets of sweat. 'She's a goer, is mine.' He wiped his forehead with the back of his hand. 'Have you seen Bruce?' And laughed. 'He's all for it, man. All over the slapper. There'll be a dose of clap by the end of the night.' And on that amusing note, he swigged his drink, lit his fag, and went off in search of his girl.

My head was throbbing. My heart was aching. The god of darkness had set up a permanent camp in my soul.

'I can't take any more of this,' I finally wailed, and buried my face in my hands.

Someone was touching my shoulder. I didn't look up.

Andy's voice. 'Come on. Let's get out of this place.'

Now I raised my head, for a brief second uplifted, expectant, hoping for great things. But this was no olive branch. The face that looked down on me was cold, aloof, distant, his invitation not given in warmth; more out of a sense of duty, I sadly, and rightly, supposed.

We didn't say goodbye to the others, we just got up and left.

We walked side by side physically, but emotionally we were as far apart as the sky is from earth. Even so, somehow I managed to put one foot in front of another, and somehow I managed to keep it together, meaning I kept my mouth shut.

Back at the house, we went straight to the office, to our bed. I couldn't be bothered to undress. I just flopped on the cushions and stared at the ceiling. Andy, over on the other side, took off his boots, unzipped and pulled down his jeans, and threw off his T-shirt.

Naked, he lay down, his back to me, at the farthest side of our makeshift bed, his feet almost touching the floor.

The blinds still open let in the moonbeams, they flickered prettily, and danced above our heads.

Time passed. A minute, an hour, I really don't know.

From somewhere, a violent banging on doors. And shouting.

'Christ.'

'What the fuck…'

And in they all came, Bruce, Steve and Graham.

'Happy New Year,' they screamed, stumbling, laughing, all of them drunk. Certainly *they* were as happy, as happy can be.

'Hey, what time is it, man?' Andy, bolt upright, peered at the trio.

'Two hours into 1974, you crazy bastard,' hollered Graham, and fell over. He landed right across my legs. 'Oh, darling,' he slurred. 'Come here and give me a nice juicy kiss.' I didn't move, couldn't move and wouldn't move; unperturbed, Graham crawled over and landed me a smacker. His breath smelt like a brewery. 'Happy New Year,' he hiccupped, before moving on to Andy. He got a full kiss on the lips too. And there was more of the same from Bruce and Steve, slobbery greetings from them all.

We reciprocated. 'Happy New Year,' we dutifully said; but nothing between us was spoken, Andy didn't even flick me a glance.

'Coming for a nightcap?' invited Steve, standing up, and doing his level best to stay straight.

'Yeah, come on,' mumbled Graham, trying hard not to wobble.

'You can't not,' slurred Bruce, with a very silly grin, his teeth bright white in the light of the moon.

We both shook our heads.

'Count me out,' Andy muttered. 'I'm beat.'

'Me too.' In the semi-darkness, my voice sounded hollow and flat.

So the boys, who were far too pissed to care, left us. 'If Auld acquaintance be forgot…' they sang at the top of their voices, as bang shut went the door.

Silence.

Silence.

Silence.

'HAPPY NEW YEAR,' one of them screamed from the roof tops.

It was the saddest New Year of my life.

CHAPTER 7

January 1974 – the first couple of days

I awoke to an empty room. The blinds were still open and sunlight streamed in.

It was a new day. It was a brand spanking New Year.

'Oh, God,' I moaned, and buried my face in the pillow and cried. And cried until I could cry no more.

Rising at last, with the night's events still going around in my head and the pain still deep in my belly, I searched for my cigarettes. Bending down to get my red leather bag, fumbling for the packet inside, I noticed something was missing. Not in my bag, but in the room.

Andy's rucksack!

Wildly I looked over to the cushions, the sleeping bag was gone, I remember Andy pulling it away from me in the darkness of night, and I'd let him, of course I'd let him, there'd been no fight in me left.

Where was his hat, his little book of poems, his flip-flops and sandals? All gone. All packed up in his bag. Just my stuff and Steve's paperwork filled the room.

Oh, my God, he's left me.

But then I heard his voice. In the distance, from the veranda, I heard them all talking and laughing. Relief, first, followed by sadness and apprehension. How would Andy be? And what about the others? Could I face them? And did they care?

Five minutes, and a couple of fags later, I crept out of the office, up the path, with my washbag in my hand. Ran a cold bath; the water went 'spitter-spatter' and came out a nice, rusty brown. Unperturbed, I undressed, got in, and lay in the cooling water, sank back beneath it, and let my dark locks float out around me. Like Ophelia, beautiful and... *But didn't she go mad?*

I washed my hair and my bits and bobs, climbed out, dried myself, and returned from whence I came with a towel wrapped around me, and began to pack. All the stuff from my old worn out bag was taken out, my numerous tops, skirts, trousers, and undies, and several pairs of shoes. These I put in my newly acquired basket

– was it only yesterday? – and still there was plenty of room. Andy will be pleased about that, I thought optimistically. Visions of the two of us traipsing the misty Cameroon mountains hand in hand, the past and all its horrors firmly behind us, and the basket resting nicely on my back.

Yes, Andy will definitely be pleased about that.

I got dressed, put on a long, red cotton skirt, white cheesecloth blouse, and a string of sandalwood beads; my hair, still wet, I left loose. Now I was ready to join the others. Well, as ready as I'd ever be. With mixed feelings, of course. Maybe they didn't care whether I joined them or not and were rather relieved to have me out of the way.

Fuck them. Fuck the lot of them. I'll be aloof, I'll be cool; I'll show them what being mature is all about.

I lit up my sixth fag of the day, picked up my basket, and was about to vacate the room. Then the door opened.

It was Andy.

'Leaving for somewhere?' Cold eyes appraised me.

I shrugged, tried to be the person I wished I could be – steady as a rock and as cool as a mountain spring – with a dash of sophistication, and a sprinkling of rock and roll chic.

'Yeah.' I tossed back my hair, just a little. 'The Cameroon.' And began to put my arms through the straps and lift the basket on my back.

'Over my dead body,' Andy said quietly.

'What do you mean?' I stared at him stupidly.

'Jee-ee-sus Christ!' Andy banged the door shut, and walked into the room with fists clenched tight. His knuckles were white. 'You're totally, fucking deranged.' His face shone red like the sun. 'Hasn't the message sunk in?' He talked through gritted teeth. 'Or do I have to spell it fucking out for you?'

I felt a trembling within. A knife in my heart. A sickness in the pit of my stomach.

The cool, cat queen had gone, in her place, a sad, little girl. 'But you said – you said – you...' (I wanted to say: you said you loved me, I will love thee still my dear 'till all the seas gang dry...) but Andy grabbed me, got hold of my arm, gripped it, and swung me around. My fag flew out of my hand and fell on one of the cushions. Ignoring the possible consequences, a blazing inferno, Andy shoved me back up against the wall.

'I don't love you,' he shouted at the top of his voice. The whole

226

of the population of the Mambilla Plateau surely had heard him. 'Do you get it, you crazy, fucking woman. It's over. Finished. You and me.' Nose to nose. Mouth to mouth. 'Forever.'

It was like poison being pumped into my soul.

'No. No,' I screamed, recoiling, trying to wrench back my arm, trying to throw myself into his. But he pushed me back, and I fell hard on the cushions, on to the cigarette. I barely felt the burn on my skin.

'I love you, I love you,' I whispered, my voice thick with tears.

Andy sneered. His lip curled. 'You make me fucking sick.'

I was now on my knees, on the floor, had thrown myself at his feet. I looked up at him, and implored. 'You – you – don't mean that, Andy.'

'Every. Fucking. Word.'

'Please, Andy.' My hands together in prayer, tears rolling. 'I can't bear to lose you.'

All dignity gone.

Andy turned. 'I'm out of here.' And opening the door, like my dignity, he too was gone.

Really gone.

Over the hills and far, far away.

That kind of gone.

I lay on that floor, in a crumpled mess, broken in pieces, for how long I couldn't say. I heard voices, sounds, knew the world was still out there, they came and they went.

Footsteps, a knock, the door opened gently. Movement, as someone stepped inside. Dear, sweet, kind, darling Bruce. Oh, how I so wished he were Andy.

'You okay?'

I sniffed, and wiped at my eyes with the hem of my red cotton skirt.

'I'm okay.'

'Sure?'

'Mmm,' I whimpered. And then I cried a little more.

Patiently Bruce waited. He sat there with me on the floor, stroked my damp hair, and waited. Lit cigarettes, gave them to me, and still waited. Finally, I said, 'Has he gone?'

Bruce nodded. 'Yes, Janni, he's gone.'

With slow movements I pushed myself up, leant back against the wall. 'Where to?'

227

'The Cameroon.'

I sat dazed, my heart heavy. 'How's he getting there?'

Bruce shrugged. 'Not sure, really. He needed a letter from the DO's office in town, giving him permission to re-enter Nigeria. Steve gave him a lift, dropped him off there. I expect he'll catch a mammy-wagon,' Bruce shrugged again.

More tears swelled my eyes. 'I can't believe it's over, Bruce. I mean really, really over.'

'No.' Bruce picked at a thread on the hem of his T-shirt. 'I don't suppose you can.'

Silence fell upon us, Bruce pulled at the thread; it began to unravel. Three inches long, and he snapped it off.

'What are you going to do?'

I closed my eyes. And a knot closed my throat.

'I dunno,' I said finally. 'Go back home, I suppose.' But the thought, the idea, filled me with dread, Gombe, my parents, Lizzie et all; the return of the prodigal daughter. No more Maiduguri. Paradise well and truly and totally lost.

'Jesus, this can't be happening.' I grabbed Bruce by the shoulders and buried my fingernails deep into his flesh. 'Tell me this is all just a fucking bad dream. Please. Please. Please.' Releasing my grip, I began banging my fists hard on the floor. Again and again and again.

'Shush, shush, don't.' Bruce had a firm hold of my wrists. 'Don't do this to yourself.'

'Oh, Bruce,' I cried, and fell into his arms like a baby, 'I want Andy. I want him so much.' And the tears – where did they all come from? – poured thick and fast. On, and on, for another thirty minutes, maybe longer, and Bruce, dear, kind Bruce, patiently waited for the deluge to stop.

'Do you want me to come back with you to Yola?' he said, after a lull in the watery proceedings. *No, of course not. I want to travel on to the Cameroon and find Andy.*

'What do you mean?' I sniffed.

'I mean, do you want me to come back with you to Yola? It's a fair distance, and I don't much like the thought of you out there in the bush on your own.'

It hit me.

I'm all on my own. Andy's left me. We'll never be together again. No more poems, no more beautiful nights under the stars. No more walking in moonlight, no more dappled sunbeams across our bed. No more love at its deepest, no more love at its best. Dreams are shattered. I'm walking in the rough part of Hell.

'I want Andy back,' I wail. 'Without him my life is in shreds.'

Beseechingly, I look to Bruce, look for a magic wand, there must be something he can do. But there isn't. And facts are facts. I'm on my own and Bruce has changed his plans. He is taking me home.

It took me a long time to get my act together, in-between sobs and howls, and rants and raves. I finally managed to wash my face, brush my damp, sticky hair, but abandoned the idea of lipstick and mascara. Especially mascara. I knew there were many, many, many more tears to fall before the day – if it ever did – came to an end.

'Here,' said Bruce, handing me a coffee. He'd gone off, heated the kettle, and told Steve of our plans. Now he was back with refreshments.

I took a sip. The liquid was black, hot and very, very sweet.

'Right,' said Bruce, emptying the ashtray in a small wicker bin, and bringing the empty receptacle back over to where I was, all hunched up on the cushions like a child, my arms wrapped round my knees. 'Steve has offered to take us to the lorry park after lunch.'

'I'm not hungry.'

'You've got to eat.'

'I'm not hungry.'

'Well, I'm starving. So, after lunch…'

'I can't face him.'

'Who?'

'Steve.'

'Oh, for fuck's sake, Janni, why?'

'Because –,' I shrugged, sniffed, '– because he'll laugh at me.'

Gently Bruce took my hand. 'No, he won't,' he said softly. 'He's really sorry about all this, really, Janni. He wants to help.'

Help? Like I'm some poor, pathetic animal who needs putting down.

'Is Graham still here?' I drew on my cigarette, and watched a lizard launch itself from one of the ceiling rafters, sailing through the air like a hang-glider.

Bruce shook his head. 'No, he went back to Masai-Mari quite early this morning. With…' Bruce chuckled, '…a bit of a bloody hangover, I might say.'

'What about you?'

'I feel like shit.'

I gave Bruce a ghost of a smile. 'You and me, both.'

The final plan was this.

Steve would drop us off at the Government Rest House where we'd eat lunch – I couldn't bear to go up into Steve's house where there were too many recent memories of Andy – and from there our host had arranged for a Forestry Land Rover to take us to Ngorogi. 'We'll stay at Pete's house tonight,' I heard Bruce say, but I wasn't really listening, I was over the hills and far, far away, in search of my Andy.

'Hey, kid,' smiled Steve, as I, and my basket, finally stood in the sunshine. It was a glorious day, blue sky and cotton wool clouds and dappled lights, in a world of birdsong, heady perfumes and gentle breezes. The kind of glorious day that makes you so glad to be alive – but only if you weren't me.

'Hi,' I mumbled, avoiding eye contact.

He was handing me something. 'You almost forgot this.' I looked at the notebook. My poems.

Thanks.' They were pushed down, far down, in amongst all my stuff.

'Ready?'

I nodded, and slowly picked up my basket.

'Hey, I'll take that.' I whispered a, 'Cheers,' and Steve slung it on his back. Bruce was already loaded up, rucksack, Fulani hat, sunglasses – oh, God, I wanted him so to be Andy – but I kept it together, and tried to be brave.

All of us were ready for moving. Slowly we made our way down the track, me in-between the two boys, none of us talking, our feet crunching on twigs and dry leaves, crackle and snap, and from a long way off I heard the thump, thump of a drum.

And I wondered if Andy might hear it too.

The Land Rover was waiting for us at the bottom of the hill. It was parked under an umbrella of trees, a little way off the road. 'My garage,' explained Steve, searching his pockets for keys.

'You must keep pretty fit, with all this climbing every day,' commented Bruce, as we, or rather they, slung the loads into the back, and opened up doors. Glumly I climbed in and sat in the middle.

'Yeah,' agreed Steve, swinging himself into the driver's seat, Bruce sliding in the other side. 'I could have had a place in town, but I prefer being off the beaten track, and kinda like the location. And, like you say, the walk up and down the hill does me good.'

He started the engine. And we chugged, chugged, chugged,

and bumped and rattled down the road. The same road Andy and I had walked together, singing songs, hand in hand – was it only yesterday?

The Government Rest House, a pretty pink construction covered in red bougainvillea, sat on its own on top of a rolling hill. The vehicle crunched on gravel, and stopped.

'I'll get your basket,' said Steve. Doors opened. I slid out Bruce's side and turned to the hills – *where are you, Andy?* – Steve was standing beside me, saying something about his driver being back in an hour. 'But don't rush your dinner,' he smiled, and gave me a kiss on the cheek. Shook Bruce's hand. 'Take care of yourselves. And have a safe journey home.'

Home. The word was like a stab in the heart.

Doors banged, the engine started, tyres moved, a hand waved to us from the window, and Steve was gone.

It was just me and Bruce. *Oh, how I so wished he were Andy.*

Bruce hitched up his rucksack, and picked up my basket. 'Come on,' he ordered, 'you'll feel better with something inside your tummy,' and led the way up the concrete steps, into the coolness of the Rest House.

A steward, delighted to see a couple of Europeans grace his establishment, was over in seconds. 'Madam. Master.' He relieved us of our loads.

'We're not staying,' explained Bruce. 'We're here for lunch.' A mite disappointed, our man led the way across a mahogany floor that shone like a mirror, and into the dining room. A large ceiling fan rotated slowly with a monotonous 'chunk chunk' over fourteen or so tables adorned with white(ish) linen cloths and white(ish) linen napkins. There was an Indian family, about six of them, mum in her sari, dad in his black patent shoes, and four children frilled to the nines, all tucking in to their groundnut delights in one corner of the room, and an old colonial with skin resembling the Dead Sea scrolls, nursing a bottle of beer, in the other corner. I vaguely smiled at him, at the Indian party, and even managed to reciprocate their 'Happy New Year' greetings.

We sat down.

The table was by a large window that looked out onto the plateau.

'Drink?'

The steward was hovering.

'Beer.'

'Two beers. And the menu.'

I screwed up my eyes. Far, far away I could see something in amongst the hills, and it was moving.

'What do you fancy?'

'Nothing.' *Yes, it was definitely moving.*

'Aw, come on, Janni. You've got to eat.' *If only I had my Dad's binoculars.* Bruce tapped my hand. 'Hoi, are you listening to me. We might not get a chance to have another proper meal for a while.' He passed me over the tatty menu, sighing, I picked it up, there was, as always, very little choice. No choice, actually. Groundnut soup for starters; beef curry the main, and guava jelly for afters.

'Soup. I'll have some soup.'

I passed back the menu, and returned to my dot in the distance. *Where the fuck was it?*

'Two soups, one beef curry, okay.' I vaguely heard the steward repeat the order and scuttle away. Desperately I scanned the hills. *Was it Andy? Had the dot been him? Hang on, there's something, or someone, over there.*

Two bottles of beer and two glasses, plop, plop, plop, fizz, fizz, fizz. Absently, I picked up my drink and drank, and continued to look out of the window. For the whole of the time we were there, through the soup course, Bruce's beef curry course, and his two helpings of guava jelly, I stared out the window to see if I might see Andy. Just one last glimpse, that's all I asked. Him, and his old rucksack, and the hat with the tartan patches walking away into the misty mountains.

But all I saw were three goats and a cow.

Steve's driver was late by thirty minutes, which was fine by me. I could have sat on the steps of the Rest House, in the warm sunshine, smoking cigarette after cigarette, and scanning the hills, forever and forever. It gave me something to do and helped block out the pain.

When the Land Rover finally arrived, my heart sank, and the truth of the matter hit me. Big time. I was leaving. Going the other way.

Remember me when I am gone
Gone far away into the silent land,
When you can no more hold me by the hand
Nor I, half go, yet turning stay...

Bruce had to literally push me into the Land Rover. I was inconsolable.

'I can't – can't leave. Don't make me, Bruce. Please – please – please – don't make me.' Tears – yet again – flooded my face, I tried to get out, but with the driver on one side, and Bruce on the other, I was wedged.

'Drive,' he ordered the driver, and the driver, a tad gob-smacked, drove.

We crunched over the hard, stony ground. I saw the Indian family standing on the Rest House steps, frills and bows and saris and black patent shoes, twinkling and sparkling in the afternoon sun. To the left of the building the water tank, our steward leaning against it having a crafty fag. And beyond the Indian family, the water tank and steward were the hills, soft, rolling, beautiful, wonderful hills.

And somewhere in amongst those soft, rolling, beautiful, wonderful hills was my beautiful, my wonderful Andy.

We took a right, and bumped along a single-track road. Past the turn off to Gembu, and Steve's house, a long, winding trail lay ahead of us. Like a slither of silver, it cut through the plateau, and like a slither of silver, it cut me to pieces. The road to nowhere, taking me away, and I leaving my heart and soul with a boy somewhere in the very hills I could see.

'Oh, Bruce,' I sobbed, burying my face into his neck, 'I miss him. I miss him so much.'

And Bruce patted me, and soothed me, and gave me a hanky. And the driver, being a canny chap, lit me a fag.

'No cry, Madam, it be good year,' he said with a smile.

'New Year,' corrected Bruce.

'New Year be good,' nodded the driver.

'It isn't,' I said flatly, taking a puff and drying an eye with the hanky. 'It be bad, bad year.'

'No, Madam.' The driver shook his head. 'It be happy year. I hear Master Steve say. He say, 'Happy New Year, Moses'. Happy not be bad, that for sure. So it be good year not bad year. So you see, Madam, no cry.'

If only it could be that easy. Still, I dried the other eye, blew my nose, and said, in a faint, whispering way, 'Thanks, Bruce,' and passed him the snot-ridden hanky back.

'No, you keep it, pet.'

'Sure?'

'Sure.'

And so we journeyed on. Over hill and dale, passing furtive

233

baboons and herds of cattle, shuddering through one village after another, with kids, goats and chickens running along by our side, Bruce with his arm out of the window, Moses dishing out the odd philosophical thought, and me, red-eyed and miserable.

It was a horrible ride. To go along that same rutted track, where only a few days before I had gone with Andy. In every bend, I imagined I could see him, every person, every inanimate object was Andy; I would sit up, expectant, ready to order Moses to slam on the brakes, ready to crawl over Bruce and…

The vision would fade. Andy resting with his rucksack would turn out to be an old man leaning with his back against a rock, Andy striding through the grasses would be a young girl walking with a basket of wood across her shoulders. But I never gave up; I carried on looking, and carried on hoping. Certain I would catch a glimpse of him in those hills.

Three hours on we were back at Pete's house. The Land Rover juddered to a halt, and Bruce and Moses got out.

'Come on.' Bruce took my hand. I said nothing, and stayed glued to my hot, sticky seat. 'Come on,' he said again. A limp lettuce, I let him prise me out, I let him lead me up the stony path, the herd of village goats were still there, dining on the hibiscus, their three minders, with sticks, still squatting in the cropped grass under the shade of the cotton tree.

We mounted the steps. We crossed the veranda. A couple of lizards were engaged in a ferocious battle. We stepped over debris and insects. Bruce opened the French doors, pulled a cobweb aside as if it were a curtain. Inside, nothing had changed. But it had really, hadn't it? Everything had changed.

'Put the bags over there, Moses.' Moses put my basket and Bruce's rucksack down on the dusty, scratched, dirt encrusted dining room table. With now empty hands, he hovered by the door. Bruce dug deep into his pocket, took out some coins. 'Cheers, Moses. Thanks for the ride.'

'Good year, Master. Good year, Madam.' And Moses pulled back the cobweb, and disappeared down the steps.

Bruce pottered about. Lit a fag and searched through his bag, for a book and a few other things, then wandered off into the kitchen.

'Tea?' he called out.

I couldn't be bothered to answer. It was all too, too much. To be back in this dark, dismal house, with the memories of being here with Andy, it was all too, too much. I picked up a butt from off the floor. I knew it was Andy's. His hands had crafted this fag, his lips had touched this fag, his breath had – oh, fucking hell, it was all too, too much.

Dazed, I walked round the eerie rooms. The Bogey Man and Miss Haversham were gone; the ghost of Andy was now in every cupboard, hiding in every corner, and I prayed that he would jump out and haunt me, but all I encountered were dark, silent voids that reflected my sadness.

I wandered back into the sitting room. Bruce was in one of the mouldy, old chairs, reading his book. He turned a page, and looked up. 'The kettle won't be long,' he said cheerfully. I said nothing, there was nothing to say. I wandered out onto the veranda. Ignored the debris, the insects, the dead lizard loser minus a head, and sat down on the step, looking up at the cascade of purple bougainvillea, at the rose bush that tumbled and formed an arch. The rose bush from where Andy, in romantic mood, had plucked the flower: 'To my love,' he had said.

I felt choked with the memory of it all.

On the step, I watched the sun go down. It was as if a vast fire had lit up the sky. Drifting clouds became large balls of candyfloss, and the silent plateau turned into an endless ocean of rippling gold.

I was in a beautiful setting. It was a glorious sunset. Just like yesterday…

Yesterday

All my troubles seemed…

A steaming cup of tea materialised next to me. Black, there was no milk.

'Thanks,' I said. There was nothing else to say.

'We'll have a trip into town later,' suggested Bruce, 'and do some shopping. And I'll build a fire. It'll cheer the place up a bit.'

I nodded but said nothing. There was just nothing to say.

Bruce went back inside the hellhole, I mused on the step for a little while longer, waited for the sky to turn silver and purple. Then I picked myself up, stepped over the debris et al, and headed for my basket. Bruce was already kneeling down by the blackened fireplace, cracking sticks in half, rolling up paper and throwing in rubbish. Certainly there was plenty, enough to build a bonfire.

Taking my bag off the table, I had a rummage around, found what I was looking for, my notebook, and picked up my fags. 'Is there a pen anywhere?' Apart from thanks, it was the first words I'd said in over an hour. Dear, darling Bruce – oh, how I wished he were Andy – looked up from his chore, and smiled. It was a kind, gentle smile. He was so bloody nice.

'I spotted one over there,' pointing to the rubbish-ridden desk, the one where Pete probably spent many a happy hour getting through his paperwork, and afterwards, writing upbeat letters home to his extremely proud parents.

I walked over. A dead spider lay right next to the biro. Gingerly I picked it up, not the spider, but the biro, and headed back out of the house. Bruce, I noticed, had a match in his hand, and was lighting the fire.

Back on my step, I drank in the silence for a while, my chin cupped in my hands, my eyes staring at the red bands of bush fires burning down the hills. The sun had long since gone but there was still a hint of its valedictory splendour, a streak of magenta tinted with gold. It was dusk but still there was enough light for seeing. The notebook on my knees, I flicked through the poems – was it only yesterday, it seemed such a long time ago – and found a blank page. I lit a fag, picked up the pen, and wrote a letter to Andy.

Andy,

What are you doing now as the sun sets? I know you're among these hills. Happy? Free? What was inside you? What is inside you? Contempt? Hate? Love? Sadness? Joy? Loneliness?

A tear dropped on the page. I wiped it away.

You just live inside yourself and you just can't get out but now, among and alone in these hills, under these stars, you'll perhaps find yourself.

A second tear plopped, followed by another. I wiped them away. The ink smudged but I really didn't care.

The sunset is wonderful tonight, and the mountains are more than beautiful. Sleep well, Andy.

A knot closed my throat tight. I wrapped my arms around me in a trance of longing. 'Oh, Andy, I want you so much,' I whispered to the huge African moon that had edged its way up behind distant hills, and now hung over the silent plateau like a bulb in the sky.

Inside the house I heard the hiss of a gas lamp being lit, the scraping of a chair, the creaking of floorboards, and footsteps. 'Here.' Bruce set down the lamp. 'You'll see better with this.'

I said nothing. There was nothing to say. Bruce turned, and went back through the doors, and I went back to my writing. It helped. Made me think I was talking to Andy.

236

There's a fire burning away in the distance, and there's a fire burning inside the house. Bruce is sitting there…'

Too much. I closed the book, unable to carry on. Alone, on the step, looking up at the moon, I let the memories and the pain come and take me away.

I must have sat there for an hour, quietly sobbing. In the dark, in the silence, the only clear sounds, the fricative churring of the cicadas and the hissing of the hurricane lamp.

A cool breeze picked up a leaf; it danced for a few seconds around my bare feet, and then was dropped near a stone. Gathering my cigarettes, my matches, my pen and book, I headed inside. Bruce, in the lamplight, lounging in one of the dusty, government-issue uncomfy chairs, with his feet up on another, was still reading his book.

Like Andy.

Smacking and pursing his lips, turning the pages, getting stuck in. Just like Andy.

Bruce looked up

'Ok?'

'Ok.'

'Sure?'

'Sure.'

Bruce smiled, and returned to his book. I removed a load of papers off the one other uncomfy chair, and dragged it nearer the fire. Spotting an old, leather pouffe, with the kapok stuffing exposed in the splits, I kicked it across the dirt-ridden floor, into place. With my pen and my notebook, my fags and my matches, I sat down, put my feet up, and resumed writing.

…and I've come to join him. It's cold outside. Are you cold? I saw you in Bruce, but it wasn't you. You're far away. So far away, and yet so near. To see the setting sun, and remember that only yesterday, we had watched the same sun slip away behind the hills.

The fire felt warm on my face. I moved my chair back a little.

I sat and thought of you, and I tried to picture you as you look, how you smile, how you laugh, how you talk.

'Hungry?'

I looked up at Bruce, pissed off at the interruption. 'Not really.'

'I am.' Putting his book down, he got up, stretched, and moved over to warm his hands by the fire.

A white T-shirt/ Faded blue jeans

'It's eight, already. Fancy a walk into town?'

'In a minute.'

Hair blonde, long/ Falling around a face/ A sculptor's perfection.

'I'll check what we need from town. I don't think there's any foodstuffs, tins or the like in the kitchen, but I'll have a root round the cupboards.'

'Ok.'

Hands long, and creative/Smile wonderfully strange/And eyes so blue

'No, there's nothing. Like Old Mother Hubbard, the cupboard is bare.'

I looked up. 'Isn't there?' But really, I didn't care. And wished Bruce would fuck off, and leave me alone.

'I'll go to the loo, and then, if you're ready, we'll make a move.'

'Ok.'

There's mystery in their depth/Voice soft and low/Sends peace to a listener/Around his neck/A chain, gold against brown skin/His wrist hidden by a band/Of leather, entwined with beads/His arm, a snake/Silver, against brown skin/

'Ready?'

'Just a sec.'

'I'll be out on the veranda.'

'Ok.'

His mind, pure but strange/To one who cannot understand/But he's just a boy/That comes and goes/And sings his songs/And leaves only a memory of/A white T-shirt/And faded blue jeans

Bruce and I made our way along and down the steep, winding track, following the torch beam, and headed into the village of Ngorogi. It took us about half an hour. We didn't talk about much on the way, I was too preoccupied, and Bruce seemed quite happy with the silence.

Like Mubi, Ngorogi was dead. Hardly anyone was around, and the sloping, narrow streets were pretty much shrouded in darkness. We wandered around like a pair of lost souls in search of food and sustenance, but found nothing.

'Christ, I'm hungry,' moaned Bruce. 'There must be somewhere open.'

'Well, there doesn't look like it. Let's head back,' I suggested, wanting to return to my book and my pen so I could resume my conversation with Andy. Food was the last thing on my mind.

But Bruce wasn't for giving up. 'There's a light over there. C'mon on, Janni, let's take a look.' Bruce led, and I, sighing, followed.

Bingo! It was a shop. Or rather, it was a crumbling shack of mud and wattle and scraps of rusting tin that sold bottles of beer, candles, paraffin, matches, tins, and an assortment of other bric-a-brac – including women, I'm sure, if that's what the customer wanted.

We bought the mundane stuff, vegetable salad, sardines, bread, chicory, tinned milk, a box of cubed sugar, and then made our way back, through the steep, narrow streets, and up the dirt track, to the hellhole on the hill that Bruce was already referring to as home.

'Nearly there,' he said, as we took our last few weary steps up to the house. In the dark, all lit up with hurricane lamps, it actually didn't look too bad. 'Funny how you can get used to a place, any place, after a while,' he continued, as we climbed the veranda steps.

'Do you know Pete?' I asked, in an effort to be sociable. Bruce had, after all, abandoned his plans so he could look after me. It was the least I could do, although I'd have loved to have just gone straight for the book and the pen, because that's where I felt closest to Andy.

'I've met him a couple of times, in Maiduguri.'

We stepped across the rubbish. Termites had already made a meal of the headless lizard, and all that was left was bone.

'What's he like?'

'He's okay. Good company, actually, the life and soul. Loves his drink and loves his dope. And he can tell a good joke.'

Inside, the fire was dying. Bruce dumped our buys and piled on some more wood. The flames crackled and hissed as they burst into life. We moved on, into the dark, dingy kitchen, Bruce bringing along a lit hurricane lamp because, as you might have guessed, Pete's house had no electricity.

'Does he look dirty?'

'Who? Pete.' Bruce chuckled. 'No, he doesn't look any different from the rest of us.' Bruce was bending down and re-lighting the wood-burning stove. Flames and black smoke billowed out. We both took a step back, and opened windows and door. Cool, fresh air wafted in.

'Fill the kettle up, would you,' said Bruce, unwrapping bread from a thick layer of newspaper.

I went to the one single tap and turned. For a second or two, nothing, then out came a trickle of water, followed by a splutter and a burst. I filled the dirty, black kettle and placed it on top of the stove.

'It'll take a while to heat up,' Bruce stated. He was opening drawers. Most were empty of kitchen things, but full of crawly things. One, though, held a couple of items of cutlery, a few forks, spoons, knives, a wooden ladle; Bruce had a rattle around and found what he was looking for, a tin opener.

'Shit, we forgot to buy margarine. D'you mind?'

He was peeling back the top of a sardine lid, using the key that went with it. I shook my head. Why the fuck would I mind about something as piddling as no margarine when I'd just lost so much. Besides, I wasn't even hungry. All I wanted was a cup of coffee, a thousand joints, and my notebook and pen. The words of a song came and I sang them in my head.

So lock me away/And don't allow the day/Here inside where I hide/With my loneliness/I won't stay in a world without love... lah..lah..lah

Depressing stuff, but then again, it was a depressing day.

I wandered out of the kitchen where the smoke still billowed, and left Bruce to his culinary preparations. Picked up my cigarettes from off the table, and watched a cockroach crawl out from under a book, it dropped on the floor with a thud. I lifted my foot, and stamped; there was a dreadful cracking noise as it died.

With a sigh, I threw myself in a chair, found Bruce's handkerchief in the pocket of my skirt, and blew my nose; then lit a cigarette and stared at the flames in the fire. Tears welled up; I ached with longing and loneliness. A noise from behind, from somewhere near the French doors, I looked around quickly.

There was nothing and nobody.

Oh God, I would have given anything for Andy to have walked through that door. I imagined him smiling. Putting out his arms and saying: 'Come here, Janni.' And I'd come, of course I would, I'd throw myself in his arms. And he'd say, as he kissed and caressed me: 'God, what a fool I've been.'

A moth bumped up against the hurricane lamp, a beetle droned nearby. I could hear Bruce in the kitchen, a clattering of plates, kettle, and forks and knives. I smoked my cigarette and stared at the fire. And began to go through every moment Andy and I had spent together, starting at the beginning, with the first day, when we were all standing outside the Woodruffs' house, he'd come along on his bike, and had slowed down and smiled, saying, 'Hi, how you doing,' in his beautiful voice. Had I known, even then? It felt as if I'd always known.

So why had it all ended like this?

I buried my face in my hands.

Bruce had gone to great efforts. Somehow, he'd managed to toast the bread, and used the oil from the sardines as a margarine replacement. He'd cut up the fish, and mixed them with a chopped onion and some sliced up tomatoes. 'Found them in the vegetable plot out the back,' he said rather proudly.

I couldn't be bothered to ask why someone like Pete, who lived in utter, total squalor, would do something so prissy as grow vegetables. It just didn't make sense. But then again, nothing made sense anymore.

Next to the sardine mix, was a little mound of vegetable salad; again, Bruce had added tomatoes and onions to give one of the Heinz 57 varieties a fresh touch.

'Enjoy,' he said, tucking in.

As if?

Ten minutes later his plate was empty, and mine was still full.

'Christ, you've got to eat, pet,' he exclaimed, eyeing up my untouched dinner.

'I'm really not that hungry, Bruce,' I replied. 'Here, you have it.'

'Well, if you're sure.' Already his hand was out, his empty plate down on the floor.

'I'm sure.' I leant over the side of my chair and picked up my mug of coffee. I took a sip. 'Have you got any dope?'

Bruce nodded. His mouth was full of sardines and tomatoes. 'There's some in my rucksack. In the side pocket. In a tin.'

I put down my mug. 'Can I make myself a joint?'

'Help yourself.' He wiped away a blob of something that had begun to run down his chin. 'Are you out, then?'

'Yeah.' I got up, and went to the bag, and had a fumble around. Like he said, the tin was in the side pocket. 'Andy had all our dope,' I explained, sitting down again. Just saying his name and I wanted to cry. Sniffing, I tried hard to focus on the job but was all fingers and thumbs.

'Here, let me do it.'

Willingly, I passed it over. Sat back in the old, mouldy chair, and stared at the fire, and stared at the fire for ages, watching the flames flicker and dance.

Time passed. Absently, I took the joint from Bruce; absently, I puffed and let the drug do its business.

And stared at the fire, watching the flames flicker and dance.

From somewhere far away, I heard Bruce moving about. Now he was speaking, saying something about mattresses, about making up our beds for the night. 'I think it's best we both sleep together tonight.'

'What!' I dragged my eyes away from the flames, and looked at Bruce. 'What did you say?'

He looked ever so embarrassed. 'I don't mean sleep together,' he quickly explained. 'I mean the both of us sleep here in this room.' He pointed to a small, single-sized mattress that lay on the floor. 'I found this in one of the cupboards in the spare room. I thought you could have it. There's a blanket, as well, if you want.'

'Thanks,' I said, not really caring. I doubted if I'd be sleeping at all tonight.

'I'll sleep over here,' Bruce continued. Proving his point, he now had a hold of his sleeping bag, and was opening it up, and laying it down some distance from my mattress and blanket.

'Thanks,' I said once again.

Bruce pottered off to the bathroom, taking the tilly lamp. I watched his shadow disappear into the gloom. Oh, fuck I wished he were Andy. For a while, I sat in my chair and continued to do nothing except stare into the fire and try to figure out what life was all about. But my mind, like my stomach, felt hollow and empty; I just couldn't figure anything out.

In the end, I picked up my notebook and began to read all my poems. And when I'd read them, I wrote a few more. And when Bruce returned from the bathroom, a mite sheepish dressed in his Y-fronts, I asked if he minded me reading him out some of my current creations. Being a nice bloke, if he did mind, he didn't say.

'Go ahead,' he nodded and quickly got into his sleeping bag. Vaguely – it was just a brief, one-second passing thought – I did wonder if he were really still a virgin. Funny how all the good guys usually always were.

'I'll go and get washed first,' I said enthusiastically for even in my darkest moments, I always liked an audience. I got out of my chair, grabbed my sponge bag from my basket, picked up the tilly lamp, and headed off down the murky, dirty corridor where ghosts hung about in the shadows. And Dracula probably, there were that many bats.

My night-time ablutions didn't take long.

Quickly, I washed my face in the trickle of water that drip-drip-dripped out of the rusty old tap that hung half off the wall. Cleaned my teeth, and did a pee in the foul-smelling toilet, watched on by a couple of lizards who were peeping at me from over the fungus-ridden cistern.

Five minutes later I was back in the sitting room. Bruce, leaning on his elbow, was rolling a joint. 'Here,' he said, chucking me another, 'this one's for you.'

'Cheers,' I said, and took off my skirt. Bruce pretended not to look. Grabbing my matches, and my notebook and pen, I settled myself down on the mattress, and pulled up the blanket. With my head against the chair, I lit up, and turned to the first page.

'I dreamt a dream one night,' I began.

Bruce took his glasses off, moved his arm and lay back on the floor, with his eyes to the ceiling. Smoke drifted out of his mouth. Oh, God, how I wished he was Andy.

'A dream of long ago.'

Outside, the endless churring of the crickets and the metallic chinking of fruit bats infiltrated the room, and mingled with the crackle and spit of the fire.

'How I went with you, along a distant shore, Beneath the world of now...'

And so I went on. Until I came to the very last page – where the poems ended, and my letter to Andy began.

Bruce let out a very loud snore.

Goodnight, I said silently. Not to Bruce really, but to Andy. Oh, God, I thought, why aren't you here? I wanted to talk to him; so wanted to sort out this dreadful business with him once and for all.

Quietly, I got out of bed – if you could call it that – and dragged the mattress nearer to the fire. And there I sat, on the lumpy bolster, with a heart full of lead, watching the dying embers, for quite a while, making up conversations with Andy in my head.

Conversations, where I always, but always, had the upper hand, and could always, but always, come up with a sharp, clever, witty retort. And where Andy would always, but always, throw himself at my feet, and would always, but always, beg for forgiveness and plead with me to take him back. And I would toss my hair, just a little, and I would...

I picked up my pen, my notebook, and lit up a fag.

My darling Andy, I wrote…
Nights in white satin,
Never reaching the end,
Letters I've written,
Never meaning to send…

I didn't get much sleep that night, as well you can imagine. Tossing and turning, and thinking about Andy. Wandering around the shadowy room dimly lit through the open windows by the distant moon and stars; with its cobwebs and lizards, and spiders and moths, smoking cigarette after cigarette, and thinking about Andy.

Stepping over Bruce, gently snoring, to the French doors to gaze into the night; out to the silhouettes of the distant hills, and thinking about Andy.

All in all, it was a tortuous night.

Next morning, very early, I made my way to the steep outcrop overlooking the plateau where Andy and I had sat – was it only just a few days ago? It was still dark, but on the very edge of the hills silhouetted to the eastern horizon, the sky was fading from the deep dark velvet of night to a pale powder blue flecked with gold. Stars still flickered in the sky, dimming as lighter shades of the purest jade spread over them. Dawn was approaching.

I found our rock, and sat down on the precise bit where I thought Andy had planted his bum. 'Oh, Andy,' I croaked, 'where did it all go wrong?' From far away the call of a village cockerel echoed faintly. Had Andy heard it too? Tears swelled my eyes, and dripped down my face. 'This can't be the end, surely,' I sobbed. 'We meant so much to each other. We were so happy. You gave me so much love. Remember?'

A harsh kee-kee from way up above, a bird sailing over the treetops. Oh, to have wings, oh, to be able to fly. It would be so easy then, all I had to do was follow the mountains to the east, and somewhere in amongst them all, I'd find my beautiful, my wonderful-

'Oh, Andy.' I buried my face in my hands, and my sobs echoed around the hills. 'I can't believe I'll never see you again.'

I cried uncontrollably for a good twenty minutes.

And all the while the sun was waking up, creeping over the edge of the escarpment, turning the sky from black, to red, to blue. And as the world turned from dark to light, the faint but unmistakeable sounds of African village life intruded on my grief; the demented call of an elderly rooster, the insistent blatting of a goat, the rhythmic pounding of wood on wood.

I wiped my eyes, sniffed hard, and took a deep breath; and a fag, from the packet beside me. The breeze blew out the first match, but I managed to light the cigarette with the second.

Slowly I puffed.

The sun was now high in the sky, with puff candy clouds drifting lazily over the green, rolling hills of the plateau. A misty-blue haze of wood smoke hung low over a patch of trees in the middle distance. It was a beautiful sight; it was a beautiful morning.

And enjoying the scenery, gave me time to reflect. And time to come up with a plan. A plan that might, just might actually work.

Yep! I hadn't given up all hope as yet. Down but not out – so the saying goes.

'I've come to a decision.'

I was kneeling down, shaking Bruce. He stirred, lifted an arm, yawning. 'Huh?'

'Here, I've made you a coffee.' I set the cup down on the floor.

'Mmm.' Bruce stretched, and rolled away, on his back. 'Cheers.' He didn't move, and his eyes were still closed.

I shook him again. 'C'mon, it'll get cold, Bruce.'

Yawning, like a sleepy cat, he opened one bleary eye, and gave a little groan. 'What's the time?' Then blindly reached for his glasses, picked them up, put them on, and blinked at me several times.

I peered at my watch. 'Seven – just gone.'

'Cor, that's a bit early.' He pushed himself up into a sitting position. I passed him his cup. 'Cheers.' He took a sip.

Mission accomplished, I got to my feet, and sat down in the nearest chair, and lit up a fag. 'I've come to a decision, Bruce…'

'Pass us one over.'

I took a cigarette from the pack next to me, chucked it, and a box of matches, down to him. 'I'm going back to Maiduguri.'

The first fag of the day, and Bruce coughed. 'Oh, yeah,' he said, when the splutter had finished.

I nodded. 'Yeah, I'm going to wait for Andy to come back.'

Bruce looked at me quizzically. 'What do you mean?'

'I mean, I'm going to wait for Andy to come back from the Cameroon. He's due back in Maiduguri around the fourteenth. I'll stay at his house, and sort it out with him when he gets back.'

Bruce took another sip of coffee – and grimaced (maybe the

245

coffee was already cold). 'What,' he asked, 'are you planning to sort out?'

I rolled my eyes up to heaven, or rather the rafters where hung the cobwebs. 'Whatever it is that's gone wrong.'

Bruce took another puff. Smoke swirled out of his nose. 'I suppose it's up to you, pet, whatever you do,' he said, after a while. But he didn't sound convinced.

'Don't you think it's a good idea?'

Bruce shrugged. 'I'm not sure…'

His lack of enthusiasm for my grand plan was pissing me off.

'Oh, come on, Bruce, you said Andy needed some space, right?'

Scratching his armpit, he nodded.

'And now he's got it,' I cried triumphantly. 'Give him two weeks, alone, in the Cameroon and he'll have all the time in the world to think about me – and things.' I dropped my finished fag into my empty coffee cup – there was a sizzle as it fell into the dregs – and immediately lit another. 'Don't you see, Bruce?' The spent match joined the drowned cigarette.

Bruce had taken off his glasses, and was rubbing his eyes. He put them back on. 'Yeah, I hear what you say.'

I leaned forward, and looked at Bruce intently.

'He loved me, Bruce. He really loved me, you know. It was –' the frog popped up in my throat – 'the best love that could ever be.' I stopped for a second, and swallowed the frog. 'I can't tell you, Bruce, what it's been like these past couple of weeks. Horrible. One minute Andy's so nasty, but the next minute he's wonderful and loving. If he's really, really gone off me, then why does he tell me he still loves me?'

Bruce gave another shrug.

'Exactly!' I declared, 'He wouldn't would he, if he didn't?'

A rather baffled Bruce had another scratch under his other armpit, and dropped his butt into his half-drunk coffee cup. The sizzle sound came as quickly as it went.

On a roll, I leaned even further forward in my chair, so my knees were almost touching the ground.

'Last week, for example, when we were in Mubi, he was foul. It was a fucking nightmare. He wouldn't talk to me. He ignored me. It was the loneliest Christmas Eve I've ever had, Bruce.' I swallowed hard; the memory of it all had brought the frog out again. 'But two days later, on the river, he was fantastic to me. We had the best time ever.' This time I smiled, even though the frog had got stuck. 'And, in the middle of the bush, he actually said to me, 'I'll search all of Africa for you, Janni, if you ever went away.'

Dramatic pause.

I took another puff, and wiped away a solitary tear that had escaped over my eyelid.

'So don't you see, Bruce?' My bottom lip trembled. 'I can't possibly give up now. I have to wait for Andy. I have to see how he feels after his time away from me. I can't possibly go straight back to Gombe, with everything still hanging in the air.' Another tear dropped.

Bruce, still looking a bit weary and bleary, gave me an ever so gentle smile. 'Looks like you've made your mind up, pet.'

'I have,' I said, sniffing.

'Well, come on then.' He unzipped his bag, exposing baggy Y-fronts and hairy, brown legs; for his sake, and for modesty's sake, I looked away. 'We'd best get a move on.'

We packed our stuff, and said a final – thank God – goodbye to Pete's horrible house. Marching down the track, we made our way to the Forestry office. It was a small building made up of mud-blocks, on the outskirts of town – if you could call Ngorogi a town. Walking up the dusty gravel path, we spotted a couple of Land Rovers parked under a coula tree, where a couple of village women, with baskets, were gathering the hard-shelled nuts to sell in the market. They giggled when they saw us, and we, because we didn't know Mambilla speak, giggled back, and gave them a nod and a 'how are you?'

Anyway, to cut a short story even shorter, as luck would have it, one of those very grey Forestry vehicles was just about to leave for Beli – remember, the fat-bellied (no pun intended) women smoking hemp in their pipes, that place – and we were given a ticket to ride.

So once again, we were off, back over the hills and down through the African savannah. The only difference being, of course, that Bruce, not Andy, was now my travelling companion. I can't tell you how many times I wished it were the other way round. And how many times that old frog came up in my throat as we passed places like Masai-Mara and Serti, and I'd think, the last time I was here, I was with Andy. And, even though the memories I had weren't all good, I quickly brushed the painful ones aside, and remembered only the best.

It was all very sad, but Bruce cheered me up, or did his very best to.

At Pete's house, amongst the cobweb-ridden books on the cobweb-ridden bookshelves, Bruce, when browsing, had come upon a paperback, entitled 'Candy'. Flicking through the pages he realised he'd picked up a real gem of a novel and had put it in his rucksack, to read at a later date.

'I know what will put a bit of a smile on that face,' said Bruce, as we shunted and juddered our way down the plateau. I gave him a withering look; then turned to gaze once more at the hallowed spot where Andy and I had shouted out our 'hello's to the passengers who'd been flying overhead in the aeroplane.

'Listen to this, Janni.' Bruce had a book in his hand, and was turning some pages. He smacked his moustached lips, and began.

'*Candy unzipped Mike, and his pink penis stood exposed, a throbbing, pulsating, eight inch member. Lovingly, Candy gave the stiff dick a lick. 'Mmm,' she sighed, 'I absolutely love the taste of cock...'*

I was aghast. 'Here. Let me have a look,' I said now giving Bruce, and his book, my full attention.

There was page after page of the same. '*Candy spread her legs, and moaned softly. His tongue was finding places inside her that she didn't know existed...*'

I'd never come across any book like it before in my life.

'Puts old DH Lawrence's tales quite in the shade, doesn't it?' said Bruce, chuckling.

I was pouring over a page.

'Bloody hell, Bruce, listen to this bit...'

And the following page... 'My God, Bruce! That *is* revolting.'

And further on... 'Yuck, how could she?'

And over the page... 'That's impossible!'

By the time we reached Beli we'd almost finished the book.

'I can't believe we're already here,' I exclaimed, as our driver slammed on the brakes, missing a donkey by an inch, and we went hurtling forward.

The usual inquisitive crowd gathered around as we jumped out, grabbed our bags, and paid off the driver.

'Na godi,' we shouted to him, as he whizzed the wheels, and hurtled away in a cloud of red dust, scattering people, donkeys and goats and chickens.

'Now what?' I turned to Bruce – wishing, with all my heart, he was Andy.

'We wait for a lorry.'

I looked up and down the empty, red henna road, at the seemingly endless straw-coloured vegetation, at the hot baking sky, at the mud-thatched huts, at the naked urchins with snot-covered noses, and flicked away at a fly.

'That could be forever, Bruce,' I sighed.

Bruce gave me one of his silly grins – the one that made him look like a mentally deficient amoeba – and hitched up his rucksack. 'Have faith,' he said, strolling over to shelter under the shade of a large baobab with massive roots, 'one will be along any minute, I'm sure.'

Six hours later, and we were still there, sitting on an old mat – kindly donated to us by one of the villagers – under the old tree, waiting and waiting for some old lorry to turn up, that was going to Yola.

It could have been a very miserable six hours, as well as you know. But actually it wasn't. Bruce had me in stitches a lot of the time by pretending that we were an old Yorkshire couple visiting a seaside resort. My name was Mabel, and Bruce was Fred.

'Eee, fancy an ice cream, luv?'

'Aye, I wouldn't say no.'

'Lyons Maid or Walls?'

''I think I'll have Walls, luv. They make a right proper sausage.'

'Aye, they do that. So, what will it be, luv? Cone or wafers?'

'I think I'll have a bit of both.'

'Eee, yer a canny lass. You don't miss a trick, do you, Mabel.'

And up got Fred. And the village kids, who had all turned out to stand in a semi-circle in front of us, staring round-eyed and silent, fascinated by our very presence, all scattered to make way for Fred.

'Eee, luv, I'm so sorry. The ice cream van's just gone. So, instead, I've got you a nice bowl of warm yoghurt from that nice man over there, who's looking rather splendid, don't you think, in his mother's dress.'

'Aye, lad. Didn't you say he came from Cleethorpes?'

'Aye, originally. But he said he took a wrong turn in Rotherham on the 601 bus, and ended up here.'

Well, we thought it was funny.

We also had a theme song: *What a Drag it is Getting Home.* We sang it a hundred times as we sat under the tree, and several hundred times, thereafter. Truly, the words befitted our predicament.

At long bloody last, as the sun was sinking in a huge red ball of fire behind the cassava tops and flights of birds were gorging themselves on invisible insects, darting and flickering in the dust-riddled air; and as Fred and Mabel were seriously toying with the idea of building themselves a nice bungalow and setting up home permanently here in Beli, a lorry rumbled into the village.

It was packed. There were about a dozen young lads hanging onto the sides, their black skins barely visible under a thick layer of red dust, and about forty people and their loads, plus thirty or so sackfuls of grain, piled high in the wagon. And only a few passengers got off, but many more – including us – got on. The back of the lorry was beginning to look like it was carting around Tangali Waja Mountain.

'Jesus,' I moaned, as I scrambled my way up the wooden slats, and poked my head over the side. 'There's hardly any room, Bruce.'

Bruce, already in the wagon, and already being shoved and elbowed by several grumpy passengers who quite obviously resented him, and his rucksack, and my basket, taking up their God-given space, gave me his hand. 'Just get in, and then we'll sort ourselves out.'

Easier said than done.

Not one of our fellow passengers would budge an inch. We scrambled hither and thither, desperate for just one itsy-bitsy bit of space, that's all we wanted, but the passengers weren't for moving.

An old fuddy-duddy, who we nicknamed 'Mallam', muttered every time we caught his eye, and prodded us with his umbrella if we got to within an inch of its length, and there were the 'Misses Fulani', who kept giving poor old Bruce 'drop dead' looks because, just once, his rucksack accidentally hit one of them on the head when we were doing the circuit around the lorry. In the end we climbed the summit, moving away from them all, and, like Hilary and his sherpa, had a magnificent, if somewhat precarious, view of the world in all its glory.

Or would have, if it hadn't been so dark.

'I don't feel very safe, Bruce,' I screamed, as the lorry trundled its way through the pitch-black bush, with the warm wind howling and blowing my hair in a zillion directions.

'Just hang onto me and you'll be fine,' Bruce screamed back. So I hung on, my arms around him, and his arms around me, for the whole of the bumping, rolling, dusty, uncomfortable journey. And all the time, for the whole of the bumping, rolling, dusty, uncomfortable journey, I so wished he were Andy.

At around about midnight we hit Jalingo town, and the lorry park. Here, almost all of the passengers got off. It was total chaos for about twenty minutes as stuff was unloaded, people grabbing and gabbling, and delving and digging for whatever, literally under our feet. And not once an, 'excuse me', or, 'do you mind'.

'How rude,' I snorted, as 'Mallam' gave Bruce a final prod with his brolly before scuttling over the side and disappearing into the midnight throng.

Bruce just laughed, and lit a cigarette. 'Man-fowl, he no de maka wahalla in other man-fowl compound,' he said, leaning back against the wooden slats to make way for a desperate Fulani who was after a bundle in our vicinity.

'What?!' I lifted my right foot, as the Fulani dived and retrieved his precious whatever, from beneath.

'It's an African saying. Surely you've heard that one before?'

'No.' I moved again, to make way for an old crone who was on hands and knees, sniffing as a dog, around my legs.

'I can't believe it, all us VSOs were told it almost as soon as we landed.'

'Oh, fuck off, Bruce.' I lit my own cigarette, and watched as the old lady, as nimble as a spring chicken, leapt over the wagon and disappeared with a sack full of rice and a pot full of yams. With her gone, Bruce and I were the only people left in the lorry. We threw ourselves onto a couple of sacks, and stretched out our legs.

'Cor, that feels better,' sighed Bruce.

It certainly did. The mountain had gone, and the interior of the wagon was now a soft, rolling hill. 'So, tell me, Bruce, what exactly does this stupid old African saying mean? Enlighten me, do.'

'Well –' Bruce smiled – and I thought: God why can't he just turn into Andy? – 'It means, only a very foolish cockerel would dare to trespass on another's territory and think he could rule the roost there. Get it?'

I shook my head. 'Not really.'

'It's not rocket science, Janni. Basically, it just means strangers in strange lands should maintain a low profile and should be prepared to obey the law of the land and not get freaked out too much.'

'Oh, I see,' I said, not seeing at all. I fiddled with a bit of the weave that had come loose on my basket. And felt somewhere inside me, a sob about to explode. Oh, God I so wanted Andy.

'Fancy a stretch?'

I did. It was the only way to deal with the inner ache that was threatening to turn me into a total, snivelling wreck. And, anyway, I wanted the loo. So we hid our stuff under one of the sacks, and scrambled down the sides of the lorry.

Due to the lateness of the hour, the lorry park was deserted, just a few lost souls aimlessly wandering around, either that or having a kip in the dirt. Apart from them, and a group of about six or seven men gathered around a small fire by the only stall open, it was just me and Bruce, and two bush dogs having a poke in the rubbish pile.

Quickly, before the riga clad lot by the fire spotted me, I did a piddle behind the back wheel of the lorry and Bruce duly did his bit for England on the other side.

Relieved, we wandered over to the stall to see what was cooking.

In the spectral moonlight, with the fire brightening up their black faces and their white robes, the group of hunched-up men looked quite surreal. It was definitely a very African moment.

'Sannu,' we said.

Mumbling, they 'sannued' us back, and then silently stared. After the African moment, it was now a bit of a scary moment. In the middle of the bush, in the middle of the night, with this lot, made me feel a tad vulnerable, especially when one of the bush dogs came and poked its nose up my privates. Gingerly, I stepped back, and hid behind Bruce, glad of his 6ft 3in massive frame.

'Shoo, go away. Bugger off.'

The dog had followed me round. Bruce gave it a kick in the bollocks. Yelping, the mange-ridden, possibly rabid-riddled hound, scuttled off.

'Hungry?' asked Bruce, as I returned to his side.

'A bit.'

'Let's see what they've got.'

Bruce led the way to the makeshift stall constructed out of some old pieces of corrugated tin (the walls), a couple of old wooden crates (the counter), and a piece of zanna matting (the roof). The proprietor of this rather grand establishment was squatting behind the boxes, and in the light of the small hurricane lamp that was flickering and hissing beside him, we could see he was having a piss, right by a couple of large pots of food that were bubbling away on top of a tiny, smoky fire.

That does it, I thought, I'm not eating any of that shite.

Next to mine host, almost hidden in the shadows, we noticed our lorry driver sitting on another wooden box, eating. He barely gave us a glance.

I whispered to Bruce. 'Ask him when the lorry's leaving.'

'How long the lorry leave?' Bruce's voice, so loud, so Yorkshire, so alien echoed around the empty lorry park and probably woke up most of Africa.

Shoving a rolled-up handful of what looked like Plasticine into his mouth, the driver shrugged. 'No go until tomorrow.'

'Oh, fuck, no,' I grumbled.

'What time tomorrow?' asked Bruce, unperturbed.

The driver, with another ball of Plasticine wiped the gravy off his plate. 'Six, maybe seven.'

'That's okay.' Bruce turned to me. 'It'll give us a chance for some shut eye.'

'Where?' I looked around the dusty, dirty lorry park half hoping the Hilton would flicker in neon somewhere over the mud, thatched edifices.

'In the lorry.'

'The lorry!'

'There's nowhere else. Unless you want to sleep in one of the doorways.'

'No thanks,' I said, and sighed. What a total, bloody nightmare. Abandoned, rejected, and subjected to spending a night on a fucking sack in the back of a flea bitten lorry, in the middle of the African wilderness, with bush dogs and sinister natives sniffing and loitering around. It was enough to make any young girl burst into tears.

'Hey, what's up?'

My life's in fucking ruins, and he asks what's up. 'Nothing,' I managed to say, in between ear-racking sobs.

A tad embarrassed, Bruce patted me gently on the back, like I was a baby with croup. 'Here, have a fag.' He was fumbling around in the pockets of his shorts. Out came matches, and a brand new packet. Through tears, I saw him break open the cellophane, and get me one out.

With shaking hands, I lit up, and puffed. Bruce took a drag on his. He passed one over to the driver, and the stallholder. 'Na godi,' they said, beaming. The blokes around the fire stirred. Bruce handed more cigarettes out. A dog started barking, a bundle of clothes fidgeted in the dirt. The moon came out, the stars shone. The night air vibrated to the songs of crickets and the rhythm of bat wings. Far away, a hyena gave out a laugh.

I dragged a hand across my sticky face. The sobs had subsided, even though my heart felt as heavy as a hard lump of granite. 'Sorry about that,' I mumbled.

Dear Bruce smiled and gave me another gentle pat on the back. 'It's okay,' he said, relieved that the moment of crisis was over. 'It's been a really long day. We're both tired. Let's get something to eat and have a kip, hey?'

'I'm really not hungry.'

'Janni, you've got to fucking eat. You'll waste away.' That suited me perfectly. But Bruce wasn't having any of it. 'Hey,' he said to the stallholder, 'give me two,' and pointed to the pots still bubbling away on the circle of fiery stones.

There was a clatter, bang of tin plates. A ladle, fashioned out of a small calabash, scooped up the mush.

'I'm not eating any of that,' I insisted.

'You are.' Bruce pointed to a mat in the dust. 'Sit down.'

I sat down. Bruce handed me a plate with a mound of steaming Plasticine, and a tin spoon that was bent.

'Eat.'

'I'm not eating…'

'Eat.'

Reluctantly, I dug into the mound. 'Look, Bruce, I'm really not that hungry…'

'For fuck's sake, Janni, just eat it, yeah.'

Sighing, I surrendered and popped the spoon into my mouth. It actually didn't taste that bad but the frog in my throat made swallowing a mite difficult and I had to gulp really hard.

With his own plate of mush, Bruce joined me on the mat. Thrusting out his long legs he made himself comfortable, and tucked in. One of the dogs bounded over. The stallholder picked up a stone, and threw it; a direct hit, there was a yelp, as the dog scuttled off.

'This is delicious,' said Bruce, munching.

'It's ok,' I agreed, shovelling in titbits.

And so we ate on. Above us, a bat flitted. Beside us, the hurricane lamp flickered and hissed.

'Want a drink?'

'Yeah.' A lone mosquito zoomed in and bit my arm. I gave it a slap but missed. 'Does he sell drinks?' I asked, scratching the spot and making it bleed.

'Dunno.' Bruce turned to the stallholder, who was now curled up, half asleep in the dirt, by his pots and his fire. Bruce leaned over, and prodded him. 'Hey, you have drink?' Sleepily, the bloke raised himself, and from behind his counter produced two bottles of orange Fanta. Bruce gave the thumbs up and handed over some kobos.

We drank the warm, sweet, fizzy liquid, and I managed to spoon in several more mouthfuls of food. Finished, we quietly passed our plates and our seriously misshapen spoons over to the stallholder, who raised himself, yet again, from off his mat, and chucked them in a large tin bowl full of murky, brown water. Then he settled himself down again, curling up, like a foetus in the dirt. Our lorry driver, on the other side of the makeshift edifice, resting his back against a piece of rusted, corrugated tin, was already fast asleep. His snores beat a rhythm and blended well with the distant beat of a drum and nearby whirr of the crickets.

We got out our cigarettes, lit up, and smoked.

It was a beautiful night, warm, but not too warm. Above us, a huge African moon bathed the empty lorry park in silvery lights and velvety shadows, and the dark silhouettes of the tropical trees and pointed thatched roofs beyond reminded me of a Christmas Nativity card. Nearby, the men around the fire talked in hushed tones; they were the shepherds awaiting the angel.

Andy, my Andy. He looked like an angel…

'Ready?' Bruce had stubbed out his fag. I nodded.

My darling Andy, I'm thinking of you, and I'm wondering what you're doing now…

We both got up. 'Sai gobi,' we said to the men by the fire.

Together, they turned and bade us goodnight.

Across the moonlit compound, we made our way home. A bloke, who looked like a pile of rags, except for the fact that we could hear him breathing, was tucked up under the lorry, by the front tyre.

'I hope he moves before the lorry does,' chuckled Bruce, as we climbed the wagon. Inside, there was one other passenger, fast asleep, on a sack. We clambered across to the place where we'd hidden our bags. Bruce delved into his rucksack and got out his sleeping bag. It reminded me so much of Andy – rucksacks and sleeping bags. I could feel tears welling up.

'Must go to the loo,' I croaked, and clambered back down the lorry.

At the bottom, I looked up at the sky, at the moon, and the stars. *Where are you, Andy, where are you*, I cried – but quietly, so quietly, so no one would hear. *I miss you so much.* And I let a tear fall.

'Psst.'

I glanced back at the lorry. Bruce's head was leaning over the side. His glasses gleamed in the moonlight. 'Are you alright?'

'Fine,' I managed to say. 'I'll be up in a minute.'

The tears spiralled down, and I wiped them away. More came, and I wiped them away. The bundle of rags under the lorry coughed and stirred. Quickly, I went round the other side, did a wee, and then clambered back up.

Bruce was already under the blanket. I lay down beside him.

'Night, night,' he said, turning over. I think he was a tad embarrassed, the both of us up close, almost intimate. Had I not been so choked up, so bereft, I might have found it really quite funny.

'Night, night,' I whispered back.

For a long time, I lay on a sack filled with grain, staring up at the heavens, listening to the endless buzz of the cicadas and the metallic chinking of fruit bats high up in the trees, making up fantasy stories, about Andy, with fairytale endings.

Until, at last, sleep overtook me.

Just as I was about to walk up the aisle and become Andy's bride.

The sun on my face, and a fly up my nose.

'Morning,' smiled Bruce, as I sat up and sneezed. *Zzzzz* went the fly as it got caught in the jet stream.

'Morning.' I blinked, and glanced at my watch. It was almost seven.

'Sleep alright?'

'Yeah, not bad. You?'

'Like a log.'

Yawning, I looked around. The lorry park was a hive of activity. Hawkers, cigarette sellers, meat-on-a-stick sellers, passengers getting on, and passengers getting off, all the usual lorry park crowd were there, milling around.

'Fancy some breakfast?' asked Bruce, sticking his legs out from

256

under the sleeping bag.

I threw my legs out too. It was so bloody hot.

'I could do with a drink.'

'Hang on.' Bruce scuttled off, crawling across the sacks, and to the side of the wagon. And, because I had nothing better to do, I followed suit. We both leaned over the wooden slats. There was a bit of a flurry as the crowd spotted us; before we knew it, several dozen entrepreneurs, and the just very curious, had gathered around the lorry. 'Changi, changi.' 'Abinche, abinche.' One little lad wanted to sell us a banana, another had an orange, and somebody else chucked up a grapefruit. Bruce tried to catch it but missed and it fell back into the crowd and was lost in a scrum of kids who went hell for leather, battling for possession.

'What's that he's selling?' I pointed to a bloke who was wheeling around a little cart filled with blue plastic mugs, and a rather large copper kettle.

'Hey,' shouted Bruce. 'Come here.'

Grinning, the lad pushed himself and his mobile shop through the mob, still fighting over the grapefruit, and ignoring the shuffles and shoves, looked up and gave out a bellow. 'Hot choc-o-late. Hot choc-o-late.'

'Oh, yeah,' I smiled. 'I'll have some of that.'

'Nowa, nowa?' Bruce was leaning right over, another inch and he'd be down there with the grapefruit – which, by the way, was now totally and utterly squashed.

The boy gave his price, two cups for fifteen kobo. 'Ten,' shouted Bruce. Fifteen it was.

A few minutes later, we were sitting on our sacks, sipping Bournvita. Meanwhile, other passengers were now starting to join us. One man, with an embroidered Muslim cap, and chewing coula nuts, perched himself down, and began spitting straight sprays of stained, rusty saliva at a dangerous angle, over the side of the lorry. Just what you want first thing in the morning. Then there was a funny old bloke, with a wizened old face, wrinkled, and as black as a prune. His body was as scrawny as a skeletal bush dog, and the only thing he was wearing was a singularly grubby pair of tattered shorts of indeterminate colour draped round his skinny loins. A collection of mammies also clambered on, some with tiny babies slung on their backs, with only their little round heads visible above the swathes of brightly coloured cloth wrapped around them. And one very attractive woman, with large velvety eyes, sat right next to

Bruce. I could see he was sweating, and I'm not sure that was just from the heat of the sun. She was beautiful, sensual, and knew it, with her glass beads round her neck, and her braids, and her shimmering, ebony body.

'I think she likes you,' I said to Bruce, winking.

'Fuck off,' responded Bruce, and turned, blushing, the other way.

By the time we were ready to hit the latterite tracks, the lorry was as jam-packed as usual, except that this time Bruce and I had got there first, and we had prime position – two sacks, one for each of us, and no one, not even Velvety Eyes, was allowed to share. Like Bruce said, man-fowl, he no de wahalla in other man-fowl compound – we were just obeying the law of the land.

Six hours later, dirty, filthy, knackered, exhausted, and any of a dozen other descriptive words that may best sum up two people who have just crossed the dusty African bush in an open-topped, jam-packed mammy-wagon. Basically, as we chugged into Yola, Bruce and I were fucked.

And I was a little depressed. Going over the bridge, with the river stretching out either side, I glimpsed distant islands, and felt bereft. Oh, God, I so wanted to go back to those happy, carefree few days.

'We'll head for the Forestry Rest House,' Bruce was saying.

I was sailing down the Benue with Andy, in our dugout boat.

'Sorry?' *We were in the water, splashing about.*

'Come on, Janni. Get your basket.'

The fantasy faded. We were at the lorry park and everyone was piling off. I grabbed my stuff. Bruce was already over the side, and out of the lorry. 'Here,' he said, looking up at me, hands ready to catch me and my loads. I passed him my basket, and made my way down.

Back on terra firma, we hitched up, and set off through the throng. Hawkers and beggars zoomed in, but we did our best to ignore them. Out of the lorry park we spotted a Ministry of Agriculture Land Rover coming towards us. We hailed it, and the vehicle stopped. The driver, with quite startling tribal facial markings, leaned across the passenger seat and wound down the window. 'Where you go?'

'To the Forestry Rest House. You know it?' answered Bruce, already with his hand on the handle.

'I know it. I take you.' Bruce opened the passenger door. I

jumped in, the bags were chucked in the back, and Bruce slid in beside me.

'Thanks,' we both said, and gave the driver a smile.

And so we chugged through the clogged-up traffic, and the kamikaze Africans, in baking heat. And I was thinking about Andy. *We walked up this street together, hand in hand, so in love, with not a care in the world. Oh, God, Andy I miss you...*

'Where you come from?' the driver was asking.

'Maiduguri,' replied Bruce, fanning his face with Candy's book.

'Ah, Maiduguri. Maybe you know my brother who lives there-'

I wasn't really listening. In fact, I wasn't even there. I was miles away, on an island with Andy.

The journey went really quickly, and before I knew it, we were at the Forestry Rest House. We piled out, and grabbed our bags. 'Cheers,' said Bruce, and handed the driver a tip. He smiled, wished us well, reminded Bruce to give greetings to his brother, and was gone. Picking up our stuff, we traipsed across the sandy compound, and made our way up the veranda steps, and into the cool of the house.

'Janni! Bruce!'

Anne, under the 'chunk chunk chunk' of the fan, sitting reading a book, sprang to her feet. 'My God, I wasn't expecting you to turn up. How lovely.' She rushed over and gave both of us a hug. Disentangling ourselves, Anne looked at me, quizzically, 'Weren't you and Andy going to the Cameroon?'

Tears pricked my eyes and the frog came up and croaked. Quickly, Bruce intervened. 'A bit of a change of plans,' he said, almost apologetically, as if he was the 'Boo Hiss' villain of the story.

'Oh,' replied Anne, not quite getting it. She looked over at the door, and beyond, expectant. 'Where's Andy?' Just the mention of his name, and I burst into tears.

'Whatever's wrong?' Anne's arms were around me, she drew me to her, and I buried my face in her rather large bust. 'What's up?' I couldn't answer, I was totally in pieces. Crying and crying. 'What's happened, Bruce?' I heard Anne ask.

'It's a bit of a long story, Anne,' I heard Bruce say.

I sobbed even more.

'Shush, shush.' Gentle hands steered me down into a chair, gentle hands stroked the wet hair off my face. 'There, there, let it all come out.'

And it did finally, everything, from beginning to end. Right up to this very moment.

'Oh, God, I'm so sorry, Janni,' Anne said, as I paused for breath, and blew on my hanky. 'I can't believe it. You've been through a terrible time.'

I had. Whimpering pathetically, I blinked back a few more tears. Bruce passed me over a lit cigarette. I drew on it, and sniffed. 'So, what do you think, Anne? Do you think I should go back and wait for Andy in Maiduguri?'

I'd have gone anyway, even if she'd said no, but I still needed reassurance, still needed to cling on to some vestige of hope, someone to say that it would all end up alright, that there would be a Happy Ever After finale.

Anne blew smoke out of her mouth. I waited, and fiddled with the ring on my finger. '*Let this be a symbol of our love…*'

'Yeah, I do.' Anne took another drag, and nodded. 'He might feel quite different after a couple of weeks on his own.' She glanced round at Bruce. 'What do you reckon, Bruce? Do you think it's a good idea?'

Bruce, dear, sweet Bruce, totally out of his depth when it came to the affairs of the heart, threw me a sympathetic look. 'What have you got to lose, Janni?'

Precisely. I'd already lost it all, anyway.

'So,' Anne reached for the ashtray, and flicked, 'when are you planning on going back to Maiduguri?'

'I'm not sure,' I said, looking at Bruce for the answer.

Bruce, it seemed, wasn't sure either. He shrugged. 'Dunno, really. I was still thinking about making the return journey and going on to Baissa, as originally planned, but,' he scratched his ear, 'if you want, I can do that some other time, and travel back to Maiduguri with you…'

'Hang on!' Anne smiled, radiant with inspiration. 'You can come back with me, Janni. I'm flying back the day after tomorrow.'

Did I hear right? 'Flying?'

'Yeah,' nodded Anne, happily. 'They've got a little airport here in Yola, didn't you know?'

I didn't know. But I liked the idea of flying back to Maiduguri. I'd had enough of mammy-wagons, and dust, and endless savannah.

'Will it cost much, the ticket?'

Anne shook her head. 'No, about thirty naira, not much more I reckon. Have you got money? I'll lend you some if you haven't.'

Weren't people nice? Bruce. Anne. After all the horrors, their

260

kindness meant such a lot. 'No, I think I've got enough, thanks.' Actually, I had loads of money left. Mum had given me about a hundred naira, and I'd hardly spent any of it. The African bush doesn't have that many shopping centres, and a kobo here, and a kobo there, still doesn't add up to much.

Bruce, relieved I think that his babysitting days were finally over, got up and out of his chair. 'Well, now that that's all sorted, I think I might grab a kip. I'm knackered.' He looked at Anne. 'Any beds free?'

'Plenty. Apart from you two, there's just me and a bloke from Kano, Mark, who's heading off to Gwoza tomorrow. Amy and the others went back to Maiduguri yesterday by road but I couldn't be bothered with a ten hour bus ride, that's why I'm flying.'

Bruce picked up his rucksack. 'Well, it's a good job it worked out the way it did, I'm glad you're here' He smiled at us both, and gave out a yawn. 'See you in a bit, hey.'

'Thanks, Bruce,' I said, still a bit sniffy. 'You really have been ace.'

Patting my shoulder, he gave me another really nice smile. 'Don't mention it. What are friends for?'

'He's a good bloke, isn't he?' I said to Anne, when Bruce had pottered off down the corridor in search of a bed.

'Yeah. You were really lucky he was there.'

Lucky is hardly how I'd have described my world at the moment, but I knew what she meant, and mumbled an, 'Mmm,' in agreement.

'God,' Anne continued, shaking her head, still quite baffled by it all. 'I can't believe Andy would do something like this to you. It's just so – so out of order.'

Sighing, I nodded, and wiped away another blob that threatened to trickle. Cue for Anne to rise to her feet. 'Why don't you have a bath,' she suggested. 'It'll make you feel so much better.' She pointed to the lethargically moving fan, 'The electricity's still on so there'll be plenty of hot water.'

I looked down at my black, grimy hands, at my red, grimy trousers, and laughed, despite myself. 'I could do with one, couldn't I? I must stink.'

Anne wiggled her rather big nose. 'Just a bit.'

Well, I had a bath, and it was lovely. The luxury of lying in hot, hot water – when did I last do that? – cleansing myself of all the muck and the shite picked up on my travels. Of course I felt better after it; still weighed down with sorrows and sadness, and my eyes still sore with the crying, and my face still a bit red and blotchy, but I did feel better.

When I returned to the sitting room, I found we had company.

'Have you met Vernon?' asked Anne.

No, I hadn't. He was a big monstrosity of a man, with a moustache that was equally massive – the tips actually touched his collarbones, and curled round his shoulders.

We exchanged greetings.

'Janni's from Gombe,' explained Anne. 'She and Bruce just got in, they've been down in Mambilla for the New Year.'

'Lovely place, Mambilla,' responded Vernon, moving his large bulk around in the chair, and making the springs squeak out in pain. 'I was there a few weeks back, visiting Pete in Ngorogi. Do you know Pete?'

'No.' I fumbled around in my bag for a fag. 'But we did stay at his house.' I made a face, wrinkled my nose. 'It was a bit, well, a bit awful.'

'It's certainly that,' Vernon chuckled, getting a box of matches from out of his pocket, and striking a light. He leaned over, and I lit up and puffed. 'So where are you and Bruce heading off to next?' Vernon leaned back in his chair; 'bo-in-gg' went the coils.

Embarrassed, I looked quickly at Anne. She laughed. 'Bruce and Janni are not an item, y'know.'

'Whoops, sorry.' He winked at me. 'I thought Bruce had just got lucky.'

Flicking ash in the ashtray, I took another drag and wondered whether I should make my position clear; tell Vernon all about Andy, all about my boyfriend, Andy. But then he'd ask me why I was here, and Andy was off somewhere in the Cameroon mountains. What would I say to that?

So I diverted the subject. 'Where are you from, Vernon?'

'Here. Yola. I teach.'

'VSO?'

'No, contract. It's my second tour. I was in Makurdi last time, but got posted here for my sins. Actually,' he said, delving into the top pocket of his denim shirt, and bringing out a pipe, and a pouch of tobacco, 'Yola's not that bad really. There's far worse places, I reckon.'

Yeah, like Gombe, I wanted to say. But I didn't, because at that point Bruce walked in. He looked all tousled and sleepy.

'Hey.' He smiled at Vernon. 'Good to see you, mate.'

Vernon stood up – he was enormous, made Bruce look almost petite – and gave him a buddy slap on the shoulder. 'Yeah, good to see you, too. Anne told me you were in town.' That said, they both sat down, and gabbled in a blokish kind of way, as blokes do. Meanwhile, Anne went off in search of the houseboy to see if he would rustle us up a pot of tea. 'Make mine a coffee,' Vernon called out, as she disappeared through to the kitchen. Then he turned back to Bruce, and sucked on his pipe, Bruce lit up a fag, and they both carried on talking in a blokish kind of way, as blokes do.

As for me? Well, I just sat there playing with my cigarette packet, and thought about Andy. *Where was he? What was he doing this minute? And was he thinking about me?*

'Meet anyone on your travels?' Vernon was saying.

'Half of Maiduguri for a start,' chuckled Bruce. 'There was a whole crowd down in Serti, staying at Richard's. I expect Anne's told you. Most of them went on to Baissa, which was where I was planning to go after the New Year but I...' Bruce stopped; remembered me, glanced over, '...I decided to come back to Yola with Janni.'

'Did you travel down to Mambilla together?' asked Vernon. Bruce said yes. I nodded. And so their conversation continued.

And I went back to my daydreams and thoughts. Back to the day when Andy and I were last here in this room. *He sat over there, and I was here, in this same chair. He wouldn't look at me, would he? Remember? But then–*

'Yeah, I heard Andy was down that way. So he's gallivanting around in the Cameroon, is he? Hasn't he got some girlfriend or other...'

A bolt of lightning seared through my body.

'–who's with him, somebody mentioned she...'

The door flew open, and in came Anne, carrying a tray. 'Sorry, no coffee, Vernon, and only condensed milk.' She plopped the loaded tin platter down on the floor. 'Is that okay?' She looked at us all. And we all nodded our heads. 'Shall I be mum then?'

Cups chinked, and Anne poured, and while we sipped, the conversation turned to more topical issues, like where shall we go for supper tonight, the Government Rest House versus the club on the hill. Decisions, decisions, decisions.

I was relieved.

Not about making plans for supper – I still wasn't at all hungry

– I just didn't want anyone else knowing about me and Andy. Rejection was humiliating enough without having the added embarrassment of everyone cottoning on to the fact that Andy had dumped me in the middle of the African bush without a backwards glance.

It had been worrying me this. Ever since I'd made the decision to return to Maiduguri, I'd been wondering: What do I say to everyone there? That we've split up? That I'm hoping for a reconciliation? I imagined the pitiful looks. The bombardment of helpful advice. The suggestion – maybe – that I was being a silly, young fool. Go home – save face – it's over – were words I really, really did not want to hear.

And it was whilst sitting here in the Rest House that I finally came up with a plan. I would lie. Just a small lie, a little porky, so no one, not Hamish, not Rosie, not Buggy, would be any the wiser. We'd run out of money, that's what I'd say. We decided, therefore, as I wasn't that bothered about visiting the Cameroon and Andy was, that he venture onwards, and I go back to Maiduguri to await his return.

Yep, that's what I'd say.

It was an excellent plan.

CHAPTER 8

January 1974; the first couple of weeks

'So what shall we do with ourselves today?'

Anne and I were out on the veranda, it was early morning, and we were having an early morning cup of tea. Inside, we could hear the houseboy hard at work, the harsh scraping of a rattan broom, the creaking of floorboards as mosquito nets were un-tucked and the big iron rest-house beds were made.

Bruce was long gone, Vernon had given him a lift before sun-up, and he was probably half-way back to Mambilla, re-tracing his footsteps, as Anne spoke. And the guy from Kano, well he was still fast asleep in his pit, and was planning to catch a mammy-wagon to Gwoza sometime later this afternoon.

'Dunno?' I shrugged, not really that bothered about doing anything. I could have sat here on the veranda all day. After almost two weeks of travelling, and sleeping rough, and baking under a hot, hot sun, it was lovely to be still and out of the heat.

Besides, I had other things on my mind.

'Oh, come on,' insisted Anne, placing her chipped cup down on the floor, and picking up her fags and her matches, 'we can't just sit and do nothing.' She chucked me a ciggie, I grabbed my matches, and in synchronised fashion we lit up. 'Y'know it's the first day of Sallah today,' she said puffing.

I didn't.

'Oh, look,' exclaimed Anne, pointing a finger, 'isn't that a parrot?' A bright green-feathered bird had landed just a few feet from us and was pecking away at something on the veranda wall. I turned abruptly in my chair to get a better look, and instantly it flew off, the sunlight illuminating its plumage in all its iridescent splendour. 'How lovely,' cooed Anne, 'I don't think I've seen a green parrot here before in Nigeria.'

'Mmm,' I mumbled, with total disinterest. As you know, I really did have other things on my mind.

'So,' said Anne, returning back to our plans for the day, 'how about you and me checking out the Durba? The houseboy says it's being held in the old part of Yola. What do you reckon?'

Not a lot.

Having spent most of my life in Nigeria, I'd been to many a Durba, all part of the Sallah/Muslim celebrations. It was just a load of turbaned blokes riding madly on a load of dressed-up horses. Throw in the odd sultan, or two, a hundred trumpets, a few thousand swords, and a heck of a lot of dust, and there you have it – a Durba.

But Anne had never been to one, and really, really wanted to go.

An hour later we were walking down an empty road under a hot, shimmering sky.

'The town's miles away,' I grumbled, sweat pouring off me. Where was a blooming Forestry Land Rover when you really needed one?

'A bit further on, we'll hit the cross roads,' said Anne brightly, to keep up my spirits that were plummeting with every footstep. 'We're bound to get a lift somewhere along the way.'

'Mmm,' I replied, a tad sarcastic.

We plodded on. And the sun got hotter and hotter. And at the crossroads we took a left, and still we plodded on. To our right, about a mile away, was the river, a gleaming muddy-brown expanse of water cutting through yellow plains dotted with acacias and mud-thatched villages. Another mile or so away, in front of us, was Yola town, tins roofs shining like mirrors in the sun.

'Sannu,' we chorused to a woman walking sedately towards us. She had a huge pan on her head, piled high with market produce, balanced perfectly, while behind her four children in single file walked, in order of size, each with a bundle on their heads.

All of them, mum and the kids, giggled and 'sannued' us back.

A bit further on I scrambled into a tall thicket of grasses, all papery and dry, and did a piddle. As I emerged from my open-air latrine, a taxi-van hurtled down the red-rutted road. Anne stepped into its path and flagged it down. Skidding to a halt, and creating the usual mini dust storm, the taxi driver stuck his head out of the window. 'Where you go?'

'Yola town,' we both trilled.

'To the Durba,' Anne further explained.

'One naira.'

'One naira,' exploded Anne. 'You've got to be joking.'

The man obviously was. 'Ok. Ok. Fifty kobo for two.'

'That's more like it,' smiled Anne.

There was a lot of scrabbling about. We were VIP's after all, and so the four passengers already squashed up in the front seat of the taxi were herded into the back where there were about ten others all on top of each other. Anne and I did mildly protest, 'No, no, we'll go in the back,' but thankfully they all said, 'Ba komi,' 'No worry.' So we didn't and got the best seats in the house.

And so we rumbled on down the hill, and into town. Already, even before we hit the Durba proper, you could see Yola was in celebratory mood. The busy streets were heaving more so than ever, and the usual din had become a strident, incessant racket, with gangs of hawkers, and mutilated beggars, grabbing at passer-by's from every dusty, street corner. It was pure, utter mayhem.

'Exciting, isn't it?' whooped Anne, from our front row seat.

'If you like that sort of thing,' said I, unimpressed, wishing I was back on the quiet veranda.

It took us ages to get through the clogged-up mess of humans and traffic. We sat in a crawling line of ceaseless honking and tooting vehicles in baking heat. Petrol and exhaust fumes shimmered, and as soon as our two white faces were spotted our taxi was like a honey pot to bees. Beggars – including several lepers, oh how I shuddered – surrounded us, sticking their hands first through the windows; quickly Anne wound her side up, then pressing their noses against the glass, leaving silver lines of runny snot.

Yuck!

Finally, after we were fully roasted and ready for carving, we reached our destination. We were out of the business end of town now and in the old part where the Emir's palace and the mosque, both large mud-built edifices, loomed over their smaller mud-thatched and/or tin roofed counterparts.

'Bloody hell,' exclaimed Anne, wiping her wet, dripping brow with the hem of her skirt as she got out of the taxi, 'that journey was horrendous. I thought I was going to faint.'

For the first time that day I agreed with Anne. It was horrendous. And it was still horrendous. The heat was still there, intense, the beggars were still there, hundreds of them, and we were covered in bluebottles and flies. And the smell – oh, my God, the smell – was overpowering. An evil stench of rotting fruit, vegetables and decaying rats, all inextricably intermingled with the penetrating pong of vaporizing urine and human excreta.

Lovely.

Meanwhile, Anne was dragging me through the throng. 'Look,' she was saying, 'there's a couple of Europeans over there. Come on, let's join them.'

'Where?' I was saying, trying to spot two white faces in a sea of ebony-black.

'Over there. Come on.'

We managed to find a way through the mass, to a less crowded spot where, yes indeed there were two Europeans, a bloke and a woman, sitting in the shade of a colossal kapok tree, on a mat. 'Hi, there,' they said, with welcoming smiles, and foreign accents. They shifted over, and patted the mat. 'Please take a seat.'

'Phew, thanks,' Anne said gratefully plopping her melting body down, and fanning herself with an old newspaper grabbed from somewhere along the way.

I flopped down too. 'Yeah, thanks.' And smiled at the couple. 'It's bloody hot, isn't it?'

'And crowded,' nodded the man, pleasantly. 'I'm Karl by the way. And this,' he put out his hand, indicating his companion, 'is Heidi.'

'I'm Anne,' said Anne.

'And I'm Janni.'

We all nodded at each other and smiled.

'Where are you from?' asked Heidi, brushing her blonde hair back from her luminous open face. She wore a long white caftan and lots of bangles and beads. She was really rather pretty.

'I'm from Maiduguri,' replied Anne, happily looking from Karl to Heidi, 'and Janni's from Gombe…'

Quickly, I interjected. 'Well, half and half. My boyfriend lives in Maiduguri –' I glanced over at Anne, she nodded, thank you God, '– so I'm sometimes there and sometimes in Gombe, if you see what I mean?'

'A lot of travelling,' smiled Karl.

'A lot of travelling,' I agreed, ignoring the reality and believing the illusion. 'But it's worth it. What about you? Where are you both from?'

'Mubi.'

'Mubi,' I exclaimed. 'Goodness me, I was there only last week.' (Was it only last week? It seemed like a hundred years had passed; so much water under the bridge.)

'Were you visiting friends?' Heidi looked at me, smiling, interested.

'Well, no, not really. Andy – my boyfriend – and I were-'

'Look, look,' interrupted Anne, all excited. 'It's starting.'

We all turned, and followed her pointing finger. The mob had cleared a path; or rather the police with their wooden batons had cleared a path, and were still whacking an unfortunate few who had strayed out of line.

'It is so inhumane,' muttered Karl, as if to himself. Out of politeness, Anne and I nodded, and went 'Mmmm,' in agreement.

'Crikey, look at all the horses,' exclaimed Anne.

We looked.

Out of the palace gates they thundered all tarted up in their finery, embroidered leather saddles and ostrich plumes, with turbaned gents sitting astride them, their lean bodies wrapped in flowing blue robes, their hands brandishing enormous curved swords that flashed in the sunshine.

'Jesus, they look fearsome,' commented Anne. She stood up, to get a better look. So did Heidi and Karl. Feeling silly, the only one sitting down, I reluctantly followed suit.

After the swordsmen, came the trumpeters on their horses. What a racket they made, like farts that had been squashed by a hammer. Incessant. Ear-splitting. Oh, God, how I longed for the quiet cool of the veranda, so I could dream my dreams of Andy.

'Who's that?' Anne was jigging up and down, really excited.

I was lighting a fag. 'The Emir probably,' I said with a disinterested shrug of my shoulders.

It was.

Out he came in a sedan chair, all swathed and covered in silken cloth, with four lackeys either side carrying him, and another four lackeys fanning the poor, comfortable bastard with blooming great ostrich feathered fans.

'He certainly looks impressive,' whooped Anne, totally awe-struck. And he did. In fact he looked like a bandage. A big bandage. All you could see were his little black eyes peeping out of a white turban that was about a foot high, and his little black hands protruding out of his crisp, white pure cotton robes.

Much fanfare, and galloping, and trumpeting followed the Emir's procession, until at last, with much relief on the lackey's part I supposed, the Emir was put down at a spot where stood a silk covered podium with a rather grand chair. Many willing hands helped him off his mobile throne and he was given additional help as he ascended the steps, and then more help to sit down. And all the time the fanners were fanning, and once the Emir was seated, they took their positions, and went hell for leather. The silk podium quite billowed.

'This is amazing!' Anne looked at me, and her eyes crinkled with delight.

'Mmm,' I muttered, a tad sarcastically. When you've seen a dozen Emirs a hundred times, it takes away a bit of the gloss.

'What's he doing now?' enquired Anne, squinting from the bright rays of the sun.

'I think he is about to make a speech,' quipped Karl.

He was. In Hausa. It went on for over three quarters of an hour. After ten minutes, Anne sat down. 'This bit's a bit boring,' she grumbled. I couldn't disagree. I joined her back on the mat. So did Karl and Heidi. Fags were offered around. We all lit up. And smiled at a collection of naked urchins, who equally bored, had decided we four baturis were much more interesting, and were standing in front of us, watching our every move.

'I have sweeties,' Heidi said gleefully, fumbling around in her massive leather bag. 'Maybe they would like some.'

Oh, no, I thought, now we'll never get rid of them. I was right. We were stuck with African kids for the duration. They came from all over Yola, and beyond.

Anyway, after the long speech, and more pomp and ceremony – with dancing girls, naked from the waist up, shimming around the dust – and more charging of horses, and more trumpeting farts, and more kids than ever hanging around, and the crowds swelling to biblical proportions, and the heat getting worse, and the flies, and the smells, even Anne began to get a little tired. Her bubble had burst.

'Do you want to go, Janni?'

Did I? 'Wouldn't mind,' was my whole-hearted response.

So we said our goodbyes to Heidi and Karl who were hanging on for the afternoon races – more fool them – and thanking them for the use of their mat, and with promises we'd all meet up again sometime in Mubi – never in a million years – we made our leave. Through the throng we went, and after a half an hour of nightmare pushing and shoving, and horrible wafts and pongs, we hit the back streets of old Yola town. And very pleasant it was too.

There was hardly anyone about; just the odd, old girl hobbling down the path, by the plantains and bananas and patches of yams, and the odd scrawny cow, and the odd scrawny goat, and a handful of scraggy, clucking chickens.

'This is very peaceful,' Anne sighed, as we meandered our way under a shady canopy of trees, in dappled sunlight. We ambled past a couple of thatched huts. An old boy wandered out of one of the mud houses ahead of us. He was dressed in full Muslim regalia, meaning he had on a dirty old cap that was probably once very white, and a dirty old riga. He saw us. He stopped his wanderings and grinned. We ambled nearer. He watched our every move. We smiled. His grin became even broader. Saying nothing, he beckoned us with a finger. He was walking backwards into his hut. The finger continued to beckon.

'What's he doing?' I asked Anne. Silly old fool.

'Looks like he wants us to follow him,' she replied, stating the bloody obvious.

'Not on his Nelly,' I snorted. 'Probably enslave us, sell us to someone like the Emir. It goes on, y'know. I heard a rumour once that a girl my age in Kano was kidnapped and sold as a white slave in some Arab country.'

Anne laughed. 'Yeah, but not an old idiot like him.' She grabbed my arm. 'Come on, let's go and see what he wants.'

Oh, for fuck's sake.

Sighing, I followed Anne, who followed the old man, who was still grinning and beckoning us with his finger. We were taken into a neat little compound where a couple of chickens were scratching a seemingly impossible living from the dust, and where a satanic-eyed goat gazed lecherously at us from the shadows.

The finger still beckoned, and we followed.

Through an empty mud hut that had blackened interior walls and smelt of wood-smoke, out the other door, into another compound, much the same as the last except a couple of naked urchins were playing around in the dirt. When they espied us, they wailed and fled into the inner sanctums of another mud hut. Old Man Finger laughed, and beckoned. And on we went, through another mud hut where there was a cooking pot, some wood, and a rolled-up mat, and out into another compound.

'Bloody hell, this is like a rabbit warren,' whispered Anne.

'Where the fuck is he taking us?' I whispered back.

Another compound, another mud hut, all much the same and all pretty empty until we reached the final compound. The epicentre. The wives' quarters. There were four of them, and about twenty kids. The latter all screamed, well the younger ones did and hid behind their mothers' long, brightly coloured wraps, while the older ones stood silently and gawped at us with wide-eyed astonishment. As for the mums, well the Emir didn't get as warm a royal welcome as were given us by them. After the initial shock, they couldn't have been more delighted to have us visit their home. The grinning old man left us to our fate but not before issuing out a long list of instructions to his spouses, and as soon as he was gone, we were sitting down on freshly brushed mats, given cool yoghurt to drink, and dish after dish was brought out and placed in front of us.

God knows where the food came from. One of the wives would disappear and emerge seconds later from out of a hut with a calabash filled with cooked rice, and a calabash filled with gari. No sooner had that lot been put in front of us, another wife would disappear and return with an assortment of cooked vegetables. Not to be outdone wife number three scuttled off, and was back with a stew. And wife number four brought out another dish, yam cakes and a lentil curry.

Then, when our banquet was complete, they all sat back on a mat opposite, the mums and their twenty or so kids, and waited for us to commence with the feasting.

'They haven't given us any cutlery,' whispered Anne, while smiling happily at our hosts.

'Or plates,' I whispered back, also smiling at the group before us, who were all smiling back.

'It's a hand job, I reckon,' tittered Anne.

'Reckon it is,' I tittered back.

And so we tucked in. It was the first proper meal I'd had in about three days, and was delicious, but by the end we were well and truly stuffed. We finished one dish, and the empty bowl was taken away, and the next one put in its place. They insisted, with various clucks and signs that we eat every bit up. And, out of politeness, we couldn't refuse.

By the time we left, after much bowing and shaking of hands, with the old man and his tribe all watching us as we wobbled our way down the path, I felt sick. Really sick. So did Anne. As soon as we turned a corner and were out of their sight, we both puked up in a ditch, observed by one very astonished, tethered-up goat.

'Jesus,' grinned Anne, after her final gob. 'That feels better.'

'Mmm,' I agreed, having done this kind of thing many times before. My stomach felt really nice and empty. I laughed. 'Shall we go back for some more?'

And would have done, if Anne hadn't thought I was joking!

The next morning Anne and I flew back to Maiduguri.

It felt great to sit on a plane and get to one's destination in less than an hour. The same trip, by mammy-wagon, took almost two days.

'How are we getting from the airport?' I asked Anne, as we buckled up, and prepared for landing.

'Amy said she would be sorting something out.' Anne, leaning down to get a hankie out of her handbag, glanced up. She smiled. 'I must say, she'll be really surprised to see you get off the plane.' Anne blew her nose.

Thoughtfully, I gazed out of the porthole window. At the dry, arid land, at the mud dots that were villages, at the brown fields waiting for rain.

Shifting my gaze, I turned back to Anne.

'Anne, you wouldn't do me a big favour, would you?'

My companion looked at me whilst stuffing her snotty hankie up the sleeve of her red and white polka-dot blouse. 'Of course,' she smiled. 'If I can, I will.' She raised an eyebrow, and waited while I tried to think of the right words to explain the plans I had up my sleeve.

'It's not so much about doing something big – well, it is for me – but not for you. I just thought...' I trailed off, shrugging, and sighed.

'Spit it out, girl,' Anne said, not unpleasantly. She gave me a reassuring smile and inclined her head, eyebrows still raised expectantly.

So I did. 'Look, Anne, I know you know all about what happened between me and Andy.' She nodded. 'But, would you mind if you keep, y'know, keep it to yourself. Like, not tell people. It's not that...' My lips began to tremble, the old frog was there again, always loitering, always ready to jump up and take control of my throat when a whiff of sadness threatened my psyche, '...that I'm...' My voice petered off. A little choking sound fell out from my mouth.

'It's okay,' Anne said gently. She took hold of my hand, and squeezed it. 'I won't give out too many details, I promise. But –' she frowned slightly, '– people will ask questions, Janni. Have you thought about that?'

A tear dripped. Anne dived up her sleeve and handed me the hankie. I took the rumpled square of linen, wiped my eye, remembered she'd just blown in it, and quickly gave it back. 'Does running out of money sound reasonable?' I shouted over the engine

273

roar. My ears popped. We were going down. The combination, popping ears, dripping eyes, and a frog in my throat, didn't feel at all nice.

'What do you mean?' Anne spoke like a fish, opening and shutting her mouth; her ears obviously popping too.

So I told her. Screamed out my plan. Focker Friendship aeroplanes make a hell of a noise, especially when taking off and landing.

'It sounds pretty plausible,' Anne hollered back. 'Anyway, who cares? It's nobody's business, just yours and Andy's, so you say what you like, love. And I promise –' Anne got hold of my hand again, and her voice went up a further twenty decibels, '– your secret's quite safe with me.'

Rosie was at the airport to meet us. As Anne predicted, after initial greetings, with Rosie running across the tarmac, whooping with delight and hugging us both like we'd been away for a hundred years, the questions began.

'Where's Andy?'

We hadn't even left the runway. We were walking across it, arm in arm, the three of us, like we were in an advert for Pan-Am.

'In the Cameroon,' I replied with a nonchalant air. And my heart sinking lower and lower. In fact all my internal organs were heading south, pretty rapido. Back in Maiduguri, seeing Rosie, and suddenly it brought it all home. Andy was gone. We were no longer a pair.

'Why aren't you there?' Rosie, all wide-eyed and pretty, asked the dreaded question so innocently. So sweetly.

Affecting an expression of carefree indifference, that not being with Andy was down to something quite trivial, I said, rather casually, 'Well – it's a long story, Rosie. I'll tell you about it later. It was to do with money, not having enough of it – you know how it is – and well, I wasn't feeling too good either, got a bit sick…'

'Oh, no, did you? What did you get? Tummy palaver?'

I nodded, and smiled. Full beam. If it had been dark I'd have lit up the runway. 'Yeah, kind of. Really bad.'

'Oh, I'm so sorry…'

'But we had a good time,' I added, quickly. 'A really good time. There's so much to tell you – and I will, later.' We were approaching the barriers. That was when I saw Mike. Remember him? He of the blonde hair and lovely smile. He was resting his hands on the bar, and as our eyes met, my tummy went all wobbly. 'Hiya, Mike.' And

274

I tossed my hair back, just a little.

'Well, this is a surprise.'

'Mmm,' I nodded. 'Isn't it just.'

He gave me a questioning look. 'No Andy?'

'No Andy.' And my lips stretched in the direction of a smile. 'He's still in the Cameroon but he'll be back soon and...'

'Janni got ill,' explained Rosie, interrupting. What a godsend she was. Squeezing my arm, she shot me a doleful-eyed look. 'Poor thing.'

'Oh, I'm sorry to hear that,' Mike responded, an expression of concern etched on his very handsome face. 'Are you better?'

'Much better, thanks.'

He smiled. I smiled. And my heart, strangely enough, missed a beat.

'Where to first?'

We were whizzing down the smooth tarmac road from the airport, in Mike's jeep. It seemed funny, a ride with no lumps or bumps or red-gritty dust.

'Mine,' answered Anne. 'It's the nearest.'

'Where are you staying?' Rosie looked at me, pausing for breath. She'd been babbling away nineteen to a dozen, filling Anne and I in with the gossip; Buggy had got really pissed Christmas day; Sally and Richard had had a barney – 'but they've made up now' – Claire had slept with an American – 'by the way, I love your basket' – Phil and Hamish won the Boxing Day treasure hunt...

'At Andy's. Why?'

Rosie tucked a blonde strand behind her ear. She looked concerned. 'Won't you be lonely, all on your own?'

Anne, in the front seat next to Mike, turned around. 'You can stay at my place if you want, Janni. There's plenty of room.'

'Or at ours,' invited Rosie. She giggled. 'It'll be fun. With Andy out of the way, you and I could get up to all sorts of mischief.'

I smiled, even though I didn't feel at all like smiling. We were just about to go under the 'Welcome to Maiduguri' arch, and the neem trees were beckoning. This place, this spot, all reminders of happier times. The last time I'd sped down this road I was on my little Honda 50, full of the joys, high on anticipation, a girl with the world at her feet and a boyfriend by her side. Now I'd nothing, only a heart full of lead and a hollow in my tummy.

'Thanks for the offer, girls,' I said with as much cheer as I could muster. 'But I'll be fine.' I glanced out of the window, a bloke on a motorbike sped by, blonde hair, white T-shirt, and faded blue jeans – he could have been Andy. The hollow in my tummy expanded. 'But if I get too lonely,' I turned back to Rosie, 'I'll be round yours in a jiffy, I promise.'

Rosie shrugged, twirling her fingers around a golden lock of hair.

'Well, if you're sure…'

'When's Andy due back?' chipped in Mike. He was, I noticed, looking at me through his rear view mirror.

'Umm.' I fought the frog in my throat, and pretended to cough. 'Sometime next week, I reckon. Around about the fourteenth.'

'So what? Has he gone on to the Cameroon?'

'Yeah.' I coughed again.

'So, what actually happened?' Mike turned his head briefly around. 'I know you were ill, but I don't get why Andy didn't come back with you?' Facing the road again, Mike's eyes shifted back to his rear view mirror.

I felt sick. Words failed me.

'You've missed the turning,' pointed out Anne, and saved me.

'Sorry.' Mike braked, reversed, and turned down a tree-lined track. 'Here we go,' he said breezily, stopping outside Anne's little bungalow.

'Cheers for that, Mike.' Anne grabbed her stuff, a bag and a rucksack, from off the front seat. She looked over at Rosie and me in the back. 'Shall we meet up later at the club?'

I nodded.

'Yeah,' Rosie agreed. 'What time?'

'Dunno?' Anne put her rucksack back on the seat, and looked at her watch. 'Bloody hell, it's two already. I didn't realise it was so late. What about eight, nine? I'm not bothered really, earlier if you want?'

'No, eight's fine by me,' I lied. The club, at any given time, was the last place where I wanted to be, I dreaded the thought of turning up and all and sundry asking me the same dreaded questions.

'Yeah, me too,' said Rosie. 'We'll see you at eight.'

Anne nodded and re-grabbed her bags. 'Cheers, again, Mike. See you all later.' She banged shut the door. 'Take care,' she mouthed to me as Mike put the jeep into reverse.

I gave her a sad, little wave.

Mike dropped Rosie off at her house. 'Are you sure you don't want to come in?' she asked me, her long legs half out the door, Che and Guevera panting and wagging their tails, and sniffing her ankles. 'Sam can drive you back later?'

I smiled appreciatively. 'No, cheers, Rosie, I'm beat. I need to get back and get myself sorted first. Have a shower, wash my hair. But I'll see you later, yeah?'

Rosie beamed her golden beam. 'Yeah, see you later.' She grabbed her bag, and got out. 'Thanks, Mike. See ya, Janni,' and blew us both a kiss.

'Aren't you going to come and sit in the front?' asked Mike, as Rosie, with her rabid dogs, stood by the veranda steps, waiting to wave us off.

Suddenly, it felt a bit weird, being on my own with Mike. I wavered. But not for long.

'Yeah, okay.' I got out the back, and slid into the front. 'Bye, Rosie, see you later,' I shouted, as I pulled the door to.

She shouted back: 'Eight o'clock. Don't be late.'

Mike put the jeep into first gear and slowly we made our way down the drive.

'You look fucked,' he commented matter-of-factly, pulling out onto the main road.

'Cheers,' I replied, keeping my eyes straight ahead, on the dappled tarmac, my heart thump thumping inside.

'Glad to be back?' His tone was casual.

I shrugged. 'Not really.'

Mike, with his right hand on the wheel, felt for his cigarettes on the seat between us. 'Want one,' he asked.

I did.

We lit up.

'So what happened?'

There was a sort of silence. I took a deep puff. We were turning into the Forestry zone. I felt something I imagined was grief. 'Nothing,' I said flatly.

We were passing the Woodruffs' house. Mrs Woodruff was out in her garden, on her knees by a flowerbed, like my Mum she was probably trying to grow English flowers from the best English seeds.

'So why didn't Andy come back with you?' Mike still had his eyes on the road. His tone still very casual.

The Bat Cave was to our left. We turned right.

I tried to keep it casual too. Difficult, especially as we were

277

now approaching the house, Andy's house, my house. Our two bikes, my little one and his big one, were still parked outside; there was a towel, my towel, hanging on the line. It all looked just as we'd left it. Nothing (but everything) had changed.

I swallowed the toad.

'Andy wanted to come back with me, but it was me who told him to go on to the Cameroon.' I shifted uneasily, looking briefly at Mike. His eyes were still on the road, negotiating the twisty turn up to the house. I ploughed on with the lies. 'He's always wanted to go, you see, but I've never really been that bothered, and we'd run out of money – actually we didn't run out, I had my purse nicked in Mubi…'

Mike drew up by the side of the bikes and switched off the engine. I noticed the empty porch opposite. Hamish was out. And Buggy's bike was nowhere to be seen. I was slightly relieved. '…which was a bit of a disaster, as you can imagine. Not that that bothered Andy, he didn't mind paying for everything but it bothered me. Anyway…' I shrugged, '…we still had a great time, spent Christmas in Mubi and then headed off to Yola…'

My voice broke.

Suddenly thinking all sorts of sad things.

It was all too, too much.

'Are you okay?'

Every resolution, every decision, deserted me. Great sobs rose up from within. Blindly, I felt for the door handle.

'Janni, what's the matter?'

'I'm sorry, I'm sorry…' I stumbled out of the jeep, somehow managed to pull out my basket and bag. 'I'm sorry, I'm sorry…'

Mike was saying something, was opening his door; was getting out, was coming around to be by my side. But I was already gone. Across the sandy drive, up the veranda steps, through the unlocked door, and into the little house, dropping my basket and my bag, I flung myself onto the bed, moaning and groaning.

And that's where I stayed for God knows how long.

When the wailing finally subsided, the pillow was sopping. Miserably, I got up, off the bed, and looked out of the window. There was an empty space where Mike's jeep had been. He'd gone. Of course he'd gone. What did I expect?

I plopped myself back on the bed and noted, for some bizarre reason, that the sheets were fresh. The cook, who sometimes doubled as a houseboy, must have come in and given the room a bit of a spring clean while we were away. It so pissed me off. I wanted to smell the two of us together but all I got, as I bent down and sniffed, was a whiff of powder-blue Omo.

Mournfully, I surveyed the room.

In the corner, on the chest of drawers, I could see our photo, with beautiful little butterflies dancing around it. I went over. Stood for a moment and gazed at our two happy, smiling faces, Andy looking down at me, me looking up.

'Oh, Andy,' I whispered, touching the photo, stroking his face, 'I love you so, so very much.'

More tears sprang into my eyes. Where did they all come from?

I opened a drawer, inside were a small collection of bagged-up dope, ready for sale. I took one of them out, and a packet of Rizlas, then picked up the photo, padded across to the tape recorder by the bed, selected a tape, put it in, rewound, and pressed the 'on' button.

Leonard Cohen's melancholic voice drifted across the room.

I loved you in the morning
Your kisses sweet and warm
Your hair upon the pillow
Like a sleepy golden storm……

I sang as I cried. The taste of salt strong in my mouth as the tears dribbled in. Plonking myself on the floor, I rolled a joint. A motorbike purred up and stopped right outside. I got up and peeped out of the window. It was Hamish. Quickly I pressed the 'off' button. Silence ensued. Back to the window, I saw Hamish take his veranda steps two at a time. He disappeared into the house.

I returned to the floor, and lit up. Through the window the afternoon sun poured in, dappled squares of brilliant light fell across the room, on the bed, on the chest of drawers, on my basket. A fly buzzed around the lampshade, a lizard ran down the wall.

I took a pillow off the bed, curled up on the cool, cool floor, and with the photo clutched to my bosom, I fell fast asleep.

Dreaming of Andy.

Time passed. The sun moved away. The last of the light came in through the windows. Another motorbike roared up. I stirred and looked at my watch. Six o'clock. Seconds later I heard voices, Buggy's and Hamish's.

Were they talking about me? Had they heard? Did they know about Andy? I stood in the half-light, by the window, and listened. They were having a chin-wag about supper. What should they eat?

279

The cook was having a day off.

'Let's go to the club,' I heard Buggy say, 'I can't be arsed to faddle about in a fucking kitchen.'

'Aye,' agreed Hamish, 'neither can I.'

Ten minutes later they sped off back through the trees.

Silence again.

I switched Leonard Cohen back on. Andy's song drifted across the room. I sang it out loud, tears down my face. It felt good to indulge in total self-pity.

And when the song finished, I rewound, and played it again.

And again.

And again...

Darkness fell. Moonlight came through the window. I turned the tape off. Quietly I opened the door, and ventured out on to the veranda, smoking a cigarette. I looked up at the stars and wondered if Andy, in his Cameroon wilderness, was doing the same thing.

I plopped myself down on the little stone wall.

Ten minutes, fifteen minutes passed.

Lights on the driveway.

A vehicle pulled up.

I heard a door open and slam shut. Footsteps, soft in the sand, padded nearer. I turned as a figure appeared on the bottom step of the veranda. It was Mike.

'Hi,' he said, his voice gentle and soft.

'Hi,' I replied, my heart suddenly beating a tad fast.

Hesitating for a second, considering, he climbed the steps.

'What are you doing out here?'

I shrugged. 'Just chilling.' But my voice trembled a little and despite the cool of the evening I felt rather hot.

Mike moved across the veranda. Leaning against a wood pillar he removed a crushed pack from his back pocket. 'Fag?' he asked, offering me one.

'Cheers,' I nodded, and got up from my perch on the wall. Mike felt his shirt pockets for a match. We lit up and puffed as moon beams washed over us both.

'So,' said Mike, looking at me thoughtfully. Smoke hovered in front of his face. 'Things haven't been so good, have they?' There was a pause. I inhaled deeply. 'I know all about it, Janni. You and Andy. About what happened in Mambilla.'

Anne! The fucking, bloody cow!

My eyes stung. The frog and the toad were hopping about in

my throat. 'It's none of your business,' I said finally in a voice that had more tremors than an earthquake.

'S'pose not.' In the light of the spectral moon, Mike shrugged. 'But...' he hesitated, took another drag, '...it does help to talk.'

Talk! Screaming more like.

'Oh, God,' I moaned, and buried my face deep in my hands. And somehow out it all came. In gasps and sobs amidst tears and splutters. But Mike was right. It was good to talk. All the sadness therein fell out of my mouth and seemed to be carried away on the back of the gentle meanderings of the cool evening breeze. I even smiled as I concluded my tale. 'Thanks for listening, Mike,' I sighed, wiping my eyes with the back of my hand, and wiping my hand on the side of my jeans.

Mike shook his head, 'I'm sorry,' he said, 'I really am.'

We were both sitting close on the little stone wall.

'Mmm, me too,' I replied, half attempting another smile. I cupped my chin in my hands and rested my elbows on my knees. 'Story of my bloody life.'

Mike looked at me sweetly and gave me a gentle nudge. 'Things can only get better, y'know.'

My eyes rolled up to heaven. 'Yeah, sure.'

I peered at the moon, tried to work out which were the mountains and which were the craters. But if my eyes were focused on the light in the sky my mind was actually focused on Mike. A yearning stirred deep within. It was all rather strange, especially when Mike suddenly grabbed my hand; it was actually what I'd been hoping for. 'Fancy a walk?' he asked.

A walk?

'Okay,' I murmured, rising with him.

He held on to me and I followed him through the trees. We were on our way to the dried-up river beyond the Bat Cave. By-passing lit up little bungalows we made a detour off the main track, and headed down to the ridge. Moonlight flooded the sandy basin and apart from the crickets, all was quiet and still. For a few minutes we walked along the earthen ledge not saying much, just a few words about how lovely it all looked and how peaceful it all was. A bit further on and we both agreed it would be nice to take a seat and rest for a while. I sat down on a rocky mound, my legs dangling over ten foot of red, sandy wall. Mike joined me. He was up close. So close, I swear he could hear my heart beating.

'What am I going to do, Mike?' I asked, addressing the air. I was trying to focus my mind, trying to dwell on the dark side of things, trying to ignore the flutter of wings that flapped in the pit of my stomach.

'Stay here in Maiduguri, and wait.' I could feel his breath warm on my cheek. 'That's all you can do.' We were both silent for a moment. Mike rummaged about in his pockets, took out a tin. I watched his fingers as they deftly rolled up a perfect little joint. He licked the Rizla. My eyes wandered up. His handsome profile; perfect in moonlight, his blonde hair like Andy's, a shining halo.

Weird things in my tummy went weirder.

'Do you really think I should wait then? For Andy?' I asked breathlessly.

Mike shifted. He struck a match. He inhaled deeply. His shoulder touched mine, our bodies pressed even closer. 'Yeah,' he nodded slowly. Smoke rolled out of his mouth. 'I reckon you should.' He took another long, drawn out drag, and passed me the joint. Our fingers brushed. I jumped at the jolt. Fuck! What was happening? I'm in love with Andy. No one comes close. Not even Mike, he of the lovely blonde hair and lovely, lovely smile.

I wiggled about; I'd been sitting on a small stone that was sticking right into my bum. A puff on the joint and I watched the smoke drift with the breeze. The night air vibrated, I could hear them now, the rhythm of faraway drums in harmony with the song of the crickets.

'I'm married, you know,' Mike suddenly said, his voice quiet and low, and really rather husky.

I flinched. 'Are you?' My hand shook as I put the joint again to my lips. 'I didn't know.'

He shrugged, and his shoulder nudged against mine. 'Why should you. Isabelle's back in England...' there was an itsy-bitsy pause, a nanosecond of silence. '...with the kids.'

'Oh,' I murmured, and watched again as the smoke from my mouth wafted up and away into the beams of the moon.

Silence.

I passed back the joint. Our fingers touched again. Another jolt shot through my body. The weird things in my stomach went haywire. 'So, why isn't your wife here with you?' I asked finally, thinking Mike didn't look old enough to be married. Or have kids. Blimey, he couldn't be more than what, twenty-five, twenty-six?

'She hates Nigeria.' Mike was so close now I could smell his breath, a mix of baccy and peppermint.

'Oh,' I replied. Our fingers weren't just touching now. Mike had reached out and was caressing our two hands together. It felt so very lovely. Like the warm sunshine had risen and kicked away the dark cold.

We sat silently this way for some time. Considering. The both of us considering the odds. The fors and the againsts. The pros and the cons. The shall we or shan't we's?

Oh, to hell with it!

His arm went around me. He pulled me towards him. There was no turning back. Thinking about Andy, and my lips met with Mike's. He was probably thinking about Isabelle, the both of us, our minds on absent folk, as we disappeared and lost ourselves in one another. Rolling, rolling and tumbling down the ridge under the silvery light of the moon.

'Where were you last night?' Rosie enquired, a tad crossly.

I was standing on her veranda having pootled up the next morning on my bike.

'Sorry,' I said, trying to fend off Che and Guevera who were both having a good sniff up my privates. 'I got a bit waylaid, Rosie.'

'We were really worried,' said Rosie, after she'd thankfully shooed off the dogs and I was safely in the sitting room with the French doors firmly closed between me and the more than likely rabid canines that were laughingly called pets. 'No one said they'd seen you, Hamish and Buggy didn't even know you were back. I got Hamish to give me lift over and you weren't in,' she continued as I followed her through the cool, quiet house to her bedroom.

'Sorry,' I said again, plopping myself down on her low-lying bed.

Rosie chucked me a fag. 'So where were you?'

What could I say? What should I say?

That I spent the whole of the night with Mike. In his house, in his bed, after we'd shagged in the sand. That he comforted me and soothed me, but it was all still a crock of shit? That even in his arms, I was thinking only of Andy? My Andy. My beautiful, my wonderful Andy – who dumped me on New Year's Day in the middle of nowhere, who told me he no longer loved me, that I was a pain in the neck, that I was a...

I sniffed.

Rosie in an instance was beside me, had her arm around me, and was stroking my hair.

'Something's happened, hasn't it?'

Miserably, I nodded.

'Andy?'

'Yes,' I whispered, biting my lip.

'What?'

I buried my face in her lap.

It was all too, too bloody much.

The proverbial cat was out of the bag.

By the end of my second day in Maiduguri, everyone who was everyone – and a few who weren't – knew of my plight. Well, about Andy. Not about Mike. Even Rosie didn't know about him.

'I'm so sorry to hear of your news,' said a concerned Mrs Woodruff, giving my shoulder a gentle squeeze.

It was four days later, I was sitting in the club, having been dragged there by Rosie, Amy and Anne as way of a 'cheer up, Janni' plan. They were convinced, I think, that I might slash my wrists or drown myself in the shower. Which was daft, I'd at least wait until Andy came back from the Cameroon and ascertain the outcome before I resorted to such desperate measures.

'Sorry?' I replied, pretending to look bemused. 'What news?'

Mrs Woodruff put her hand to her mouth, ever so delicately. 'Oh, dear,' she muttered, and gave a slight cough. 'I really don't mean to pry but Colin and I did hear about – well, that things went quite wrong for you and Andy in Mambilla.'

I gave her a smile. A jolly smile in fact. With a 'fuck off' hidden message. Tossing my hair, I laughed nonchalantly.

'Oh, no, Mrs Woodruff, nothing's happened. Andy and I are fine, it was just that I was getting a bit fed up with travelling, that's all.'

My three friends nodded, going along with the lie. Mrs Woodruff, a tad perplexed, coughed again. 'Oh, dear,' she said, 'I must have got my wires crossed, my dear. Chinese whispers, it's always the same, the truth gets drowned in the muck that gets dished out, especially out here. Still, I'm glad to hear it's not bad news after all. That you and your young man are still going strong. I can understand you wanting to come back.' She looked at us all. 'Certainly I wouldn't want to be cavorting around Africa the way you young things do.' She smiled, revealing bright, even white teeth. We all gave a polite chuckle as if what she was saying was a funny old thing. Her eyes beamed back on me. 'Your Mother must have been frantic with worry. She'll be so relieved to know you're here in Maiduguri, *quite* safe and sound.'

She smiled again. Her teeth glinted.

I smiled again.

Her hand returned to my shoulder, vice-like. Years of gardening in hard African soil had made the five-fingered member as tough as a trowel. 'You will take care, won't you, Janni?' Her laser beam eyes bored into mine, the trowel dug deeper. 'I promised your Mother I'd watch out for you, so if there's anything, anything…'

I nodded, and flashed another smile. 'Thanks, Mrs Woodruff. You're very kind.'

Mrs Woodruff nodded appreciatively. 'Perhaps when Andy gets back, the both of you might like to come over for supper…'

'Lovely,' I said. Just hearing his name and I wanted to cry. So I bit my lip and pretended to look tranquil. 'Thanks ever so much.'

Mrs Woodruff loosened her grip. She bestowed her beam upon each and every one of the four of us. 'Enjoy your evening, girls.'

'Thanks,' we all trilled.

And off she trotted.

I watched her go. Watched as her rather large bottom waddled its way through the table and chairs, stopping now and then to greet fellow friends, and over to hubby who was having a gay old time with a group of his chums on the far side of the club. I watched as Mrs Woodruff kissed Mr Woodruff, it was just a peck on the cheek but it reminded me of how nice it is to have a partner, how nice it is to have someone you can call your very own.

I stood up.

'Where are you going?' asked Rosie, my number one minder, as she stubbed out a fag.

I threw my bag over my shoulder.

'Out'

'Out where?' enquired Amy, minder number two, setting down her bottle of Coke with two straws bobbing out of the top.

'The fuck knows,' I muttered, not caring. I just wanted, suddenly, to be on my own.

'Hey, sit down.' Anne, minder number three, patted my chair. She gave me one of those caring kind of smiles that are saved for wheelchair bound ancients and senile delinquents. 'You can't just go off like that.'

But I could.

And I did.

Back to Andy's. Back to the quiet little house, back to the quiet little room, full with all my happy little memories.

To sleep, and dream.

And wait.

Actually being back in Maiduguri wasn't all bad. After the first few days of unmitigated grief, and after the initial outpourings of sympathy from well-meaning friends, I managed to settle back into mainstream life. Meaning, I had occasional sex with Mike, it was nice but not spectacular, I was always thinking about Andy when we were doing it, and he was probably thinking about Isabelle, his wife. Still, it helped pass the time and gave me a bit of a boost. And after all the recent crap with Andy, a bit of a boost was just what was needed.

Of course, I didn't tell anyone – not at first anyway; didn't want to scupper my already fragile relationship with Andy as news in the bush travels fast. But, in truth, I'm not very good at keeping secrets, as you now know, and in one of my many heart-to-hearts with Rosie I spilt the beans.

'Promise you won't tell anyone, Rosie, if I let you into a little secret.'

We were sitting in deckchairs on her veranda, smoking cigarettes, drinking homemade lemonade, and listening to the latest Pink Floyd tape, 'Dark Side of the Moon'. A weird title for an African afternoon what with the sun shining, the birds singing, and everywhere honey-dew warm.

'I promise,' said Rosie, twirling a golden lock of hair in her fingers.

'Promise.'

'Promise.'

She waited with baited breath. And I took a deep one. 'I've been seeing someone. Well, not seeing as much as…' I shrugged '…well, you know…'

Rosie laughed. 'Yeah, I do know.' I looked at her blankly. So she explained. 'Are you talking about you and Mike?'

'What!' I almost leapt out of my chair. Certainly I kicked my glass of lemonade over, and Che and Guevera were there in an instant, lapping it up. 'What do you mean, you know?'

'Oh, for fuck's sake, Janni, it's bloody obvious. He's always liked you, and I know you've always liked him. You were with him that first night, weren't you, when we couldn't find you?'

Gobsmacked, I scratched my head. And bent down and grabbed my cigarettes that were slightly lemon-sodden. Just in time, the dogs were all for sucking the juice out of the packet. Could you catch rabies that way, I wondered, dog saliva on filter tip cigarettes? Quickly I dropped them, and went for one of Rosie's.

'Yeah, but how did you know?' I lit up and popped the match back in the box.

Rosie chuckled and rolled her eyes up to the cloudless sky above. 'Because his jeep was outside Andy's house, idiot, when we came to look for you.'

'Blimey,' I said. And then I had a horrible thought. 'Does Hamish know?'

'Oh, yes,' nodded Rosie, still twiddling her locks, 'Hamish knows.'

'Oh, fuck.' I gave a deep sigh and puffed out a load of smoke. 'He'll tell Andy.'

Rosie shook her head. 'No he won't, Hamish's not like that. He's a friend.'

'Yeah, but he's Andy's friend too.'

'Do stop worrying,' said Rosie, reaching for her glass. She took a swig. Pink Floyd was still trilling away. 'Did you hear that?' she asked, changing the subject entirely. 'On the tape? I swear I just heard a voice say something about Nigeria Airways flight stopping at Rome and Kano.'

Rosie flicked off the tape and rewound.

But I was worried.

Later, back at Andy's I meandered my way over to Hamish's. He was in his usual spot, on the veranda, in his rocking chair, sucking contentedly on his pipe, a bottle of beer and a glass by his feet, the hurricane lamps all ablaze.

'How's it going?' he asked kindly, vacating the rocker just for me.

'Okay,' I lied, and plopped myself down.

'Want a beer?'

'Please.'

'I'll get you a glass.' He descended the veranda steps and wandered over to the cookhouse. I went on sitting there rocking myself to and fro, my feet on the ground, vaguely comforted by the rhythm. Hamish returned. He poured some beer into a glass. 'Cheers,' he said, handing it over.

'Cheers,' I said, and took a sip.

287

For a moment or two we sat in silence, in the still of the evening, Hamish with his pipe, and me with my beer.

'So, how are you bearing up?' he asked finally.

I sighed. Didn't really know what to say, except I wanted to make everything right now that everything was wrong. Nightmarishly wrong. 'I'm doing alright, I s'pose,' I muttered miserably, 'considering.'

Hamish on his stool, leaned over, and took hold of my hand. 'Och, you've had a tough time,' he declared kindly. 'But I reckon it'll turn out alright.'

The hurricane lamp hissed. Or maybe it was me? 'Will it?' I drew back my hand, and pushed back my hair. 'It's a mess, Hamish. A fucking mess.'

'Aye,' he nodded. 'At times like this, we all feel powerless, but life has a way of springing surprises, nice surprises, just as we think everything is lost. Just have faith, Janni, and trust me, it'll turn out okay.'

What a bloke? What an incredibly tranquil bloke.

'I wish I was like you,' I whispered, really meaning it.

Hamish chuckled. 'Och, no, you don't. Don't always take what you see as gospel, I have my bad times just like everybody else, I can assure you.'

Another companionable silence ensued. Hamish puffed on his pipe and I smoked on a fag. I shifted in my rocking chair and it squeaked.

'Do you think I'm mad waiting for Andy?'

Hamish and I had had this conversation a dozen times since I'd got back but I still hadn't grasped the concept that I might be boring the pants off him – or anybody else for that matter. I reckon half of Maiduguri had indulged me with the same topic almost as many times in the last week.

Hamish lifted his glass and stared at the amber fluid absently. I in my chair, rocked to and fro, listening to the endless churr of the crickets. 'You have to do what you feel is right,' finally came the answer. He looked at me. 'It's your life. Your decision.'

That wasn't what I wanted to hear. I wanted Hamish to tell me, to assure me, that *he* thought what I was doing was right. That Andy was just going through a weird moment and that he'd come back from the Cameroon and love me more than ever. But Hamish never said anything that specific. He just talked in riddles.

'I'm pretty sure what I'm doing is right,' I insisted, not

altogether truthfully. As it was, I wasn't at all sure about anything anymore. Come to think of it, I'd never been sure about anything, ever – except about Andy, I was certain, that I truly loved Andy.

'Oh God, I miss him so much,' I blubbered, my eyes stinging with freshwater tears. Or they may have been stagnant pools, simply recycled.

'Aye, I know,' nodded Hamish, kind and concerned.

'He means the world to me.'

'Aye.'

'There's no one, Hamish, ever, ever, ever, that will take his place. You know that, don't you?'

'Aye.'

'Nobody. Never, ever.'

'Aye.'

Oh, for fuck's sake, we were going in circles. Spit it out, Janni, spit it out.

Deep breath, along with a bit of a sniff, and a tear down my cheek. 'Mike means nothing to me, nothing, Hamish. You've got to believe it. You do, don't you?'

I was leaning over, my hands on Hamish's knees, my nails digging into his flesh. If it hurt, Hamish didn't say. I looked at him beseechingly. I could feel the sweat warm on my face. 'Please don't tell Andy, please.'

'Och, Janni.' Hamish put down his pipe, and gently prised my hands from off his knees, and held them as if he were about to drag me off for a bit of a country and western jig. 'People do strange things all the time, and sometimes there's no rhyme or reason.' He smiled. 'Sometimes we have to find comfort elsewhere when times are bad, it gets us through and out the other side. It's the way of the world.'

Relief overwhelmed me, the guilt almost but almost went away. 'Oh, you're so right, Hamish,' I said, smiling through tears.

'Aye,' he agreed. 'So quit worrying.'

'I will,' I promised.

And gently I rocked myself to and fro.

Andy was due back around about the fourteenth of January.

That day dawned.

I cancelled all social invitations and waited at the house like a cat on hot bricks. Every voice, every vehicle, every itsy-bitsy sound, was Andy. Please, please let it be Andy, I'd pray as I positioned myself for the umpteenth time out on the veranda with pen and notebook in hand.

I had it all planned, you see.

I'd be looking lovely, my hair flowing down my back like a gypsy, bare feet, not much make-up, totally focused on penning a poem. Andy would arrive, he'd walk round the corner and there I'd be sitting composing my epic. I'd pretend not to notice him, of course, and for a few minutes he'd just stand there, in his old worn out hat, rucksack on his back, taking the vision of beauty before him all in.

Finally he'd say, 'Hello, Janns.' The soft voice; the beautiful Scots accent.

Startled, I'd look up. 'Hello, Andy.' And I'd toss my hair, just a little.

Time, for a while, would stand still.

We'd stare at each other across the vast expanse of veranda, our hearts beating as one. Then slowly he'd walk towards me. Nearer, and he would reach out and touch me. 'You look beautiful dressed in the afternoon sun,' he'd whisper hoarsely. Tears of joy would spiral down my cheeks. He'd bring his hand up to my face and gently wipe away dewy drops. Then put his fingers in my hair, and push back my dark, tumbling locks. 'Don't cry, my darling,' he would say. 'Don't cry.'

And he'd kiss me, like in the song. And like a butterfly, I'd float away in his arms.

'Oh, Andy. Oh, Andy.'

'Oh, Janni. Oh, Janni.' Cupping my chin, his beautiful blue eyes would bore into mine. 'I've never stopped thinking about you, you must believe that. You've always been on my mind. Always.' Then, miserably, wretchedly he'd throw himself into the deckchair, and cover his face with his hands, moaning, 'Oh, man, I've been cruel to you, shit I've been so fucking cruel.'

I'd throw myself at his feet, like some fairytale Beauty at the feet of the Beast. 'Don't be angry with yourself, Andy, please?'

But he'd moan and he'd groan, and I'd hold him and hold him. 'I've been so fucking cruel,' he'd wail, in between heart-racking sobs.

'Sssh, sssh,' I'd soothe, 'sssh, sssh.'

Finally, with tear driven eyes, Andy would lift up his head. 'I wish I could explain it, Janns,' he'd say with a whimper, 'but I can't.'

'Don't then, Andy.' My voice would be gentle, forgiving, because I'm that kind of girl.

290

Another heart-wrenching moan. 'But I want to try. I just wasn't sure – about you loving me. I didn't want to get hurt so I hurt you.'

I knew it, I knew it. Halleluiah, God be praised. 'It's alright, Andy. It's alright.' And my heart would be singing. And I'd bury my face in his long, golden hair.

But Andy still needs to confess. Gently, oh so gently, he pushes me away. 'No, no, it isn't alright.' From somewhere deep within, he lets out a sigh. 'I killed you, didn't I?'

'Yes,' I whisper, but like Jesus I have risen from the dead. God lives and so too does Janni!

He shakes his head. 'What an idiot I've been.' And with wet, sticky hands he pulls me towards him again. 'I'm so glad you waited. If you hadn't, I'd have found you, even if it meant searching every inch of this world.'

My head is dizzy with joy. 'Why?' I ask, my heart standing still.

We just look at each other. I know the answer before he says the words.

"Cos, Janns, I've never stopped loving you.'

Cue, a mad passionate kiss, followed by wedding bells and roses round a rustic cottage door.

And thus we lived happily ever after.

All day I waited but Andy never came.

But still there was hope in my heart. I went to bed that night and prayed that he would come in the early hours and see me there, like a sleeping Princess. I'd be turned away from him, my face to the open window. He'd come across to the low, double bed and the moon would shine on me like a spotlight. Quietly, he'd lie down beside me, kissing my neck through my hair. I'd smile in my sleep. Then gently he'd roll me towards him, on to my back, his hand moving under the sheet, touching me in just the right place.

And I'd begin to cry. 'I love you, I love you…'

'I know,' he'd say simply. 'I love you, too.'

And together the both of us would soar up to Heaven.

But I awoke on the morning of the fifteenth and there was just me in the bed. With heavy heart I quickly got dressed and headed over to Hamish's.

'He's not back yet,' I declared miserably, climbing the veranda steps.

Hamish was spreading thick marmalade on a piece of charcoal

crunchy toast. 'Och, he'll be back soon, I'm sure,' said Hamish, doing his usual thing and giving me his chair.

I threw myself in it. 'You don't think he's had an accident, do you?' Fear gripped my heart.

'Och, no.' Hamish was pouring, he handed me a cup filled with steaming hot tea. 'Toast?'

'No, thanks,' I replied, feeling totally flat. Moodily I took a sip. 'So, where is he, then?' I banged the cup down, spilling brown liquid into the saucer.

'Probably in Maiduguri lorry park as we speak,' soothed Hamish, patting my hand.

'Mmm,' I mumbled, feeling fit to explode.

Footsteps.

My stomach jolted and my heart nearly flew out of my mouth.

'Morning.'

Instant deflation.

'Morning, Buggy.'

Buggy, all tousled-haired and sleepy-eyed, grabbed and dragged over another deckchair. 'I take it the wanderer has yet to return,' he observed, stating the fucking obvious.

'Aye, he's not back yet,' nodded Hamish.

'Oh, dear,' said Buggy, chuckling, and raising an eyebrow at me, 'maybe he's got waylaid by Cameroon bandits.'

'Oh, my God, do you think so?' I squealed.

'Who knows,' shrugged Buggy, grabbing himself a piece of toast. 'Anything could have happened.' He smeared half a pound of margarine across the burnt offering, and then dolloped a load of marmalade on top.

'Like what?' I squealed again. Visions of all kinds of horrors filled my brain. Masked men, bullets in Andy's head, decapitation even. The list was endless.

'Well...' said Buggy, thinking while he crunched into his toast, sending little black bits flying into the air, 'I knew of a bloke...'

'Shut up, Buggy,' said Hamish, a tad crossly. He looked at me kindly. 'Don't listen to him, he's only winding you up.'

Buggy assented. 'Yeah, course I am, Janni.' He smiled showing teeth that were covered in black. 'Andy can look after himself.'

'So, why isn't he back yet?' I demanded.

Buggy was smearing more marge on another piece of toast. 'He's only a day late, for Christ's sake, Janni. Give it a break.'

That was it. On edge all day yesterday, all last night, and those

292

words finally pushed me over. 'You don't understand,' I bawled, 'you just don't fucking understand.'

I cried for a full ten minutes, while the boys patted and comforted me, and spread the message of hope.

'He'll be here soon.'

'I bet he's already on his way.'

'It'll all turn out alright.'

'He'll be so glad you stayed.'

After I'd finally dried my tears, and washed my face, and re-applied my make-up, and had returned back to the breakfast table, Hamish had already decided to take a day off from his artwork and spend a day with me at the Lake Chad swimming pool. 'And then you and me and Buggy will have dinner at the club tonight,' he declared as he put a rolled-up towel and a pair of black trunks into a brown leather satchel. He smiled at us both. 'The treat's on me.'

'Can't say no to that,' laughed Buggy, as he lit up a fag and swatted a fly. 'Rarely does a Scotsman put his hand in his pocket.'

'Away with you,' chortled Hamish, picking up his pipe and brandishing it like a weapon.

'On that note, I will.' Buggy scraped back his chair, and with fag in hand, he bade us farewell. 'See you two shirkers tonight,' he called over his shoulder as he descended the steps.

I watched Buggy get on his bike and head off to work. Hamish was already up and out of his chair, gathering his tobacco, his matches and book, pondering on what else he might need for a day of frivolous fun, sunning himself by a pool.

Inwardly, I felt very pissed off.

The last thing I wanted to do was spend a day at the Lake Chad with Hamish, and then spend the evening supping with him and Buggy at the club. What if Andy comes back while I'm there? What about my grand poetic plans and our romantic encounter? What about...?

'A quick pee and I'll be about ready,' Hamish said, putting his stuff into the brown leather satchel.

I managed a smile. 'I'll go get my costume and towel.'

As it was, it wasn't too bad a day. Hamish and I had the pool pretty much to ourselves for most of the morning, and later my three minders turned up, plus a couple of Dutch guys, three cool Americans, and Phil and Jamie. Oh, and Mike. No problems there, we just chatted to each other like we were old mates, which we were really, except – well, we knew each other just a little more intimately, I suppose.

At five we all headed back to our respective homes. If I'd had my own way I'd have gone earlier, just to check things out, but stupidly I'd agreed to leave my bike and let Hamish drive me to the hotel, so I couldn't and had to bide my time. As it was, it would have been a fruitless quest as Andy still wasn't back anyway. To say I was a little depressed is putting it mildly.

Still, I had a date with a couple of guys and they weren't going to let me get out of it. By 7.30 we were sitting in the club tucking into steak and chips. Well, Hamish and Buggy were, I declined (that was the one good thing to come out of all of this – my decreasing appetite meant less visits and pukes in the porcelain bowl – clouds and silver linings, and all that malarkey). Instead, I was supping vodka, large double vodkas recommended by Buggy as being the perfect solution to any problem one may have, big or small.

And he was right.

I had a great evening. A fabulous evening, in fact. Surrounded by friends, and I loved them all, even those I didn't know very well. I believe I even planted a kiss on old Mr Woodruff's withered cheeks, and took him for a bop around the tables.

'Come on,' I shouted, stamping my feet to 'Those Were The Days'. Now Hamish was in my arms, whirling and twirling. By the end of the evening I think I'd danced with every man in the club. But the fun still wasn't over. Even after the club closed there was a whole crowd of us singing, and when finally the bar steward politely shooed us all out, we went round to a bloke's called Roger for coffee where we smoked copious amounts of dope.

Finally, at three in the morning, Hamish dragged me home.

The lights were still not on in Andy's house, but did I give a toss? Not a bit of it. 'I'm starving,' I declared, as I stumbled across to the cookhouse. So was Buggy and Hamish. We raided the fridge that was pretty much empty, except for a big, round glob of processed cheese, and a few loaves of freshly baked bread. With carving knives out, and a sword fight in between, we cut ourselves great doorsteps, and found some mango pickle to spread on our cheese.

'Delicious,' I exclaimed, as we sat on the wooden kitchen table, chomping, the three of us, all very happy and all very pissed.

Until the next morning – mega hangover.

Thank God Andy didn't turn up that day.

Three days later, still no Andy. Christ, I was panicking. Where was he? I tortured myself. I conjured up every conceivable scene possible. My entire nervous system was fit to explode.

'Cool it,' soothed Rosie, as once again, she was the recipient of my ongoing tales of misery and woe.

'How can I?' I screamed, so loud, Che and Guevera bolted off down the veranda steps and hid behind the back of the house (at least I'd finally found a way of dealing with them).

'I'll tell you what,' Rosie said, unfolding her lovely long legs, and tucking a golden strand of hair behind her ear, 'let's go to the market. That'll take your mind off things. A bit of shopping always helps.'

Market! Market! How could a browse around a dirty, smelly, poxy market help?

For fuck's sake.

'Rosie, be serious,' I begged. 'This is hard.'

'I am being serious. It's better than just sitting around here doing nothing.'

She did have a point.

'Oh, all right,' I said, half-heartedly, getting up and stuffing my fags in my bag.

I drove, Rosie rode pillion.

We were just going past Bata's, Nigerian shoe shop extraordinaire, when my eye happened to alight upon a silver Ford Cortina. Now, you don't get that many flashy silver cars out here in Nigeria, as well you might know. Blimey, I thought, that looks just like my Dad's car. But the thought left me as quickly as it came.

We sped on.

Through the squalor and the mayhem, through the mutilated throng, to the market place, a large square of open stalls that sold everything from fabrics to dog meat (meaning dog meat for human consumption not tins of Pal). I parked the bike by a ditch filled with rubbish and all kinds of other horrible things, and where a man, quite unabashed, was having a shit in full view of the general public.

'Come on.' Rosie grabbed my arm. Darting and weaving in and out of traffic and people and donkeys and goats, we crossed the road to the stalls, kicking up little clouds of dust as we did so. 'I'm after another bag,' said Rosie, pushing away a beggar with only one arm who already had it outstretched and up in our faces. 'This one's falling apart at the seams.'

'I suppose I could do with another one,' I commented, ignoring another dozen hands battling for our attention. 'Look, all the tassels have nearly fallen off.' I pulled one, just to make my point, and it came away in my hand.

We, along with half of the beggar population in Maiduguri, eventually found the bag stall. The crowd surged forward as we surveyed the brightly coloured display of leather goods, pouffes, holdalls, bags, purses, wall coverings that were once part of an animal's backside.

'What about this one?' suggested Rosie, half bent down, examining a rather splendid carrier of ladies' goods that was made out of crocodile skin.

'Mmm,' I said, 'let's have a look.'

She passed the bag up. It was very nice, long strap, the bumps on the croc superimposed in decorative fashion on the front. Undoing the zip, I peered inside. Very roomy. And how many, three, no four compartments – just what a girl with a load of make-up, and an addiction to fags, and dope, needs. 'I'll have that,' I said, ready to go into barter mode with the man in the riga and bright orange, coala nut teeth. 'Hey, Mallam. Nowa, nowa?'

To get things off to a good start, the proprietor of this rather grand handbag stall turned and spat a straight spray of stained, rusty saliva in my direction. As you do. It missed my foot by a mere inch.

Disgusted, I turned away for a second.

My God! By the second-hand tool store, in amongst a pile of jerry cans up for sale, and a load of old rubber tyres, was my Dad having a rootle around. My Dad!

Fuck!

'Rosie, Rosie.'

'What?' Rosie wasn't really listening, she was knee-deep in bags, on a mission; every single one was being prodded, inspected, and poked.

I grabbed her arm, and dropped the croc. 'Rosie, we've got to get out of here. Quick!'

Rosie struggled, tried to wrench back her arm. She was half up, half down. 'Janni, what are you doing, for Christ sake?'

'My Dad,' I hissed. 'Quick!'

'Your Dad?' Rosie looked at me in a way that suggested she was convinced I was, as she'd always suspected, quite mad.

'Yeah, my Dad! There. Look.'

I pointed. She followed my finger. The crowd, the kids, the panhandlers, the just down right inquisitive, all turned their heads as well and stared at my Dad who was now squatting down, rummaging through an old tea chest full of car jacks.

'Is that your Dad?'

'Yes,' I hissed. 'Come on.'

We fled. Through the throng, jumping over piles of putrid rubbish, knocking into women in bright cloths and pans on their heads, I think I even collided with a leper – but who bloody well cared?

'Quick,' I demanded. 'Get on the bike.'

Turn the key, into first gear, and we were off.

'I'll have to hide?' I shouted over the engine noise, and the din.

'Mine?' Rosie shouted back.

'No. Dad knows he might find me at yours, and he'll look, believe me, he'll look.'

'Where then?'

'Anne's.'

'Anne's?'

'Yeah, Anne's.'

Anne's it was.

I stayed there all day, and Anne very kindly went to the club on my behalf to sniff out any information about my Dad's sudden appearance here in Maiduguri.

'Well?' I asked, when she finally came back after two bloody long hours and I was half-way climbing the walls.

'Yeah, it was your Dad,' said Anne, flopping down in a chair, and taking off her sandals.

'I know it was my Dad, you idiot. What I mean is what was he doing? Why was he here?'

'Some business meeting, I think.' Anne lifted up her left foot, and inspected the skin underneath. Shit, I think I've got a verruca.'

'So he hadn't come looking for me then?' I said, mildly relieved.

'No,' said Anne, picking at the small black bit on her foot. 'Ouch!'

Ignoring her plight, I ventured on. 'Did my Mum come with him?'

'I don't think so,' answered Anne, putting her foot back down on the floor. I made a mental note not to walk around her house in bare feet.

'So, where's he now?'

'Gone home, I think'

'What? Back to Gombe?'

Anne nodded, and lit up a fag. I followed suit. 'Where did you get all this info from?' I asked, puffing like an old locomotive. Today's events had made me feel very on edge. I was already contemplating the next cigarette even before I'd halfway finished this one.

'Colin Woodruff.'

That figured. I blew out a dark cloud of smoke. 'Did Mr Woodruff say anything about Dad asking about me?'

Anne inhaled, and exhaled. 'Not really. He just said that your Dad now knows you're here, and he now knows Andy's not.'

'Oh.' I pondered this little titbit of information. What, I thought, would Dad make of that? Would he be glad or sad? Would he be crowing – 'told you so, Janni' – or worried about the state of my heart? A trickle of sweat ran down my back. I gave it a wipe. It was sweltering. The kind of heat made worse when you know your Dad's hot on your trail.

Except he wasn't. Or was he?

'Did Dad look for me, Anne? Did Mr Woodruff say whether he went round Andy's?'

Anne shrugged. 'Oh, I don't know, Janni. Does it matter?'

'Yes, it does.'

Then I thought: no it doesn't. Dad was gone. Crisis over – for the time being at least.

I sighed, a deep, meaningful sigh. 'I don't suppose you've heard anything about Andy while you were out?'

Anne shook her head. 'Not a tweet.'

CHAPTER 9

Maiduguri; January 1974 – and the wanderer returns

I stayed at Anne's that night – just in case – and returned to Andy's the next day.

Still no sign of him. Where the hell was he?

Depressed, helpless, I wandered out on to the veranda and spotted Buggy coming out of his little thatched house. I raced over.

'Buggy, when's Andy due back at work?' As if I hadn't asked the question a million times.

Buggy gave me a reasonably patient look. 'He's got pretty much the whole of January off, you know that, Janni.'

'Yeah, but originally he was aiming for the fourteenth, we were going to do a couple of weeks in the Cameroon and then come back here and head north into Chad...'

'Yeah,' butted in Buggy, 'but that was before, well you know, you and he – er – went your separate ways.'

Someone else saying it out loud was like a dagger severing my heart. I could feel tears welling up. Buggy sensed it too. Quickly he looked at his watch. 'Got to go, Janni. Old Man Woodruff's on my case, I was late twice last week.' He patted my shoulder. 'Stay cool, hey.'

'Yeah,' I mumbled.

As if?

I stood and watched Buggy go off in a cloud of powdery dust, then headed for Hamish's. The veranda was empty, and so was his house. Fuck! It was one of those days when I didn't want to be on my own. So I jumped on my bike and purred off to Rosie's.

'She's at school, sweetheart,' said her Mum. Her bangles jangled as she tucked a lock of grey/golden hair behind her brass ashtrays that had doubled-up as earrings.

'Course,' I said, glumly, 'I forgot.'

I dithered by the door, not sure what to do. 'Do you want to come in, and have a drink?' asked this most unusual of mums, putting a hennaed hand on my shoulder. Her invitation was out of kindness, she seemed enormously busy, through the French doors her overloaded desk looked more overloaded than ever, and she'd

299

been clacking away at her typewriter when I arrived. Part of me wanted to bury myself in her low-hanging bosoms and gush out my woes (I was certain she'd understand, she was that kind of woman) but I did the polite thing, being a well brought up young lady, and declined.

'No, no thanks. Just tell Rosie I'll be up at the Chad pool. Perhaps she can meet me there later, if that's okay.'

Rosie's Mum smiled. 'Not a problem.'

'Thanks. Bye.'

'Bye. Enjoy your day.'

As if.

I jumped on my bike, and headed back to the house – just to make sure Andy hadn't come back in the fifteen minutes I'd been away. He hadn't. Despondently, I gathered my towel and my cossie, and my little notebook that was now more like a journal, an outpouring of daily events and up and down emotions, plus a smattering of poems, and headed off to the Lake Chad pool. Tucking myself away in a corner, as far away from the mums and kids as I possibly could, I spent the morning penning my thoughts.

I waited for you, Andy. Full of expectations, and thought about what I'd say when you arrived. But today, like every other day, you never came. And still I wait. Sitting in a chair, in an empty room, staring at an empty wall. Alone in our bed. The tears filling my eyes and silently falling, falling away. Oh, the sadness, the very heaviness of it all.

What is this thing called love? I hate love, because love hates me. I want you now. Now, now, now. Please come back to me, Andy.

Heart-rending stuff. But, then again, it was a heart-rending time.

Around about one, I headed back home, just in case. A useless quest. So distraught was I, I ended up getting hopelessly lost in a neem street nightmare on my return journey back to the pool, and encountered parts of Maiduguri I'd never yet seen. And how I didn't end up having an accident, I'll never know. Blinded by tears I wasn't fit to be on the road, more than once I nearly ended upside-down in a ditch and almost came a cropper when I zoomed out of a side road and very nearly collided with a kit-car.

'Bugger off,' I screamed, as the driver tooted and honked. 'Bugger off, bugger off, bugger off!' Poor bloke, he didn't know what to make of it, a baturi girl, a demented baturi girl, losing her marbles in a ditch.

300

Anyway, after a bloody good cry across the handlebars of my bike, watched by a couple of humpedback cows aimlessly meandering by, I wiped my eyes, took a deep breath, and started over again. And somehow I managed to get back on the right road, and half an hour later I was by the pool, bottle of Sprite by my side, fag in hand, penning more of the same. Until, of course, when Rosie and the mob arrived around about three o'clock, then I abandoned my written observations on my sad, fucking life, and made concerted efforts to be one of the gang.

It wasn't easy, believe me.

At five, we all agreed we'd had enough of the Lake Chad, and decided to resume social interaction back at the club.

'I'll just pop home,' I said to Rosie. 'Just in case.'

I didn't have to spell it out to her, she knew what I meant. 'Okay, see you later,' she said, and sped off on her bike, her golden locks flying like golden threads in the late afternoon sun.

No Andy. No flipping Andy. The house as quiet as a church, only a fly buzzing around the window, and our resident lizard running amok down the wall.

With heavy heart, I jumped again on my bike, and headed off to the club. They were all there, Rosie, Anne, Amy, the Dutch guys, Roger the midnight-coffee-maker, Phil, Sally, Mike, and many others.

They were all talking about stupid things; well, stupid to me, my mind, as always, was on much more important matters, I couldn't have given a toss about Hanks' forthcoming fancy dress party.

'I've got this lovely ball gown that belonged to my grandmother,' Amy was blathering. 'It's all frilly with lace. I wish I'd brought it out with me. I could have gone as – what's her name in 'Gone With the Wind...'

'Ruby, isn't it?' quipped one of the blokes.

'No,' laughed Sally. 'Scarlet. Scarlet O'Hara.'

'Oh, yeah,' nodded Amy. 'That's right.'

'I loved that film,' sighed Anne, rolling herself a fag.

'Chuck us your tin over, Annie.' This came from Roger. Anne passed it to Mike, who passed it to me, who passed it to Roger.

The conversation continued. Anne spouting on about Rhet bloody Butler – and 'frankly, my dear, I don't give a damn' – Roger and Mike comparing the qualities of the Stones music versus the Small Faces, Hank going on about building a ruddy great bonfire complete with a Guy.

'Bonfire Night's in November, man,' Phil was saying.

'Ya, I know this,' shrugged Hank. 'So vot?'

So vot indeed. All this inane conversation was driving me crazy.

'You okay?' asked Mike, when Roger had headed off to the toilet for a slash, bringing the Stones/Faces debate to a pause.

I tossed my hair back, just a little. Mike and I were now just friends, a mutual, but unsaid agreement had somewhere along the way been made that our sexual encounter was but a brief interlude and was now at an end. And that suited us both fine.

'Yeah,' I lied. 'I'm okay. Well, I'm not really – but, well – you know–'

Mike smiled his lovely smile. 'Yeah, I know…'

'Hey, drink, Janni?' Rosie was waving my empty glass.

'Please.'

'What?'

'Tomato juice.'

'Yuck.' This came from Buggy who'd just walked in. Dragging a chair over, he flopped down and sprawled out. 'How can you drink that shite? It looks like female menstrual blood.'

'Well, it wouldn't be blokes' menstrual blood, would it?' quipped Sally.

Everyone laughed. Even me.

'Oh, I dunno, I knew a bloke once, who had periods,' came Buggy's bright response.

'Fuck off,' everyone trilled.

'No, man, I mean it. There was this bloke who…'

See what I mean? All of it totally inane.

And so the evening wore on. More people came and more chairs were dragged over, everyone settling themselves down for a sociable chit-chat. Normally I'd have loved this kind of get-together, cool folk, with me in their midst. But not tonight, not any night since I'd got back from Mambilla. There was this invisible, empty chair next to me, and it was there all the time. And the person who should have been sitting in it was – well, you know, don't you? I ached with the pain.

Around seven Richard breezed in. 'Sorry I'm late, babe.' He gave Sally a kiss on the top of her head. 'Work issues got in the fucking way.'

'Get us a drink,' said Sally, not bothered.

'Hey, Janni...'

I was talking to Phil, telling him about my stay on the islands in the middle of the Benue River. This was my kind of conversation. It reminded me of the good times, of which there were many.

'Fuck me, crocodiles. Man, weren't you scared,' enquired a wide-eyed Phil.

'Terrified, Phil. I couldn't get in the friggin' boat. If Andy hadn't...'

'Hey, Janni...' Richard, over the other side of the table, Sal's empty glass in hand, was trying to get my attention.

'What?' Mildly pissed off, I was just getting to the good bit.

'You know Andy's back, don't you?'

'What!!!!????'

'Yeah, I've just seen him.'

I was up, out of my chair. 'Where?'

'Back at his place. He got in about six.'

Jesus Christ!

'Got to go,' I squealed, grabbing my two-tasselled bag.

If anyone said anything to me as I bolted out of the club, I didn't hear, words, faces, furniture, all had become a blob.

I zipped down the darkened road like Stirling Moss, zig-zagging and flying over potholes; goats, donkeys, unassuming women on their way home from market, were scattered in my wake.

And my bike wasn't the only thing that was racing. My mind was going like the clappers. *What will he say? What should I say? Will he be sorry? Had he missed me? Oh, dear God, please let him have missed me.*

Reaching the house, I did a skid, and left a figure of eight in the sand.

Oh, shit! What do I look like?

Throwing the bike down – who gives a fuck? – I quickly scrabbled about in my bag, found compact case and lipstick, and rapidly did a repair job on my face using my headlamp as a torch. Quickly I scrutinised my clothes, a tie-dyed coffee coloured smock over red loon trousers, not quite what I'd imagined I'd be wearing but there you go – it would just have to do.

I approached the veranda steps nervously. Butterflies swirled. My legs were like jelly.

Nearer, and I heard the mutter of voices coming from inside the house. Andy's. His soft dulcet voice sent me all in a quiver. The other was deeper, African. Shit! A threesome. This wasn't in my fantasy script.

One at a time, I ascended the veranda steps, and tiptoed up to the door. It was ajar. Stopping for a moment, my back against the shadowy wall, I breathed slowly, deeply, in, out, and counted to three, four, five, six- tentatively I poked my head round the door.

Andy sat on the bed, his long, fair hair in a ponytail, his skin deeply tanned, the silver snake glinting in the light of the hissing hurricane lamp. He looked utterly, utterly gorgeous. A warm, funny feeling gushed through my body and settled in my nether regions. But I stayed still, and I stayed quiet, and I bided my time.

Opposite Andy, squatting on the floor and puffing on a joint was Lowan the night watchman, his lean coffee-coloured body wrapped in a flowing blue robe. Together they made an exotic ensemble – black and gold, east and west.

Lowan was talking, in Hausa of course, and must have said something funny. Andy laughed, a Celtic, throaty sound. Oh, God how I loved his laugh. Actually I loved all of him, everything, from the top of his golden head to the tip of his sun-brown toes.

Still, I bided my time.

Neither of them was aware of my presence. The night watchman took another drag, then leant across and gave Andy the joint. Chuckling, Andy put the butt to his mouth, inhaled deeply, exhaled slowly–

It was now or never. I stepped out of the shadows and into the room.

'Hello, Andy,' I said, rather too brightly.

Lowan looked up, Andy turned round. Lowan grinned. Andy frowned.

There was a moment of dreadful silence. I could hear my watch ticking.

'I heard you were still around,' he said, finally, in a voice that was cold, and in a voice that was dark.

That wasn't in my fantasy script either. In this room, finally together, and he was about as distant as the moon in the sky. I could have wept. Stupidly, I managed to smile as barbed wire wrapped itself round my innards. 'Did you have a good time?' I asked, edging towards the bed.

'It was okay.' He didn't look at me, and the wire pulled tight.

Feeling a bit dizzy, I put my arm round the bedpost. Andy glanced up. In his face was everything I'd ever feared: an expression of unequivocal rejection.

I swallowed, and it hurt.

Silence. A dreadful, awful silence.

Desperate, I tried hard to think of something to say, something that would change the whole situation, and make it all right. But my head was fuzzy, and my tongue was tied up in knots.

Tick, tick, tick went my watch.

Boomedy, boom went my heart.

Amphibians crowded my throat. I tried to swallow the lot. But they stayed. And I thought I might die on the spot.

And still the silence continued.

Andy swatted a fly. Missed, and it flew away, over the net. He bent down and picked up his cigarettes and a box of matches that were lying by his feet on the floor. Ignoring me, he lit up, and chucked down the matches. In the quiet, they didn't half make a rattle.

Clutching my bedpost, I gazed upon the man I adored as he smoked. Not being able to put my arms around him was terrible. It was if I was standing on one side of a great impassable divide, between what I longed for and dreamed of, and what was real.

Truly, I hurt.

Andy blew out a smoke ring, and watched as it floated up and away, and blew out another one, and another. And I stood there, and, even though the temperature was probably in the hundreds, I shivered with cold.

Another smoke ring drifted high in the air.

My tongue, all big and floppy, moved inside my mouth. I couldn't bear the silence any longer.

'Andy–' I wasn't sure what else to say, so I stopped.

He looked at me, he stopped blowing smoke rings, and looked at me, and my heart raced. 'Why did you come back?' he muttered, under his breath. 'After everything, why did you still come back?'

Because I love you.

I stumbled to find the right words, a suitable explanation that would make him stop looking at me like I was something a hyena had spat out – believe me, hyenas eat almost anything. 'Because – because I – because Anne invited me back–' My voice croaked. 'We met up in Yola, she wanted me to–'

Andy turned away, and summed up the floor.

I ploughed on. 'She – well, she invited me back to Maiduguri…'

The groan that came out of his mouth sounded totally unnatural.

305

'…so…so I came back…'

Another alien-type groan and Andy put his head in his hands.

'…I came back – and – and waited for you. Because…' I trembled, as I said the final words '…I love you. Oh, God, I love you, so, so, much, Andy.' And I held onto the bedpost, and blinked away splashing water, and through the blur, gazed upon the man I adored who still had his head in his hands.

And that's how it was for a moment or two.

Then he spoke. Because his hands were over his mouth, I couldn't quite catch what he said. 'Huh?' came my miserable, wretched response.

The golden head lifted. And through gritted teeth, he repeated himself. 'Have you no dignity?'

I couldn't quite comprehend. 'Huh?'

Andy kicked the box of matches across the floor. Then put his head back in his hands.

It finally clicked. Jesus! At least now I could empathise with Dick the Prick. Delusions make you believe so many daft things.

Boom, boom, boom went my heart and tick, tick, tick, went my watch. Clutching onto my post like the drowning man who hangs onto a useless rubber-ring that has a hole in it. I was going down, and I knew it.

'Why?' His head still in his hands, his voice so muffled, I barely heard him. 'Why? Why? Why?'

Still hanging onto the post, I swung myself round, and sat down on the bed. We were just a couple of feet away from each other, so close, so fucking close. 'Because I love you,' I blubbered. 'And want to be with you…you don't mean what you say…'

Delusions again. Except they seemed so fucking real.

'…you don't, do you, Andy, you love me…'

This groan was like an elephant's bellow.

'…Andy, please.' I put my hand out, and almost touched him. He flinched, and I drew it back. 'Andy, please…'

'You shouldn't have.' Andy raised his head, turned, and faced me. In the lamplight his handsome features had turned ugly. He snarled. 'There's no way you should have come back.' He hissed. He spat. He glared. 'You're fucking pathetic.'

I whimpered. 'Don't say that, Andy, please.'

'Jesus Christ!'

Lowan moved. We'd forgotten all about him. 'Sai gobi,' he muttered, and left us both to it.

I might be pathetic, but I didn't care. 'Andy...' He turned a shoulder, a very cold shoulder. 'Andy...'

I couldn't help myself, he was always the magnet, I was always the pin. My trembling finger touched his arm, ever so lightly. He bolted, and moved as far away as was possible, to the other side of the room.

Oh God, how could he do this to me?

A cold fear spread through my chest and curled around my ribcage. The real reality had finally kicked in. Andy definitely didn't love me anymore. It was worse than I could have imagined.

Silence. Dreadful, dreadful silence.

I sat on the bed. Andy, his back against the wall, crouched on the floor.

Silence.

Tick, tick, tick, went my watch, the hurricane lamp hissed. A moth bumped against the ceiling, and there were faraway sounds as a motorbike screeched up the road.

More silence. And more silence. Tick, tick. Hiss, hiss. And a bumpety-bump.

'Can I ask you something?' he asked suddenly. From a great distance, his voice was quite soft.

Hope springs eternal. He's changed his mind, it's going to be...

A blaze of anger screamed from the shadows. 'Are there any brain cells in that fucking brain of yours? Are there? Are there?'

It was like a bloody great spear, the type hunters use when they're tracking bloody great animals. It ripped me apart. 'Don't, Andy,' I moaned. 'Don't talk to me like this...'

'Like what, you fucking moron?'

The words stung me. A moron? A fucking moron? My God, he just called me a fucking moron – this definitely wasn't part of my fantasy script! 'Don't you dare call me a fucking moron, you bastard.' Even I surprised myself. I jumped up off the bed, grabbed the box of matches from the floor, and chucked them. Good aim. Right on the head.

Like quicksilver let loose, Andy charged across the room. I tried to duck out of his way, but too late, he had my arm, he swung me around, his other hand gripped me, his fingers dug hard into my flesh. 'You're hurting me,' I screamed. 'Get off me, you're hurting me.' But the fingers dug in.

'Don't you get it?' he shouted, his voice shaking. 'Don't you get it? It's over, over, over.' He pushed me onto the bed, roughly he pulled me up, and roughly he pushed me down again. I kicked him in the balls. That made him let go. 'Aaagh,' he howled, clutching the tender spot.

'Serves you right,' I screamed back.

'You make me sick,' he spat.

'Not half as sick as you make me, you bastard.'

'Then why don't you go and be sick somewhere else, and leave me to be sick here.'

He glared at me, from a safe distance.

I glared back. Then I crumpled. It was all too fucking much.

I ended up sprawled across the bed, heaving with tortured sobs and gut wrenching moans.

So much for happy-ever-after- finales.

This was the pits.

I cried on that bed for ages, and Andy returned to his spot and stayed there for ages, the two of us, once joined at the hip, now separated, set adrift, like two astronauts lost in space. Except, he still had his rocket, and I had nothing, not even a tank of oxygen to help sustain what was left of my life.

It was truly the end. I could hear Jim Morrison singing the words. I carried on crying and gulping for breath, grieving the loss of my love, and all that that loss entailed. So many no mores. So many, so many, so many...

My God! How would I cope? I wouldn't, I wouldn't, I wouldn't. I couldn't, I couldn't, I couldn't.

I howled to the moon.

But even in dark hours such as this, when all hope was gone, when I couldn't envisage ever laughing again, and when I couldn't imagine anyone ever kissing or holding me again (Mike didn't count), despite all this, the sobs finally subsided. My wails became a moan, my moans became a whimper, and my whimpers became a sniff.

And silence.

Five minutes passed.

Horizontal on the bed, I couldn't see Andy. In fact, I didn't even know if he was still in the room. If he was, he was certainly keeping quiet. The only sound was a tick-tick-tick, a hiss-hiss-hiss, a bumpety-bump, a screech in the distance, and the occasional sniff that came from me.

Ten minutes passed.

I shifted myself on the bed, and in the gloom stared at the ceiling. If I really, really looked hard I could just about see the moth playing kamikaze through the folds in the net.

Twenty minutes passed.

Aside from the tick (there was no longer a hiss as the wick on the hurricane lamp had burnt out) and the bump-bump-bump, another sound now drifted around the room. Someone moving. Bare feet across the floor. A light went on in the bathroom, the door slammed, then water ran through pipes, a few minutes later I heard the flush of the loo. The door opened, the bathroom light went off. The pad of bare feet again, going across the room.

And more silence. And more minutes passed.

And still I lay on my bed, because I really didn't know what else to do.

Then I heard the sound of a tin being opened, the lid coming off. A rustle of papers, Rizla papers. The strike of a match.

I smelt smoke, dope smoke.

Lifting my head, I had to squint through shadows because my eyes were all puffed up from crying, and located Andy still sitting in his spot on the floor. I saw him draw on his joint, a tiny red glow lighting his face as he did so.

I shifted myself, sat up, and felt the ache in my bones.

'Smoke?'

He speaks!

I moved my legs over the bed.

The amphibians in my throat croaked a, 'Yeah.'

Andy and the red glow came over. His fingers touched mine (oh, God!) as he handed it to me. 'Thanks,' I managed to say.

Andy walked back to his spot.

I inhaled. It felt good, really good. For as long as I could I kept the intoxicating smoke down. Then I exhaled. And the drug hit my brain. My tense body began to relax. I could feel the blood flowing. I took another drag – just as long, and just as deep, and another, and another. The dreadful pain became less dreadful pain, it was still there, like a knife in my belly, but the blade didn't feel quite so sharp.

One more drag, and I got up, a little unsteady, and walked across the room to Andy, with his back against the wall, his legs spread out in front of him, his eyes studying the void. 'Cheers,' I managed to say, passing the little red glow stick back to him.

He took it without saying a word.

And me, wanting to throw myself down and feel warm in his arms, returned through the shadows to my cold, miserable bed. Another five minutes passed. I deliberated on whether it might be worth my while letting out a scream – just for the sheer hell of it. All this saying nothing was really getting on my tits.

'I'm sorry.'

He speaks again!

'Huh?'

'I'm sorry.'

I swallowed, and it really, really hurt. 'About what?' *Duh!*

'About us not working out.'

He said this so sweetly, too sweetly, a soft, gentle voice handing me over the gritty reality that this truly was the end. My insides were wrenched apart. Better to be cruel, I reckon. The impact on the emotions is less.

I opened my mouth and nothing came out, except the frog. The usual tear welling malarkey began, of course, drip, drip, drip as the drops spilled down my face. But we were so far apart, and it was gloomy, and I was quiet, so he didn't notice a thing.

'We had some good times, didn't we?'

Still I couldn't speak, so I grunted.

Andy shifted himself on the floor. I heard the lid of the tin come off again, and the rustle of dope-making paraphernalia. The match flared, he lit up, and out came a sigh. 'Och, Janni, it's a funny business is life.'

Never was a truer word spoken, except I'd have swapped the word funny for shite.

'Smoke?'

Again I grunted.

Again Andy got up and came over with the joint. Taking it from him with one hand, I pushed back the hair off my face with the other in an effort to look appealing, which was a bit daft as I had blotchy cheeks and eyes like puff pastry. Anyway, it didn't make any difference, he barely gave me a glance, just passed the spliff on, and returned to his shadowy spot on the floor, the spot that was as far away as possible from me on the bed.

Am I that revolting? I asked myself, as I miserably puffed away.

'You know, I got arrested in the Cameroon,' said the voice from the other side of the room.

'Huh?' I wasn't really listening, too much shit in my head, plus

310

I'd knocked the end of my joint with my hand trying to wipe away a tear, and was busy putting out the sparks that were threatening to burn holes in me and the bed sheets. Not that I really cared.

The voice continued, oblivious. 'Jeez, it was a bad, fucking nightmare.'

Welcome to my world.

'It was a good job you weren't with me, y'know.'

Oh, I don't think so, Andy. I really don't bloody well think so.

Opening my mouth, and in the tears spilled, all salty. 'What happened?' I managed to croak.

Dramatic pause while Andy lit a cigarette. 'It was in Yaounde, the capital.' Another pause while he took a couple of puffs. 'Man, what a scene. I hit town at around two in the morning, hitched a ride on an old cattle truck, and was dropped off on the outskirts- the driver said something about soldiers, I didn't know what the fuck he meant, he was speaking mostly in French, but I guessed right. There I was traipsing along this road into town, minding my own business, when a load of drunk soldiers with guns suddenly appeared out of the bush...'

I coughed. 'Blimey!' I said quietly.

'Yeah. This bozo with sunglasses and a rain poncho tossed over his shoulder like a cape, started screaming, 'Drugs, drugs.'

'Blimey,' I said again, and for a second, my grief took a backseat. This was heavy stuff. 'No shit!' I exclaimed, pretty loudly.

Andy was on a roll. It was like old times.

'Fuck, I'm telling you, Janns, I was panicking. My stash was in my bag, and this freak made me open the bag up, with an automatic aimed at my head...'

'Jesus!' I was perched on the edge of the bed, the pain almost, but almost forgotten.

'Yeah, I was praying. He lifted everything out, took my torch, a book, my Zippo lighter-'

'No?' Not his lovely Zippo lighter. What bastards. 'I'm sorry...'

'Fuck, I didn't give a toss about my lighter. He could have it, it was the bag of dope that worried me, it was in my side pocket.'

'Did he find it?'

'He found it. Oh yeah, he fucking found it. The next thing I knew, I was being bundled into an army truck surrounded by armed, drunken soldiers, going to fuck knows where. Man, I was shitting myself.'

'Oh, Andy.' Poor, poor, Andy. I should have been there. He

shouldn't have had to face such a thing on his own.

'They took me to this shit-hole of a place, stinking of piss, full of rats, and locked me up with about twenty other guys. Africans. Real hard nuts. And that was it.'

My hand was to my mouth. Quelle horreur! 'What happened next?'

'Nothing.'

'Nothing?'

'Yeah, fucking nothing. I've spent the last two weeks in a shit-hole gaol in the Cameroon.'

'You're joking!'

'I wish I fucking was.'

'So what – I mean, how have you – did you escape?'

Andy chuckled. It really was like old times. 'Man, no one escapes from a Cameroon prison. Ten feet deep walls, armed guards, it was like Alcatraz…'

'So how come you're here? I mean, what happened?'

'Well, just as I was beginning to see no light at the end of the tunnel…'

'Was it really dreadful?'

'Horrific. Hell on earth.'

'Did you have to go to court?'

'No. What happened was this bozo comes from the British Embassy, a right tosser in a panama hat with a public school accent, and tells me I'm being deported, and that I'm a very lucky young man because I could have faced ten years…'

'Jesus!'

'Yeah.' I saw Andy lean over, and pick up something. 'Cigarette?'

'Yeah.'

Eagerly, I got up off the bed, and moved across the room. A match flashed in the dark, Andy passed the red glowing tip over. 'Cheers.' I slid down and sat on the floor, just an outstretched arm away from his spot. Another match flared. We both blew smoke rings in the air.

It was definitely like old times.

'So, I get bundled into this Citroen, with two French dudes wearing sunglasses and Inspector Maigret hats, and this bozo in his panama hat, and I'm taken to the boarder – this was three days ago–'

'I wondered where you were, we all did.'

'Well, now you know.' Andy took a puff. So did I. 'Anyway, I get an armed escort across the border, and then the Nigerian authorities re-arrest me.'

I edged an inch closer. 'You're joking!'

'I wish I was. They banged me up in another rat-infested cell, and I'm thinking, shit man, what's happening? But, then they let me go after four hours.'

Another inch. 'Thank God!'

'But I don't think it's all over just yet...' Andy took another drag, and the glow glowed. '...I think I'm out on bail...'

Another inch. 'No, way!'

'Yeah.'

'Did you have to pay any money?'

'Naw. That's just it, I don't know what the fuck's going on.' He looked at me, and almost, but almost, put out his hand. 'I think I'm up shit creak without a paddle.'

'Oh, Andy.' I almost, but almost, touched him. Restraining myself, keeping my arms by my side was agony.

'Still, I'm here to fight another day,' he said, shifting. Which disturbed me, he was moving a couple of inches away. 'But I reckon my dope dealing days are over, and I'll have to keep my head down.'

'Yeah,' I concurred. 'You will. You really will.'

Silence.

'Andy...'

'Yeah?'

Oh, no! He was pushing himself up. He was flicking on the light switch.

Blinking, I swallowed, cleared my throat. *Hold me. I am in pieces. Please hold me.* 'I'm – glad you're back.'

From his lofty perch he looked down at me, and I, in love and fear, looked up. Our eyes met directly. For a moment, just for a moment, there was something of the old warmth in his expression. It was as if he was going to give me his hand, was going to pull me into his arms.

He turned away. The moment was gone. My stomach felt like it had been kicked.

'I'm fucking beat.' He yawned. He stretched. 'I've been on the road all day and really need to get some shut-eye.'

Sleeping arrangements? What about sleeping arrangements? Maybe all is not lost. I sat on the floor, and waited and watched, with fingers crossed. Padding across the room, Andy went over to his rucksack, and began to unpack. Out came his hat, his little collection of sponge bag items that weren't in a sponge bag, his toothbrush, toothpaste, a small bar of soap wrapped in a flannel. His book. His little anthology.

Oh, God, I willed him to open it up, turn a page, and read me out a poem. But the book and the anthology were tossed aside.

Next, out came some T-shirts, then a pair of jeans, some underpants; these were all chucked in a pile in a corner of the room. The cook-cum-houseboy would take them away in the morning, and bring them back, all freshly laundered, by teatime the same day.

Last out was the sleeping bag, our sleeping bag, inside the nylon padding, where so many dreams and erotic moments had been shared.

'I'll take the floor, you take the bed.'

He didn't even look at me. My heart seared into two, and the two pieces sank.

'I don't mind sleeping on the floor,' Saint Janni the Martyr whimpered lamely.

Andy, shoving his now empty rucksack into his almost empty wardrobe, glanced over. Briefly.

'Naw, I'm used to it, after two weeks on a shit, stinking rat-infested, piss strewn, dirt floor, this floor, believe me, will feel like cotton wool on my bones.'

A tear dribbled. Thank God it was semi-dark. The bulb that hung from the ceiling light was just 40 watt.

I managed to keep it together, and struggled to my feet.

We moved about, I went to my basket and had a pretend sort-out. Andy picked up his toothbrush, his toothpaste, and pottered off to the bathroom. The door closed.

Quietly, I howled.

The door opened. Quickly, I put my head back in the basket, and aimlessly moved things about.

'It's all yours.'

'Cheers,' I said, almost brightly. Randomly I picked out something from my basket, a pair of trousers, and hoped he'd think it was a towel. Not that he was even interested in me, his back was turned, he was laying the sleeping bag out, taking a pillow off the bed, and a cushion off the chair.

In the bathroom, I turned on the taps, sat on the toilet, and howled again. Cranking pipes and gushing water helped dim the moans. Oh, God, what was I going to do?

Turning off the taps, and pulling the chain, some ten minutes later, I opened the bathroom door, and crept out.

The room was in darkness. Just a dim light from the far distant moon came through the window. I tiptoed across to the bed, hoping against hope that Andy might have changed his mind, and would be tucked up in there. Telling me it was all a silly joke. He wasn't, and he didn't. All this heartache was seriously real.

'Night, night,' I said softly, as I dragged my wretched body into my cold, empty bed.

No response, just one gentle snore.

My head touched the pillow.

At least we're here together, I thought.

CHAPTER 10

January 22 1974 – the return of the Prodigal daughter

Sleep didn't come easy. But that goes without saying.

It was somewhere around five in the morning, and the dawning sun had coloured the sky a golden red, when my eyes finally shut, and I succumbed to a few hours of restless oblivion.

I say restless, because when I awoke I was all wrapped up in the sheet like an Egyptian Mummy, and the mattress was soaked with my sweat. Rubbing my eyes that were still sore from last night's crying, I glanced over at the sleeping bag still on the floor. It was empty. I peered at my watch. 8.30.

My head hit the pillow again. It was so sodden it squished like a sponge.

And what will happen today? I wondered glumly, as I stared up at the folds in the net. A fly had found its way through a gap in the mesh, and was trying to find its way out again; it buzzed from fold to fold but no could do. Poor wretched fly.

Poor wretched me.

I was just about to kick my legs over the side of the bed and grudgingly make for the loo, when the door flew open, and Andy strode into the room. He looked like a man on a mission. A no nonsense mission; death to all, no prisoners taken.

Meaning, he had plans for me.

I quaked on the bed.

'Get up,' he barked, the gentle side of him, glimpsed for five minutes last night, truly gone. 'Your transport's going to be here in half an hour.'

'What?' My legs already over the side, I sat on the edge of the bed, paralysed with fear. 'What transport?' I squeaked.

Ignoring me, Andy marched over to my Mambillan basket, and began throwing in some of my debris from off the floor, a pair of sandals, a jumble of clothes, my damp bikini and towel. He headed for the chest of drawers. Swept all my make-up off, my Agatha Christie book, for a horrible second his hand hovered over the photo, our photo, I heard myself screaming, two horrible seconds later it and everything else was in my basket, thrown like rubbish in a bin.

My screaming continued. 'What are you doing, Andy?' I'd bounced off the bed, and was racing round the room stark bollock naked, trying to stop him, as everything, my poems, my box of Tampax, my knickers, clean and dirty, my hairbrush, my earrings, everything that made up me, my life, my whole personae, was flung furiously into the basket. Yesterday's clothes, the red loons, the tie-dyed coffee coloured smock, were in a pile by the bed, he gathered them up, and threw them at me.

'Get dressed,' came the order. Then he flounced off to the bathroom.

Kicking cheesecloth and cotton to the side, I raced after him. 'What's happening? What are you doing?' I howled. He had my toothbrush in his hand, my cotton wool buds, my fake tan that I'd carefully hidden behind the shampoo and pot of Pond's moisturising cream. All were swept up. 'Don't,' I begged. I tried to grab them off him, grappled with him, but he pushed me to the side, and set off back to the sitting room with his haul. Hysterics ensued. 'Jesus! Jesus! This is insane.'

I fled the bathroom, threw myself at his feet, like a nun does when she wants to be a saint, and clung on to one of his legs. But in his head I didn't exist, he walked on, dragging me across the floor, over to the bookshelf, scanning, picking out stuff that was mine; another Agatha Christie book, another notebook of poems, a water-colour painting I'd done of the house. 'Oh, Jesus, Andy, please...'

I was still holding onto his ankle.

'Let go.' The voice was insistent, determined.

'Andy...' Beseeching, like Mother Mary at the foot of the Cross. 'Andy – please – please...'

'I said, let go.'

Oh, God, help me.

He kicked out. 'I said, let go of my fucking leg.'

With tears gushing, I looked up at a stranger's face. The angel had gone. Something, or someone (me?), had sucked out his shining soul and replaced it with something quite sinister.

I let go.

He headed straight for the basket, and in the stuff went.

'You've got ten minutes left. Get dressed.'

He was leaning back against the wall now, casually, oh so casually, lighting up a fag.

Broken, totally in bits, so utterly, utterly bereft, with rivers streaming, I looked at him as he coolly puffed away. 'Why – why...'

317

I could barely get the words out, my throat was so full of gunge.

'You know why.' The cold eyes appraised me. 'Now fucking get dressed.'

A little giddy, a little dizzy, with the last vestige of hope truly gone, I staggered, held onto the bookshelf, and raised myself to my feet.

'You've got five minutes now,' he said, and took a puff. 'I've arranged for a Forestry Land Rover to take you back to Gombe.'

My chest heaved with a sob.

'Here.' Andy had left his patch of wall, had picked up my loons from off the floor, and had kindly chucked them my way. The tie-dyed coffee coloured smock came next. Both landed by my feet.

All fight had gone. Whimpering and crying, I began to get dressed.

Outside, a vehicle drew up. Andy went to the door, and popped his head out. Shouted out something unintelligible to whoever, and popped his head back in. 'Your driver's here,' he said smoothly, like he was doing me a really, really big favour. 'Hurry up.'

Slowly I did up my buttons, it was difficult, my hands were trembling so much.

'Come on, come on.' Andy was hovering, half in, half out, by the door. So eager to get rid of me, well he just couldn't wait.

Dressed, with flip-flops on, whimpering quietly, and barely holding it together, I glumly looked around the room. Andy already had my basket, and was already out of the door.

It was too much. It was all too fucking much.

'My bag,' I wailed. 'My bag.'

Andy strode back into the room. 'Will you come on,' he shouted, the Cadbury cream smoothness now totally gone.

'My bag,' I wailed. 'My bag.' Madly, insanely, I was looking around this, oh so familiar room, for my two-tasselled bag.

Grabbing hold of my arm, Andy dragged me across to the door. 'It's in the fucking basket.'

Sunlight flooded the veranda; birds were singing happy songs in the trees. But there was no time to stop and ponder on the more delightful things in life. Determinedly, Andy hauled me down the four little steps.

A man was putting my bike in the boot of the Land Rover. On the front seat was my basket. 'Ready, Ibrahim?' asked Andy, as he steered me towards the grey coloured vehicle.

'Ready, Sah!' acknowledged Ibrahim, tugging on a rope that

held my little Honda in place. A final knot and he was done. The back door slammed shut, and he flip-flopped his way to the driver's seat in the front.

Meanwhile, I was sobbing. 'Don't send me away. Please, Andy. Not like this.'

But my words fell on deaf ears. The back passenger seat door was opened. 'Get in.' It was an order not a request.

I struggled a bit, just a bit, not enough to make an impact. Firm hands pushed me up, firm hands pushed me in. 'What about Rosie? Hamish? Buggy. Everybody?' I screamed, as the door slammed shut. Snot and tears ran down my face as I desperately banged on the window.

My God, I was going away without saying goodbye to any of them. My friends, all my friends. Would I ever see them again?

'I'll pass on your goodbyes,' sneered Andy, on the other side of the dirty brown, mucky glass.

And that was that. He turned away, and didn't look over his shoulder. I saw him casually stroll back into his dear little house. I let out a desperately sad, little whimper as the driver started up the engine, put the gears into reverse, and spun the Land Rover around.

And so began the longest journey of my life.

And the funny thing was. Today was my nineteenth birthday.

What can I say?

I could use a thousand words but none of them would truly describe how I was really feeling as I sat on that hot, plastic seat, and ate up the miles in the back of that Land Rover. I thought I'd already gone through the whole spectrum of emotions in my short up and down life but nothing, not even the experience of being a six-year-old child saying goodbye to my parents, saying goodbye to sunshine and happiness; winging my way back to England, back to grey fog and drizzle, back to evil, nasty nuns and bleak, grim, cold, dark, scary boarding school, had prepared me for something like this. I'd never felt pain quite like it.

To make matters worse, I had nobody to while away the hours with on that long, lonely journey home. No Bruce, no Anne. No shoulder to cry on, no wise cracks or banter that had brought a smile to my lips even in the darkest of hours. No ray of hope. No nothing.

Fuck, it was awful!

The first fifty miles, and I couldn't stop crying. One sob after another, the front of my tie-dyed coffee coloured smock was drenched. The driver, bless him, looked straight ahead, smoked his fags, hummed his little African tunes, and said virtually nothing for the whole of the two hundred and fifty mile trek through the Nigerian bush lands. Maybe Andy had prepared him for this. 'She be a bit mad, Ibrahim. The head no done right.'

'Yas, Massa.' Ibrahim nods, of course he understands, he's got an aged uncle just like it.

'No, worry, hey, Ibrahim. She no make harm.'

'Yas, Massa.' Uncle Musa was a harmless twit. All the family ignored him. So that's what I'll do with this mad baturi girl.

And so that's what he did. Ignored me. I could weep and wail to my heart's content, and Ibrahim would just hum his tunes, light up his fags, and look straight ahead. Perfect.

By the time we reached Damaturu, I'd pretty much exhausted the reservoir of tears, and now sat slumped in my hot, plastic seat, silently miserable. The town, if you could call it a town, was, as it always was, a dry, desert dump. Even more so in fact, it being bang in the middle of January, there hadn't been rain for months. The red, yellow dust swirled and got in everywhere, up my nostrils, in my hair, especially it clung to my wet, sticky face. But did I care? Oh, the fuck, no.

Passing the sand pit that was the lorry park, Ibrahim turned right, instead of carrying on straight. We bumped up a track towards a low concrete building. 'Ministry of Forestry' proudly proclaimed the board at the entrance of the dry, arid compound. This, as I've said, always amazed me. As far as I could see there was only one fucking tree in the whole vicinity, six foot high it was, and with bare branches, it looked positively dead.

'Two minutes, Madam.'

Ibrahim had switched off the engine, was gathering up a couple of files, and had opened the door.

Too wretched to care, he could take as long as he liked, I stared miserably ahead, not really taking in what I was seeing. A white bloke, a quite handsome white bloke, with fair curly hair, wearing jeans and a faded blue denim shirt, was leaning on the handlebars of a bike, fiddling with a screw that had probably come loose.

He looked up. Saw Ibrahim first, watched as he ran up the veranda steps and disappeared into the Forestry offices with his files, and then was just about to return to his screw, when he must have spotted me.

Too late, I should have ducked down. The guy was striding

320

over. My God! My face! Puff pastry eyes! Possibly snot on my chin! Jesus!

'Hi, there,' said the guy with the fair curly hair, popping his head through the open window.

'Hello.'

'You're not from around here, are you?' He was smiling, it was a nice kind of smile, the sort of smile that would have made me want to toss my hair back, just a little, if I hadn't looked so appalling, and felt so horrendous, that is.

'No.'

'Me neither.'

'Oh.'

His arm came through the window. 'I'm Pete.'

I gave a limp smile, took his outstretched hand, and shook it. 'Janni.'

'Pleased to meet you, Janni.' He still had a hold of my hand. Oh, God, it felt so fucking nice. After everything, a warm handshake, a warm greeting, felt so fucking nice. 'So, where are you from?'

I could barely say the word. If I said it, it would mean that it was true. It would mean that Andy, Maiduguri, everything, was all in the past. All just a dream.

'Gombe.'

I said it so quietly, the guy barely heard. 'Where?'

A bit louder this time. 'Gombe.' And just to be polite. 'You?'

'Mambilla. A place called Ngorogi.'

Jesus Christ! It's Pete from Ngorogi! 'My God, you're Pete from Ngorogi!' Despite the pain, and the grief, and the horrors within, I actually found myself smiling.

Pete was grinning, too. Excitedly, he opened the driver's door, slipped into the seat, turned round to face me, took a packet of fags from his pocket, handed me one, himself one, and then pulled out a lighter. 'Do I know you?' he asked.

'No, but I know you. Sort of.'

Pete flipped open his lighter, and flicked the switch. 'How?'

Putting cigarette to flame, I puffed. 'I've actually stayed in your house.'

Pete pushed back his fair curly hair, and gave out a whistle. 'Fuck me, that's amazing. Really bizarre.' He lit up. 'So tell me, when did you visit my place? Was I so out of it, I didn't even know you'd come and gone?'

'No,' I said, laughing. Then remembered, and stopped laughing. My voice became sombre. In fact, it croaked. 'It was, er, over the, er, New Year. I think, er, you were, er, away in Jos.'

Pete nodded, not noticing a thing. Maybe he thought I always spoke with a deep, froggy accent. Or just that I smoked too much. 'Yeah, I was. But how come you got to stay at my place? It's a bit – how shall I put it?'

A shit hole. I was too polite to say it. And cut up. All this was bringing everything back to the fore. 'I was there with Andy,' I whispered, my guts churning with sludge-ridden grief.

'Fuck me!' Pete slapped the seat with his hand. 'Fuck me.' And he pointed a finger. 'I know who you are. Fuck me. You're Andy's girl, aren't you? Janni from Gombe.'

That did it.

The howls I emitted from my mouth were horrendous. And they began just as the driver came out of the offices, so he got the full brunt, as did Pete.

'Jesus, man. What the fuck's wrong?' Not getting any intelligible answer from me, Pete turned wildly to the driver, and begged the question. 'Hey, man, what's wrong with her?'

'She no be well,' answered Ibrahim, thinking probably that he'd got there just in time. A couple of minutes later I might have run amok, and killed all the chickens that were clucking out the back in the compound.

Pete, still in the front seat, slipped out to make way for my minder. 'Hey,' he soothed, as he opened my door, and slid in the back, 'whatever it is, it'll all be cool, Janni.'

That made it even worse. Tears spilled, gushed, and bucketed down. It was like the rainy season had come early.

'Jesus, man. What did I say?'

'She no be well,' was the obvious answer.

'I can't just leave her like this, man.'

'No worry. I take her home.'

'You make sure you do.' Pete had his arm round me. 'I'm heading to Maiduguri right now. Is there anything you want me to pass on to Andy?'

I screamed. At the top of my voice, I screamed. Quite what the content was, I'm not sure, but it certainly scared the hell out of Pete and the driver. 'Fuck me, man, she's crazy.'

'She no be well.'

'There's something wrong, definitely.'

322

By now I was sprawled out across the back seat, sobbing my heart out. It had definitely gone. There was a big hollow space in my chest.

'You take care, now, hey.' I think that's what Pete said, as he scrambled, pretty pronto, out of the Land Rover. 'Lock the door, just in case, hey, driver.' The door slammed, there was a click. I carried on with my howling, beating my fists on the hot plastic seat.

'Jesus, man,' was the last words I heard Pete say.

'She no be well,' followed, as always.

By the time we reached Bui, I'd calmed down somewhat. Enough to get out of the Land Rover, have a drink at the lorry park, and hide behind the shacks, with the usual crowd looking on – did I care? not a bit of it – and spend a penny.

The final lap of the journey was much more subdued. I knew the road so well, every inch of it had a memory, that bump there was when I...that tree there was when I...see that hill...that bush...like I said, every inch of it had a memory.

Closer to Gombe, and I really began to feel it. It being whatever it was that was bad in my life. With the sun, my heart sunk lower and lower. The gritty realisation that everything had gone horribly wrong, that I was back at square one, literally, overwhelmed me.

And, to top it all, just to make things just that little bit worse, as if I hadn't got enough on my plate already, I would have to face my parents, and the likes of Lizzie and Dick, and everybody else (it was so long ago, I'd almost forgotten their names), and they'd all know what a fuck up I was.

Oh, the horror, the hell, and the total humiliation.

And now we were going down the hill into Gombe. Tin roofs glinting in the early evening sunshine. A town of mud walls, dirt-pitted streets, ten thousand or so natives, several million humpbacked cows, a billion donkeys, several trillion goats, countless bush dogs, and thirty or so barking mad colonials.

And only one, stupid, boring club.

A club where nothing much happens.

In fact, nothing much happens in Gombe. It's a bush town, for God's sake. A poxy, two-horse bush town (three actually, if you counted Ginyadi), a million miles from nowhere, bang in the middle of the African savannah – oh God, it was all too horrible to contemplate. I wanted to run away in the opposite direction. Jump on my bike, and head straight back to Maiduguri.

To Andy.

Oh, my God, Andy – Andy, Andy, Andy. Black waves, dark thoughts. Nowhere to run, nowhere to hide. And the nightmare was beckoning. My hands gripped the hot plastic seat. We were driving through the native part of town, through squalid streets, the stench of putrefaction filling the air, onwards and forwards, past the Catholic Mission, Father John parking his Land Rover, Brother Damian in his white cassock, having a laugh.

And, oh, look! There's the Paradise Hotel. Gosh, it still looks the same. And don't the memories just come flooding back. Dick the Prick. Crab-scratching whores. Spunk-ridden beds and shit-riddled walls. Oh, happy times.

And so we drove on. To our left, Shittu Bakari's, can't wait to scour the shelves for that must have bargain buy. A hundred-year-old bar of melted Camay soap. Lovely! An antique packet of dry crumbed-up tasteless biscuits. Wow!

It was all too much. It was all too, too much. Depression, of a serious kind, had definitely set in.

We had reached the roundabout. Mr Loony was there in his usual place, bang in the middle of the road, barking out orders. But I didn't take much notice. Didn't take any notice, in fact. If someone ran over him, squashed him right this minute, I wouldn't have cared. Wouldn't have seen it, you see. Hot, gushing tears had blinded my eyes.

But when Ibrahim turned left, I began to take notice. Oh, yes, I really began to take notice. This was, literally, too close to home.

'Stop! Stop!' I screamed. And I was up, and out of my seat.

Ibrahim, a tad concerned, (he was probably thinking: I've managed to come all this way, two hundred and fifty miles, with this barking mad woman in the back of the Land Rover, and *now* she loses it!) pushed hard on the brakes. Everything, my bike, my basket, my two-tasselled bag, Ibrahim's head, my body, shot forward. And gravel and stones went 'ping!' as they whirled in the air and hit the undercarriage.

'Madam?'

I had straightened myself up, and was opening the door.

'This is good, Ibrahim. You leave me here, yeah.'

My feet touched terra firma.

Ibrahim looked a little perplexed. There were no houses to speak of along this bit of the road, just a few ramshackle mud edifices, some scrubland, and a few obligatory humpbacked cows

324

wandering aimlessly through the dry, papery grass. We hadn't even reached the little bridge that straddled the arid riverbed. I was already opening up the back, had a hold of the rope, trying to untie the knots; but my hands were shaking, my heart was beating, my legs felt like jelly, and there was a big hole where my stomach should have been.

As hard as I tried, I couldn't untie the bloody knots.

Helpless and hopeless, I sat down on the gravel and cried.

'Madam?'

Gently he shook me.

'Madam?'

I raised my sad, fuzzy head. Ibrahim, standing proudly next to my bike and my basket, and in his hands, my two-tasselled bag.

'Thanks, Ibrahim,' I managed to say, as out came a hiccup of sobs.

'No problem, Madam.'

I pushed myself up, staggered a bit, Ibrahim gave me a hand.

My bag now lay on the top of the basket. I fumbled through the interior, located my purse, opened it up, and drew out two ten naira notes. Money was of no use to me. 'Here, take.' She really is mad, this woman. Twenty naira was probably more than he earned in a month. Eagerly, gratefully, Ibrahim tucked the notes in the top pocket of his rather grubby shirt. Now it was time to go. Ibrahim had completed his task. Master Andy, he was sure, would be very proud.

'Thank you, Madam.'

I gave him a watery smile.

Back in the driver's seat, bang shut went the door. A three-point turn, a quick wave, and Ibrahim and the Land Rover sped away.

My last link with Andy had gone.

The thread was broken.

It was truly the end.

Standing on the side of that dusty, little road, with my Honda 50 bike and my Mambilla basket, I felt totally alone, and so, so very sad. Rejected and dejected.

Could things possibly get any worse? Sighing, I picked up my basket, heaved it onto my back, and pulled the straps over my shoulders. Then, clutching the handlebars of my bike, I slowly began pushing.

It was Woggles barking that alerted my Mum. Dressed in pink shorts, a striped, sleeveless top, and cork-heeled sandals, she was watering her beloved plants, the smell of fresh, damp earth lingering in the air, as I turned the corner, and began my weary trudge down the drive. Her back to me, she had to turn to see who or what Woggles was barking at. The evening sun, lancing through the canopy of trees surrounding the compound, must have slightly blinded her. She squinted, and shaded her eyes with her hand.

Then the hand went over her mouth.

Down went the hosepipe. Precious water wasted, as it spurted out on hard, stony ground.

'Tony! Tony!'

With open arms, she came running. Running, running, never have I seen my Mum run so bloody fast.

'Tony! Tony!'

Nearer, and I saw tears pouring down her face. My face was pretty wet, too.

'My darling, my darling,' she screamed. 'Oh, my darling, darling, dear, little girl.'

'Oh, Mum,' I cried, as she gathered me in her arms, and I could smell the sweet scent of her hair. 'Oh, Mum.'

'Oh, darling. Oh, darling.'

Mother and daughter, under a rippling, roseate sky, clinging to each other, me sobbing, Mum howling. Woggles, meanwhile, went barking mad, jumping up, licking us; running rings round the both of us, as doggies do.

It was a very emotional moment.

Then Dad appeared. He'd wandered out on the veranda to check out what all the fuss about, took one look at the scene before him, hitched up his riding trousers, and was over like a shot.

'Janni-Pinksy. Janni-Pinsky.'

Oh, God.

His blue eyes wet with tears, his voice croaking with emotion, he dived in, and swept me, and my basket, up in his arms. 'Welcome home, my darling daughter. Welcome home.'

Oh, God.

Without exaggeration, I think it's fair to say then that Mum and Dad were pretty much over the moon. Their prodigal daughter was back safe, if not entirely sound.

They picked the latter up almost immediately. It was the tears and the howls that gave it away.

'Darling, has something happened between you and Andy?'

Talk about stating the obvious.

We were all now in the sitting room, me, Mum, Dad, Woggles, even Pussy-Mew, who normally preferred hanging out in the stables, had curled herself up on one of the comfy chairs – so as not to miss out on the excitement, I suppose.

A tear, the millionth that day, spilled down my face.

'What's happened, darling?' Mum, concerned, worried, took hold of my hand. With the other she gently pushed matted hair off my brow.

'Don't, Mum.' I jerked my head away.

'Darling, tell us what's happened?'

Another tear hurtled down my cheeks. 'I don't want to talk about it.'

My parents exchanged meaningful looks.

Mum, next to me on the sofa, was not about to give up. Something was wrong with her darling daughter, and she needed to know what that wrong was. 'Darling…'

My voice was thick. 'Mum, please…'

Dad, opposite us, in his favourite chair, took off his spectacles. I'll give him his due, up to now he'd kept pretty quiet, was saving the 'do you have to put your hand in the fire to know that it burns' lectures for later.

Whatever, the 'oh, no, here we go moment' was probably about to begin.

Resting his hands on his knees, and fiddling with his glasses, he leaned forward. 'My darling, we need to understand what it is that is making you so unhappy. We want to help…'

'Well you can't,' I screamed, and leapt to my feet. 'There's nothing –oh, my God – there's nothing…'

Jonathon, who'd just bustled in with a tray laden with goodies, a pot of tea, homemade bread bacon sarnies, and what looked very suspiciously like a coffee sponge birthday cake, saw me fly across the room, weeping and frantic.

'Janni.' Mum's voice, full of anguish.

'Leave her, Peg. Leave her.' Dad was sounding pretty cut up, too.

But not half as cut up as I was. Jesus, I was in pieces.

I fled down the corridor, into the sanctuary of my bedroom, and prostrated myself on the bed, grief stricken.

All I could think of was Andy.

327

My beautiful, my wonderful Andy.

And all that I had lost.

Never again would I hold him in my arms. Never again would I hear him read me a poem. Never again would we take a walk in the moonlight. Or search for the stars. Or float on a boat down a river. Or make love as the dawn breaks over the bush. Or sit by a crackling fire and hear the waterfalls tumble.

Never, never, never again.

How could I ever relinquish the dream?

Early evening, a little cooler.

Someone tapped on my door. I didn't answer.

I was staring up at the void that was my ceiling, going over the many precious memories that were stored and treasured in my mind. Our first encounter, remember? Outside the Woodruff's house, he came past on his bike...

'Janni?' My Mum's voice. She tapped again. Again I didn't answer.

...with his soft Scottish accent, he asked us all how we were? Little did I know then that it was the start of something wonderful...

The handle turned, the door opened, Mum popped her head round. 'Can I come in?' she asked, already halfway in.

She stepped into darkness.

'May I put the light on?'

'No.'

So she left the door ajar instead, and let the corridor light do the business. I turned away, and stared at the shadows on the wall. Mum sat down on the edge of the bed, the net was still up, the mosquitoes were buzzing. She took my hand. I didn't pull it away, I felt too drained of energy to pull it away.

For a while she just sat there, saying nothing, just stroking my hand. And I just lay there, dry-eyed with grief, staring at the wall. There were no more tears; there couldn't possibly be any more tears. Over the past few weeks, over the past few days, I'd shed enough droplets to fill up the new reservoir, *and* the Benue River. And still there'd be enough for a soak in the bath, if the water tank happened to run dry.

'I'm here you know, darling,' she said finally. 'I just want you to know both Dad and I are here. And we're –' she hesitated, obviously wanting to get it right – 'we're sorry you're sad.'

I'd turned my attention to the curtains. A light breeze was

blowing through the open window, and they were being sucked in, and sucked out, and sucked in, and sucked out – it was all quite mesmerising. And if I closed one eye, I could almost imagine that the window was the one in Andy's house, the one where the spectral light of the moon shone in and covered our bodies with silver.

Mum, still holding my hand, was still talking. 'You might think Dad and I are old, and we don't always understand, but darling, we do. We were young once, we know what it's like when – when.' She'd hit an obstacle. When what? What could be anything, when could be anything. What when? When what? Oh, dear.

So Mum tried another tact. 'Darling, do you want to talk to me? Mmm?'

I couldn't take being reminded of Andy's window anymore. I shut my eyes, and tears – yes, more tears, can you believe? – rolled on to the pillow. I think Mum was having a little problem with her waterworks too. Either that or there was a leak in the roof. Something from above, a drip and a drop, definitely plopped down on my hand that was still being held by my Mother's.

'Poor Janni. I'm so sorry.'

'Oh, Mum…'

She gathered me up in her arms, and I cried.

'It hurts.'

'I know. I know.'

She was rocking me, holding me close.

'He said he'd always love me, Mum. So why – so why – has he been so-'

'So what, darling?'

'So cruel.'

'Cruel?' Mum raised her voice in fury. 'Has this man – this Andy – this, oh, my God, what has he done to you, darling?'

'Oh, Mum…'

'What darling, what? What has he done to you?' Mum was shaking, I could hear it in her voice, and I could feel it in her body. Desperate for me to tell her the truth, so she could sort this wicked man, Andy, out. So I told her. Slowly, and painfully, I told her everything. Well, not everything, I left all the sex and drug bits out and the romp in the sand dunes with Mike out, but pretty much everything else, I laid bare my soul.

'Darling, I am so sorry.' We'd finally reached the end. Up to today. The day of my nineteenth birthday. 'He's a wicked, wicked man.' This was said with much venom.

329

'No, no, Mum, he's not.' This was my Andy she was talking about.

'He is. How dare he treat a daughter of mine like – like…'

'Shit, Mum?'

'Yes. Yes. Like shit.' She spat the word out. 'If ever I get my hands on him I'll…'

'Don't, Mum.' The tremble in my voice did the trick.

'I'm sorry,' said Mum, drawing me back in her arms, stroking wet hair off my face. She sighed softly. 'I'm just glad you're home safe, darling.'

'Yeah,' I whispered, wishing I wasn't. Wishing, with all my heart, that I were back in Maiduguri with Andy. Together. For always.

Like I said, it's hard to relinquish a dream.

Especially when the dream was real.

CHAPTER 11

January to March 1974 – Gombe days, yet again

I sat on my bed, picked up my pen and notebook, and began to write.

Where you ever really there?
Did your hand touch mine?
Or where you a spirit
Standing by,
A figment of my mind?

I paused, looked round for my cigarettes, saw they were on the chest of drawers, put my pen and notebook down, got up, went over, took a fag out of the packet, a match from the box, lit up, returned to the bed, remembered the ashtray, got up again, grabbed it off the dressing table, returned to the bed, placed the ashtray on the floor, picked up my notebook and pen, and resumed writing.

Did you say you loved me?
Or was it whispers of wind in my ears?
Did your eyes look into mine?
Or was it the just the stars in the sky?

Something twittered. I looked up. A little bird with blue velvet wings had perched itself on the windowsill. It looked happy enough, pecking away at the ants, hopping hither and thither. That is, until Pussy-Mew, hiding in the bushes below, jumped up and pounced. It was ginger on blue, a close shave. Front paws almost but almost clawed the poor little thing.

'Tweet,' went the bird, spreading its wings. Up, up and away.

'Meow' went Pussy-Mew, totally pissed off. And, with tail twitching, she curled herself up on the windowsill, and sulked.

I ignored her, and returned to my writing.

Did you ever laugh with me?
Or was it the tinkle and ring of a bell?

Did you ever cry with me?
Or was it the rain softly falling?

Footsteps padded down the corridor, stopped outside my bedroom. A gentle tap-tap-tap on the door.

I knew that knock.

'Come in, Jonathon.' He came in, his arms full with my freshly laundered stuff, knickers on top of the pile, trousers, skirts and tops underneath, all ironed, all ready to be put away in my wardrobe and drawers. Smiling, Jonathon awaited his instructions.

I patted the bed. 'Just put them down here, Jonathon. I'll put them away later myself.'

He did as I bid, knowing full well that the pile would still be there at six o'clock when he came into the bedroom again to put down my mosquito net. Then he'd do what he could have done now, put it all neatly away in my cupboard and drawers.

'Cheers.' I bent down, steered the ashtray nearer with my foot, and stubbed out my fag. He nodded, smiled, and left me to it.

I returned to my writing.

I will wait, my love
I will wait and see.

Done.

I got up, and headed for the dressing table. Opening the top drawer, I placed the notebook in amongst the knickers and bras, making sure that it was well hidden. Then I checked out my visage. Not bad. Quite pretty, really. I liked the new lipstick Mum had given me. Max Factor. It had come in a parcel last week, compliments of Granny, but the old girl had cocked up the colour, Mum had requested cherry red not blossom pink. 'No, I don't think it suits,' Mum had said. She was sitting at the dressing table, her lips smeared with the stuff. 'What do you think, darling?' She swivelled round.

I made a grimace. 'God no! It's definitely not you, Mum.' Actually, I was lying. Mum looked lovely. But my lipstick supplies needed replenishing. A couple I'd left in a faraway place and some Mubi stallholder's wife was probably walking around with Rimmel Frosted Calypso on her dusky lips as we speak.

'Any use to you?' Mum was replacing the top.

'Mmm. Might be?'

332

'There you go, have it, darling. I'll ask Granny to send me out the right one next time.'

'Cheers, Mum.'

And off I scuttled with my pink blossom prize.

One more glance in the mirror. One more pout for the road. Picking up my fags and matches and popping them into my brand new orange leather bag, abundant with tassels, I headed for the sitting room. Mum on the sofa with her feet up on a pouffe, was flicking through the October issue of the Woman's Weekly magazine. It had arrived only yesterday, just a tad out of date.

'This looks a nice recipe,' she murmured, more to herself. 'I might have a go at it myself. Dad loves tripe.'

Yuck.

'Where's my keys, Mum?'

Mum turned a page. 'Where you left them. Over there.' She pointed to the bookshelf.

'Where?' I scanned the ornaments, nothing. Moved two candles holders out of the way, looked behind the small silver box, nothing. 'I can't find them, Mum.'

'Second shelf, darling.' Mum flicked over another page. 'By the brass pot.'

I looked. Indeed they were.

'I'm off out.'

'Lizzie's?' Mum's head popped up over the magazine.

'Yeah.' I was half out of the door.

'Have a nice time. Supper's at seven. Don't be late.'

'I won't. See you, Mum.'

'Bye, darling.'

And off I went.

Amazing how back to normal it all seemed.

A month had passed.

It wasn't getting any easier. Then again, it wasn't getting any worse.

The first few days back in Gombe had been horrific. Everything hit me with one God almighty blow.

Andy hates me.

No man could say the things he'd said if he had even a little love in him left for me. He hated me. And to be hated by someone you still love so much, and who had once loved you so dearly, sent me spinning off into the realms of total despair. I couldn't sleep. I couldn't eat (clouds? silver linings?). I refused to leave my room.

333

Even washing was a chore. I'd splash my face with cold, rust-coloured water, limply pass a toothpasteless toothbrush once, twice across my teeth, and that was basically it. I mean, what was the fucking point?

Back in my room, I'd lie on my bed, with the curtains always drawn, and stare at the wall for hour after hour after hour. And I'd smoke. Fag after fag after fag. When supplies got low, I'd send Jonathon out to replenish my stock of tobacco. He'd say, 'Maybe I bring back some nice fruit.' And I'd mumble, 'No, just cigarettes will do, thank you, Jonathon.' And he'd sigh, and go about his business before heading off to the market, emptying the full to over flowing ashtrays, flicking the feather duster round the gloom-ridden room, and removing the mounds of tear-sodden tissues that I'd just chucked willy-nilly on the floor.

I couldn't wait for him to piss off so I could get back to my wall gazing. It was a kind of perverse indulgence. On my own, in a darkened room, with no outside distractions, I could wallow in my misery, I could contemplate the mess of my life, and dwell on the losses I'd gained, and know that no one, not one other person in the whole, wide world, had ever, ever, been as deeply wounded as me.

I think some might say I was suffering from a broken heart. But it was more than that, much more than that.

My soul had been crushed.

Mum and Dad, of course, were always fussing.

Mum especially.

On that first morning, after a night of sleepless torment, she bounced into my room, pulled back the curtains without a 'please may I?' or a 'do you mind?' and then, as I lay blinking from the unfamiliar golden shards of light that poured through the window, she sat on the edge of the bed, took my limp, lifeless hand, and said, ever so sweetly, 'May I suggest you have a bath before lunch? It would make you feel so much better, darling.'

I could have screamed.

How could a bath possibly make me feel better?

Would it bring back my Andy? Huh?

Would it make him love me again? Huh?

Would it bring back my nice, easy life? Huh?

My friends. What about my cool, chilled out friends? If I sat in a bath, would I magically be beamed back to Maiduguri? Huh?

Back to where I belonged? Huh?

So you see, there was absolutely no point whatsoever in me

334

taking a bath. Mum was lying. 'Leave me alone,' I said dully, my eyes glued to the wall.

'You'll smell, darling. And,' she twiddled with my hair, 'your lovely curls are all covered in dust.'

'I don't care.'

'You must care.'

'I don't.'

And I didn't.

'What about something to eat then, darling? You'll feel better after you've eaten. I've made some nice chicken soup for lunch-'

She was doing my head in. Chicken soup? Why the fuck would I want chicken soup? My whole world had collapsed, my entire reason for existence had gone, and here she is going on about chicken soup.

Don't parents take the fucking biscuit?

My parents especially.

In my self-imposed prison I could hear their little chats out on the veranda. They thought I couldn't but I could.

'I wish she'd never laid eyes on that man, Tony. Why didn't we stop her? Why?'

It was early evening, the end of the first day.

'How could we, Peg? She has a mind of her own. She has to learn these things for herself.' A glass chinked. A bottle clanked. Dad, it seemed, was pouring himself a beer.

'But look what he's done to her, Tony. I tell you, if I ever set eyes on that dreadful, dreadful man, I'll...' Mum growled, it might have been Woggles, but in context, it was more than likely my Mum '...I'll give him a piece of my mind. I will, Tony. How dare he treat Janni this way.' There was a bit of a scrape, it was either a chair moving, or Mum's nails.

'Have you ever thought that it might be our daughter who's in the wrong, that this Andy man couldn't put up with her behaviour, maybe?'

What!

There must have been a little bit of life left in me. I actually raised my head off the pillow – the first bit of exercise I had had that day. How dare Dad suggest such a thing!

'No, Tony, I can't accept that (my head went back on the pillow). It's him. There's something about that man, I just can't put my finger on it-'

'I have to admit, Peg, I agree. He's not the kind of man I'd want

335

as my son-in-law. But you see, right from the start I had my doubts...'

And on and on, they went.

I couldn't bear it. They were attacking the man that I loved. They didn't even know him, and yet here they were, pulling him apart. Andy wasn't a bad influence. He wasn't a bad man. He was good. He was kind. He was beautiful.

It all came flooding back.

Every precious moment together.

It all came flooding back.

After two days of total withdrawal from the world, I ventured out on the third day. Not far, mind, just to the sitting room.

Mum smiled when I made my entrance. 'You look nice, darling.' Relief was etched on her face. I'd finally had a bath, see, and washed my hair. And had had a bowl of chicken noodle soup. There still wasn't any point, mind, but Mum was right. It did make me feel a little better, physically, if not spiritually. Spiritually, I was fucked.

Sighing, I collapsed on to the settee, pulled my legs up, put my arms round my knees, and stared blankly at whatever.

'Lizzie said she might pop round.' Mum, sitting at the dining table, polishing her collection of silver and brass object d'art, glanced over my way, and gave me another of her uplifting 'we can get through this together' nauseating smiles.

'Is she?' Glumly I picked at a spot on my knee. 'She knows then, does she?' The spot had begun to bleed, I watched as a small river of red trickled down my leg.

'Oh, darling, of course we told her. Why wouldn't we? She's your best friend.'

Is she? I thought. What about Hamish? And Rosie? And Anne? And Amy? And Buggy? And Mike? And Bruce? And Phil? And Sam? Weren't they my best friends, too? And thinking about them, my throat went all lumpy. Oh God, I so wanted to be back in Maiduguri with them all. Not here, in this sitting room, with my Mum, watching her polish her bloody brasses.

Life was so, so unfair.

Everything I'd ever wanted, I'd got in the last few months, everything. Romance. Friendships. Travel. My God, what an amazing experience that had been, bumping about in the bush in a mammy-wagon, sailing down rivers in a dugout boat, camping on desert islands, sleeping rough by the side of the road, every bit of it had been an incredible adventure. And now, just like that, gone. In a puff of smoke, it had all disappeared. Memories were all that was left.

Mum was still talking. 'Henry and Kevin did say they might come over later. I think they were planning on having chop at the club, and thought you might like to join them. Of course, Dad did explain that you might not be feeling up to it, and they said they'd understand if you didn't want to, darling-'

That was it. I fled to my room.

After a bawl, I lay watching the curtains sucking in and out in the air that came through the open window. The curtains were all covered with flowers, bright bunches of them – anemones, carnations, poppies, cornflowers – and they were lined with pink; when they wafted out into the room they let in a golden light from outside, when they drifted back to the window the room looked sunset pink.

Red-eyed, I glanced over at my basket. It was just as I'd left it on my first night back, full to the brim with my stuff. Unpacking hadn't been high on my agenda, you see.

Slipping my legs over the side of the bed, I padded over the cool concrete. My two-tasselled bag was still there on the top. Diving my hand into it I scrambled around, and found what I was looking for, a small leather pouch Rosie had given me ages ago. I opened it up, and inside was my secret stash of dope, the bag of grass that I'd nicked from Andy's drawer. A packet of papers was in amongst it.

I glanced over at the door. Shit! Why didn't I have a bloody lock on it? Even Rosie, years younger, had more privacy than me. Still, now was not the time to query the whys and the why nots. Quickly I rolled myself a joint, and when done, I switched on the fan full blast, propped my dressing table chair up against the door handle, and then headed for the window, drawing back the curtains, and pushing the glass frame so it was open a little wider. Pussy-Mew, who was curled up on the sill, tentatively opened one eye, saw it was only me, and went back to her sunny dreams where the world was made up of pretty little birds and she was the only cat in it.

Lighting up, I inhaled, kept it there, and then exhaled, blowing the smoke straight out of the window. When the drug hit, I felt a bit dizzy, but that was all right, dizzy was actually quite nice.

Afterwards, when the joint was finished, and I'd sneaked off to the bathroom and grabbed a bottle of Dettol from the cabinet and poured most of it over my bedroom floor to hide the smell, I returned to my basket and started unpacking.

Everything I took out was a memory. Even my clothes had a story to tell. I could place the location, the event, with each and every item. There was sand from the island still in my brown, leather sandals. My rubber flip-flops were still red with the dust from the bush. I could smell wood-smoke on the top I wore Christmas Day, when we sat round the fire and sang Christmas carols with the locals. This skirt still had an oil stain. Remember, a whole load of it leaked out in the back of that lorry, on our way to Mambilla?

I dug further into my basket. Out came my little bottle of perfume. Twisting the tin top, I whiffed the heady mix of what was it? Jasmine? Frangipani? And instantly I was back there, on our island of dreams.

A little emotional, and a little bit stoned, I pulled out the photo next. There we were the two of us, proof, if ever I needed proof, that Andy and I were once very much in love. I sat on the bed gazing at it for ages, letting the memories come and take me to another much kinder place.

And afterwards, I sorted through my poems and all the other little bits and pieces I'd written on my journey.

'Are you all right, darling?' Mum asked, popping her head round the door.

I nodded. 'Mmm, I'm okay.'

She wrinkled her nose. 'Is that Dettol I smell?'

'Yeah.' I showed her the scratch on my leg. 'I thought it better to be safe than sorry.'

This from the girl that had hurtled around the bush like a native; without mosquito net, without paludrine, without boiled, treated drinking water; from the girl who went jumping in rivers where crocodiles, hippos and the bilharzia snail dwells; from the girl who slept on the ground in the bush, alongside snakes, scorpions, and a million other creepy crawly things. And ate bush dog for dinner

Mum sniffed again. 'You don't need much, darling. Just a dab will do.'

'Mmm,' I muttered, not really listening, my mind on far greater things.

Her eyes settled on my notepads and the photo on the bed, and

338

all my clothes that were scattered on the floor. 'I'll leave you to it,' she said wisely.

The door shut.

'Mum?' Quickly, I ran out of the bedroom, she was across the way, checking out the almost empty bottle of Dettol in the bathroom cabinet. She was, I think, a tad perplexed. Pondering on the amount usually required for just one little scratch.

'Yes, darling?'

'Dad hasn't got any of those hardback exercise books has he? You know the ones I mean, don't you?'

'Umm, I think so.' Mum put the Dettol back in the cabinet, picked up the bath towel I'd left on the floor, and replaced the bar of soap that was lying in the bottom of the bath. On a normal day she'd have moaned, but not today. It pleased her enough me just having a bath. 'If they're anywhere, they'll be somewhere in Dad's desk.'

So we trotted off to the sitting room. And Mum had a rootle around, and found a brand new exercise book in the middle drawer. Quickly I grabbed it, and a pen. 'Can I have it, Mum? Dad won't mind, will he?'

'No, of course, he won't,' smiled my Mum. She gave my face a gentle stroke with her hand. 'It's good to see you getting interested in things again, darling.'

'Mmm,' I said, already halfway gone.

Back in my bedroom, I sat on the bed with my pen and my pad. Remembered my cigarettes, got up, grabbed them and the ashtray from off the dressing table, and, thus equipped, returned to my bed. Plumping up the pillows, I leant back, and made myself comfortable. Lit a fag, picked up my pen and my pad.

And began writing the first edition of this book that you're reading!

I dedicate these thoughts, poems, and memoirs to Andy, for he gave me, for the first time, love. Now that we've gone our own ways, I feel dreadfully alone, but I know that the fire of the love he had for me will always burn within, and I will never forget him.

To Andy
25.1.74

An hour later, I was still beavering away.

Mum poked her head round the door. 'There's someone to see you, darling.'

339

'Huh?' Mildly irritated, I looked up from my prose. 'Who?'

'Me.' Lizzie, like a sideways Jack-in-the-box, popped out from behind Mum.

I half-smiled. 'Hiya, Lizzie.'

She pulled a funny face. 'Aren't you going to invite me in?'

'Yeah, course.' My voice wobbled a bit. In preparation for the outpourings of emotions that were bound to come next, it was inevitable really. And I was right. Seconds later, I had my face buried in her chest, and was sobbing. It went on for a good twenty minutes, me babbling unintelligibly, Lizzie rocking me, going, 'There, there, there.' Finally, when the storm had subsided, and Lizzie was still no closer to understanding why, how or what really happened, she suggested I wash my face, and do a pee, and then both of us should take a walk. 'To blow the cobwebs away, pet,' she explained. 'Your Mum says you've been holed up in this godforsaken room for the last couple of days, and it'll do you all the good in the world to get out, and breathe in some fresh air.'

It made sense. Besides, I was gagging for another smoke on a joint.

Ten minutes later, in the still of the late afternoon, our feet were leaving prints in the soft earth, as we made our way towards the dried-up riverbed. We walked slowly, silently, listening to the buzz of the insects and the distant beat of wood pulping maize from a far away village.

Out of my pocket, I took a tissue and blew my nose.

'So,' Lizzie said, finally kicking off the conversation. 'What's happened between you and Andy?'

Putting the tissue back in my pocket, I bent down, picked a twig up, and hurled it into the bush. 'We've split up,' I replied miserably.

'I know that, you wally.' But her voice was gentle. 'What I want to know is, why?'

'I don't know.' I kicked a stone. 'One minute we were all lovey-dovey, and the next-' (the amphibians in my throat croaked) '-the next thing he's telling me it's all over.'

Lizzie said nothing; just flicked away a fly that had buzzed in her ear. We walked on. Past my old bridge playing friend's house, I barely gave it a glance.

'So when did this all happen?'

'Just before Christmas.' I swallowed a toad, but it popped back up almost immediately.

Lizzie gave me an odd look. 'Before Christmas?' She seemed shocked. 'You've got to be kidding me. That's four weeks ago. I saw you in Yola, when was that, the 27th, 28th, and you were still together. You were fine then.' She stopped walking. 'Weren't you?'

'Not really,' I whimpered.

Lizzie looked at me in disbelief. 'Are you telling me that you were with this bloke…'

Quickly I jumped in. 'His name's Andy.' My Andy. How dare she refer to him as 'this bloke'.

'…Andy for four weeks, travelling around with him, and all that time you knew he didn't…'

My lips tightened and paled. 'He didn't what?' I challenged her, as if all this was her fucking fault.

To the point, as always. 'Didn't love you,' Lizzie said.

My fingers were fiddling with my Bida brass ring. I shot her a dark look. 'He did love me, Lizzie.' My bottom lip trembled. 'He loved me very, very much. But then he didn't, before we set off, and then when we did set off he loved me again on the islands – and then he didn't, just before we bumped into you in Yola but he was beginning to love me again…'

Lizzie interrupted. She was totally bemused. 'I'm sorry, Janni, but you've lost me. You're not making sense.'

A blob welled over my eyelid. 'That's because none of it makes sense.' The blob dribbled down my cheek. 'Oh God, Lizzie, you know how much he loved me, how everything was so beautiful at the beginning.' My voice cracked and more blobs dribbled. 'He would have given me the whole world if I'd asked for it.'

'Mmm,' muttered Lizzie, not, it would seem, entirely convinced.

Which pissed me off. So I gave her facts.

'He came all those miles to be with me, Lizzie, who know he did. He gave me this ring. Look.' I showed her the fourth finger of my left hand. The Bida brass ring sparkled in the sunlight. 'He even…' I stopped. I was going to say he even wanted me to have his baby, but it was all too much. Instead I covered my face.

I felt Lizzie's arm curl round my shoulder. 'Oh, Janni, what am I going to do with you?'

'I'm sorry,' I spluttered.

'Don't apologise to me, I'm not the one hurting.' She drew me closer. 'Cry all you want. It's the most natural way for us humans to get rid of our shit.' If only it were that easy, but I heeded her advice, and cried. Not howls just quiet sobs, for a while, as we walked slowly, Lizzie's arm round my shoulder, under a honeydew sun, in the hot, lazy hours of an African afternoon.

'Better?'

I nodded my head. The sniffs had subsided.

We were at the little bridge now that crossed over the dried-up riverbed. As always, there was no one around, just shady trees and silken brown-yellow earth; and the still air full of whistling birds and the chatter of insects. Plopping myself down on one of the low, concrete posts that was the upper part of the bridge, with my feet dangling over the red, arid gorge, I pulled out of my pocket 'one that I'd prepared earlier', in between Lizzie going off to have a word with Mum, and me washing my face.

I lit up. 'Those bloody joints of yours,' Lizzie tutted. But she wasn't really that bothered.

And I didn't bother with a reply. I just inhaled deeply, and exhaled slowly. And wondered what it might be like if I jumped now, and landed on the stony ground, twenty, thirty, feet below. Would it hurt more, or less, or the same as the hurt I was experiencing now?

'Right,' said Lizzie, parking down next to me, the other way round so her feet were firmly on the little track that went over the bridge, 'let's start from the beginning. Tell me exactly what happened.'

So I told her. It was probably the most honest account of this sad, sorry tale I'd given so far. With the others, with Bruce, Rosie, Anne, Hamish, et al, I'd always kept something back. With Lizzie I left nothing out, nothing. I even told her about my brief encounter with Mike, and about Andy's arrest in the Cameroon. Lizzie, you see, had a canny knack of asking the right questions, and wheedling out the most honest answers.

'Why did you wait for Andy, Janni, go back to Maiduguri, when it was obvious he wanted out of the relationship?'

The words stung. I prickled. 'Because – because, well wouldn't you, Lizzie?'

'No.' Lizzie shook her head. 'I wouldn't.'

No, of course Lizzie wouldn't. I was silly to have even suggested such a thing.

'But I loved him, Lizzie, adored him. That's why.'

'I know you did, but obviously things had changed for Andy. He told you, in no uncertain terms, it was over. Yet you couldn't accept that. And you can't make someone love you, Janni. Events have proved that, haven't they?'

Her voice was gentle, but she was digging the knife in.

My eyes lingered on a small herd of cattle munching through the grasses, a long way away. A white bird flew down from the sky, and settled on the back of one of them, in for a free ride. Chucking the end of my joint, I took a cigarette from the packet beside me, and lit up. 'You don't understand, Lizzie…'

Lizzie fluttered a hand, waving the grey stuff away. 'I do understand, very much as a matter of fact…'

Tears of pain and fury spurted out. 'No you don't.'

Lizzie furrowed her brow. 'What makes you say that? Don't you think I've ever been in love before?'

I shrugged. I wasn't interested in Lizzie's love life. Drawing on my cigarette, I gazed yonder, and watched as another white bird flew down from the blue, blue sky, and joined its mate on the cow.

I addressed the air.

'Andy's the best thing that ever happened to me. I can't just give up on something so wonderful – I can't just stop thinking about him, I can't pretend he never existed…'

'No one's expecting you to,' replied Lizzie, her hand on my trembling one.

'Then what–' I took a drag, and sucked in tears, 'are you bloody well saying?'

Lizzie leant back, not too much otherwise she'd have fallen twenty feet into the dried-up riverbed, and that would have been catastrophic. 'Do you really want to know?'

'Yes.'

There was a pause. I watched as one of the white birds on the cow's hump flew away and perched on a tree stump. Seconds later, its mate was there too.

'If you really, really love Andy, you'll let him go.'

Oh, Jesus!

'True love wants what's best for the other person,' Lizzie continued. 'Romantic love wants the other person.'

I looked at her, through tears and fag smoke. 'What!?'

Lizzie gave a wry smile. 'I got that out of the Reader's Digest – rather good, isn't it?'

'Oh, fuck off, Lizzie,' I said, half laughing, half crying, not sure about anything anymore. Only that my life was definitely the pits. But talking it through with Lizzie had made feel a little better. She was rather like an old comfort blanket, always there when I needed her, sorting me out in her no nonsense way.

'In all honesty,' said Lizzie, still on the subject, 'I haven't got the answers at all, no one has, no one knows what tomorrow might bring, what will happen next week, who will be with who a year after next. Although I'm certain of one thing...' She paused. I threw down my fag, watched as it landed bang in the middle of what looked like a big pile of cow dung. '...I bloody well won't be married to Henry.'

She chuckled. I chuckled, not much, just a bit.

'Is he still pining after you?' Three days back in Gombe, and this was the first time I'd really thought about anyone else apart from myself.

'Like an old faithful dog, poor thing.'

'How's Barb?'

'She's good.'

'And the Prick?'

'Still a dick.'

'Nothing's changed then, hey.' I tapped out another cigarette from the packet. Lit it. Smoke drifted up towards the overhanging branches of the old koala nut tree and away towards a cloud of midget like insects that had begun to dance above the path.

'Nope,' said Lizzie, stretching out her arms, and inspecting her fingers. 'While you've been away on your helter-skelter journey, experiencing all manner of things, everything and everyone here has stayed just the same.'

'Great,' I said, a tad sarcastically, and stared glumly ahead, at hills, at bush, at a red, setting sun. Memories of the same scene, somewhere else, with someone else, and I'm dreaming of Andy. He's wearing a white T-shirt and faded blue jeans...

Lizzie gave me a nudge.

'What?'

'Come on,' she said, jumping up. 'I'm gasping for a cup of your Mum's lovely tea. After my Nan, no one makes a brew quite like her.'

Sighing, I turned away from the hills, the bush, and the red blob in the sky, and struggled to my feet, picking up my fags and my matches. Lizzie linked her arm in mine, and we ambled our way back down the track.

'What are you doing tomorrow evening?'

What I always did in Gombe. Nothing. 'Not sure,' I shrugged

my mind still on sunsets and Andy. If I closed my eyes, I could almost believe that it was his arm in mine. That I was walking with him.

'Why don't you come round for supper? We could have a bit of a girlies' night. Pru's down for the weekend, and I'll get Barb to come over. What do you say?'

I couldn't think of anything worse. Well, I could.

'Promise you won't get the Scrabble board out.'

'Promise.'

'Then I'll come.'

I spent the rest of the evening in my room, on my bed, writing. I spent the next morning doing much the same, but this time I ventured out into the garden, and sat in a deckchair, in the shade.

'Lunch,' Mum called from the veranda.

If she was half expecting me to come out with my usual 'I'm not hungry' bit, she was in for a surprise. I'd just had a crafty joint out the back by the stables, and now had the munchies. I downed three bread rolls with my soup, and dug into a massive great bowl of Mum's homemade ice cream, and finished the lot. She was thrilled. Especially, when after a quick visit to the loo, I asked if there was anymore of anymore left.

'Plenty, darling,' she said ecstatically. Not for her to reason why I should go back to firsts, after I'd had seconds. So I had two more bowls of soup, three more bread rolls, *and* another helping of ice cream. Which must have gobsmacked Mum a bit, I suppose.

After lunch, I returned to my deckchair in the shade, and carried on writing.

…I remember when we met at Yankari, the first real meeting. I really fancied him…

Dad returned home at his usual time, three. As the car crunched its way down the drive, quickly I closed my notebook.

'Hello, darling.' He smiled as he got out of his car.

'Hiya, Dad.'

He hitched up his shorts, always a sure sign that he wanted to talk.

Oh, Gawd.

Actually, I'll give him his due, up to now he'd not really said much about anything, not a word about my great escape, or a word about my meanderings in the bush, nothing in fact, which was not like my Dad at all. But here he was, hitching up his shorts, making his way over to me in my deckchair in the shade.

I braced myself.

'What have you been up to today?' Dad parked his butt down on the little stonewall that was the roundabout.

I shrugged. 'Not much, Dad, just a bit of reading and sunbathing.'

'And writing, by the looks of it.' He nodded at the pad closed on my lap.

'Mmm.' Protectively, I put a hand over it, as if I was expecting Dad to steal it away.

'Does it help?'

'What?'

'Writing.' He looked at me enquiringly, and did one of his facial tics.

I shrugged, not sure quite where this conversation was going. 'I suppose.'

Dad crossed, and uncrossed his legs. And sniffed, passing his hand under his nose, another of my Dad's funny little habits. He nodded again at my book. 'It is good to write things. It focuses one's mind and helps put fragmented thoughts in some kind of order.' Dad paused. 'Would you not agree?'

I pondered the question. Certainly I found refuge in my book, reliving memories, putting them into a story, writing them all down. And even though there was a big empty space where my stomach should have been, when I scribbled, it seemed to get just that little bit smaller. Maybe that's what Dad meant.

Slowly I nodded. 'Yeah, Dad, I think you're right.'

We both went quiet. Dad was thinking, and so was I. About fags actually, I wanted one but didn't think now was the right time to light up. It had something to do with my Dad, the two of us together, and me feeling like a little girl. Not a bad feeling, mind, just sort of weird.

'You know,' said Dad, flicking away a fly with his hand, 'when I was a young man I used to write a lot.'

Did that surprise me? Not really. By all accounts my Dad was a bit of an old romantic. 'What? Poetry, that sort of thing?'

Dad nodded. 'Yes, some poetry, sometimes just words to understand how I was feeling about myself.'

This time I nodded. Dad was spot on.

'Have I ever told you about the diary I kept when I was escaping from Poland?'

'I can't remember, Dad.' Knowing my Dad he probably had but

it would have gone in one ear and out the other as soon as possible.

Dad spread his hands on his knees. He gave a little twitch. 'As you know, I was only nineteen, your age.' Dad paused, allowing time for the information to sink in.

Nineteen. My age. Blimey! Even though I knew the facts, it was hard to imagine Dad ever being that young. 'I had to leave my family, my mother, your grandmother, my father, your grandfather. I had to leave my brothers and sisters, and all my childhood friends. I had to leave my home, and my country.'

Again, I knew all this but I'd never really taken it on board. Nineteen. My age. Blimey!

'Can you imagine, darling, what it must have been like? Leaving behind your loved ones, and not knowing if you'll ever see them again.'

I gave Dad an empathic 'mmm' and a wry kind of smile. 'It must have been horrible, Dad. I suppose a bit like me going off to boarding school, leaving you and Mum behind.'

Dad weighed this up. He nodded. 'Maybe it was. I never thought of it this way, but yes, perhaps there were the same feelings.'

There was a moment of silence as we both pondered on that.

'The difference, I suppose,' Dad was thoughtful, 'being that I was in fear of my life, do you think?'

'It must have been awful, Dad,' I said, meaning it.

Dad half-smiled. 'It was but I was young, like you, and full of bravado, and I believed I knew best. My mother didn't want me to go, you know?'

Was Dad trying to say something here?

'But I went,' Dad continued. 'And there were some incredible adventures, but there were also some dreadful, dreadful times when I felt so alone, so frightened, and I thought I would never survive this.' Dad sniffed, and passed his hand under his nose, as was his want. 'My diary helped me in these times. Every night, in the snow, high up in the mountains, with Germans lying in wait, I would still write my feelings in this little diary of mine, it was a pocketbook size, and, just for a while, I could almost forget what was happening around me.' Dad leaned back, his blue eyes glistening. 'So you see, darling, writing is good. And you and I are lucky we have discovered this tool that helps us in times of hardship, do you see my point?'

I did.

There was another pause. Dad pushed himself up from his seat on the wall, and hitched up his shorts by the waistband. He smiled. 'Are you coming for a ride with your old Dad tonight?'

Oh God, we were back to this were we? Some things just never bloody change.

I leaned down and picked up my fags. Took one out, and struck a match. 'Sorry, Dad,' I said with a puff, 'I'm going round to Lizzie's.'

The girlies' night suddenly seemed like a very, very good idea.

Somehow I got through the first week. Somehow I got through the second week. Somehow I got through the third week. By the fourth week it was like I'd never been away.

Let me elaborate.

22nd February '74

I sunbathed practically all day and am now a mass of beautiful brown freckles. Lizzie accompanied me in the sunbathing extravaganza, along with Mum, and what a jolly threesome we were. And boy, did we have a laugh this morning! Henry came round with some mail (one letter from Granny for me!) and there we all were drinking tea, and having a natter. What fun! On impulse, I suddenly had a brainwave. Up I got, and nipped off to the bedroom, where I raided Dad's cupboard and found what I was looking for. Five minutes later I was dressed in Dad's baggy shorts, khaki shirt, trilby hat, boots, socks, and cravat. I looked a cracker. The 'old colonial' emerged out on the veranda, and Mum, Henry and Lizzie were in fits. Henry just had to get his camera and capture the moment, except he didn't have his camera so Mum lent him hers. He took three shots. I can't wait for them to be developed. I bet I look funny!

Later on this afternoon I decided that I would go for a horse ride, on my own, just to impress Dad, and so I did. I took the usual path but instead of carrying over the old bridge, I turned off and went under it instead, and trotted down the riverbed towards the Tangali road. It was so quiet, so peaceful, down there. And it gave me a chance to really think about you, Andy.

I've tried to expel you from my thoughts, and sometimes I can, but most of the time I find you're there, living in my mind. Otherwise you're just hiding there. When I go somewhere, I feel that I'm going to you, and I pretend that everything I see, the flowers, the trees and hills, I'm showing just to you. In little things, in songs, I drift to where I think you are, and wish that you were here to listen to the words. At night, I make-believe that we'll meet again, and we'll love one another the way we did, before sadness entered our souls. You see, although you're gone, you're within me still, and perhaps that's why you're always on my mind.

Night, night, Andy. Until tomorrow.

23rd February '74

God, it's hot. Another day thick with hamartan. There's dust simply everywhere, even in the house, along with that cloggy smell. It's hell 'cos it literally is going to harm my tan!

Dad and Henry went early this morning to Bauchi on business. I felt really bored in the morning (what's new!), no sun, no sunbathing. But I did a little bit of work on my book and it's coming along nicely.

At about 1.30 I went up to the hospital for a cholera jab. The state of the hospitals are terrible and, as always, there were just masses of sick people milling around. I certainly wouldn't want to leave my life in the hands of that lot up there.

In the afternoon I got on my bike and headed over to Lizzie's. She was a bit cross with Ian and Gordon because it was the houseboy's day off and they went out and left her with the washing-up. I gave her a hand, good old me! But she was so mad with them both so she decided to come over to mine for a break. We stopped at the market on the way and bought some oranges, and had a walk around. God, the smell!

It's now gone ten, I've just had a bath, and I'm writing this by the light of the tilly lamp as the power has gone out. Outside, the light from the moon makes the trees seem as if they are painted in different colours of silver. I look at these trees and watch as their branches move when the night breeze gently passes through them, on its way to somewhere. Like that breeze, my mind always seems to be going somewhere, but I don't make the trees move, only my tears which fall softly down my face. My mind is far away, travelling with that breeze, on its way to where I left my heart behind, to Maiduguri, to Andy.

Goodnight, my love. Goodnight.

See what I mean? Everyone thought that I was getting on with it, that the love thing had passed; that the moment of whatever was over. Janni was back. Normal service had resumed.

Wrong!

Every night I cried myself to sleep. Every morning I awoke with a lump in my throat. I was hurting all the time.

And so life ticked on. I got up, drifted through the day, and went to bed. The routine rarely changed. Sometimes I went to the club and played table tennis with Henry and Kevin, or we might play a game of Scrabble. Other highlights would include a visit to Lizzie's, a horse ride with Dad, occasionally I'd go and bake cookies with Barb and the kids. I even made polite conversation with Dick the Prick if he happened to be around. He was a nothing to me now, as significant as a half-dead fly stuck in pig shit.

As for my bridge playing friends, well here things weren't quite the same as before. Mum's version of events goes something like this.

It was a few days after I'd bounced back into the land of the living.

'Darling, what's that nice young man called down the road?'

We were lounging in deckchairs, out in the sun.

I lit a cigarette. 'What road, Mum?'

Mum pointed. 'This road, darling. Our road.'

'Oh, you mean the Canadians?'

'That's right. That nice young man…'

'Which one, Mum? Duggie?'

'No, the one you played bridge with.'

'I played with them both.' *Whoops! That sounded a bit naughty.*

'No, no. You know who I mean, the French one.'

Gawd! 'You mean Francois?'

'That's right, Francois. We never got to know him that well, not like you, darling…'

I took a nonchalant drag.

'What about him?'

'His wife. What's his wife's name?'

I took another nonchalant drag.

'Sonia.'

'That's right, Sonia.'

And nonchalantly blew smoke rings in the air.

'What about Sonia?'

Dramatic pause from Mum.

'Had a heart attack, darling.'

'A heart attack!'

I almost fell through the canvass padding.

'Yes, while eating her Christmas dinner.'

'Her Christmas dinner? Blimey!'

'Yes, a dreadful situation. At first they thought she'd choked on a roast potato but luckily Duggie knew all about heart attacks, his father apparently died of one...'

'She's dead!'

Mum shook her head. 'No, not as far as I know. But they had to take her to the hospital in Jos.'

'Blimey.'

'Dreadful, isn't it? She can't be that old.'

'No, but she was fat, Mum.'

'Mmm, she was, wasn't she, poor darling?'

'So where is she now? Is she okay?'

Mum shrugged. 'The last thing I heard they flew her back to Canada.'

'Blimey. What about Francois?'

'Oh, he's back with her, of course.'

'In Canada?'

'Of course.'

'Oh.'

'Madge says he's totally devoted to her.'

'Who is?'

'Francois. To his wife, Sonia.'

'Did she?'

'Mmm. It's all such a shame.'

Wasn't it just. No more bridge games then for me.

February went, March arrived. And all the time it was getting hotter and hotter, the sands of the Sahara hanging like a suspended red blanket in the sky, the dust clogging, the air thick with boiled smog.

I was in my bedroom, and had two fans going, the ceiling fan and a table fan. The curtains were shut, another vain attempt to make it feel cooler. Pen in hand, I was writing.

...and so on Christmas Eve, as the sun painted the sky in colours of gold, we went away, on our search for the misty

351

mountains that were somewhere out there in the infinite wilderness of the African bush. There were two of us, a boy and a girl, searching for dreams of love and freedom, leaving behind an artificial society that mocked life and the whole concept of love.. No, I'd used that word already, I crossed out love...*the whole concept of Christmas...*

The fans made such a din, it was virtually impossible to pick up on any noise outside my room, but I was sure I could hear Woggy barking. Heralding a visitor, perhaps? Shit! Lizzie probably. I so wanted to get on with my book.

...We had said our goodbyes to our friends, leaving them to go to their parties and their orgies, and in that silent dawn of Christmas Eve, we slipped away into our own world. But my heart was heavy as we crossed the sands...

The bedroom door opened. 'Darling, there's someone to see you.'

Oh, shit.

'Who?'

'Mike.'

Bloody hell! I threw down my pen, slammed shut my book. 'From Maiduguri, Mum?'

Mum shrugged. 'I don't know, darling. He didn't say.'

Excitedly, I rushed past Mum, raced down the corridor, and into the sitting room.

'Mike.'

'Janni.'

We hugged.

'How are you doing?'

'Fine.'

We un-cuddled ourselves. Holding hands, we looked at each other. It was still there, that lovely smile. 'God, it's so good to see you, Mike.'

'And you.'

Mum, plumping up cushions, offered Mike a seat, and refreshments. Jonathon, by the kitchen door, hovered and awaited the order for drinks.

'A beer would be good.'

A beer duly arrived. I had a Fanta.

'Let's sit out on the veranda,' I suggested. Mum, pretending to be busy rearranging magazines and books on a shelf, was all ears.

352

Picking up our bottles and tumblers, we headed outside, and sat amidst the pot plants, in deckchairs.

Mike offered me a fag.

'Cheers.'

A light.

'Cheers.'

We both sat back and puffed.

I opened my mouth, so too did Mike.

Nervously I laughed. 'You first.'

'No, no, what were you going to say?' And he gave me one of his oh, so nice, lovely smiles.

'How...' I gulped '...how is everybody?' Everybody being Andy, of course.

'Everyone's good, Janni.' Mike paused. Putting his hands in his jeans pocket, he pulled a crumpled envelope out. I leaned forward, expectant, hopeful. 'Rosie's written you a letter. Sorry about the state of it. It's been sitting in my pocket for most of the journey.' He passed it me over.

'Thanks,' I said, hoping I didn't sound too disappointed. Not about the crumpled envelope, of course. 'How's everybody else?' I know I'd already asked the question but I was digging.

Mike pretended not to notice. 'Fine,' he said again. 'Buggy's as mad as ever. He told me to tell you...'

'Yes?' My heart was thudding.

'...that he might be down this way sometime next week, he's got some job on at Yankari, and said to tell you he'll probably pop in on his way back – if that's okay.'

'Oh, I'd love to see him. Will he – will he be coming on his own?'

Mike nodded. 'I think so.'

I managed a smile. 'It's nice to know that some of you haven't forgotten me.'

'Oh, Janni.' Mike leaned forward, put his hand on my knee (I felt a little quiver in that place where my stomach had once been). 'How could anyone forget you?' Blues eyes looked at me searchingly. I felt weak. If I hadn't been sitting down I'd have keeled over on the spot.

'Has it been tough?' he asked gently.

'What do you reckon?' Tears were welling up.

'I'm so sorry.'

A tear trickled down. I contemplated the hand on my knee.

Long, perfect fingers, just like – well, you know who.

'Have you seen him at all?' I whispered the words.

Mike nodded.

Sniffing, I brushed off a tear that had blobbed on my nose. 'Is he okay?'

Mike nodded again.

That wasn't the answer I wanted. 'Oh, God.' I dropped my cigarette, it fell on the mat, and I buried my head in my hands. 'He's not with anyone else. Please don't say he's with anyone else?'

'No, he's not with anyone else.' Gently, Mike pulled my hands away from my face; I saw his foot on the smouldering cigarette. 'Don't torture yourself like this, Janni. Please.'

'I'm sorry.' I wiped my eyes and pushed back my hair. 'I'm sorry.'

'Don't be.' Mike was looking at me so sweetly. 'I think you're handling it all really well.'

If I wasn't feeling so upset, I'd have laughed. That was what everyone said. How little they knew. I leant down, picked up my bottle of Fanta, and took a swig. 'Anyway, what brings you here to Gombe, Mike?' Now that I knew there was no welcoming news on Andy, I thought it best to change the subject.

Mike picked up his beer glass. 'I made a bit of a detour. I'm on my way to Zaria, actually.'

Despite myself, I chuckled. 'Zaria! Bloody hell, that's miles away, Mike. Gombe's nowhere near the place.'

He gave me another of his oh, so lovely smiles. 'No, but what's a few miles between friends?'

How nice was that. How bloody nice was that.

'Oh, Mike, you're a sweetheart.'

There was that smile again. 'Tell that to the wife,' he said, with a sheepish grin.

Mike didn't stay long. He still had about two hundred miles, give or take fifty, to go, back in the opposite direction – silly pudding. But it was so good to see him. His visit made my day, my week actually, and the rest. I know I cried at the news that there wasn't any news on Andy, that nothing had changed, but at least I could die happy in the knowledge that I'd not been totally forgotten, that I still had friends in Maiduguri who cared. That was so bloody reassuring. Buggy was visiting me next week, and Rosie's letter was filled with gossip, and all the other kind of stuff you'd expect from a dear friend who wanted to remain a dear friend.

354

It quite warmed the cockles of my heart.

Buggy came
I was doing a spot of sunbathing when he rolled down the drive.

'Buggy,' I screamed.

'Wotcha,' he said, jumping out of the Land Rover before his driver had even put his foot on the brake. His stoned eyes appraised me. 'Fuck, you look good.'

I giggled. 'And you look awful.'

'Mmm,' he grinned, scratching his wild, woolly hair. 'Too many late nights, too many early mornings. But what can you do, hey? You just got to go with the flow, man, it's the only fucking way.'

'Oh, Buggy.' And I threw my arms round him, and gave him a big hug.

'No chance of any grub is there, Janni?'

We were crunching across gravel, arm-in-arm, heading for the house.

'Sure. What do you want?'

'A fry-up would be very nice.'

So a fry-up it was, made actually by my very own fair hands. Jonathon had already legged it to the market you see, as had Mum. Thank God. Buggy was so stoned, even someone as naïve as my Mum would have spotted that something was dreadfully amiss with the way Buggy walked, talked, and moved.

'It's ready,' I shouted down the corridor.

Buggy was in the loo. Had been there for about twenty minutes, the whole time it had taken me to fry up the goodies. A muffled groan, toilet paper crackled, the chain pulled. Seconds later Buggy was back in the sitting room. 'Phaw! You don't want to go down there for a while,' he grinned.

He was right. I could smell it from here. Uggh!

'Sit here, Buggy.' I pulled out a dining table chair, and patted the seat.

Buggy stumbled over, bumping into several of my Mum's object d'art in the process.

'Yum, yum.' Buggy smacked his dehydrated lips as the gooey mess was placed down in front of him. Squirting a load of tomato sauce, and a dollop of Colman's English mustard (sent via one of Granny's Red Cross type parcels), Buggy picked up his knife and

355

fork, and dug in.

'So how are things, Buggy?' I puffed on my fag, and flicked ash in a saucer. 'Hamish alright?'

Buggy threw a forkful of runny egg, charcoal bacon, burnt baked beans, and underdone sausage into his gob. 'Yeah, he's good.' Bits of the above flew out of his mouth, and one particularly revolting blob of salivary mush managed to fly across the table and land on my hand. If he hadn't been one of Andy's closest friends, and if his presence hadn't made me feel like I was nearer to Andy, I'd have well and truly gone off Buggy the instant that blob of food hit my middle digit.

Unobtrusively, I used a bit of the curtain as I was sitting with my back to the window, and wiped the mucky stuff off.

'Lowan alright?' As if I cared about the bloody night-watchman.

'Yeah, yeah.' More food went in, more food flew out.

I stubbed out my fag, and lit up another one. And wisely I waited for Buggy to finish eating before I carried on with the conversing. It didn't take long, a world record maybe, one minute max to polish off a full to overflowing plate of gooey mush that was laughingly called a fried breakfast.

'That was fucking ace, man!' Buggy threw down his cutlery on the now empty plate, bang clatter they went. Woggy, a mite miffed that there'd be no leftover delights for him, abandoned Buggy's side where'd he'd been hopefully waiting, and sloped off to have a sulk in his dog basket out on the veranda. 'Smoke?' Buggy already had the paraphernalia out, papers, baccy, dried bits of grass. Quickly, I glanced out of the window, down the drive. No sign of Mum just yet, even so…

'Err, not here, Buggy, if you don't mind – my Mum and Dad, you see…'

'Yeah, yeah, sure.' Buggy gathered the paraphernalia up, including a couple of stray baked beans that had fallen off his plate. All went into the top pocket of his denim shirt.

'Here.' I chucked him my packet. 'Have a fag.'

'Any chance of a sit down over there?' Buggy beckoned towards the sitting room chairs.

'Yeah, course you can.'

We vacated our hard seats and headed for comfy ones. Buggy threw himself on the sofa, feet up on my Mum's prized handmade Polish cushions – he didn't care.

'Any chance of a coffee?'

I'd just sat down, was about to get straight to the point – how the fuck was Andy. Talk to me about Andy. Tell me everything, Buggy, everything. Does he mention me, does he regret what he's done, does he...

Sighing, I got up.

'How do you take it, Buggy?'

'Milk, four sugars.'

'Won't be a minute.' I left Buggy on his back blowing smoke rings in the air, and headed for the kitchen, remembering to pick up his dirty plate as I did so. That got slung into the sink with the rest of the utensils, the frying pan, the spatula et al. The pan with the baked beans I'd already thrown out, the bottom of it had been burnt well and truly. I lit the stove and filled the kettle with just enough water for two cups of coffee. While waiting for the water to boil, I grabbed mugs out of the cupboard, spooned in coffee from a jar, and four sugars for Buggy, one sugar for me. The kettle sang quickly, and I poured, stirred, and added milk.

'Coffee,' I said brightly, re-entering the sitting room.

'Zzzzzz,' came the noise from the comfy settee.

Shit!

Buggy, glasses akimbo, was dead to the world.

I never had a chance to speak about the subject closest to my heart. Buggy was out for the count for the duration. I tried waking him a couple of times but no could do, Buggy just carried on snoring, even when I slapped his face and gave him a kick.

And then Mum came back.

'Goodness me,' she exclaimed. 'Who's that?' pointing to the horrific sight of a sleeping Buggy, feet up on her beautifully embroidered, prized Polish cushions.

'Buggy, Mum.'

Mum pursed her lips, like she'd sucked on a lemon. 'Isn't he a friend of that – of Andy's?' She spat out the name like a cobra spits out its venom.

I gave her a head butt stare. 'Yeah, as a matter of fact he is, Mum. So what?'

Mum sniffed. Not as in nose runny, but as in 'hmmm'. 'Well, he can't just stay there,' she said. 'Dad'll be home soon.'

'So.'

Mum threw her hands in the air. 'Be it on your own head, darling. But I don't think Dad will be altogether pleased to see...'

357

At that precise moment Buggy stirred. It was a bit like a volcano erupting, he sat bolt upright, his glasses hanging down rather than across his face, and screamed, 'Jesus Christ! Where the fuck am I?'

Mum looked appalled. Good Catholics don't like to hear their savour's name being taken in vain.

'You're here at mine, Buggy.' I'd fled to his side. 'At Janni's.'

Wildly he looked around, as blind as a bat, then remembered his glasses, and put them properly back on. 'Jesus,' he said, focusing on me. 'That dream I just had was like a fucking acid trip, man…'

Quickly, I interrupted. 'Er – my Mum's back, Buggy.'

'Huh?'

I beckoned with my head. 'My, er, Mum, Buggy, she's back.'

Buggy's eyes swivelled round, and took in Mum. He broke into a lopsided grin. Bits of his brunch still stuck to his teeth. 'Oh, hello, Mrs K. How're you doing?'

'I'm very well, thank you, Buggy,' her voice clipped and flat. 'How are you doing?' As if she cared.

'Cool, Mrs K. Really cool.'

'I'm so pleased.' Quickly she glanced at me, and back to Buggy who was now in the process of taking his feet off Mum's cushions, and getting himself back into a sitting position. 'Are you staying long?'

As a way of an answer, Buggy peered at his watch, and jumped up. 'Fuck me, oh, sorry, Mrs K, but is that the time?' It was. Ten minutes past two to be precise.

'Christ, Janni, I've really got to go. I didn't realise it was so bloody late.' He made for the door. 'See you, Mrs K. Cheers for the breakfast.'

I followed him out.

By the Land Rover he gave me a hug. 'Take care of yourself, mate. I'll see ya soon.'

With sinking heart, I responded accordingly. 'See you, Buggy. Safe journey.' Every bit of me wishing I was going with him.

'Come on, wake up, you old fucker.' Buggy banged on the Land Rover roof. His driver, lying across the front seat fast asleep, went from horizontal to bolt upright in seconds. Buggy climbed in, slammed the door and stuck his head out the window. 'See you, babe,' he shouted once more, as the driver started the engine.

'Bye, Buggy,' I mournfully cried.

And in a cloud of dust, the Maiduguri bound Land Rover

zoomed away.

A week or so later.

I was up at the club. Kevin ambled in. I was playing a game of table tennis with Henry. 'Hi,' I shouted, dropping my bat and racing over to be by Kevin's side. He'd just got back from Maiduguri, hence my enthusiasm regarding his arrival.

'Did you have a good time?'

Kevin told me he had, in his usual boring manner.

'Did you give the letter to Rosie?'

Yes, Kevin said he had.

'And the book to Anne?' (Roger Ackroyd by Agatha Christie)

Yes, Kevin had. 'By the way,' he said, 'do you fancy coming over to my place for a bit of a get-together tomorrow evening?'

'Love to,' I replied. Well, I had nothing better to do. 'Who's coming?' As if I didn't know. The usually bloody lot, as always.

'Well, now let me see?' Kevin gave me a tantalising smile, as if he had some great surprise up his sleeve that would knock me bloody backwards. 'John and Abdu from Bauchi...' (Two bores if ever there were two bores) '...and the girls from Bui...' (Even worse) ...and the lot from here...' (No comment necessary) '...and also Sam's coming...' (Wow! Now that was more like it) '...and...' dramatic pause '...Andy!!!!!'

Well, you could have knocked me bloody backwards.

I couldn't believe it. I didn't know what to think. Was he just coming down for something to do or was he coming down to actually see me? Kevin was totally useless, he couldn't enlighten me on the subject at all even though I bombarded him with a million and one questions. 'All I know,' he said, in his boring, pompous way, 'is that Sam expressed a wish to make another visit here and that Andy told him he might come along for the ride.'

That night I wrote in my diary.

All evening I've walked and talked as if in a dream. I mustn't hope too much, but maybe God has, after all this time, finally heard my prayers.

Andy never came.

All day I lived in hope. All day I imagined the moment. For twenty-four beautiful hours I floated once again like a butterfly, up in the air, on a radiant pink cloud.

But it was not to be.

Sam came. He walked through the door of Kevin's house on his own. My heart, already in my throat, jumped out when I saw the empty space that followed behind him. 'Andy not coming?' asked Kevin, in a matter-of-fact voice.

'Nope,' said Sam. And he didn't say why.

Never have I felt so disappointed. The flicker of light at the end of the dark tunnel went out.

Sam did greetings. He wended his way over to me. 'Hey, how's it going? Rosie says cheers for the letter.'

I swallowed. 'Hiya, Sam.' It hurt. Not just my throat, every bit of me hurt. Sam seemed not to notice that anything was wrong. Or maybe he did but couldn't be arsed to saddle himself with the problem. He had, after all, just completed a two hundred and fifty mile journey on the back of a bike.

'I'll just get myself a drink, have a slash, and I'll catch up with you in a mo,' he said cheerfully.

'Fine,' I said, in a dull, monotone voice. 'Take as long as you like.'

And he did. In fact, we barely spoke all evening. Or rather, I barely spoke to him or anyone else, for that matter, all evening. I just sat staring at nothing on my own in a corner (actually it wasn't a corner because, remember, Kevin's house was round).

'You're being silly.'

I looked up. Lizzie was looming down. 'Get a grip, Janni, for God's sake.'

'It's alright for you,' I muttered. 'You haven't just had your hopes raised, and then had them crashing down around you, have you, Lizzie?'

'No, I haven't. Shift over.' Sighing, I shifted just enough so Lizzie had space to plant her butt. 'But you're acting as if it's everybody's fault, you know, especially poor old Sam's. He's come all this way over from Maiduguri, and you're the only person he really knows here and you won't even speak to him, Janni. It's awful.'

'Thanks, Lizzie.' God, she pissed me off.

'Come on, Janni, snap out of it. Please. Moping and sulking isn't going to help in any way shape or form, now is it?'

'S'pose not.' I took a swig of my drink that had sat in my hand, untouched, for over an hour, and took a fag out of my bag. 'The thing is, Lizzie,' I said, lighting up, 'I just wish Kevin hadn't said anything, if he hadn't mentioned that Andy might have been coming then I'd have carried on as normal. Now though,' I took a drag, and sighed, 'now it's different again, if you see what I mean.'

Lizzie pondered on this. 'Yeah, I do see what you mean,' she said finally, waving away my smoke that had drifted her way, 'but try not to let it spoil the whole evening for you, Janni.' She gestured at everyone in the room. There were about a dozen or so folk lounging about, smoking, drinking, and having a laugh while Canned Heat beat out a jolly tune on Henry's old, cranky record player. 'We don't get many evenings like this in Gombe, so why not enjoy it, hey?'

I shrugged, and I sighed. 'Mmm, suppose you're right. Can't let a good party go to waste, can we?'

'No we can't.' Lizzie jumped up, and pulled me up with her. 'Go sock it to them, baby,' she laughed, pushing me into the throng.

So I did.

In the end, it wasn't a bad party after all.

Chapter 12

April 1974 – the final bit of my African tale

And so life in Gombe slowly ticked on.

Nothing much happened. Nothing much changed.

Until one day, a day in April that started off as a hundred other days. A day that saw me get up, have a coffee and a fag for breakfast, saw me lie out in a sun half-hidden by sands from the Sahara for most of the morning, saw me consume three heavily buttered rolls and knock back two bowls of soup for lunch, and more after a quick trip to the loo, saw me jump on my bike and drive off to Lizzie's, saw me amble over for a chat at Barb's, saw me jump on my bike and head home at five with a promise that I'd be up at the club at seven for a game of table tennis with whoever so happened to be there.

Just another day.

I parked my bike under the old tree, walked across the sandy drive, patted Woggy who was standing guard out on the veranda, stepped over Pussy-Mew who was curled up on the mat, and through the French doors, and into the house.

Mum and Dad were deep in conversation. They were sitting around the dining room table, Dad was nursing a beer; Mum had her hands gripped round a glass of pink gin.

'Hiya,' I said, chucking my keys and my bag down on the coffee table.

The talking stopped, they both looked my way. Even from where I was standing, on the other side of what was quite a large room, two rooms actually, a dining room cum sitting room divided by a rather grand bookcase, I could see Mum was crying, or had been crying, her face was all red and blotchy, and her mascara was smeared down her cheeks.

Oh, Gawd.

'What's up, Mum?'

I stood looking at them looking at me.

'Janni, would you come and join us, please.' This request came from Dad. There were no splodges on his face but he certainly didn't look happy. And his voice was monotone and flat.

'What's up?' I said again. Had somebody died? Granny? Grandpa? With thumping heart, and trembling knees, I made my way over to them and the table.

'Sit down, please.' An unsmiling Dad gestured to the empty chair, already pulled out, already waiting for me.

I sat down. 'What's happened, Dad?'

I looked at him, his face resembled what can only be described as being the same as the sky when a storm's about to break. Nervously, I turned to Mum. She sniffed and gave me one of her 'oh, darling, what have you done now?' kind of looks.

I gave them an, 'oh, Christ, what have they found out?' kind of expression.

All sorts of things zipped through my head, Dick the Prick, the brothel, Francois the Frenchie, oh, God what else – um, um, um – the list was fucking endless...

'I'll get straight to the point.' Dad's face twitched, as he moved his chair slightly, positioning himself so eye to eye contact was direct. 'And I want the truth here, you understand.' The voice was low, clear, and terrifying. His blue pupils bore into mine. 'You understand?' he said again, just to make the point sink home.

I nodded. I couldn't speak, my throat was so constricted I could barely breathe, let alone move my tongue and say words.

'Have you ever, ever had anything to do with drugs, Janni?'

'What?!' Like a frightened gazelle trapped in headlights, I stared round-eyed at my Dad.

'You heard me.' Dad's face twitched. 'But I'll say it again just to make sure. Have you ever, ever had anything to do with drugs?'

Wiping my, oh, so sweaty palms on my, oh, so sweaty knees, I gulped, and tried desperately to come up with the right answer. Which was difficult because I wasn't sure whether Dad was just guessing, or whether Dad had hard facts. Had he found my secret stash? No, he couldn't have, all my dope was in my bag, and my bag was on the coffee table, and my bag had been with me all day. Oh, Jesus, my mind was racing.

'I'm waiting.'

Quickly, I glanced at Mum. 'Tell us the truth, darling. Please.' Wet-eyed, she gave me what she believed was an encouraging smile. I didn't see it quite like that.

I turned back to Dad, and shrugged in a rather nonchalant fashion. 'I don't know what you're talking about, Dad. What do you mean – drugs?'

Dad perused me. Like the hangman peruses the condemned man, weighs him up before he goes to the gallows. 'I think you do.'

My palms were dripping. 'No, I don't.' My voice squeaked.

'Very well.' Dad picked up his spectacles that were lying on the table. Put them on, his blue eyes, all magnified, looked more frightening than ever. 'I have a letter, here.' He gestured to said letter; a letter I'd not really noticed before, that was lying on the table. He picked it up. 'This letter,' Dad said, waving it in my face, creating a gentle breeze, 'is a letter from the Commissioner of Police in Maiduguri.'

I gulped.

Dad removed his glasses. 'Would you like to know what it says?' Dad didn't wait for an answer. It would have been a long time coming, anyway. I was swallowing so hard my tongue was now half way down my throat. Dad put his glasses back on. 'I won't read it word for word but I will give you the general content.' Dad's voice was now so calm, you could almost be forgiven for thinking he was about to read me a bedtime story – a very scary bedtime story, mind, that didn't have a happy ever after and they went off into the sunset ending. 'The Commissioner tells me that there has been some concern regarding this friend of yours, Andy...'

Andy!!!! Jesus!!!

'...and drug dealing in Maiduguri.' Dad paused. He glanced at me over his spectacles. 'Ring any bells?'

Clang! Clang! Clang! The death knoll, certainly.

'Um, no.'

'Sure?' Fuck, the voice was so calm.

I gripped the chair. 'Absolutely.' Sweat trickled down the line that divided my buttocks.

'Then why?' Dad held the letter in one hand, and hit it lightly with the other, so you could hear the paper crack. 'Then why does the Commissioner feel that in some way you are implicated in this...' Dad paused, cleared his throat, '...in this drug dealing with this Andy?'

The silence that followed was solid. All I could hear was my own mind befuddled with my own muddled thoughts. Court – prison – rats – lice – lepers – dirt – mud – wardens – being thwacked – carrying water across bush – Ben Hur – my Granny – my Mum – my Dad – dirty knickers – my hair all shaved off – no make-up – guns – lesbians – visiting hours –

The enormity of it all had really sunk in.

'I don't know what you're talking about,' I screamed. I'd pushed back my chair, and was holding my hands up to Heaven. 'I haven't done anything, Dad.' Imploring, pleading. 'Please, believe me, Dad.'

Carefully, like it was a fragile object, Dad placed the letter down on the table. He looked at me with his steely, blue eyes. 'Are you certain of this? You can honestly say you have no part in any drug dealing, Janni?'

I slammed my hands down on the table. Tears of pure, unadulterated fear spurted down my face. 'No, Dad. No. Of course, I haven't. You must believe me.' Wildly, I turned to Mum. Pain was etched on her face. 'Please, please, believe me.'

Mum nodded, her face also dripping with tears. 'We so want to, darling. We so want to.'

She held open her arms, and I got up and threw myself in them. 'Then you must, you must.' And I'm sobbing, and I'm crying. 'Don't let them take to me prison, please, please, oh, God, Mummy please, don't let them send me to prison.'

'Shush, shush.' That came from Mum.

'Listen to me, Janni.' This came from Dad.

I raised a tear-splattered face, and listened. Like never before in my life, I listened to what my Dad had to say.

'No one is going to send you to prison. Understand.'

Oh, thank you, God.

I whimpered a, 'Yes'.

'The Commissioner is someone I know well, and this letter merely expresses concern regarding your association with...' again Dad had difficulty saying his name '...with this Andy. No one is accusing you of anything. Understand.'

Another whimpered 'yes' fell from my wet, sticky lips.

'But...' Dad tapped the letter that was lying on the table, several times '...this is very serious, all the same. Understand.'

I nodded. Oh, God, I could taste the bile in my throat.

'I have no idea when, or if, the police will be acting on the information they have on this – this Andy.' Dad paused. 'Possibly they will.' Another pause. *Oh, my God, poor Andy.* 'Possibly they won't.' *Please, God, let them not.*

Dad picked up his glass, and took a slow sip of beer. From my Mother's lap, I watched Dad, and waited for what would come next. Nothing, I hoped.

'Now, young lady.' Dad placed his glass down, and looked straight at me. 'Mum and I want to believe you, and we hope sincerely what you have said is true. That you have had nothing to do with the selling of these drugs.'

'I haven't, Dad, I haven't.' Which was partly true. I mean all I did was go to a drawer, get a bit of dope out, hand it over, and put some money in a tin. In my book, that was hardly a sin. And I only did it a few times. Six, seven, eight, nine, ten times at the most. Give or take a dozen more.

'The next thing we want to know,' said Dad, ploughing on. 'Is have you ever taken any drug? It would seem to me...' Dad glanced at Mum, '-us, that you would have most certainly been exposed to such things having spent quite a bit of time with this...' Dad cleared his throat '...Andy.'

I thought of my bag, sitting innocently on the table. Of the dope nestled deep in the bottom, amongst the lipsticks and the mascaras.

'Um, not really, Dad.' I knew I couldn't deny it completely. 'I've tried hashish once or twice.' Dad raised an eyebrow. 'But I didn't like it much,' I added hastily.

Dad shot a look at Mum, then back to me. 'Do most young people smoke this hashish?'

What could I say? Of course everybody smoked hashish. It was part of being young, part of being in with the in-crowd. Even the out-crowd bloody partook of the weed. Well, some of them did. Although I couldn't really think of anyone at the moment. Kevin, maybe? No, not Kevin? Henry? Definitely not. Ian and Pru? No bloody way. I think I might have seen that drip John from Bauchi have a puff.

I shrugged. 'Dunno, Dad, really. Some do, some don't.'

'Does Lizzie?' piped up Mum.

I jumped up in her lap. 'Oh God, no.'

'Henry? What about Henry?' asked Dad.

Oh, Christ, I was getting a headache. With the threat of prison now out of the way, I now wanted out of the Spanish/Polish Inquisition.

'No,' I said, 'of course not.'

Dad nodded his head, clearly relieved, as too was Mum. She even picked up her glass of pink gin, and had a sip, a sure sign that everything was getting back to normal. So normal, I removed myself from off my mother's lap, and sat back in my own chair, expectant, politely awaiting Dad to give the nod. 'You are dismissed, Janni. You can now go off and play.' Or something like that.

But something like that didn't happen. Something else happened instead.

Dad cleared his throat. 'I am glad to hear that you have been honest enough to tell us that you have tried this hashish. And…'

'Do you mind if I smoke, Dad?' I was gasping. Especially after all that had just gone on, I needed a fag more than ever.

'If you must,' tutted Dad. He took another sip of beer; Mum took another swig of pink gin. Quickly I went to my bag, quickly I took out my fags and my matches, and just to be on the safe side, I came back to the table with my bag tucked under my arm.

'You were saying, Dad?' I said, lighting up. Mum stretched her arm over to the drinks trolley and grabbed an ashtray. She placed it in front of me. 'Cheers, Mum.'

Dad continued. 'I am glad that you have been honest about trying this hashish…'

I nodded, and drew on my fag.

'…and I am glad to hear that you don't much like it.'

Again I nodded, and blew smoke out of my mouth.

'And I am pleased to know that two young people we respect very much – Lizzie and Henry – do not take this drug, either.'

I gave another nod. And took another drag.

'Now the thing is.' Dad paused. He and Mum exchanged rather odd looks.

I turned to Mum. She gave me a ghost of a smile. I turned back to Dad. 'What?'

Dad cleared his throat again. And he twitched. Always a sure sign that something was going to come out of his mouth that I knew I wouldn't like. 'This letter…'

Oh, God, we were back to the bloody letter. In an instant, my palms felt sweaty again.

'This letter is serious.'

'I know, Dad, I know.'

'The Police Commissioner expressed his concerns…'

My heart thumped. 'I know, Dad, but you've got nothing to…'

'We hear what you have to say, and we believe you. But there is still a problem that needs sorting out.'

Oh, God! What now?

'You have been implicated, rightly or wrongly, in this mess.'

I could have screamed. Sensibly, I kept my gob shut.

'There maybe repercussions for this – this Andy…'

'I know that, Dad.' I flicked ash in the ashtray and kept my eyes on my Dad.

'So,' said Dad, obviously choosing his next words carefully, 'I have spoken to the Commissioner about what he advises…'

I flicked more ash into the ashtray. 'What do you mean? Advises? What advice?'

'If you let Dad finish, you'll find out,' piped up Mum. I looked at her. She was dribbling again, there were drops coursing down her cheeks. Why?

I turned back to Dad. I noticed his knuckles were white. His hands were clenched – his body was rigid. Why?

Was there more?

Dad opened his mouth to speak. I waited with baited breath. In truth, I could barely breathe. Something was about to said, of that I was sure. Something I wouldn't much like, of that I was certain.

'Now, Janni…'

At that precise moment Jonathon, our devoted houseboy, popped out of the kitchen door with tray in hand ready to clear the decks in preparation for supper.

'Not now,' ordered Mum, waving the poor bloke away. Quickly, without a murmur, he scuttled back into the kitchen. I would have dearly loved to have joined him, would have dearly loved to have cleaned up some pots. Even given him a hand with the cooking.

'Where was I?' Dad placed his clenched fists on the table, and gave up a moment to think. I stubbed out my fag, and considered lighting another but in view of the situation, I decided against it. Now was not the time to provoke a lecture on the dangers of chain-smoking, I don't think I could have taken it with everything else.

Dad cleared his throat.

'So, I have spoken to the Commissioner and it has been decided that the best course of action is for you to be removed from the situation.'

I definitely lit up another fag when I heard that. What the hell did he mean?

'What do you mean, Dad?' My hand trembled as I held the match to the fag, and inhaled.

'I mean, you must return to England.'

Smoke bellowed out of my mouth. 'What!' I turned to Mum. 'Mum?'

'Listen to your father.' Mum leaned across and got hold of my arm that lay prostrate across the table.

I snatched it away. 'I can't believe this.' Angrily, I turned on Dad. 'What do you mean, return to England? It's only April. I'm supposed to be out here for a year.'

And then it suddenly dawned.

Am I...' I turned back to Mum, to Dad, to Mum, to Dad, '...am I being kicked out of the country?' My voice rose. 'Am I?'

'Shush,' from Mum, as tears plopped down her cheeks.

'Stop overreacting,' from Dad, as the eye tics doubled their speed.

Overreacting!

'You're kidding me, Dad.'

Dad shook his head slowly. 'Sadly, I am not. You return to England next week.'

'Next week!' Back to Mum, back to Dad, back to Mum, my head was swivelling. I felt dizzy.

'Mum will accompany you,' Dad said, trying to keep his voice very matter-of-fact. 'It is for the best.'

'What!!!'

This was a fucking farce.

Back to Mum, Dad, swivel, swivel, swivel, God I was dizzy.

Dad continued, outlining the plan. 'You will fly from Maiduguri to Kano next Thursday, and then take a plane to London the same day. It is all booked.'

Maiduguri!!!! Did I hear right? Maiduguri?

'Maiduguri?!'

In all this madness, all I could now think of was I was going back to Maiduguri.

Back to Andy.

'Yes, I need to speak to the Police Commissioner in person. About certain things,' Dad was saying. 'And the Police Commissioner wants to ensure your safe departure. He will be at the airport to see you off.'

Oh – My – God!!!!!!!

One week. Seven days.

All of a sudden life in Gombe ticked over very quickly.

Out came the packing cases, everything in a muddle, Mum and Dad's room, my room littered with stuff, clothes, shoes, belts, scarves, beads, earrings, bags, bangles, Tampax, bras, and whatever else that is essential to an old woman's and a young woman's needs.

'Don't forget we're only allowed forty-four pounds,' Mum

369

trilled every so often as yet more of the same was pulled out of my drawers, and more of the same was bunged into my suitcase.

Meanwhile, in the bathroom Jonathon spent his mornings washing and washing, backwards and forwards he went with the laundry basket, hanging everything out in the sun. In the kitchen Jonathon spent his afternoons ironing and ironing, pile after pile, and when each lot was done, the mountains of fresh laundry were left stacked up on the bed, on the chairs, on the drawers, on the floor, all ready for packing.

He shouldn't have bothered, I thought, as I chucked everything in willy-nilly, and immediately all his hard work became rumpled and crumpled and wrinkled and creased.

Meanwhile, Mum, in between packing her Jaeger winter sweaters and her M&S bras, sat at the dining room table writing out endless lists, for Dad, for Jonathon, the must-do's and the must don'ts – basically an essential guide for any man left to fend in the bush on his own without his wife.

Example: *When buying eggs from natives, test them in cold water first. Fresh eggs are heavy. Bad eggs will float.*

Example: *Furniture should be wiped over inside and out every few weeks with a cloth soaked in paraffin. This discourages ants and spider nests.*

Example: *Two cakes of soap for washing day. A cake for dish-towels. Ensure saucepans, baking tins etc are scrubbed with sand or ashes and put out in the sun.*

After a hundred pages of the same, Mum was up and out of her chair and into the pantry to do her final inventories, counting and checking the stocks, the bags of sugar, the tins of cheese, the sacks of flour, adding the must-haves and the must gets to her good housekeeping list that was now blossoming into a 'Household book for Africa'.

A sack of potatoes. Empty the sack and spread the potatoes on mats. If ants are rife spread on iron raised on bricks. Get Musa to plant sprouted and shrivelled potatoes in the garden.

1 case of washing soap.

6 packets candles.

50 lb. Sugar sealed in large biscuit tin

6 tins scouring powder

Next, on the veranda, in the garden, Mum watering and weeding, Musa the horse boy following her around, Mum giving him instructions on how to take care of that plant, not too much water, this plant, not too much sun, the one over there, not too much shade – and adding her 'must never forgets' to that long, long, housekeeping manifesto.

And while Mum anticipated every possible contingency in every part of her house, Dad would be going apoplectic. He always did when his life was going through a particularly stressful phase. Off the silver rocket would roar first thing in the morning, ten minutes later the silver rocket was back. Leaving the car door open, Dad would tear into the house.

'Passports, Peg? Have you got your passports?'

'Passports? Mmm?' Mum, with pen poised, would consider the question. 'In my drawer, Tony, in our bedroom, I think.'

'Check, Peg, check.'

And Mum would check, and she'd be rifling through her drawers for a good fifteen minutes, wondering where the hell my passport was, and Dad would be going mental, blood pressure rising by the second. 'For God's sake, Peg, try to think when it was you last saw it.'

And Mum would think.

And I'd just happen to pop my head round their bedroom door, and say. 'Have you got any room in your case for some of my stuff, Mum?'

'Where's your passport?' Dad asked this whilst jumping from one foot to another, like he was training for an Olympic marathon race.

'In my room, Dad? Why?'

'Are you sure?'

'Of course I'm sure.'

'Get it. Get it.'

And I'd traipse back into my room with Dad hot on my heels, and with Mum, mildly worried, loitering in the background. And after a few tense-ridden minutes, with me fruitlessly searching through piles of knickers and halter-necks tops, I'd brandish said passport triumphantly in the air. 'Here it is.'

Phew! Panic over.

Dad would get in his car and he'd be off down the drive again. One hour later he'd be back. Some papers he needs from out of his desk. A quick powwow with Mum, more of: 'Have you got this?' and, 'Have you seen that?'

'Yes, yes,' says Mum, a mite frazzled.

And so Dad's back in his car, and off like the clappers.

Important letters to write. Important people to see.

In that last week the K's home was definitely as busy, as busy could be. And in the midst of all this chaos, there was me. A little bewildered, a little bit dazed. A little bit of everything really.

It took a while for the enormity of the situation to sink in. Indeed, in an upbeat moment I thought it all rather cool. Janni, the hippie drug dealer. My God, what would my old friends at school have to say about that! And I liked – no I loved – the fact that my name was linked with Andy's, that I was implicated with him; that made me feel rather special. It was quite Romeo and Juliet, in a funny sort of way.

But there was little else to be over the moon about.

The suddenness of it all, the fact that I was leaving so much behind, the possibility that I might never, ever return, was utterly heart rendering. Those horrible old feelings came up, those horrible old feelings that went with 'goodbye sunshine', 'hello fog and drizzle'.

I loved Africa, you see.

Really loved it. It was in my blood. It was in my soul. It was etched on my heart.

And now, with just a few days to go, everything around me began to take shape, everything around me began to have meaning. I noticed all the familiar things, all the smallest details. Mum's garden suddenly seemed to be the most gorgeous garden in the world. I never realised there were so many lovely plants and flowers growing in it. For the first time I'd notice that everywhere was ablaze with bougainvillea and hibiscus. That blue starlings gathered on our roof top, crowds of them, their metallic gleams shining brightly with the sun, that there were doves, weavers, parrots with green feathers (I'd have to mention that to Anne if I ever saw her again) picking at the small crusts of bread and peanut shells that Mum and Jonathon chucked out to them each and every day. That bumblebees circled Mum's potted plants; that multi-coloured butterflies danced and hovered around the bright yellow flowers that grew in abundance over my window sill. And I took note of how lovely and cheerful the pepper-bird's warble sounded, and how I enjoyed the querulous croak of the go-away bird as it called from its nest in the trees. Simple things like cows doing their usual thing through the scrub now brought a lump to my throat. Donkeys copulating even stirred the emotions. The white bird that flew down from the sky, the jewelled sun on its wings, actually made my eyes water. The woman with a pot on her head, her ebony skin against the colours of a golden afternoon, the way she moved, the graceful swing of her hips. Seeing her and my heart would miss a beat.

To stand under a vast tropical moon, to feel the warmth of the evening breeze, to hear the plaintive cry of a hyena, the churr of a hundred crickets, the trill of a thousand frogs, to sway to the rhythm of a far away drum, to hear the thump, thump of wood pulping the maize. And my soul would be bursting.

To watch a collection of naked urchins standing in the bucketing rain, to walk down a dusty red track in the still heat of an African day, to hear the tilly-lamp hissing and flickering as rhino-beetles went bump in the night.

How could I give all this up? How could I leave behind the smell of the wood-smoke, and the jasmine and the frangipani, and the peppery aromas that tickled my nose? How could I? How would I?

Now, instead of lying in bed for as long as was possible, I was up with the dawn, and out on the veranda. I'd watch the sun rise, and in the evenings I'd watch the sun fall.

And with silent tears spilling, I'd whisper my heartfelt farewells to my wonderful, my beautiful Africa.

God, it was awful.

How quickly that last week went.

We were leaving for Maiduguri early Wednesday morning and flying to England on Thursday. I'd pretty much said my goodbyes. There'd been a farewell party for me at the club on the Saturday night. Everyone was there, which I know in the great scheme of things isn't that many, but in Gombe a gathering of thirty people counts for a lot.

It was quite a tear jerking do.

Mukaji presented me with The Lord of the Rings Trilogy. 'I was in the SIM bookshop in Jos the other day, and I saw it, and thought of you,' he said, as he handed the gift over.

I was touched.

Barb gave me a really lovely bracelet. Like my ring, it was made of Bida brass, and she had had my initials etched on the inside of it, JK and the date. 'Honey, you take the greatest care of yourself. It's been a real privilege to be your friend,' which made me feel really, really bad, especially as Dick the Prick was standing right by her side.

I gave her a hug, a big hug. Our bangles jangled and our earrings clanged as we buried our faces in each other's hair. 'Take care, hey,' she said again.

'Will do.'

'Write,'

'I promise.'

We disentangled ourselves. I turned to Dick and shook the loathsome prick's hand. 'Bye, Dick.' I smiled at him. He smiled at me. We were, oh so, bloody polite.

'It's been good knowing you, kid.'

Kid! How rude was that!

'And you.'

Quickly I let go, and moved on, to Kevin, to Geoff, to Ian.

'Take care…'

'See you…'

'Safe journey…

To dear, darling Pru.

'Oh, sweetie, sweetie, Gombe won't be the same…'

To my good old friend, still with that quiff.

'Oh, Henry, thank you for everything…'

'Keep in touch, yah.'

'I will.'

And so it went on, shaking hands, hugging and kissing.

Madge and Duggie.

'We'll miss our little bridge playing pal…'

'And I'll miss you too-'

'I just can't figure out why you're going so soon-'

A lot of people said that.

'Got to sort out college,' I explained, when anyone asked, which was partly true but, as you know, not wholly true. Even though I thought it quite cool, I think most of the good folk of Gombe might not have seen my brush with the Nigerian law in quite the same light.

'Oh, Father Delaney, guess what, I've got myself into a bit of a bother with the drug squad, and that's why I'm leaving. Dad's got friends in high places, and I'm having to flee the country because things are getting just a little bit too hot here for me. And no, I don't mean the weather. Ha, ha!!'

Actually what I said was: 'Goodbye, Father Delaney. I hope I'll see you again soon. And hopefully when I've got my college all sorted out, I might well be back for the Christmas hols.' Or words to that effect.

And Father Delaney put his hand on my arm, and kissed me on my cheek. 'You're a grand girl,' he said. 'And you've done your Mother and Father proud.' Or words to that effect.

And now it was Tuesday.

We were very nearly packed. We were very nearly ready to go. I felt like a condemned man for all of that day, everything I did, I knew I was doing for the very last time.

First thing, pulling back my curtains and perusing the scene; the early morning sun as it peeps through the twisted branches of the kapok tree, a cow as it plods through the scrub, two frisky donkeys banging away, the old teacher with his raggedy mob.

One final look, one final time.

And the sounds. The liquid song of the birds, the incessant chatter of insects, a moo and a hee-haw, a screech and a cackle, the non-stop chants from ten little boys.

One final listen, one final time.

A lump in my throat, and it stayed there for all of the day. I wandered aimlessly about, out to the stables to say goodbye to the horses. Patting old Smokey on the nose, smelling the sweet smell of hay, standing with my back against the rough muddy walls, watching Musa shovel shit from the floors, and I wanted to stay here for ever. I wanted to saddle up my nag and ride down the old beaten track to that lonely place where I could sit and think; where there were shady trees and little red butterflies with soft velvet wings, and dragonflies, a shimmering blue. I'd tether old Smokey under the cool of the mimosa tree where birds, doves, weavers and scarlet-breasted sunbirds, whistled from the branches and fluttered and flitted about.

And I'd want to sit there forever.

'You ride, Madam?' Musa, leaning on his spade by the compost heap, asked the question.

Sadly I shook my head. 'Not today, Musa. I plenty busy.'

Musa, his dark body glistening with sweat, wiped a hand across his brow.

'Master say you go back to England with Madam.'

I couldn't speak so I nodded.

Musa gestured to Smokey who was poking his head through the top half of the stable door, and was trying to nibble my ear. 'I think he miss you, Madam.'

'I will miss him, too,' I croaked.

And I would.

I wanted to be out there on the plains with my Dad, on the back of Smokey, perusing the view as dusk came. With the richness of Africa spread out before us, golden bushes and silhouetted trees, hills rising up, and the distant peak of Tangali Waja reigning supreme. We would gee up the horses and trot across the stony earth, over rocks and dunes, and granite mounds –

Oh God, I so wanted to gallop with my Dad across Africa forever.

'Goodbye, Musa' I put out my hand, as tears leapt over my lids.

Musa wiped a sweaty palm on his very grubby, raggedy shorts. 'Allah be with you, Madam.'

It was gut-wrenching stuff this goodbye business.

Later, after lunch, after the final paludrine experience when I sat at the dining table and opened up that little aluminium pot and popped a tablet, I went out on my little Honda 50 cc for the very last time. The adventures we'd had together could have filled a book, and never once had it let me down.

Off we went, heading up the hill and out of Gombe. I wanted to stop by the gates of the old Stirling Astaldi Camp and take in the memories but grief overwhelmed me, so I moved on without giving the place even a glance. At the top of the rise the road to Bauchi lay before me, a straight gleaming line like a black mirage that cut its way for nigh on a hundred miles through the bush. I opened up the throttle, revved up the engine and went like the clappers with the wind in my hair. Dan Iska, that was me, I was an adventurer, an explorer, an angel, a witch; I was whatever I wanted to be as I sailed through the air on my beloved Honda 50 cc.

I went for miles.

Somewhere along the way I stopped. I was all on my own. Surrounded by dried grasses and yellow plains dotted with baobabs and thorn trees. Far away, a misty-blue haze of wood-smoke hung low, a sign that somewhere out there in the wilderness was a village made up of mud, and, yes, snotty-nosed kids, goat pellets and chickens. If I listened very carefully, in the still silence of the bush, there was the steady rhythmic pounding of wood on wood. Truly, an African sound, nowhere else on earth was there a sound quite like it.

I looked up above. The galloping clouds of Africa charged across a white, baking sky. Soon the rains would come, that dry burning orb would be transformed into a harsh, watery glare. Great clattering bursts of thunder would shake the earth, and lighting would split the heavens. And down it would fall, a relentless torrent, with hardly a pause for breath.

I sat on a small rock, in the midst of the wilderness, smoking my fags, taking it all in.

And wished I could stay here forever.

It was with heavy heart that I turned on the engine and made my way back to Gombe. As I came down the hill, acacia trees lining the red, dusty road, I imagined I was coming home, not going away, that this was my first sighting of the Dadinkauwa hills, not the last. That I was seeing the whitewashed, mud-walled catering Rest House, nestling in amongst the trees, the corrugated roofs glistening in the sunshine, for the very first time.

I approached the fork in the road.

It's all as I remembered it. Nothing has changed. My house looks the same. The wide veranda and jungle of pots and plants, the rusted water tank and the brown, mud brick stables so lovingly built by my Dad. Mum has finished watering her small oasis of green, and the smell...oh, the smell...water and dry earth mingled together, steaming in the heat.

Now I'm walking up to the club on the hill. The setting sun is on fire, the world is draped in a cloak of red, orange and gold.

I touch the earth, kiss the sky, and cry with all my heart.

Oh God, I so don't want to go.

Wednesday morning.

I woke up very early, and sat alone on the veranda sipping my cup of coffee and smoking my fags. Woggles was by my side, his furry body wrapped round my legs. He always sensed when I was going, and with my Mum going too, he was doubly sad.

'What time did Lizzie say she was coming?'

I looked up, Dad with a couple of flasks for the road in his arms, was standing by my side. I peered at my watch. 'She said about six, Dad. Any minute now, I suppose.'

We both looked out at the quiet, empty road.

'We're going to have to leave soon, you know,' said Dad. He trotted down the steps with his flasks, and joined Jonathon who was tying suitcases on to the roof rack of the car. Our boy was doing a grand job but Dad had to put his koboworth in. 'Tighter, tighter, Jonathon.'

And Jonathon smiled, as he always did, and hummed his little African tune, as he pulled the rope in his hands just that little bit tighter, as he twisted the knots, just that little bit more.

The distant sound of a motorbike, it got louder, as Lizzie turned down our drive. She parked the bike where she always parked it, under the flame tree. Oh, Lizzie, I thought, as she clambered off her little metal warrior and made her way over, I aren't half going to miss you.

I chucked my fag in one of Mum's prized potted plants, and got up.

'Hiya, Tony,' she said to Dad, who was now tugging and pulling with Jonathon – Dad could never, ever leave well alone. 'Morning, Jonathon.'

Master and boy gave greetings back.

I stood on the veranda step, under a cascade of purple bougainvillea.

'Hello, little sis,' said Lizzie with a smile. She had what looked like a scroll in her hand. She marched up and gave it to me.

'What's this?'

'Open it up and you'll see.'

I untied the little red ribbon, and rolled out the paper.

'Oh, Lizzie!'

It was a poem, from Lizzie to me. From someone who thought poems were just a bit silly, yet she'd sat down, thought about it, and made one up just for me.

I plonked myself down on the steps, and as the early morning Gombe sun shined on me for the very last time, I read my poem.

'For Janni – A Parting Gesture from Lizzie, your big sister!!!'

A young lady living in two worlds
Mixing fantasy with reality
And gifted in self-expression.
One who delights all with her personality
She laughs and sings – but is she really happy?
Or is this just part of her Oscar winning performance?
And underneath it all – how does she feel?
Alone and lost – and needed to be needed.
We all need her. We all love her.
The world is yours,
Janni
Continue looking for your star in life
To touch you with its brightness every second,
And you will find it one day.
But 'Janni – never search too hard to find your star

Or it may fade away.
Out there your star is waiting
Discover it.
Got to it quickly, and with faith.
And now, Janina,
Farewell.

There were a lot of tears after that. A deluge of truly Noahic proportions.

My last sighting of Lizzie was her standing next to Jonathon, Woggy in the middle, under the old flame tree, outside our house.

I was inconsolable as I sat in the back seat of my Dad's silver Ford Cortina.

Maiduguri bound.

How weird it all was.

Heading back up the old familiar road.

A road that had seen me as high, as it has seen me as low.

I won't bore you with a description of the journey, the places we passed through, and the places where we stopped for a quick piddle, and a quick slurp on our lukewarm drinks. I expect you know the road as well as I do by now, anyway. Suffice to say, the trip was totally uneventful.

We hit the neem trees at around one in the afternoon.

It was all very strange. It was as if someone had pressed a button and I was whizzing back in time, back to that very first visit.

Oh God, how I wished it were so.

Oh, Andy. Oh, Andy. Oh, Andy.

Dad took a left. We were heading for the Lake Chad Hotel. Yes, my Dad had finally not spared the expense – Mum and I were going to spend our last night in Nigeria in style. But behind my Dad's generosity there were reasons, namely the Forestry Rest House was too close to Andy's house for Mum and Dad's comfort. They didn't say that of course, but I'm not a fool. I mean, why else would Dad put his hand in his pocket?

We parked the car. We took out our little overnight bags, and we got a salute from our uniformed man who stood to attention as we passed through the doors, and into the lobby.

'Madams? Sir?'

Dad gave the receptionist our names; the receptionist gave us our keys. Two lackeys magically appeared, with Cheshire cat grins they did their usual party trick – pretending a lightweight bag held a ton of cement.

We were shown to our rooms. Mum and Dad had a double on the second floor, and I, thank God, had a single on the third. Well away from prying eyes. I could sneak out in the dead of night, and head for – oh God, if it were only that easy. So near, yet so bloody far.

I slumped on the bed.

'Nagodi,' I said, and gave my smiling lackey a naira. Not bad for a two second job.

The door shut. I inspected myself in the mirror. At least I'd be going back to England all nice and brown. That was about the only plus in my life. How sad was that.

Half an hour later I was sat by the pool. Mum and Dad had gone off on a secret mission, probably for talks with the Nigerian Head of Police. Did I care? Not a bit of it. I had more pressing things on my mind.

So near, and yet so bloody far.

There were a few people around the pool, some basking in deckchairs, some splashing about in the water, mostly young kids with their mums, and a couple of hotel guests who looked as inspiring as a wet afternoon in Bridlington.

I smiled at a couple of ladies I recognised, and they smiled back at me. My return was of no consequence to them. They wouldn't have even known my name.

But the waiter knew me all right. 'Madam, welcome back.'

I shaded my eyes. 'Hello, Lamin,' I said, from my horizontal position on the sunbed. 'How are you?'

'I be fine, Madam. And you?'

I swung my legs over the side of the bed, and put bare feet on very hot concrete. I sat up. And gave Lamin a wry smile. 'I be okay, Lamin.'

Holding his tray like he was hiding his privates, Lamin grinned, showing shiny, sparkly white teeth. Which baffled me because I knew he smoked. How come my teeth weren't as shiny, and as sparkly, and as white as his?

'So, where you go for the last few months, Madam? You be away for a long, long time.'

I nodded. 'Yeah, Lamin. I go back to my home. Gombe.' Just saying the word heralded that old frog to jump back to his favourite haunt, my throat.

'Ah! You are from Gombe.' A thrilled expression spread across Lamin's face. 'My brother's brother-in-law's father he done come from there. Maybe you know him.'

I shook my head. 'I doubt it, Lamin.'

It was the same wherever you went in Nigeria; all Nigerians were convinced you'd know a friend or relation. Be it London or Gombe, or Paris or Madrid. To them, the world was a very small place.

Lamin hid his disappointment pretty well. He grinned again. 'So, Madam, you have come back to be with your friends, and...,' he chuckled, '...to be with your very special friend, Master Andy.'

Just the mention of his name and a jolt of electricity tore through my body. I thought I was about to spontaneously combust. Headlines in the New Nigerian: *Drug suspect girl mysteriously goes up in flames by Lake Chad pool. The work of the Mafia?*

Trembling, I picked up my fags and my lighter. Lit up, and inhaled. 'No, Lamin, I no come back to stay.' Out came the smoke, it whirled up, up and away, drifting, drifting into the blue of the sky. 'I go back to England tomorrow.'

Oh God! Saying it out loud meant it was true.

I gave Lamin a very sad smile. The saddest smile he'd probably ever encountered, he was almost fit to bursting into tears himself on hearing the news. The grin gave way to utter facial despair. 'Oh, Madam, no! Oh, Madam!' Slowly he shook his head, from left to right. 'No, oh no, no, no, no!'

Oh yes, oh yes, oh yes fucking yes.

"Fraid so, Lamin,' I replied sadly. 'I fly tomorrow morning at eleven o'clock.'

Well, it was just too much to bear. A choked up Lamin looked up to the heavens, as if already he could see me flying high in the sky. 'May Allah protect you,' he said finally, coming back down to earth.

'Thank you, Lamin,' I replied solemnly. 'Thank you very much.' I took another drag. 'Oh, and may I have a Coke?'

The grin returned to Lamin's face, the white, shiny smile dazzled in the sun. 'And some peanuts, Madam?'

'Definitely,' I said, swinging my legs back up, and resuming horizontal position.

I lay on that sunbed, in the sun, by the Lake Chad pool, on my own, for over an hour. Taking in the last rays, packing in the tan.

And thinking about Andy.

381

Remembering happier days when we were together. How he used to pick me up from the pool when he'd finished his work. We'd go to the bar for a drink. Meet up with our friends. Joyful conviviality. When life was at its best.

Two Cokes, and three bowls of peanuts later, I called it a day. No one of any interest had turned up at the pool. A paranoid voice in my head suggested that it was perhaps because everyone knew I was back. Persona non gratis – or something like that.

Fuck them. Fuck the lot of them, I said out loud in my head as I grabbed my towel, my bag, and my small bottle of vinegar and groundnut oil that had helped the sun fry my skin to a crisp.

Slowly I made my way back to the hotel lobby.

'Janni! Fuck, is that you, Janni?'

I turned to whence the voice had come. Blinked once, twice, because the sun was in my eyes. 'Richard!' He was standing by the door of the bar, fag and drink in hand. I headed his way. 'Hi,' I said, feeling slightly daft. I had one of Mum's old towels wrapped round my body like a Nigerian, and was smelling like an old fish and chip pan.

Richard didn't care. He set down his drink and his fag, and gave me a hug. 'What are you doing here?' he asked when the preliminaries were over.

I tried to toss my wet hair back, just a little. A futile effort, if ever there was one. So I just got straight to the point. 'I'm flying back to England tomorrow, Rich.'

He whistled. 'No way! Lucky you.'

I made a face. 'Do you think so? I hate the idea.'

Richard took a drag, and scratched his head, the fag singeing his hair. He took no notice of the burnt, horrible smell. 'Do you? I think England is lovely in May. All those green fields and warm sun and rain.'

I pulled another face.

'So what are you going to do?'

I shrugged. 'I dunno.'

'Then why are you going back?'

There was a bit of an awkward silence. Richard looked a tad embarrassed. As if the reason why had suddenly dawned.

Or had it?

How much did I know that he didn't know? How much did he know that I didn't know? Indeed, did he know what I knew, and did I know what he knew?

Oh, God, this was mad.

Here I was standing with one of Andy's closest buddies, and I couldn't even mention his name. Or speak about the drugs thing. Did any of them, did Andy especially have an inkling of what was underfoot. Mum and Dad had sworn me to secrecy. 'The Head of Police is putting himself on the line for you,' Dad had warned. 'You mustn't discuss the case with anyone. Understand.'

I bit my lip, and cleared my throat. 'Life just got a bit boring in Gombe, so I thought I might as well go back to England.'

'Oh, right,' said Richard, obviously not knowing what else to say. The whole me and Andy thing was like an invisible barrier between me and his friends. Pretending he didn't exist seemed the best way to go about it.

'How's – um – Sally?'

'She'll be here in a bit.' Richard smiled, relieved that the subject had been rightly diverted. 'Come and join us. Sally will be cock-a-hoop to know that you're back.'

Which was a nice thing to say.

'Give me a second to get changed.'

'We'll be inside, in the bar,' shouted Richard, as I raced into the lobby and skidded like an ice skater across the shiny, marble-effect floor, to the stairs, where I took the steps three at a time, first floor, second floor, and third floor.

In my room, it was off with the towel and the bikini, and into the shower, and out again, and on with the baby lotion. I held my head out of the window to let the sun dry my hair, while smoking a joint, courtesy of Mukaji. The drug did the business. I felt like a million dollars when I finally stepped out of my room. My gypsy curls hung down my back. I had on a beautiful green, silky top – one of Barb's specials – that went, according to the lady who gave it to me, with the colour of my eyes. My white chiffon skirt swished as I walked. Heads turned as I entered the bar. It felt good to be noticed again. It really felt good.

Richard and Sally were propping up the long granite counter, sitting on the high red, leather covered stools. 'Wow!' smiled Sally. 'You look cool.'

We hugged. We talked. General chit-chat. About this and about that. But not about Andy. And not about drugs.

'Does Rosie know you're here?' Sally blew out a match, and chucked it in the ashtray.

'I don't think anyone knows I'm here, except you two.' I popped a peanut in my mouth.

'I'll give you a lift over to hers if you want.' Richard checked his watch. 'She should be home around now.' He looked at Sally. 'Then we could meet Janni later back here, buy her a goodbye drink.' He turned to me. 'What do you say?'

We both said great.

Rosie was as over the moon as anyone could be when she saw me. With her long legs, and her flowing blonde hair, she looked like a catwalk queen as she flew down the veranda and across the compound to greet me.

'Whooee,' she screamed. 'I don't believe it!'

The horrible dogs of hers were pretty over the moon too. They jumped up, and went nose-long into my privates, one taking my back, the other my front. It was really quite obscene. 'Down, Che! Down, Guevera!' Rosie kicked one of them away. I thwacked the other with my orange tasselled bag.

'See you later,' shouted Richard over the din.

'Yeah, see you. Cheers, Richard.'

He reversed pretty sharpish, and headed back down the drive with Che and Guevera making chase, barking and trying to jump into the open windows either side. Jesus, they were evil, bloody dogs. No wonder their flipping mother had abandoned them at birth.

'Come on,' said Rosie. 'Get in quick before they turn their attention back on to you.' She pulled my arm. 'They're on heat, you see. And that sends them completely mad. '

Oh, fuck!

Like two streaks of lightning we flashed up the steps, and into the house.

'Well, hello, Janni.'

It was Rosie's strange mother, Megan, sitting at her desk, with her piles of books, and bosoms still dangling a feet off the ground.

'Hi,' I replied, out of breath from our quick sprint across the stony compound. I had to take my sandals off, bits of sand and the like had got stuck in under my feet. 'Sorry,' I said, replacing my foot in the soft, leather hide.

'Are you with us long?' Megan tucked a grey lock behind her ear with a red hennaed hand.

I looked at Rosie, who was also getting bits of whatever out of her shoes, and back to Megan. 'Actually, no. I'm flying back to England tomorrow.'

Rosie dropped her sandal, it made a slapping sound as it hit the hard concrete floor, and put her hand to her mouth. 'Oh, my God! You're joking, aren't you?'

That old frog croaked. 'I wish I was, Rosie,' I said sadly.

'Oh, I don't believe it.'

Certainly Rosie looked stunned.

'I'm sorry to hear that. Any reason why you're going back so soon?' Megan asked this while she got out her cigarette papers, her baccy, and rolled herself a fag.

I sighed, and shrugged. 'It's a bit complicated, really. Basically, Mum and Dad want me to sort out my future, y'know, college, and all that.'

Megan, licking the sticky bit on the Rizla, nodded as she did so. She picked up her lighter and smiled at her daughter. 'That's what you'll be doing, Rosie, in a few years time.'

'Mmm, I suppose,' said Rosie, getting a hold of my arm. Current issues, not future plans were what interested her at the moment. 'Come on, Janni. Let's go to my room.'

'Enjoy,' came the comment from Megan, as she lit up and puffed, and I got dragged down the corridor. 'Enjoy.'

Well, we talked and we talked and we talked.

About this, and about that, but about Andy, especially. With Rosie, censorship wasn't a word in her book. It was so good to talk freely about the man I still really loved – even though I had lost him. It made what we had, seem real again. Not just a story I'd written in the wee hours of the morning when I couldn't get to sleep. Not just something I created when I found it difficult to get through the monotony of a slow ticking day.

In fact, being with Rosie felt almost like old times. Almost.

So close. And yet so, so far away.

'Actually, I haven't seen much of him, lately,' said Rosie, as she rolled up a joint, the both of us sprawled across her bed. 'He keeps himself pretty much to himself these days.'

I followed the dappled sunlight that danced on her bedspread. 'You don't think that's because –' Did I dare say it? '– because he's found someone else.'

Rosie tossed back her hair, and gave an emphatic shake of the head. 'No. No, definitely not. He just doesn't come up to the club so often, that's all.'

'Is he alright?'

Rosie shrugged. 'I s'pose. He seems okay when I do see him. Laughs and jokes, that kind of thing.'

Thinking about him laughing and joking made my heart bleed.

'Does he ever talk about me, Rosie?'

Rosie gave me a really nice smile. 'Yeah, he has, of course.' She lit up the joint. 'You were a big part of his life, once. Why wouldn't he?'

'Oh, Rosie,' I said, all choked up, with butterflies racing round in my tummy. It was the first positive thing I'd heard in ages. I bit my lip. 'What does he say about me?'

Rosie took a deep puff. And waited for the drug to go in, and come out. 'That you were someone who he really, really had a good time with...'

'Did he really say that?'

'Yes, he did. And he said you were a crazy girl who he once loved very much...'

A warm glow filled up my entire body 'When did he say that?'

Rosie took one final drag, and passed the joint over. 'Oh, I don't know. Last week. A couple of weeks ago...'

'As recent as that!' The warm glow got warmer. 'Really, Rosie? Really?'

Rosie laughed. 'Why would I lie to you? Anyway, you know it's all true. He did love you...'

'I know, but I thought he hated me now. That he didn't care.' I pulled at a thread on Rosie's blanket, and took another puff. Smoke floated out. 'Rosie?'

'Yeah?' Rosie twiddled with her hair, her head propped up by her elbow.

'You haven't heard of any drug thing, have you? I mean to do with the police, or Andy, or anything?'

'No.' Rosie shook her head. 'What do you mean?'

So I told her. Fuck Dad's secret deal with the Head of the Maiduguri police.

She listened, open-mouthed.

'Christ! That sounds bloody serious.' She rolled up another joint, as you would when you've heard a tale about drug busts and the like. 'So that's why you've got to go back to England?'

I nodded. 'But what do you think will happen to Andy?' I sat up. 'You don't think he'll go to prison?'

Rosie sat up too, and drew her long legs so her chin rested on her knees. 'God knows. Do you think we should warn him?'

'Dunno,' I said, mulling the idea over in my head.

Actually, I'd been mulling the idea over in my head for the last seven days. Had thought about nothing else really. Did Andy know? About me and the letter from the Head of Police? About the information they had on him? Should I send a message? Flee the country as quick as you can. But I was already in a pickle myself. A shudder went through me. Might menacing eyes be watching my every move? Might menacing eyes be watching me now?

'I don't know what to do,' I said finally, and as an afterthought, 'Best not to get involved, Rosie. The less you know the better it is for you, and Andy, and anyone else that might be implicated.'

Rosie shrugged. 'I suppose.' She slapped an ant that had crawled up her arm. 'Maybe that's why Andy's keeping a really low profile. Why he hasn't been up to the club so much, of late.'

'Possibly,' I agreed. 'Has he talked about his arrest in the Cameroon?'

'No, I haven't heard it from him but I've heard rumours,' she said. 'I bet that's where it's all come from, don't you think?'

'Perhaps.' I pondered on that. 'He did say to me that he was going to keep his head down, that things might get a bit rocky.'

'Maybe he already knows the score,' suggested Rosie.

Maybe he did. Maybe he didn't.

I lay on the bed and stared at the ceiling. A shaft of afternoon sunshine speared through the quiet coolness. Golden dust hung suspended in the air. A fly buzzed. Two small geckos ran down the zanna-mat wall. My mind went back to happier times, when everything in the world seemed so total and perfect, when it was me and Andy together in our star-studded dream.

'Oh, Rosie,' I said wistfully, 'I so wish I could see him before I disappeared back to England.' I turned my head, looked at her lying next to me, her long, golden locks reminding me of a golden storm on another pillow so near, but so far away. 'I really, really wish I could.'

Rosie sighed. She flicked back a strand that had fallen in her eyes. 'Oh, Janni, it's all such a fucking, fucking mess.'

Sadly, I nodded. Wasn't it just.

At six, I jumped on the back of Rosie's bike, and with our hair flying in a million directions, we headed through the dusk to the club. I only had an hour. I was meeting Mum and Dad back at the Lake Chad at seven for our last supper together.

Oh, how my heart skipped a beat as we drew up, oh, how it thudded as we parked the bike near the whitewashed building bedecked with green climbing creepers and pink bougainvillea.

Every memory of every moment spent here came flooding back. And not for the first time, I wished I had a Tardis like Dr Who's and I could be whizzed back to that happier place when life was so nice and easy.

We flip-flopped up the steps. My heart was pumping. We flip-flopped into the club. My heart was going like the clappers. People turned, people recognised me.

'Hey, how's it going...'

'Good to see you...'

'How's Gombe...'

'Flying back tomorrow...'

'Oh, we're sorry to hear that...'

I shook hands, I waved, I stopped and chatted. Rosie skipped and weaved through tables and chairs, carried on moving to the bar. 'What are you drinking?' she shouted.

'Brandy and Coke,' I hollered back. Brandy was supposed to lift up the spirits, and if anyone needed a lift it was me.

'Mum and Dad okay...'

'Fine, thanks, they're here too...'

'Good. We might catch up with them later...'

'See you...'

'Bye...'

'Take care of yourself...'

'Safe journey back...'

Blah-dy, blah-dy, blah.

'I'll see you out on the veranda with the drinks.'

Rosie disappeared out the French doors. I made my way through the throng, as quickly as was politely possible, waving and shaking more hands as I went, and headed out to the great outdoors, where shafts of evening sunshine, dust-laden, speared through the canopy of trees surrounding the patio. Familiar faces all around, but there were just two who really were special.

Under the fairy lights, not yet lit, sat Hamish and Buggy.

It was an emotional moment as I made my way to their table. Seeing the both of them made Andy seem even nearer. In fact he was just a stone's throw away. I could so easily have jumped on Rosie's bike. I'd be there at the house in less than five minutes – in his arms – oh, God–

'Hello, Hamish,' I said, my voice all a quiver.

Hamish, as always, jumped out of his chair. 'Och,' he smiled, 'it's good to see you. Richard told us you were back, and we were

388

hoping you'd turn up sometime this evening. And here you are.' He gave me his seat. I hugged Buggy first before sitting down.

Rosie, who'd been chatting to a group of Dutch guys, came over with my drink. 'I'll be back in a second,' she said, giggling.

'She fancies that Marcus,' Buggy explained.

I turned. She was sitting on some blonde hunk's knee. Lucky old Rosie. I took a sip of my drink. My hands, I noticed, trembled a bit. I put the glass down, and sat on them.

'So, how are you both?' I asked, smiling.

Hamish took a puff on his pipe. The memories, the memories – if I could close my eyes I could be back on his veranda, with the smell of his tobacco – with Andy's golden head in my lap...

'Och, we're good.' Hamish took another puff, the tobacco embers glowed orange and red. His eyes crinkled with warmth. And concern. 'You?'

I shrugged. 'I'm okay.'

He nodded. Considering. And threw me a gentle smile. 'You're a spirited lassie, I always knew you'd get by.'

'Mmm.' I didn't really know what else to say so I took another sip of my drink.

'Richard says you're flying back to England tomorrow.'

'Mmm,' I said again. I put down my glass. 'At eleven, from Maiduguri.' I fiddled with the ring on my finger. 'I think we fly from Kano at five.'

'Are you glad?' Buggy asked casually, leaning back in his chair, his hands round the back of his head that was covered in thick, wiry hair. 'About returning to England?'

Glad? I was fucking mad.

I picked up my drink. 'Not really,' I said sadly, trying to steady my glass with both hands. I took another sip.

'What will you do?'

'Not sure.'

God! Why did everyone ask me the same bloody question? And why, apart from Rosie, was everyone so scared to mention *his* name? See, they'd even got me doing it.

I took another sip, and another. I could see through the bottom of my glass.

'Can I get you a refill?' Hamish was half up.

'No. No, cheers.' I glanced at my watch. It was 6.30. I didn't have to meet Mum and Dad until seven, but I wasn't going to last out another half hour, sitting in this place, with Hamish and Buggy, and my heart nigh on breaking. And none of us really knew what to say. 'I've got to go,' I said quietly, and swallowed hard. 'I only popped in on the off chance that you might be here so I could say cheerio. Mum and Dad are expecting me back at the Lake Chad Hotel for dinner.' I got up. 'It's been lovely seeing you, Hamish, again.' My voice broke, but I hung on in there, and kept it together. 'And you, Buggy.'

'Yeah, yeah,' they both said, a little taken aback. 'Can we give you a lift…' Hamish was still hovering over his chair.

'No, it's all right.' I turned away, and pretended I was looking for Rosie, and bit my lip. Grabbing my bag, I blew them both a kiss. 'Bye.' The tears tumbled. I couldn't hear what they said. In a blur, I marched over to Rosie who was having a fine time on her handsome hunk's lap. 'Can you take me back to the hotel?' I whispered in her ear.

'Yeah, sure.'

'I'll be out by the bike, waiting.'

And, quietly and unobtrusively, I walked out of the club without another word.

'Are you alright?'

'Yeah, I'm fine.'

'Are you sure?'

'Yeah, I'm sure.'

We were outside the hotel. Rosie sat astride her bike, with the engine still throbbing.

'Oh, Janni, don't cry.'

I wiped away a tear with the back of my hand. 'Please, Rosie, just go. I'm really okay.'

'I can't leave you like this.'

Another tear fell. More drops quickly joined it.

'Let me come in with you?' Rosie switched off her engine. 'I can't leave you in this state.'

She was about to clamber off. I stopped her. 'Rosie, please, I really want to be on my own.'

She must have got the message.

'I'll be at the airport tomorrow,' she said. 'I promise.'

'I know.' I kissed her cheek, leaving wet on her face. 'Thanks, Rosie.'

She turned her key. The engine roared back into life. 'See you.'

390

'Yeah, see you.'

I turned away, and made it back to my bedroom, and threw myself on the bed.

For ten minutes I howled. The following ten minutes were taken up with trying to patch up the wreck of my face.

I think I did a pretty good job.

'You look lovely,' smiled Mum, as I walked into the bar.

She and Dad were talking to another couple. Dad got up. 'Do you remember Mr and Mrs Greaves, darling?'

No.

I put out my hand. 'Yes, of course I do. How are you?'

Hands were shook, I sat down amongst them, we made small talk; I told Mr and Mrs Greaves about some of my plans, that I might become a teacher.

Dad smiled proudly and Mum looked pretty chuffed.

Maybe they were thinking: There's hope for our daughter after all.

At eight, after two vodka-martinis – 'That's rather a sophisticated drink, darling, I didn't know you liked that kind of thing,' Mum had said after I'd put in my order (well, here's news for you, Mum, neither did I but it tasted very nice, and certainly it hit the right spot) – we said goodbye to the Greaves's and traipsed into dinner.

'What will you have, darling?'

I checked out the menu. There was certainly plenty of choice. Should I have the soup or the melon for starters?

'What soup is it?'

'Groundnut, Madam.'

Of course, I should have known.

'I'll have-'

The waiter stood poised with his pen.

'...the soup. And...' I perused the menu again. 'And steak, chips, fried onions, and whatever else that goes with it.'

That done, I took out my fags, lit up, and blew smoke in Dad's face. By accident, of course.

'Janni!'

'Sorry, Dad.'

'Put it out, darling.' Mum passed me over the ashtray.

I took another drag. 'But the food won't be here for ages...'

'Put it out, young lady.'

This came from Dad. It was a requirement, not a request.

Inwardly, I gave a long drawn out sigh. Outwardly, my sigh was pretty brief. Didn't want to be upsetting the father too much tonight. I had enough on my plate. I stubbed the cigarette out, and with folded arms, and a bored expression, awaited my food.

'Is she waving at us?' Mum was looking over my shoulder. I was at a rather odd angle so had to turn.

'Anne,' I screamed. I was up, and out of my chair.

'Careful, careful,' ordered Dad, as I very nearly pulled off the tablecloth.

'Sorry.' Even though I wasn't sorry at all.

I hurtled over to Anne, standing by the glass door.

'Hey,' she said delightedly, 'I heard from Sal you were here.' She hugged me. 'And that you're going back to England tomorrow. What a bloody shame.'

'Mmm, it is.' I returned her hug. 'Can you hang about? I've got dinner with the blooming parents.'

'Yeah.' Anne beckoned to the patio. 'We'll be out there.'

'Who's we?'

'Hank and Phil.'

'Oh, wow. That's good.' I gave her another hug and a little excited jiggle. The vodka-martinis were certainly working their magic. For a moment I almost felt like my old happy self. 'I'll see you in about half an hour.'

'Who was that?' asked Mum when I returned to the table.

'Anne.'

'Anne who?'

'A teacher friend. She's very nice.' My soup arrived along with Dad's. Mum was having melon. There was a pause to allow the waiter to do his thing. 'I'm catching up with her after dinner,' I said, tucking in.

'Well, don't be up too, too late,' advised Mum. 'We've got a long day ahead of us tomorrow.'

I grabbed a roll, and slapped on butter.

'I won't be,' I said.

Dinner was finished. I legged it to the loo, the one that smelt of mothballs and disinfectant. Flushing all my meal down the drain, I stepped out of the cubicle and checked how I looked in the mirror. Not bad, considering.

With my bag over my shoulder, I headed out of the toilet, across the lobby, into the bar, out through the patio doors and...

I gasped.

My whole being melted.

My feet were ten inches off the ground.

I was floating on gossamer mist.

They were all there. And when I mean all, I mean all. Everybody that was anybody was there. And that anybody included Andy.

Oh, my God! Oh, my God! Oh, my God!

There was a cheer as I stepped over the threshold.

Somehow I managed to make it to the table. I didn't dare look at him. I sat down in the nearest empty chair, next to Hamish. I'm not really sure who the person was on my other side. In fact, I couldn't have cared less who any of them were. All were eclipsed by my Andy.

But I didn't dare look at him.

Everyone's talking. I am. They are.

'So what time's the flight?' someone is saying.

And I'm saying, in as natural a voice as can be, 'About eleven, I think. And our flight from Kano goes at five.'

'I'll be back in the UK, next month,' comes from somebody else. 'My three long years are up and the first thing I'm going to do is drink a fucking pint of Guinness.'

'Oh, really.' I seem interested. 'And then what are you going to do?'

They tell me. I don't hear a word.

I talk to Rosie. Roger. Richard. Sally. Phil. One of the Dutch guys. Buggy. Amy and Anne. Bruce. Yes, he's there. So many adventures together but I'm finding it hard to connect. My voice manages to form the right words even though I'm not sure what it is that I'm saying.

'Remember that bloke, Janni, with the umbrella, on the mammy-wagon, what was it we called him?'

The fuck knows. But the right name plops out of my mouth.

Bruce laughs. I laugh.

Does Andy laugh? Does he talk? I think I can hear his soft, dulcet tones.

I hear Hamish laugh. I hear Hamish say, not to me, 'Here, let's swap places.' There's a scrape of chairs, everyone's chatting, about this, about that, and I – well, I'm not sure what I'm doing, really.

I remember stubbing my fag out and taking another out of the packet.

A match strikes, a match flares.

Next to me, someone with a tiny flicker of light in their hand; like a moth to the flame, I move my head towards it, the end of my cigarette glows. That someone moves his head towards me. Our eyes meet. Our hands touch. I tell you, the surge that shoots through my body has enough electricity to light up the world.

It's a beautiful moment.

'How are you?' Andy smiles

'I'm okay.' I smile back. 'You?'

'Getting there.'

'Me too.'

A pause. Nothing awkward, nothing like that, just one of those golden silences when you know things are going to be alright, after all.

He slips his arm round the back of my chair. I take a sip of my drink and a puff on my fag. He takes one on his. The both of us blow smoke in the warm evening air.

'So, what's with the going back to England bit?'

He doesn't know. But I know I'll tell him later.

'Not sure, really.'

'Don't you want to go?'

'No.' I look straight at him. Oh God, those beautiful, blue eyes. 'No I don't.'

His fingers brush the back of my neck. The touch is so exquisite, I very nearly moan out aloud.

'Is this your Mum and Dad's idea?'

'Sort of.'

'I'm sorry.'

'Me too.'

He glances up at the moon. And back to me. 'You look lovely dressed in moonlight,' he murmurs.

'Do I?'

'You always do.'

I glance up at the moon. And back to him. 'So do you.'

He smiles. 'Do I?'

I smile. 'You always do.'

Everyone around the table, and there must be fifteen, maybe twenty people, and yet the only sound I hear is the beat of our hearts and the butterflies that dance in my tummy. A true sign that the dark cloak of winter has been shed and the warm, light mantle of spring has arrived.

'Janni?'

394

The butterflies twirl even faster.

'Do you want to make a move?'

I nod.

'Come on.'

Without a word I pick up my bag, and together we slip away.

On his bike, my arms around him, we go back to 'our house'.

Paradise calls once again.

Early, early morning, before the sun is even a light in the sky, Andy and I make one last journey together, back to the Lake Chad Hotel. He stops his bike before we get to the entrance and we say our goodbyes.

'I'll see you, sometime,' he says, pushing the tumbling hair back off my face. 'And don't worry your little head about stuff. Everything will be cool.'

I know it will. He's known about the drugs thing all along. Already he's getting it sorted. Well, that's what he tells me and I have to believe him.

I bury my face in his neck. As always, the tears. Oh God, I so don't want to go.

But dawn is breaking, as is my heart.

'I love you, Andy.'

'I know. And I love you, too. Whatever may have happened that wasn't good between us, what we had that was good was beautiful.'

And that said, he blows me a kiss, and roars away into the gold of the dawn.

'What time did you get to bed last night?' asked Mum. We were at breakfast three hours later. I was nibbling on a slice of toast.

I shrugged. 'Dunno, really. Not late.'

Which was true, I was in bed by ten.

'Well, you look awful. You've got dark rings under your eyes.'

'Thanks, Mum.'

I dropped the toast and lit up a fag.

'Dad's back,' said Mum, gathering her handbag and glasses. 'Come on, hurry up, it's time to go.'

I threw the last dregs of my coffee down my throat. Yuck! It tasted like someone had pissed in it.

'Ready?' Dad was hitching up his trousers, and twitching, as

395

was his want, when things got a bit emotional. Mum was looking a bit pale around the gills, too. Even for aged parents, this parting stuff was a heavy affair.

'Ready,' nodded Mum.

I nodded too.

We scraped back our chairs, I stubbed out my fag, Mum and I picked up our bags, and all three of us headed out of the dining room, through the lobby, and out of the Lake Chad Hotel, and into the car.

We drove to the airport pretty much in silence. Mum, I noticed, had her hand on Dad's knee for most of the journey. I had my nose pressed close to the window, taking what was out there in for the very last time. 'Goodbye from Maiduguri' said the sign as we drove under the arch. 'We wish you a safe journey'.

It brought that old devil of a lump to my throat.

Five miles on, and we turned right. My heart was pounding. I hated airports when I was flying back, loved them, when I was flying home. Dad parked the car. There was a bit of a flurry as a million baggage boys all appeared from out of the thorn trees, and hurtled towards our cases.

Dad saw them all off.

In the main building, Mum and I headed for the check-in desk, Dad went off to talk to some bloke. I paid no attention to the fact that he was dressed up in uniform. Who cared?

We were late, as always. There wasn't much time to say our goodbyes.

'Janni, Janni.'

I turned around. There was Rosie, Amy and Anne. 'We've been waiting for ages.'

'Sorry,' I shrugged. 'But my Dad – well, he had something to do.'

Rosie whispered, even though my parents where well out of earshot. 'How did it go? Last night?'

My eyes sparkled. 'Ace, Rosie. Just ace.'

'I'm so glad.' She pulled me into her arms. 'Write? Promise?'

'I promise.'

'Safe journey.'

I responded with a squeak.

Anne grabbed me next. 'Take care. And write, won't you?'

'I will.'

'So glad it worked out all right.'

My throat croaked.

A big hug from Amy. 'Take it easy, but take it.'

I promise her I will.

'Janni.'

Mum was calling.

'Got to go. Bye.'

'Bye.'

Kisses were blown.

I walked with Dad and Mum to the gate. The man in uniform was loitering. I gave him a watery smile.

Dad pulled me to him.

'I love you,' he said, his rich accented voice all cracked up and weird. 'I love you very, very much.'

'Oh, Dad. I'm so sorry.'

We clung to each other for a while.

His eyes glistened as we pulled ourselves apart.

'Take care of Mum, won't you?'

My head moved in an up and down motion. I just couldn't speak.

Mum was crying, too. It was dreadful.

'Go, go.' Dad pushed us away, ever so gently.

'Bye,' I squeaked.

Quietly sniffing, Mum and I walked through the airport lounge, it was empty. All the passengers had already boarded the plane. We walked out of the door. A nice Nigerian air stewardess escorted us across the tarmac, to our little Focker Friendship that was waiting for us in the sunshine. At the steps we turned, one last time, and waved, at Dad, at the bloke by his side, at Rosie, at Anne, and Amy. Except for the bloke in the uniform, they all waved back.

We climbed the steps.

'Welcome aboard,' said a smiling steward, waiting for us by the hatch.

One last look at the Maiduguri sun, one last look at the Maiduguri sky, one last breath of Maiduguri air, and we followed him to our seats. I sat by the window, had my nose pressed up against the (hopefully) unbreakable glass, was buckling up my seatbelt. There was Dad. There was that man. There was Rosie smoking a fag, Anne by her side. And there was Amy talking to – Jesus Christ! – Andy!

I unbuckled my seatbelt. I stood up.

'What are you doing?' asked Mum, dabbing her eyes with a hankie.

I climbed over her legs. 'I'll be back in a mo.'

I raced down the aisle. 'Stop! Stop!' I screamed. The steward was about to close up the hatch. 'Stop. Please.'

'Madam, what is wrong?'

'I must just go and say goodbye to somebody. Please. I won't be a minute.'

'But, Madam...'

Shoving the steward aside, I pushed open the door. The steps were just about to be wheeled away. 'Stop,' I demanded. 'Put them back.'

Amazingly, the four astonished blokes at the foot of my stairs did just what I told them. I flew down the steps. Everyone at Maiduguri Airport looked on, and that included my Dad and the Head of Police, as I hurtled across the tarmac. I saw Dad make a move. I think he thought I was racing towards him but then he saw me make a right turn.

'Andy,' I screamed. 'Andy.'

I jumped the barriers, and threw myself into his arms.

I wished it could have been a long, drawn out embrace.

But the plane beckoned.

'Take this,' he said. He put in my hands a brown paper bag.

'What...'

'Go. Open it up when you're high in the sky.'

'But...'

The steward was calling.

'Take care of your wee self, Janns.'

'Bye,' I shouted, as I raced back across the tarmac. 'I love you.'

'I love you, too,' rang and sang in my ears.

Once again I climbed the steps, the steward looked relieved. One last wave, one last kiss to blow from my lips, and the steward shut the door. All the passengers watched as I walked down the aisle, back to my seat. I couldn't have cared less what they were thinking. I climbed over Mum. She looked like she was about to have an anaglyptic shock. Whatever that was.

'I can't believe you just did tha...'

I didn't listen to the rest.

My nose was pressed to the window.

The engine roared into life. The plane moved. The plane turned. The engines roared even louder. Faster. Faster. I saw the buildings whiz past, a glimpse of golden hair in the sun, then desert and sky. We were up.

Up, up, up and away.

I buried my face in my hands and cried for a while.

'I can't believe you did that,' Mum was still saying, when I'd finished shedding my tears. 'Honestly, Janni, do you realise what a scene you've just caused, in front of everybody, Dad, the Commissioner? Do you realise?'

'Sorry, Mum,' I mumbled, delving into my brown paper bag and taking out a little book, the one that had been with us on so many of our journeys. Andy's prized possession. His Robert Burns' anthology. I flicked through the pages. Inside the cover, he had written.

But pleasures are like poppies spread
You pluck the flower
The bloom is shed
Or like the snow
Falls in the river
A moment white
Then melts forever.

Hope this wee book brings back happy memories, Janns. Take care of your wee self. See you when I see you.

Love you, Andy xxxx

We were flying above clouds. I was flying even higher.

I looked to see what else was in my little paper bag. Four brown biscuits, the ones that the cook used to make, Heavenly Hash.

'Biscuit?' I said, turning to Mum.

Mum tutted, she was still pissed off with me, but she could never refuse anything with chocolate.

She put her hand in the bag.

I turned back to the window, and smiled.

We both chomped away.

Dreamily.

And the plane flew steadily on.